IT STARTED WITH A WEDDING...

A two-in-one volume of fun, sexy romance!

The dresses, the flowers, the cake.
The first dance. And among the aunties and
flower girls and cousins there are occasionally
some very sexy single guys present as guests.

For both Emma and Bella,
their sisters are getting married and it's
the perfect opportunity for a little bit of flirting....

It might start at one wedding...
but it might just end at another!

NATALIE ANDERSON

adores happy endings, so you can be sure you've got happy endings to enjoy when you buy her books—she promises nothing less. She loves peppermint-filled dark chocolate, pineapple juice and extremely long showers, plus teasing her imaginary friends with dating dilemmas! She lives in New Zealand with her gorgeous husband and four fabulous children. If you love happy endings, too, come find her on facebook.com/authornataliea, Twitter: @authornataliea, or www.natalie-anderson.com.

ANNE OLIVER

lives in Adelaide, South Australia. She is an avid romance reader, and after eight years of writing her own stories, Harlequin Mills and Boon offered her publication in their Modern Heat series in 2005. Her first two published novels won the Romance Writers of Australia's Romantic Book of the Year Award in 2007 and 2008. She was a finalist again in 2012 and 2013. Visit her website: www.anne-oliver.com.

NATALIE ANDERSON
AND
ANNE OLIVER

It Started with a Wedding...

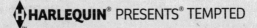

HARLEQUIN® PRESENTS® TEMPTED

ISBN-13: 978-0-373-60645-0

IT STARTED WITH A WEDDING...

Copyright © 2014 by Harlequin Books S.A.

The publisher acknowledges the copyright holder of the individual works as follows:

SLEEPLESS NIGHT WITH A STRANGER
Copyright © 2009 by Natalie Anderson

(This was first published in the U.K. as PLEASURED IN THE PLAYBOY'S PENTHOUSE).

THE MORNING AFTER THE WEDDING BEFORE
Copyright © 2012 by Anne Oliver

Recycling programs
for this product may
not exist in your area.

www.Harlequin.com

Printed in U.S.A.

CONTENTS

SLEEPLESS NIGHT WITH A STRANGER

Natalie Anderson

CHAPTER ONE

Did she want a 'sex machine' or a 'slow comfortable screw'? Choices, choices…and tonight Bella was struggling with decisions. The names were all such appalling puns, she didn't know if she'd be able to ask for one without blushing. Especially as she was sitting all alone in this bar—on a Friday night. The bartender would probably panic and think she was coming on to him. But as she looked at the gleaming glasses lined up behind the counter and the rows of bottles holding varying amounts of brightly coloured liquid, her taste buds were tickled. It had been a while since she'd had anything more indulgent than whatever was the cheapest red wine at the supermarket. Surely she was justified in having something fabulous to celebrate her day? And as this weekend had already burned one huge hole in her savings, she might as well make it a crater.

She looked back at the cocktail list, but barely read on. She'd waited all day for someone to say it. Someone. Anyone. It wasn't as if she expected a party—a cake, candles or even a card. It was a frantic time getting everything organised for Vita's wedding, Bella understood that. But surely even one of them could have remembered? Her father perhaps?

But no. She was just there, as usual, in the background, like the family cat. Present, accounted for, but blending in as if part of the furniture. It was only if she had some sort of catastrophe that they remembered her. And she was determined to avoid any catastrophes this weekend. This was Vita's special time. As uncomfortable as Bella felt, she was determined to help make the weekend as wonderful as it could be for her sister.

Volunteering to oversee the decorating had been her best idea. It had meant she'd been able to avoid most of the others. And honestly, she'd felt more at home with the waitresses and staff of the exclusive resort than with her own family and their friends.

When she'd paused at lunchtime she'd looked up and seen them out walking along the beach. The island of Waiheke looked as if it had been taken over by an accountancy convention. In truth it basically had. They were like clones. All wearing corporate casual. The men in fawn trousers and open-collared pale blue shirts. Tomorrow they'd be in fawn again only with white shirts for the wedding. Afterwards, they'd saunter on the sand in three-quarter 'casual' trousers, overly colourful Hawaiian shirts, with their pale feet sliding in leather 'mandals'. They all had crisp cut hair, and expensive sunglasses plastered across their faces. The women were using their even more expensive sunglasses to pin back their long, sleek hair. Her tall, glamorous cousins, her sister. They were all the same. All so incredibly successful—if you equated money, high-flying jobs and incredibly suitable partners with success.

She'd tried it once—to play it their way. She'd dated a guy who was more approved of by her own family than she was herself. What a disaster that had been. They still didn't believe that she'd been the one to end it. Of course, there were reasons for that. But none Bella felt like dwelling on now. Tomorrow was going to be bad enough.

After she'd finally hung all the ribbons on the white-shrouded chairs, she'd headed straight for the bar inside the main building of the hotel. She'd celebrate herself. Toast in another year. Raise a glass to the success of the last. Even if no one else was going to. Even if there wasn't that much success to toast.

There had been talk of a family dinner, but the preparations had run too late—drinks maybe. She was glad. She didn't want to face the all too inevitable questions about her career and her love-life, the looks of unwanted sympathy from her aunts. There'd be time enough for that the next day, when there was no way she could avoid them as much as she had today. For today was her day and she could spend the last of it however she wanted to.

Now, as she sat and waited to be served, she avoided looking around, pretending she was happy to be there alone. She pushed back the inadequacy with some mind games—she'd play a role and fake the confidence. She would do cosmopolitan woman—the woman who took on the world and played it her way. Who took no prisoners, had what she wanted and lived it to the max. It would be good practice for to-morrow when she'd be confronted by Rex and Celia. One of the fun things about being an actress—even a minor-league, bit-part player—was the pretending.

She read through the list again, muttering as she narrowed her choices. 'Do I want "sex on the beach" or a "screaming orgasm"?'

'Why do you have to choose?'

She turned her head sharply. There was a guy standing right beside her. One incredibly hot guy whom she knew she'd never seen before because she'd damn well remember if she had. Tall and dark and with the bluest of eyes capturing hers. While she was staring, he was talking some more.

'I would have thought a woman like you would always have both.'

Sex on the beach and a screaming orgasm? Look-ing up at him, she took a firmer grip on both the menu card and the sensation suddenly beating through her—the tantalising tempo of temptation.

He must be just about the only person here who wasn't involved in the wedding. Or maybe he was. He was probably one of her cousins' dates. For a split second disappointment washed through her. But then she looked him over again—he wasn't wearing an Armani suit and if he was one of their dates he'd definitely be in Armani. And he'd be hanging on his date's arm, not alone and possibly on the prowl in a bar. This guy was in jeans—the roughest fabric she'd seen in the place to date. They were wet around the ankles as if he'd been splashing in the water, and on his feet were a pair of ancient-looking boat shoes. A light grey long-sleeved tee shirt covered his top half. It had a slight vee at the neck, exposing the base of the tanned column that was his neck. It was such a relief to see someone doing truly casual—someone not flaunting evidence of their superb bank balance.

Those bright blue eyes smiled at her. Very brightly. And then they looked her up and down.

Suddenly she felt totally uncomfortable as she thought about her own appearance. Not for the first time she wished for the cool, glamorous gene that the rest of her family had inherited. Instead she was hot, mosquito bitten, with a stripe of cooked-lobster-red sunburn across one half of her chest where she'd missed with her 110 SPF sunscreen. Her white cotton blouse was more off-white than bright and the fire-engine-red ribbon of her floral skirt was starting to come loose—but that was what you got for wearing second-hand.

It was one of her more sedate outfits, an attempt to dress up a little, in deference to the 'family' and their expectations. She'd even used the hotel iron—a real concession given she usually got at least one burn when she went anywhere near the things. Today had been no different. There was a small, very red, very sore patch just below her elbow. And now, thanks to a day spent on her knees dressing chairs in white robes and yellow ribbons, she knew she looked a sight.

As she took in his beautifully chiselled jaw, she

really wished she'd bothered to go to her room and check her face or something on the way. There'd been some mascara on her eyelashes this morning, a rub of lip balm. Both were undoubtedly long gone. She was hardly in a state to be drawing single guys to her across a bar. She darted a glance around. She was the only female in the room. And there were only a couple of other customers. Then she looked at her watch. It was early. He was just making small talk with the only woman about. He was probably a travelling salesman. Only he definitely didn't look the salesman type. And despite the suggestion in his talk he didn't come across as sleazy. There was a bit of a glint in those blue eyes—she'd like to think it was appreciation, but it was more of a dare. And there was more humour than anything. She could do with some humour.

The bartender came back down to where they were standing. And Bella took up the challenge. Cosmopolitan woman she would be. Summoning all her courage and telling her cheeks to remain free of excess colour, she ordered. 'A "sex on the beach" and a "screaming orgasm" please.'

She refused to look at him but she could sense his smile of approval—could hear it in his voice as he ordered too.

'I'll have two "screaming orgasms" and "sex on the beach".'

Bella studiously watched the bartender line up the five shot glasses. She didn't want to turn and look in his eyes again, not entirely sure she wouldn't be mesmerised completely. But peripheral vision was very handy. She was motionless, seemingly fixated on the bartender as he carefully poured in each ingredient, but in reality she was wholly focused on the guy next to her as he pulled out the bar stool next to hers and sat on it. His leg brushed against hers as he did. It was a very long leg, and it looked fine clad in the faded denim. She could feel the strength just from that one accidental touch.

Silently, shaking inside, she went to lift the first glass in the line-up. But then his hand covered hers, lightly pressing it down to the wood. Did he feel her fingers jerk beneath his? She snatched a moment to recover her self-possession before attempting to look at him with what she hoped was sophisticated query.

His bright blues were twinkling. 'Have the orgasm first.'

She could feel the heat as her blood beat its way to her cheeks.

The twinkles in his eyes burned brighter. 'After all, you can always have another one later.'

She stared at him as he released her. He'd turned on the widest, laziest, most sensual smile she'd ever seen. Spellbound wasn't the word. Almost without thinking, she moved her fingers, encircling the second shot.

'What about you?' Why had her voice suddenly gone whispery?

'A gentleman always lets the lady go first.'

So she picked up the orgasm, kind of amazed her hand wasn't visibly trembling. In a swift motion she knocked the contents back into her mouth and swallowed the lot. She took a moment before breathing—then it was a short, sharp breath as she absorbed the burning hit. Slowly she put the glass back down on the bar.

His smile was wicked now. He'd picked up the sex shot, pausing pointedly with it slightly raised, until she did the same. She met his eyes and lifted the glass to her lips. Simultaneously they tipped back and swallowed.

Slamming his on the bench, he picked up the next shot. Then he paused again, inclined his head towards the remaining orgasm.

'You know it's for you.' That smile twisted his mouth as he spoke and its teasing warmth reached out to her.

There was no way she could refuse. She couldn't actually speak for the fire in her throat. So she picked up the shot and again, eyes trained on him, drank. And he mirrored her, barely half a beat behind.

It was a long, deep breath she drew that time. And her recovery was much slower. She stared for a while at the five empty glasses in front of them. And then she looked back at him.

He wasn't smiling any more. At least, his mouth wasn't turned up. But his eyes searched hers while sending a message at the same time. And the warmth was all pervasive. The burning sensation rippled through her body, showing no sign of cooling. Instead her temperature was still rising. And she wasn't at all sure if it was from the alcohol or the fire in his gaze.

Wow. She tried to take another deep breath. But the cool of the air made her tingling lips sizzle more. His gaze dropped to her mouth as if he knew of her sensitivity. The sizzle didn't cease.

She blinked, pressed her lips together to try to stop the whisper of temptation they were screaming to her, resumed visual contemplation of the empty shot glasses. She should never have looked at him.

'Thank you,' she managed, studying him peripherally again.

He shrugged, mouth twitching, lightening the atmosphere and making her wonder if she'd over-emphasised that supercharged moment. Of course there was no way he would be hitting on her. Now his eyes said it was all just a joke. As if he knew that if she thought he was really after her, she'd be running a mile. City slicker vixen-in-a-bar was so not her style. But she'd decided anything could be possible tonight. Anything she wanted could be hers. She was pretending, remember?

'So are we celebrating, or drowning sorrows?' He flashed that easy smile again. And it gave her the confidence that up until now she'd been faking.

'Celebrating.' She turned to face him.

His brows raised. She could understand his surprise. People didn't usually celebrate in a bar drinking all by themselves. So she elaborated.

'It's my birthday.'

'Oh? Which one?'

Did the man not know it was rude to ask? She nearly giggled. But he was so gorgeous she decided to forgive him immediately. Besides, she had the feeling his boldness was innate. It was simply him. It gave her another charge. 'My flirtieth.'

'I'm sorry?' She could see the corners of his mouth twitching again.

'My flirtieth.' So she was making an idiot of herself. What did she care? This night was hers and she could do as she wanted with it—and that might just include flirting with strangers.

'You're either lying or lisping. I think maybe both.' His lips quirked again. And the thing was, she didn't find it offensive. So he was laughing at her. It was worth it just to see the way that smile reached right into his eyes.

'How many have you had?' he asked. 'You seem to be slurring.'

Not only that, she was still staring fixedly at him. She forced herself to blink again. It was so hard not to look at him. His was a face that captured attention and held it for ever. 'These were my first.'

'And last.' He called the bartender over and ordered. 'Sedate white wine spritzer, please.'

'Who wants sedate?' she argued, ignoring his further instructions to the waiter. 'The last thing I want is wine.' The urge for something stronger gripped her—something even more powerful, something to really take her breath away. She wanted the taste of fire to take away the lonely bitterness of disappointment.

'Not true. Come on, whine away. Why are you here, celebrating alone?'

He'd do. The blue in his eyes was all fire.

'I'm not alone. My family is here too—my sister is getting married tomorrow in the resort.'

His brows flashed upwards again. 'So why aren't they here now celebrating your birthday with you?'

She paused. A chink in her act was about to be revealed, but she answered honestly. 'They've forgotten.'

'Ah.' He looked at her, only a half-smile now. 'So the birthday girl has missed out on her party.'

She shrugged. 'Everyone's been busy with the wedding.'

The spritzer arrived, together with a bottle of wine for him and two tall glasses of water.

'Tell me about this wedding.' He said wedding as if it were a bad word.

'What's to tell? She's gorgeous. He's gorgeous. A successful, wealthy, nice guy.'

He inclined his head towards her. 'And you're a little jealous?'

'No!' She shook her head, but a little hurt stabbed inside. She wasn't jealous of Vita, surely she wasn't. She was truly pleased for her. And no way on this earth would she want Hamish. 'He's solid and dependable.' The truth came out. 'Square.'

'You don't like square?'

She thought about it. Hamish was a nice person. And he thought the world of Vita—you could see it in the way he looked at her. He adored her. That little hurt stabbed again. She toughed it out. 'I like a guy who can make me laugh.'

'Do you, now?' But he was the one who laughed. A low chuckle that made her want to smile too—if she weren't having a self-piteous moment. He sobered. 'What's your role in the wedding?'

'Chief bridesmaid,' she said mournfully.

His warm laughter rumbled again.

'It's all right for you,' she said indignantly. 'You've never been a bridesmaid.'

'And you have?'

She nodded. It was all too hideous. 'I know all about it. This is my fourth outing.'

And, yes, she knew what they said. Three times a bridesmaid and all that. Her aunts would be reminding her tomorrow. The only one of her siblings not perfectly paired off.

'What's the best man like?'

She couldn't hide the wince. Rex. How unfortunate that Hamish's best friend was the guy Bella had once picked in her weak moment of trying to be all that the family wanted.

'That bad, huh?'

'Worse.' Because after she'd broken up with him—and it had been her—he'd started dating her most perfect cousin of them all, Celia. And no one in the family could believe that Bella would dump such a catch as Rex and so it was that she earned even more sympathy—more shakes of the head. Not only could she not hold down a decent job, she couldn't hold onto a decent man. No wonder her father treated her like a child. She supposed, despite her Masters degree and her array of part-time jobs, she was. She still hadn't left home, was still dependent on the old man for the basics—like food.

'So.' Her charming companion at the bar speared her attention again with a laser-like look. 'Invite me.'

'I'm sorry?'

'You're the chief bridesmaid, aren't you? You've got to have a date for the wedding.'

'I'm not going to invite a total stranger to my sister's wedding.'

'Why not? It'll make it interesting.'

'How so?' she asked. 'Because you're really a psycho out to create mayhem?'

He laughed at that. 'Look, it's pretty clear you're not looking forward to it. They've forgotten your birthday. This isn't about them. This is about you doing something you want to. Do something you think is tempting.'

'You think you're tempting?' OK, so he was. He sure was. But he didn't need to be so sure about it.

He leaned forward. 'I think what tempts you is the thought of doing something unexpected.'

He was daring her. She very nearly smiled then. It would be too—totally unexpected. And the idea really appealed to her. It had been her motivation all evening—for most of her life, in fact. To be utterly unlike the staid, conservative perfectionists in her bean-counter family. And how wonderful it would be to turn up on the arm of the most handsome man she'd ever seen. Pure fantasy. Especially when she was the only one of the younger generation not to be in a happy couple and have a high-powered career.

And then, for once, she had a flash of her father's conservatism—of realism. 'I can't ask you. I barely know you.'

He leaned forward another inch. 'But you have all night to get to know me.'

CHAPTER TWO

ALL NIGHT? Now it was Bella's lips twitching.

His smile was wicked. 'Come on. Ask me anything.'

Holding his gaze was something she wasn't capable of any more. She ducked it, sat back and concentrated on the conversation.

'All right. Are you married?' She'd better establish the basics.

'Never have, never will.'

Uh-huh. 'Live-in lover?'

'Heaven forbid.'

She paused. He was letting her know exactly where he stood on the commitment front.

Devilry danced in his eyes. She knew he meant every word, but she also knew he was challenging her to pull him up on it.

'Gay?' she asked blithely.

He looked smugly amused. 'Will you take my word for it or do you want proof?'

Now there was a challenge. And not one she was up for just yet.

'Diseases?' Tart this time.

His amusement deepened. 'I think there's diabetes on my father's side, but that doesn't seem to manifest until old age.'

She refused to smile, was determined to find some flaw. To get the better of him somehow. 'What do you do for a living?'

'I work with computers.'

Gee, she nearly snorted, that could mean anything. 'Computers? As in programming?'

His head angled and for the first time his gaze slid from hers. 'Sort of.'

'Ah-h-h.' She nodded, as if it all made perfect sense. Then she wrinkled her nose.

'Ah, what?' He sat up straighter. 'Why the disapproval?'

She hit him then, with everything she could think of. 'Did you know the people most likely to download porn are single, male computer nerds aged between twenty-five and thirty-five? You've probably got some warped perception of the female body now, right? And I bet you're into games—with those female characters with boobs bigger than bazookas and skinny hips and who can knock out five hit men in three seconds.' She stopped for breath, dared him to meet her challenge.

'Ah.' His smile widened while his eyes promised retribution. 'Well, actually, no, that's not me.'

'You think?' she asked innocently.

'I'm single, I'm male, I'm into computers and I'm aged between twenty-five and thirty-five. But I don't need porn because…' he leaned closer and whispered '…I'm not a nerd.'

She leaned a little closer, whispered right back. 'That's what you think.' Admittedly he didn't look much like one, but she could bluff.

But then he called her on it. Laughing aloud, he asked, 'Should I be wearing glasses and have long, lank, greasy hair?'

His hair was short and wind-spiked and his eyes were bright, perceptive and unadorned—and suddenly they flashed with glee.

'Do nerds have muscles like these?' He slapped his bicep with his hand. 'Go on, feel them.'

She could hardly refuse when she'd been the one to throw the insult. Tentatively she reached out a hand and poked gingerly at his upper arm with her finger. It was rock hard. Intrigued, she took a second shot. Spread her fingers wide, pressing down on the grey sleeve. Underneath was big, solid muscle. Really big. And she could feel the definition, was totally tempted to feel further…

But she pulled back, because there was a sudden fire streaming through her. She must be blushing something awful. She took a much-needed sip of her watered-down wine.

His told-you-so gaze teased her.

She sniffed. 'You're probably wearing a body suit under that shirt.' Completely clutching at straws.

'OK,' he said calmly, 'feel them now.' He took her hand, lifted the hem of his shirt and before she knew it her palm was pressed to his bare abs.

OK? Hell, yes, OK!

She froze. Her mind froze. Her whole body froze. But her hand didn't. The skin on his stomach was warm and beneath her fingers she could feel the light scratchiness of hair and then the rock-hard indents of muscles. This was no weedy-boy-who-spent-hours-in-front-of-a-computer physique. And this wasn't just big, strong male. This was fit. Superfit.

Her fingers badly wanted to stretch out some more and explore. If she moved her thumb a fraction she'd be able to stroke below his navel. She whipped her hand out while she still had it under control.

His smile was wicked as the heat in her cheeks became unbearable. 'And what about this tan, hmm?' He pushed up a sleeve and displayed a bronzed fore-arm as if it were some treasured museum exhibit. She stared at the length of it, lightly hair-dusted, muscle flexing, she could see the clear outline of a thick vein running down to the back of a very broad palm. Very real, very much alive—and strong. She was taken with his hand for some time.

Finally she got back the ability to speak. 'Is the tan all-over-body?'

'If you're lucky you might get to find out.'

The guy had some nerve. But he was laughing as he said it.

'So why are you single, then?' she said, trying to adopt an acidic tone. 'I mean, if you're such a catch, why haven't you been caught already?'

'You misunderstand the game, sweetheart,' he answered softly. 'I'm not the prey. I'm the predator.'

And if she could bring herself to admit it, she wanted him to pounce on her right now. But she was still working on defence and denial. 'Well, you're not that good, then, are you? Where's your catch tonight?'

The only answer was a quick lift of his brows and a wink.

She pressed her lips together, but couldn't quite stop them quirking upwards. 'You hunt often?'

He laughed outright at that, shaking his head. She wasn't sure if it was a negative to her question or simple disbelief at the conversation in general. 'I'm like a big-game animal—one hunt will last me some time.' His eyes caught hers again. 'And I only hunt when I see something really, really juicy.'

Juicy, huh? Her juices were running now and that voice in her head saying 'eat me' really should be shot.

His laughter resurfaced, though not as loud, and she knew he'd twigged her thoughts.

Still she refused to join in. 'But you don't keep your catches.'

'No.' He shook his head. 'Catch and release. That's the rule.'

Hmm. Bella wasn't so sure about the strategy. 'What if she doesn't want to be released?'

'Ah, but she does,' he corrected. 'Because she understands the rules of the game. And even if she doesn't, it won't take long until she wants out.'

Her mouth dropped. She couldn't imagine any woman wanting to get away from this guy's net.

Flirting outrageously was too much fun—especially when the flirt had a body like this and eyes like those.

His smile sharpened round the edges. 'I have it on good authority that I'm very selfish.'

'Ah-h-h.' She was intrigued. That smacked of bitter-ex-girlfriend speak. Was he playing the field on the rebound? 'You've never wanted to catch and keep?'

He grimaced. 'No.'

'Why not?'

For the first time he looked serious. 'Nothing keeps. Things don't ever stay the same.' He paused, the glint resurfaced. 'The answer is to go for what you want, when you want it.'

'And after that?'

He didn't reply, merely shrugged his shoulders.

Bella took another sip of the spritzer and contemplated what she knew to be the ultimate temptation before her—defence and denial crumbling. 'After that' didn't matter really, did it? He had a beautiful body and a sense of humour—what more would a confident, cosmopolitan woman want for an evening? And wasn't that what she was—for tonight?

'So, now that you know something about me,' he said, 'tell me, what do you do?'

He might have told her some things, but strangely she felt as if she knew even less. But what she really wanted to know, he didn't need words for. She wanted to know if that tan was all-over-body, she wanted to know the heat and strength of those muscles—the feel of them. Everything of him. Cosmo woman here she was.

'I'm an actor,' she declared, chin high.

There was a pause. 'Ah-h-h.'

'Ah, what?' She didn't like the look of his exaggerated, knowing nod.

'I bet you're a very good one,' he sidestepped.

Her cosmo confidence ebbed. 'I could be.' Given the opportunity.

'Could?'

'Sure.' She just needed that lucky break.

Now he was looking way too amused. 'What else do you do?'

'What do you mean what else?' she snapped. 'I'm an actor.'

'I don't know of many actors who don't have some sort of day job.'

She sighed—totally theatrically, and then capitulated. 'I make really good coffee.'

He laughed again. 'Of course you do.'

Of course. She was the walking cliché. The family joke. The wannabe. And no way in hell was she telling him what else she did. Children's birthday party entertainer ranked as one of the lowest, most laughable occupations on the earth—her family gave her no end of grief about it. She didn't need to give him more reason to as well.

'And how is the life of a jobbing actor these days?' He was still looking a tad too cynically amused for her liking.

She sighed again—doubly theatrical. 'I have "the nose".'

'"The nose"?'

She turned her head, offered him a profile shot.

He studied it seriously for several seconds. Then, 'What's wrong with it?'

'A little long, a little straight.'

'I'd say it's majestic.'

She jumped when he ran his finger down it. The tip tingled as he tapped it.

'Quite,' she acknowledged, sitting back out of reach. 'It gives me character and that's what I am—a character actress.'

'I'm not convinced it's the nose that makes you so full of character,' he drawled.

'Quite.' She almost laughed—it was taking everything to ignore his irony. 'I've not the looks for the heroine. I'm the sidekick.'

She didn't mention it, but there was also the fact she was on the rounder side of skinny. A little short, a little curvy for anything like Hollywood. But Wellywood—more formally known as Wellington, New Zealand's own movie town? Maybe. She just needed to get the guts to move there.

'Oh, I wouldn't say—'

'Don't.' She raised her hand, stopped him mid-sentence. 'It's true. No leading-lady looks here, but it doesn't matter because the smart-ass sidekick gets all the best lines anyway.'

'But not the guy.'

She frowned. So true. And half the time she didn't

get the sidekick part either. She got the walk-on-here, quick-exit-there parts. The no-name ones that never earned any money, fame or even notoriety.

She figured it was because she hadn't done the posh drama academy thing. Her father had put his foot down. She wasn't to waste her brain on that piffle—a hobby sure, but never a career. So she'd been packed off to university—like all her siblings. Only instead of brain-addling accountancy or law, she'd read English. And, to her father's horror, film studies. After a while he'd 'supposed she might go into teaching'. He'd supposed wrong. She'd done evening classes in acting at the local high school. Read every method book in the library. Watched the classic films a million kazillion times. Only at all those agencies and casting calls it was almost always the same talent turning up and she couldn't help but be psyched out by the pros, by the natural talents who'd been onstage from the age of three and who had all the confidence and self-belief in the world.

Bella thought she had self-belief. But it fought a hard battle against the disbelief of her family. 'When are you going to settle into a real job?' they constantly asked. 'This drama thing is just a hobby. You don't want to be standing on your feet making coffee, or blowing up balloons for spoilt toddlers for the rest of your days…' And on and on and on.

'Well, who wants the guy anyway?' she asked grumpily. 'I don't want the saccharine love story. Give me adventure and snappy repartee any day.'

'Really?' he asked in total disbelief. 'You sure you don't want the big, fluffy princess part?'

'No, Prince Charming is boring.' And Prince Charming, the guy her family had adored, wouldn't let her be herself.

He leaned forward, took her chin in his hand and turned her to face him. 'I don't believe you're always this cynical.'

The comment struck another little stab into her. It twisted a little sharper when she saw he was totally serious.

'No,' she admitted honestly. 'Only when it's my birthday and no one has remembered and I'm stuck in wedding-of-the-century hell.'

'All weddings are hell.' His fingers left her face but his focus didn't.

Well, this one sure was. 'Here was me thinking it was going to be a barefoot-on-the-beach number with hardly anyone in attendance, but it's massive— ninety-nine per cent of the resort is booked out with all the guests!'

'Hmm.' He was silent a moment. Then he flicked her a sideways glance. 'How lucky for you that I'm in that remaining one per cent.'

Wordless, she stared at him, taking a second to believe the lazy arrogance in the comment he'd so dryly delivered. Then she saw the teasing, over-the-top wink.

Her face broke and the amusement burst forth.

'Finally!' He spoke above her giggles. 'She laughs. And when she laughs...'

The laughter passed between them, light and fresh, low and sweet. And her mood totally lifted.

'I am so sorry,' she apologised, shaking her head.

'That's OK. You're clearly having a trying day.'

'Something like that.' The thought of tomorrow hadn't made it any easier and she'd felt guilty for feeling so me-me-me that it had all compounded into a serious case of the grumps.

'Shall we start over?' His eyes were twinkling again and this time she didn't try to stop her answering smile.

'Please, that would be good.' And it would be good. Because it was quite clear that under his super-flirt exterior there was actually a nice guy. Not to mention, damn attractive.

'I'm Owen Hughes. Disease-free, single and straight.'

Owen. A player to be sure—but one that she knew would be a lot of fun.

'I'm Bella Cotton. Also disease-free, single and straight.'

'Bella,' he repeated, but didn't make the obvious 'beautiful' translation. He didn't need to—simply the way he said it made her feel its meaning. Then he made her smile some more. 'Any chance you're in need of a laugh?'

She nodded. 'Desperately. Light relief is what I need.'

'I can do that.' He grinned again and she found herself feeling happier than she had all day—all week even. He leaned towards her. 'Look, I've got an empty pit instead of a stomach right now. Have dinner with me—unless you've got some full-on rehearsal dinner to go to or something?'

She shook her head. 'Amazingly that's not the plan. I think some of the younger guests are just supposed to meet up later for drinks. The olds are doing their own thing.'

'Maybe they've organised a surprise birthday party for you.'

'As nice as that idea sounds—' and it did sound really nice '—they haven't. You can trust me on that.'

'OK. Then let's go find a table.'

She found herself standing and walking with him to the adjoining restaurant just like that. No hesitation, no second thought, just simplicity.

He grinned as they sat down. 'I really am starving.'

'So you haven't caught anything much lately, you big tiger, you,' she mocked.

He laughed. 'I'm confident I can make up for it.'

Bella met the message in his eyes. And was quite sure he could.

CHAPTER THREE

OWEN FELT A ridiculous surge of pleasure at finally having made Bella see the funny side. And, just as he'd suspected, she had a killer of a smile and a deadly sweet giggle. Her full lips invited and her eyes crinkled at the corners. He couldn't decide if they were pale blue or grey, but he liked looking a lot while trying to work it out and he liked watching them widen the more he looked.

He'd been bluffing—if he really were some tiger in the jungle, he'd have died of starvation months ago. Sex was a recreational hobby for him, very recreational. But it had been a while. Way too much of a while. Maybe that was why he'd felt the irresistible pull of attraction when she'd walked into the bar. He'd been sitting at a table in the corner and almost without will had walked up to stand beside her at the bar. Just to get a closer look at her little hourglass figure. In the shirt and skirt he could see shapely legs and frankly bountiful breasts that had called to the most base of elements in him.

Then he'd noticed the droop to her lip that she'd

been determinedly trying to lift as she'd read that menu. And he'd just had to make her smile.

The table he'd led her to was in the most isolated corner of the restaurant he could find. He didn't want her family interrupting any sooner than necessary. Wanted to keep jousting and joking with her. Wanted a whole lot more than that too and needed the time to make it happen.

'So,' she asked, suddenly perky, 'what sort of computers? You work for some software giant?'

'I work for myself.' For the last ten years he'd done nothing much other than work—pulling it together, thinking it through, organising the team and getting it done.

'Programming what—games? Banking software?'

'I work in security.'

'Oh, my.' She rolled her eyes. 'I bet you're one of them whiz-kids who broke into the FBI's files when you were fourteen, or created some nasty virus. Bad-boy hacker now crossed over to the good side or something—am I right?'

'No.' He chuckled. Truth was the actual programming stuff wasn't him—he had bona fide computer nerds working for him. He was the ideas guy—who'd thought up a way to make online payments more secure, and now to protect identity. 'I've never been in trouble with the law.'

'Oh. So...' She paused, clearly trying to think up the next big assault. 'Business good?'

'You could say that.' Inwardly he smiled. He now

had employees scattered around the world. A truly international operation, but one that he preferred to direct from his inner-city bolt hole in Wellington. But he didn't want to talk about work—it was all consuming, even keeping his mind racing when he should be asleep. That was why he was on Waiheke, staying at his holiday home a few yards down the beach from the hotel. He was due for some R & R, a little distraction. And the ideal distraction seemed to have stepped right in front of him.

His banter before hadn't all been a lie, though. He did believe in going for what he wanted and then moving right on. This little poppet was the perfect pastime for his weekend of unwind time. So he'd made sure she understood the way he played it. Spelt the rules out loud and clear. She'd got them, as he'd intended, and she was tempted. Now he just had to give her that extra little nudge.

She was studying the menu intently. And he studied her, taken by the stripe of sunburn that disappeared under her shirt. It seemed to be riding along to the crest of her breast and his fingers itched to follow its path.

When the waiter came she ordered with an almost reckless abandonment and he joined in. He was hungry. He'd splashed up the beach over an hour ago now. He hadn't been able to be bothered fixing something for himself, figured he'd get a meal to take away from the restaurant. Only now he'd found something better to take back with him.

'Oh, no.' The look on her face was comical.

'What?' he asked.

'Some of my family has arrived.'

'It's time for drinks, then, huh?' He turned his head in the direction she was staring. Inwardly cursing. Just when she was getting warmed up.

He saw the tall blonde looking over at them speculatively. When she saw them notice her, she strode over, long legs making short work of the distance.

'Bella. So sorry,' she clipped. 'It's your birthday and you're here all alone.'

What? thought Owen. Was he suddenly invisible?

'I can't believe you didn't remind us,' the blonde continued, still ignoring him.

'I didn't want to say anything.' For a second he saw the pain in Bella's eyes. A surge of anger hit him.

He realised what she'd done. She'd tested them. And they'd failed.

'Don't worry.' He spoke up. 'She's not alone. It's just that we wanted to have our own private celebration.'

The blonde looked at him then, frosty faced. 'And you are?'

'Owen,' he answered, as if that explained it all.

'Owen.' She glanced to Bella and then back to give him the once-over. He watched her coldness thaw to a sugary smile as she checked out his watch and his shoes. He knew she recognised the brands. Yes, darling, he thought, I'm loaded. And it was one thing Bella hadn't noticed. He found it refreshing.

'It seems you've been keeping a few things to yourself lately, Isabella.'

Owen looked at Bella. There was a plea in her eyes he couldn't ignore.

The silence deepened, becoming more awkward as he kept his focus on her. And a tinge of amusement tugged when finally the willowy blonde spoke, sounding disconcerted. 'I'll leave you to your meal, then.'

'Thank you,' Owen answered, not taking his gaze off Bella. He was never normally so rude, but he could do arrogance when necessary. And when he'd seen the hurt in Bella's eyes he'd known it was necessary. The irrational need to help her, to support her, had bitten him. Stupid. Because Owen wasn't the sort to do support. Ordinarily he did all he could to avoid any show of interest or involvement other than the purely physical, purely fun. He'd made that mistake before and been pushed too close to commitment as a result. His ex-girlfriend had wanted the ring, the ceremony, the works. He hadn't. But then she'd tried to force it in a way he totally resented her for. The experience had been so bad he was determined to make damn sure it didn't happen again. He no longer had relationships. He had flings.

But now he simply hoped that his brush-off would be reported back to the rest of the family and they'd all stay away for a bit.

The waiter arrived with the first plates, breaking the moment. Bella was busy picking up her fork, but he could see her struggling to hold back her smile.

He waited until she'd swallowed her first bite. 'Am I invited now?'

'If I do, your job is to entertain me, right?' Her smile was freed. 'No eyeing up my beautiful cousins.'

He didn't need anyone else to eye up. And he'd entertain her all night and then some if she wanted. But he played the tease some more. 'How beautiful are they?'

She stared down her majestic nose at him. 'You just met one of them.'

'Her?' he asked, putting on surprise. 'She's not beautiful.'

Her expression of disbelief was magic.

He laughed. 'She's not. So she's tall and blonde. So what? They're a dime a dozen. I'd far rather spend time with someone interesting.' He'd done tall and blonde many times over in his past. These days he was searching for something a little different.

She ignored him. 'No getting wildly drunk and embarrassing me. That isn't why you want to go, is it? The free booze?'

'No.'

'Then why?'

The truth slipped out. 'I want to see you have a really good time. A really, really good time.'

He did too. And he knew he could give it to her, and how. There was a baseline sizzle between them that was intense and undeniable. He'd seen the recognition, the jolt of awareness in her expression the moment their gazes had first locked. It was what she needed; it was what he needed. And he'd happily spend the weekend at her dull family wedding to get it. He'd put up with a lot more to get it if he had to.

On top of that primary, physical attraction, she was funny. Smart. Definitely a little bitter. And he liked her smile. He liked to make her smile.

As their dinner progressed it was nice to forget about everything for a moment as he concentrated wholly on her. He pulled his mobile out of his pocket and flicked it to Vibrate, pushing work from his mind. He was supposed to be having a couple of hours off after all. Like forty-eight.

He saw her glance into the main body of the restaurant as it filled. Saw her attention turn from him to whatever the deal was about tomorrow.

'It's going to be a massive wedding,' she said gloomily. 'The whole family and extended family and friends and everyone.'

'All that fuss for nothing.' He just couldn't see the point of it. Nor could he see why it was such a problem for her.

'All that money for just one day.' She shook her head. Her hair feathered out; shoulder length, it was a light wavy brown. He wanted to lean over and feel it fly over his face.

'Do you know how much she's spent on the dress?'

So money was some of it. 'I hate to think.' His drollery seemed to pass her by.

'And I've got the most hideous bridesmaid's dress. Hideous.'

'You'll look gorgeous.' She was such a cute package she could wear anything and look good.

'You don't understand,' she said mournfully. 'It's a cast of thousands. Celia—the gorgeous cousin—is one too. And there are others.' The little frown was back.

Her every emotion seemed to play out on her face—she was highly readable. If she could control it, learn to manipulate it, then she'd make a very good actress.

'The dress suits all of them, of course.'

'Of course.' And she was worried about what she looked like—what woman wasn't? He'd be happy to reassure her, spend some time emphasising her most favourable assets.

She looked up at him balefully. 'They're all five-seven or more and svelte.'

Whereas she was maybe five-four and all curves. He'd have her over ten tall blonde Celias any day.

'Did they go with a gift list?' He played along.

'Yes.' She ground out the answer. 'The cheapest item was just under a hundred bucks—and you had to buy a pair.'

Money was definitely an issue. He supposed it must be—fledgling actresses and café staff didn't exactly earn lots. And this resort was one of the most exclusive and expensive in the country. To be having a wedding here meant someone had some serious dosh. Was she worried about not keeping up with the family success?

He laughed, wanting to keep the mood light. 'Lists

are such a waste of time. They'd be better off leaving it to chance and getting two coffee plungers. That way when they split up they can have one each.'

Surprise flashed on her face. 'Oh, and you call me cynical.'

'Marriage isn't worth the paper it's written on.' He'd been witness to that one all right—hit on the head with a sledgehammer. It was all a sham.

'You think?'

'Come on, how many people make it to ten years these days, seven even? What's the point?' Because at some point, always, it ended. Owen figured it was better to walk before the boredom or the bitterness set in—and it would set in. The feelings never lasted—he'd seen that, he'd felt it himself. Now he knew it was better not to get tied into something you didn't want—and certainly not to drag the lives of innocents into it either. He wasn't running the risk of that happening ever again. No live-in lover, no wife, no kids.

BELLA SAT BACK and thought. She had to give him that—one of her older cousins had separated only last month, a marriage of three and a half years over already. But other marriages worked out, didn't they? She had high hopes for Vita and Hamish. She had faint hopes for herself—if she was lucky.

She frowned at him. 'Yes, we already know it's not on your agenda.' He couldn't commit to marriage—the monogamy bit would get him. He was too buff to be limited to one woman. Smorgasbord was his style. Well, that was fine. She was hardly at a 'settle down' point in life. She was still working on the 'get' a life bit.

'That's right.' He grinned. 'But I'm not averse to helping others celebrate their folly.'

'So you can flirt with all the bridesmaids?' A little dig.

'Not all of them. Just one.'

The shorter, darker-haired, dumpier one with the long straight nose? He was just being nice because he hadn't actually seen all the others yet. When he did, it would be all over. She looked up from her cleared plate and encountered his stare again. The glint was back and notch by notch making her smoulder.

His stare didn't waver. And the message grew stronger.

Pure want.

She curled her fingers around her chilled wine glass. She felt flushed all over and had the almost desperate thought that she needed to cool down. Her fingers tightened. Then his hand covered hers, holding the glass to the table.

'I think you've had enough.'

She narrowed her eyes, unsure of his meaning.

He lifted his hands, spread his fingers as he shrugged loosely. 'I'm not suggesting you're drunk. Far from it.' His smile flashed, and it was all wicked. 'But the more you drink, the duller your senses become and I wouldn't want you to lose any sensation. Not tonight.'

'I'm going to need my senses?' She was mesmerised.

'All of them.'

OK.

He inclined his head to the large bi-folding doors that opened out to the deck. A small jazz ensemble was playing. She hadn't even noticed them set up. Too focused on her companion—the most casual customer in the place yet the one who commanded all her attention.

'Dance with me.' He stood. 'We can see how well we move together. Make sure we've got it right for the big day tomorrow.'

Why did she take everything he said and think he was really meaning something else?

He grinned, seeming to understand her problem exactly, and silently telling her that she was absolutely right. He held out his hand.

For a split second she looked at it. The broad palm, the long fingers, the invitation. The instant she placed her hand on top, he locked it into his. There was no going back now.

They walked out the doors together, to the part of the deck by the band where people were dancing. The waves were gently washing the beach. The evening was warm and for Bella the night seemed to exude magic.

'I like this old music,' he muttered, curling one arm around her waist while holding her hand to his chest with the other. 'Made for my kind of dancing.'

'Your kind?'

'Where you actually touch.' His hand was wide and firm across the small of her back as he pulled her towards him, and she went to him because she couldn't not. Because in reality she wanted to get closer still. Her head barely reached above his shoulders, but it didn't matter because she couldn't focus much further than on the material right in front of her anyway, and on the inviting, warm strength beneath it.

His fingers feathered over her back, skin to skin. She trembled at the sensation, nearly stumbled with the need that rose deep within her. She masked the craziness of her response with some sarcasm. 'I said yes to dancing, not having your hands up my shirt.'

'I thought up your shirt might be quite good.' His low reply in her ear made her need heighten to almost painful intensity.

Good was an understatement. He pressed her that little bit closer, so her breasts were only a millimetre from the hard wall that was his chest. Not quite close enough to touch, but she could almost, almost feel him and her nipples were tight.

She dragged in a burning breath. 'Owen, I—'

'Shh,' he said. 'Your family is watching.'

He danced her away from the others and into the farthest corner of the deck, where the darkness of night lurked, encroaching on the lights and loud conviviality of the restaurant. Gently he swayed them both to the languid music, talking to her in low tones, telling her just to dance with him. Was it one song, was it three, or five? Time seemed suspended. He muttered her name, his breath stirring her hair, then nothing. And as she moved to his lead she fell deeper into his web.

When the band took a break, she took a moment in the bathroom to try to recover her aplomb—cooling her wrists under the rush of water from the cold tap. She shouldn't have had those shots. She'd barely drunk a drop since, but she felt giddy. And as she looked at her reflection—at her large eyes, and the heightened colour in her cheeks and lips—she knew she didn't want to recover her aplomb at all. She wanted to follow this madness to its natural conclusion. Nothing else seemed to matter any more—nothing but being with Owen. Just for while she was on this fantasy island.

She stepped out of the bathroom and saw him straighten from where he'd been leaning against the wall, eyes trained on her door. She walked over to meet him, but her path was intercepted by Vita, her sister.

'Bella, where have you been all night? More to the point, who is that guy you're dancing with?' Vita looked astounded.

'Owen is an old friend.'

'How old?' The disbelief on her sister's face was mortifying.

'Well, not that old.' Bella looked up to where he stood now looming large and close, right behind Vita, his eyes keen. She just kept slim control of her voice and the hysterical giggle out of it. 'You were born what, about thirty years ago, weren't you?'

'Somewhere thereabouts.' He took the last couple of steps so he stood beside her, circling his arm around her waist as naturally as if he'd done it a thousand times.

Then he smiled at her, a glowing, deeply intimate smile that had Bella blinking as much as Vita. His fingers pressed her slightly closer to him and inside she shook. He held her even more firmly.

When he turned his head to Vita, the smile lost its intimacy but was no less potent. 'You must be Bella's sister, the beautiful bride. Congratulations.'

Vita blinked and took more than a second to recover her manners. 'Thank you…er…Owen. Will we be seeing you tomorrow? You're more than welcome.'

'Well…' he glanced back to Bella and she saw the laughter dancing in his eyes '…I'd love to be there, but Bella wasn't sure…'

'Oh, if you're a friend of Bella's, of course you're welcome.'

Bella turned sharply, narrowed her gaze on Vita. Did she stress the 'if'?

'Thank you.' Owen closed off the conversation smoothly. And with a nod drew Bella back outside and threaded them through the dancing couples.

Bella went into his arms hardly thinking about what she was doing. Melancholy had struck. Vita had seemed stunned that Bella might actually have a gorgeous guy wanting to be with her. They were probably all watching agog—amazed at the development. Oh, why did she have to be here with her perfect sister and her perfect family—when she was so obviously the odd one out?

He must have read her thoughts because he pulled her close and looked right in her eyes. 'She's not that perfect.'

She didn't believe him. Her little sister, by a year, had always been the one to do things how they were supposed to—the way her father wanted.

'She didn't wish you a happy birthday,' he said softly.

Bella sighed. 'She's preoccupied.' And she was. This wedding was a mammoth operation.

Owen frowned, clearly thinking that it wasn't a good enough excuse. Warmth flooded her. He was so damn attractive.

'So how many candles should you be blowing out tonight, Bella?'

'Twenty-four.' She hadn't the energy for joking any more—she was too focused on her feelings for him. And all of a sudden the giddiness took over—she couldn't slow the speed of her heartbeat; her breath was knocked from her lungs. She stumbled.

His hands tightened on her arms. 'You're tired.'

Tired was the last thing she was feeling.

But he stepped back, breaking their physical contact. 'I'll walk you to your room.'

Disappointment flooded her. She'd been having a wonderful night and she didn't want it to come to an end. But it had—with Vita's interruption the fantasy had been shattered. And Owen was already moving them across the deck, towards the stairs that led to the sandy beach.

She glanced up into his face, hoping for a sign of that glint, only to find it shuttered. Blandly unreadable. The sense of disappointment swelled.

As they reached the steps, Celia stepped in front of them.

'You're not leaving already?' she asked, full of vivaciousness.

'It's a big day tomorrow. Bella needs to turn in now,' Owen answered before she had the chance.

Celia turned her stunning gaze from him to Bella and the glance became stabbing. 'You'd better put some cream on that sunburn or you'll look like a zebra tomorrow.'

Oh, she just had to get that jibe in, didn't she? Bella smarted.

Owen turned slightly. Slowly, carefully, he gave Bella such an intense once-over that she could feel the impact as if he were really touching her, a bold caress. But it was his eyes that kissed—from the tip of her nose all the way to her toes. And then he did touch her. Lifting his hand, with a firm finger, he stroked the red stripe on her chest—from the top of it near her collarbone, down the angled line to where it disappeared into her blouse. His eyes followed the path, and then went lower, seeming to be able to see everything, regardless of the material.

'Don't worry.' He spoke slowly. 'I'll make sure she takes care of it.'

Bella stared up at him, fascinated by the flare

in his eyes. The flare that had been there from that moment when she'd turned her head to his voice as she'd sat at the bar. It had flashed now and then as they'd talked and laughed their way through dinner. But now it was back and bigger than before and she couldn't help her response. Every muscle, every fibre, every cell tightened within her. As he looked at her like that, his hunger was obvious to anyone. She'd never felt more wanted than she did in that moment and she was utterly seduced. The whole of his attention was on her and the whole of her responded. But she wasn't just willing, she was wanting.

She dimly heard a cough, but when she finally managed to tear her gaze from his, Celia had already walked off. Bella managed a vague smile after her general direction, but then, compelled by the pull between them, she walked with Owen—barely aware of her cousin's and her sister's gazes following her. She no longer cared. She was too focused on the burn of her skin where his finger had touched, and the excitement burgeoning now as he held her hand and matched her step for step.

CHAPTER FOUR

Down on the sand the breeze lifted and the drop in temperature checked Bella.

'Where are you staying?' Owen asked, his voice oddly gentle.

'One of the studios round the back.' She wasn't in one of the luxury villas, but a tiny unit in a building with several other tiny units. It was still nice. It didn't quite have the view and door opening directly onto the beach that the villas did, but it didn't have the price tag either.

'Show me.' Still gentle.

But her mind teased her with what it was that he wanted her to show him. It took only a minute or so to wind around the back of the building, to where the units were. At her door she stopped. She gazed at the frame of it, suddenly shy of wanting to look him in the eye. 'Thank you for seeing me through that.'

'No problem.' He loomed beside her. 'It was fun.'

Fun. Disappointment wafted over her again. Stupid, when he'd given her a victory she'd mentally relive time and time again, but there was something

else she wanted now. Something she sensed would
be much, much better.

He gestured towards the door. 'Are you alone in
there? Not twin sharing with your great-aunt Ame-
lia or anyone awful?'

'All alone. Just me.' She chanced a look up at him
then, saw the hint of the smile, the gleam of teeth
flashing white in the darkness.

'Want me to come in and make sure there are no
monsters in the wardrobe?'

Confidence trickled back through her. She stepped
a little closer. 'Quite the gentleman, aren't you? Are
you going to turn down my sheet as well?'

'If you like.' He matched her move, stepped closer
still. 'Would you like, Bella?'

Such a simple question. It needed only the sim-
plest of answers. And she already knew what he was
asking and what her answer would be. There was
no way she could ever say no to him. Probably no
one had ever said no to him and she didn't blame
any of them.

'Yes.'

His head bent. His smile was no wider, but somehow stronger. 'Good.'

His first kiss was soft, just a gentle press of lips
on lips. No other contact. Then he pulled away—just
a fraction, for just a moment. Then he was back. Another butterfly-light kiss that had her reaching after
him when he pulled back again. And as she moved
forward he swept her into his arms. Strong and tight
they held her and the next kiss changed completely.

Deep, then deeper again. The awareness that had sizzled between them all night was unleashed. Her hands threaded through his hair, his hands moulded over her curves. Together they strained closer, lips hungry, tongues tasting. Bella was lost. He felt better than she'd imagined—broad, lean, hard. Her eyes closed as his lips left hers, roving down to her jaw, down her throat, hot and hungry. The fire in her belly roared.

And then he was kissing her sunburn stripe, undoing the top few buttons on her blouse, pulling it open so he could follow the path of reddened skin with lush wet kisses that did anything but soothe. The red stopped on the curve of her breast—where her bikini cup had been. But he didn't stop. He pulled the lace of her bra down until her nipple popped up over it. And then he took that in his mouth too.

She arched back as sensations spasmed deep inside. His other arm took her weight, pulling her pelvis into the heat of his hips, and she could feel his hardness through his jeans. She gasped at the impact—and at the pleasure ricocheting through her system. He lifted his head, his hunger showing in the strain on his face and in his body. The air was cool on her bared skin but she was still steaming up.

Breathless, she pulled back, her blouse hanging half open, breast spilling over her bra. 'I think I better get the door unlocked now.'

'I think you better had,' he teased, but her confidence surged higher when she heard his equal breathlessness. 'Because the thing about sex on the beach,' he added, 'is the sand.'

Giggling, she slipped her hand in her pocket, closed her fingers around the key. Turning, she fumbled to get it into the lock. He stood behind her, ran his hands over her hips and then pressed so close she could feel everything he had to offer. Her hand lurched off course completely. He put his fingers over hers and guided the key safely home.

Pressing even harder against her, he spoke in her ear, hot and full of sexy humour. 'We are having screaming orgasms though, OK?'

'OK.' She just got the door open and the answer out before he spun her around and his mouth came down on hers again. He backed her in, kicking the door shut behind them with his foot. He kept backing her, but angled her direction so after only a couple of paces she was up against the wall. Relief flooded her as she felt it behind her and she half sagged against it. She didn't think her legs were strong enough to hold her up all on their own any more. When the man kissed, all she could think of was a bed, and her desperation to be on it and exploring and feeling and being kissed like that everywhere.

His hands held her face up to his, warm fingers stroked down her neck, but he stood back so his body didn't touch hers. She wanted it to touch again— all of it against her. The kisses grew deeper as she opened more to him—inviting him in with the sighs of pleasure she let escape and the way she sought him with her tongue.

But her confidence came in waves—ebbing again as his caresses became more intimate, as he undid the last buttons and hooks. Shyness overcame her as her blouse and her bra slipped away completely.

He looked down at her, sensing her stillness. 'You're sure?'

She nodded, but explained. 'It's been a while.'

'Me too.'

She didn't believe that for a second. But it was nice of him to say it.

Then her shyness melted as he whisked his shirt over his head and she saw the beauty of his body beneath.

Her hands lifted instinctively, and she spread her fingers on his shoulder, slowly letting them trace down the impressive breadth of his chest and then lower, over the taut upper abs down to where his jeans were fastened. He lifted his head at that, grinning wickedly. 'Stop that, sweetness. It'll all be over all too soon. As it is it's going to be a close one.'

'Very close,' she agreed, letting her fingers walk some more.

'Stop that.' His smile only widened.

'I can't. You feel fantastic. You really do have muscles.' She marvelled at it. How the hell did a computer geek grow muscles like these?

But then her own actions slowed as she became acutely aware of his—of the kisses dulling her sense of initiative. He was taking the lead and increasingly all she could do was follow. Slowly, so slowly, he was stripping the skirt off her. Dropping to his knees, he eased it down, pressing kisses to her thighs and legs.

Then he stood again, him still clad in jeans, her in nothing but knickers. Their shoes had been kicked off somewhere outside the door. He took her face in his hands again, searching her eyes and then smiling. Then kissing. And with every moment of the kiss her need grew. Until, pressing her shoulders against the wall for support, she pushed her hips forward towards him—aching for closeness.

'Something you want?' he asked.

'You know.'

He slid his hands from her shoulders all the way down until he curled his fingers round hers. Then he lifted them, swinging her arms up above her head, pinning them back to the wall with his hands. The movement lifted her breasts, her hard nipples strained straight up to him.

He paused and took advantage of the view. Looking into his eyes, she saw the passion and simply melted more—shivering as she did. Swiftly he kissed her and transferred the possession of both her hands to only one of his. He glided his other hand down her throat, then lower. Cupping her breast, he stroked the taut nipple with his thumb. She whimpered into his mouth. His hand moved again, fingers sliding down her stomach, and then they slipped inside her panties, right down, curving into her, feeling the extent of the warm wetness there as she moaned.

'Mmm.' He lifted his mouth from hers, looked into her eyes as another moan escaped her. And any embarrassment dissolved as she took in his pleased expression.

'That's what I want,' he muttered, kissing her eyes closed, one and then the other. Gentle. His fingers started to work. So slowly, gently. And his mouth pressed to hers again, his tongue exploring, just as his fingers were. Slow and gentle and tormenting. Insistent. And the giddiness was back. She kept her eyes closed, lost in the feeling, utterly at his mercy, until she was writhing and arching and wanting harder and faster. But still he kept it slow, teasing her. And then she was panting, pleading in the scarce moments when he lifted his head to let her take breath.

And he listened, watched, altered his actions. Not so gentle. Faster and deeper. Passionate kisses that bruised her lips and then roved hard over her face and then down. His mouth was hot as he nuzzled his way down the side of her throat, to her breast and back to her starving mouth.

He lifted his head to watch as her panting grew shallower, faster, louder. She started to shake, was begging for him not to stop, for him to give her more.

His eyes gleamed with satisfaction. 'Screaming, remember?'

But he didn't need to tell her. She couldn't stop it anyway, the cry that came as she came—hard and loud.

His fingers loosened on her wrists, her arms dropped down to her sides and he braced his hands on the wall either side of her. He brushed a gentle kiss on her nose.

She shook her head. 'I can't stand any more.'

'Yes, you can.'

'No, I mean literally. I can't stand any more.' And her feet began to slip out in front of her, a slow slither to the floor.

He scooped her straight up.

'Oh, thanks. My legs just didn't want to be upright any more.'

'What do they want?' He chuckled.

'To be wrapped round you. Like this.' She hooked them round his waist and felt her desire for him surge back stronger than before.

'Mmm.' He nodded. 'Feels good to me.'

'Does this feel good?' She slid one hand down his chest, eager to feel his muscles respond.

His arms tightened. 'Thought I told you to quit it.'

'Afraid you can't handle it?'

'Sure am.' His teeth flashed white and she knew he didn't mean it. This guy could handle anything—especially her.

The bed was unmissable and in four paces he had her on it, following immediately. She opened her arms, her mouth, her legs. Ready for everything.

He groaned as he pressed close. 'Condoms?'

She shook her head.

'You don't have any?' He paused and she shook her head again. Then he grinned. 'I do.'

Of course he did. She lay still beneath him as he pulled his wallet out of his back pocket, pulled a small square from inside that and then put it beside her.

'Quite the Boy Scout.'

He met her snark with an unapologetic look. 'Accidents are best avoided, don't you think?'

She nodded. She knew he was right to be prepared—to protect both of them. And then, as he kissed her, she decided his experience was something to celebrate—because nobody had kissed her like this before. No one had known how to turn her on like this. She'd never known such raw lust, or had such an ache for physical fulfilment.

He worked his way down her body, peeling her panties from her, stoking the fire within with caresses and whispers and kisses. Her hands grappled with the fastening of his jeans—she could wait no longer. But he took over, rolling to his back, tearing the denim from his body and quickly sorting the condom. Then he was back, settling over her, and the level of her anticipation almost had her hyperventilating.

He held back for a second, humour twinkling in the dark desire. 'Happy birthday, Bella.'

She closed her eyes. The first person to actually say it today. And now he was—oh! She gasped. Opened her eyes again—wide.

'Birthday girls deserve big presents.' He was watching her closely. 'That OK?'

'Oh, yes.' She squealed as he moved closer and a smile stretched his mouth. Air rushed out from her lungs in jagged segments as her body adjusted to his—to the glorious delight of it.

And then, when she was able to revel in the feel

of him, he moved, rolling her over, lifting her so she was sitting astride him while at the same time arching up into her so the connection wasn't lost.

'Let me see how beautiful you are, Bella.'

She looked down at him, marvelling that she was astride such magnificence. His chest tabled out before her and she spread her hands over it, leaning forward so she could slide up his length—and back down. Her eyes closed as she slowly hit his hilt again. And then again and again.

Shuddering, she opened her eyes to see him watching, with his head on the big pillows, appreciation apparent as he roved over her body, taking in her reaction. His hands spread wide, sliding up her thighs, lifting to cup her breasts and then take them in a ripe handful.

'Beautiful Bella,' he muttered, thumbs stroking. His heat fired her to go faster. And then he moved to match her.

'Oh, God,' she gasped. 'You really are a tiger.'

He growled in response.

Her giggle was lost in another gasp as he moved more, encouraging her to take more. And the sensations grew—overwhelming everything. Until there was nothing left in her mind—no thought, no humour, recognition of nothing but this wild passion that was all-consuming. Tension seared through her, until it could tighten no more, making her body rigid as she was thrust to the brink of madness.

His arms encircled her as he surged up with more force and depth than ever, and his hands clenched, supporting her as her orgasm tore through her, taking her strength with it. But he held her hard, making her face the intensity of it, squeezing every last sensation from her until she screamed with the exquisite pleasure of it.

She collapsed forward onto him, his shout still reverberating in her ears. Every muscle quivered—hot and bubbling, seeming to sing and so sensitive she could hardly believe it. She'd never felt anything like it.

'In about half an hour or so,' he murmured as her lids lowered, 'we're going to do that again.'

'And more,' she mumbled. She had plans for him, oh, yes, she had plans…in about half an hour…

THERE WAS A strange buzzing sound. As if an oversized bumblebee had made its way in and was trapped inside. Her warm pillow jerked up. Startled, she rolled away, and he quickly slid from the bed. Blinking rapidly so her eyes adjusted, feeling cold, she watched as he found his jeans. He swore crudely as he struggled to find the right pocket in the dark. The screen cast a cold blue glow on his face. He studied it for a moment, then his fingers pressed buttons, fast, frantic.

He glanced up, distance reflected in his eyes. 'What a nightmare.'

She wasn't sure what he was referring to—the message, or the situation. After another minute or so the phone buzzed again. He read the message.

'I have to go,' he said, pushing more buttons.

It wasn't light yet. Not even close. And this was summer in New Zealand when it got light near five a.m. Hell, he was running out in the middle of the night.

'It's so early.'

He had his jeans on and was still pressing buttons. 'In New York, it's nine a.m. and my client needs help right now.'

'But it's Saturday.' He wouldn't even look at her.

'No such thing as Saturdays, not for me. I have to get back right away.'

But what about the wedding? Devastated, she envisaged the hours to come. But she wasn't going to remind him. He'd probably had too much to drink to even remember. The idea of him being her date had only ever been a joke. Except her family knew. Everyone knew. She was on the train to humiliation central.

She drew her knees up. Face it, she was already there. Mortification spread over her skin and she was glad it was dark and her blush hidden. He could hardly wait to leave her. Silently, quickly, he found his top, pulling it over his head. His mind had already left the building.

Frowning at the screen, he spoke. 'Give me your number.'

He was taking the control—not giving her his details, but trying to make her feel better. As if he'd ever call.

'Bella.' He spoke sharply. 'Tell me your number.'

She recited it, with a cold heart and a determined mind.

He nodded, still pressing buttons. 'I'll call you.'

He made it sound sincere. But she knew for a fact he wouldn't.

THIRTEEN HOURS AND no sleep later, Bella watched Vita and Hamish walk around the beach wearing their cheesy flip-flops that left 'Just Married' imprinted in the sand. She really wished she had a hangover. That way she could blame the whole escapade on booze. Say she'd been blind drunk and shrug the thing off with the insouciance of an ingénue.

But while she was aching, the pain wasn't in her head—it was deep inside her chest and she tried to tell herself it wasn't really that bad. Fact was, she'd never had a one-night stand before. She'd had boyfriends that hadn't lasted long—OK, so all three of her ex-boyfriends would fall into that category. But she'd never had a fling that lasted less than ten hours. And she'd gone and done it in front of her entire family—who thought she was a hopeless case already. What had she been thinking?

And there was Celia, hanging on the arm of Rex, flashing victorious glances her way at every opportunity. Thank goodness he hadn't arrived until this morning and hadn't been witness to last night too. And now everyone was thinking she couldn't hang onto anyone—not the fabulously suitable accountancy star that was Rex or the laid-back, coolly casual sex god that was Owen. Thank heavens her father had spent the night talking business with his brothers—hopefully he wouldn't have heard a thing about it.

She felt a prickle inside as she saw the sheer joy on her sister's face. Maybe Owen had been right—she was a little jealous. But who wouldn't want to be loved like that? And little sister Vita seemed to have it all—she'd been the one to embrace the family profession—as all four of their elder brothers had. Vita had been the one able to do everything the way the family wanted. Even down to marrying one of the partners in the firm. She'd worked really hard to get her degree and her charter. And to cap it off, she was nice. She deserved to be happy.

But Bella worked hard too. Damn hard. Didn't she deserve to be happy? Didn't she deserve some respect too?

She was jealous. How nice it would be to have someone look at her the way Hamish looked at Vita. To have the career and the lover. But she'd yet to get the job she wanted, and she couldn't even have a one-night stand last the whole night.

As if Owen had really had to get up and go to work at three in the damn morning? On a Saturday. He'd probably programmed his phone to buzz then and the talk of the client in New York was just for believability. It was probably his standard modus operandi—enabling him to make that quick escape and avoid the awkward morning-after scene.

The morning after had been unbearably awkward for Bella. And it wasn't just because of the questioning looks of the younger members of the family—the ones who'd been in the restaurant last night. She'd gone to Reception and asked which room 'Owen' was staying in—only to be told there was no Owen staying at all. And no Owen had checked out recently either. Then she'd asked to check her tab, bracing herself for a huge bill from the bar. But she found it had been paid in full, including the accommodation cost. She'd asked whose name was on the card—but apparently whoever it was had paid in cash.

It had been him—she was sure of it. What was he doing—paying for services rendered?

She stood, brushed the sand from the horrendous dress. She wasn't going to sit around and be the object of mockery or pity any more—and certainly not her own self-pity either. It was time for action. Things were going to have to change.

CHAPTER FIVE

A LOT COULD happen in three weeks and a day. Life-changing decisions could be made and the resulting plans put into action. And it was too late for regrets now. Bella had finally pushed herself out of the nest—and it was time to see if she could fly. Thus far, she was succeeding barely on a day-by-day basis.

The minute she'd got back from that hellish weekend she'd moved out of her father's home in Auckland and down to Wellington. Movies were made there. There were theatres. It was the arts hub. She'd found a tiny flat quite easily. Above another flat where a couple lived. It was in the shade of a hill and was a little damp, but it would do. She hadn't wanted to flat-share. She was going independent—all the way.

Because she'd finally had the shove she needed. And it wasn't ambition. It was one humiliation too many. If she ever saw Owen again she'd have to thank him. His was the boot that had got her moving. The smug sideways glances of Celia, the questions in her perfect sister's eyes at the reception. Bella had explained that he'd had to leave for work. It had sounded lame even to her. When they'd asked what he did, where he worked, she'd only been able to parrot the vague answers that he'd given her.

She didn't want to run the risk of bumping into him ever again. It would have been just her luck that he'd have come into the café where she'd worked in central Auckland.

So now she worked at a café in central Wellington. The manager of that branch of the chain had jumped at the chance to hire someone already trained, and with so much experience she could step in as deputy manager any time he needed. And she'd started children's party entertaining here too. She'd had a couple of recommendations from contacts in Auckland and today's supreme effort had ensured a booking for her second party already. Several other parents had asked for her card at the end of it too. It wasn't exactly glam work, but she was good at it.

But then there was the lecherous uncle. There was always one. The younger brother of the mother, or the cousin of the father, who fancied a woman in a fairy dress. He'd cornered her as she was packing up her gear.

'Make my wish come true. Have dinner with me.'

As if she hadn't heard that one before. Then he'd touched her, an attempt at playfulness. He'd run his fingers down her arm and they'd felt reptilian. She'd made a quick exit—smiling politely at the hosts. Once out the door she'd bolted, because she'd seen him coming down the hall after her. She'd been in such a hurry to get into the car and away she'd pulled hard on her dress as she'd sat and one of the cute capped sleeves had just ripped right off, meaning that side of the top was in imminent danger of slipping south too. Well, the dress had been slightly tight. She'd been eating a little more chocolate than usual these last three weeks. Like a couple of king-size cakes a day to get her through the move. Now she needed to top up on essential supplies. And so it was that she pulled into the supermarket car park— fully costumed up and half falling out of it.

Ordinarily she'd never stop and shop while in character, but this wasn't an ordinary day. She was tired and ever so slightly depressed. She picked up a basket on her way in and ignored the looks from the other customers. Didn't they often see fully grown women wearing silver fairy dresses and wings, an eyeload of make-up and an entire tube of glitter gel?

She'd blow her last fifteen dollars on some serious comfort food. She loaded in her favourite chocolate. The best ice cream—she could just afford the two-litre pack so long as she could find a five-dollar bottle of wine. In this, one of the posher supermarkets, she might be pushing her luck. As it was her luck was always limited.

She headed to the wine aisle and searched for the bright yellow 'on special' tags. She'd just selected one particularly dodgy-looking one when the voice in her ear startled her.

'And you told me you didn't want the fluffy princess part.'

Her fingers were around the wine, taking the

weight, but at the sound of that smooth drawl they instinctively flexed.

The bottle smashed all over the floor—wine splattered everywhere, punctuated by large shards of green glass.

Oh, great. It would have to happen to her. Right this very second. She looked hard at the rapidly spreading red puddle on the floor so she wouldn't have to face the stares of the gazillion other customers, especially not… Was it really him?

'Sorry, I didn't mean to give you such a fright.'

She couldn't avoid it any longer. She looked up at—yes, it was him. Right there. Right in front of her. And utterly devastating.

'Oh, no.' The words were out before she thought better of it. 'What are you doing here? I thought you lived in—' She broke off. Actually she had no idea where he lived. She'd thought Auckland, but there was no real reason for her to have done so. They hadn't really talked details much—not about anything that really mattered.

After a disturbingly stern appraisal, he bent, picked up the fragment of wine bottle and read the smeared label. It reminded her where they were and the mess she'd just made. She glanced down the aisle and saw a uniform-clad spotty teenager headed their way with a bucket and mop.

'No, no, no and no again.' Owen, if that indeed was his name, was shaking his head.

'It's for cooking. A casserole.' Ultra defensive, she invented wildly.

He drew back up to full height and looked in her basket. Both brows flipped. 'Some casserole.'

'It is actually,' she breezed, determined to ignore the heat in her cheeks. 'Pretty extraordinary.'

'Ultra extraordinary,' he said, still looking at her with a sharpness that was making her feel guilty somehow. It maddened her—he was the one who'd skipped out that crazy night. Don't think about it. Do not think about it!

But suddenly it was all back in a rush—all she could see was him naked, her body remembering the warmth of his, the thrill. And all she could hear was his low laughter and how seductive it had been.

The heat in her cheeks went from merely hot to scorching. And he stood still and watched its progression—degree, by slow degree.

Then his gaze dropped, flared and only then did she remember the state of her dress. Quickly she tugged the low sagging neckline up and kept her fist curled round the material just below her shoulder.

His eyes seemed to stroke her skin. 'Your sunburn has faded.'

It didn't feel as if it had now—it felt more on fire than it had weeks ago when it had been almost raw.

'I'm sorry about this.' He gestured to the mess. 'I'll pay for it.'

And then she remembered how he'd left her.

'No, thanks,' she said briskly. 'You don't have to—'

He wasn't listening. He'd turned, studying the shelves of wine. After a moment he picked one out and put it in her basket. 'I think this one will serve you better.'

She caught a glimpse of a white tag—not a yellow 'on special' one—and winced. No way could she afford that bottle of wine. But she couldn't put it back in front of him.

Then he took her basket off her. 'Is that everything you need for your casserole?' he asked blandly.

'Oh, er, sure.'

He turned away from her and headed towards the checkout. She paused, staring after him, panic rising. More humiliation was imminent. She'd chopped up her credit card—not wanting to get into debt—so all she had was that fifteen dollars in her pocket. While she had the cheque from the birthday party she'd just done, it was Sunday and she couldn't cash it.

And no way was she letting him pay her bill—not again.

But he put both lots of shopping on the conveyor belt. His was all connoisseur—prime beef steak, a bag of baby spinach, two bottles of hellishly expensive red wine. She couldn't help wondering if he was cooking for a date. Then, as she helplessly watched, he paid for it all—hers as well as his—with a couple of crisp hundred-dollar bills.

Cash. Of course. But as he put the change back in his wallet, she saw the array of cards in there too—exclusive, private banking ones—and she really started to seethe.

OWEN DIDN'T GLANCE her way once during the transaction. He tried to focus on getting the shopping sorted, but all the while his mind was screening the sight of her spilling out of that unbelievable dress.

Bella Cotton. The woman who'd haunted his dreams every night for the last three weeks. He was mad with her. Madder with himself for not being able to shake her from his head.

And now here she was—real and in the beautifully round flesh he couldn't help but remember. She didn't exactly seem thrilled to see him. In fact she looked extremely uncomfortable. Well, so she should, after fobbing him off with a false number like that.

But her embarrassment only made him that bit madder. Made him feel perverse enough to drag out their bumping into each other even longer. Made him all the more determined to interfere and help her out because she so clearly didn't want him to. How awful for her to have to suffer his company for a few more minutes. He very nearly ground his teeth.

Well, he hadn't wanted her to take up as much of his brain space as she had these last few weeks either. Night after night, restless, he'd thought of her—suffered cold showers because of her. During the day too—at those quiet moments when he should have been thinking of important things. He'd even got so distracted one day he'd actually searched for her on the Internet like some sad jilted lover.

So he'd known she was in Wellington, but he hadn't known where or why or for how long. He certainly hadn't expected to see her in his local supermarket. And he sure as hell hadn't expected her to be wearing the most ridiculous get-up—or half wearing it. And he most definitely hadn't expected to feel that rush of desire again—because he was mad with her, wasn't he? He was that jilted lover. He really wanted to know why she'd done it—why when even now, for a few moments, he'd seen that passionate rush reflected in her eyes.

So while the rational part of him was telling him to hand over her shopping and walk away asap, the wounded-male-pride bit was making him hold onto it. The flick of desire was making sure his grip was tight.

HE WAS WALKING out of the supermarket already. Hadn't looked at her once while at the checkout—not even to ask whether it was OK with her. He'd just paid for the lot, ensured their goods were separately bagged and then picked them up. Now he was carrying both sets of shopping out to the car park. She had no option but to follow behind him—her temper spiking higher with every step. And seeing him still looking so hot, casual in jeans and tee again, made every 'take me' hormone start jiggling inside. She stopped them with an iron-hard clench of her teeth and her tummy muscles. She was angry with him. He'd done a runner and insulted her with his payment choices.

But she could hardly wrench the bag off him. Not in front of everyone—she was already causing a big enough scene.

Her car was parked in the first row. She stopped

beside it and sent a quick look in his direction to assess his reaction. He was looking at it with his bland-man expression. It only made her even more defensive.

'She's called Bubbles. The kids like it.'

'Kids?'

'I'm a children's party entertainer. The fairy.' People usually laughed. It wasn't exactly seen as the ultimate work and as a result her credibility—especially with her family—was low. They thought it was the biggest waste of her time ever.

He nodded slowly. 'Hence the wings.'

'And the frock.'

There was a silence. 'Do you do adult parties?'

'That's the third time I've been asked that today,' she snapped. 'You're about to get the non-polite answer.'

His grin flashed for the first time. And she was almost floored once more. Or she would have been if she weren't feeling so cross with him—Mr I'll-Pay-For-Everything-Including-You.

Her ancient Bambini was painted baby-blue and had bright-coloured spots all over it. She quickly unlocked it, glancing pointedly at the bag he was carrying, not looking higher than his hand.

Silently he handed it over. 'Thanks.' She aimed for blitheness over bitterness but wasn't entirely sure of her success. 'Nice to see you again.' Saccharine all over. She got in the car before she lost it, ending the conversation, and hitting the ignition.

Nothing.

She tried again. Willed the car to start. Start before she made even more of an idiot of herself.

The engine choked. Her heart sank. Had the long drive down from Auckland finally done the old darling in? She tried the ignition once more. It choked again.

He knocked on the window. Reluctantly she wound it down.

'Having trouble?'

She wasn't looking at him. She was looking at the fuel gauge. The arrow was on the wrong side of E. Totally on the wrong side. It was beyond the red bit and into the nothing. As in NOTHING. No petrol. Nada. Zip.

Man, she was an idiot. But relief trickled through her all the same. She had real affection for the car she'd had for years and had painted herself.

She took a deep breath. She could fake it, right? At least try to get through the next two minutes with a scrap of dignity? She got out of the car.

'Problem?'

Did he have to be so smooth? So calm, so damn well in control? Didn't he do dumb things on occasion?

'I forgot something,' she answered briefly. Now she remembered the warning light had been on—when was that? Yesterday? The day before? But it had gone off. She'd thought it was OK, that it had been a warning and then changed its mind. She mentally gave herself a clunk in the head—as if it had found some more petrol in its back pocket?

Clearly not. It had completely run out of juice. And the nearest garage was… Where was it exactly? The only one she could think of was the one near her flat—the one she should have filled up at this morning, had she had the funds.

'What?' he asked—dry, almost bored-sounding.

But she was extremely conscious that he hadn't taken his eyes off her. And she was doing everything not to have to look into them, because they were that brilliant blue and she knew how well they could mesmerise her.

She tugged her top up again. 'Petrol.'

'Oh.' He looked away from her then, seeming to take an age looking at the other cars. She realised he was barely holding in his amusement. Finally he spoke. 'The nearest service station is just—'

'Uh, no, thanks,' she interrupted. 'I'll go home first.'

There was no way she was having him beside her when she put five dollars into a jerry can so she could cough and splutter the car home and leave it there until her cheque cleared. After this final splurge it was going to be a tin of baked beans and stale bread for a couple of days. No bad thing given the way she was spilling out the top of the fairy frock.

'How far away is home?'

'Not far.' A twenty-minute walk. Make that thirty in her sequined, patent leather slippers.

There was a silence. She felt his gaze rake her from head to toes—lingering around the middle before settling back up on her face. Heat filled her and she just knew he was enjoying watching her blush deepen. She stared fixedly at the seam on the neckline of his tee shirt and refused to think of anything but how much she was going to appreciate her ice cream when she got the chance.

And then he asked, 'Can I give you a ride?' Mockery twisted his lips, coloured the question and vexed her all the more.

Get a ride with him? Oh, no. She'd already had one ride of sorts and that was plenty, right? She could cope with this just fine on her own.

She'd call the breakdown service. But then she remembered it was her father's account and she refused to lean on him again. Independence was her new mantra. They wouldn't take her seriously until she got herself sorted. Until she proved she was completely capable of succeeding alone. She frowned; she'd have to walk.

'You trusted me enough to sleep with me, I think you can trust me to run you home safely.'

She looked straight at him then, taken by his soft words. With unwavering intensity, he regarded her. She'd known she'd be stunned if she looked into his eyes—brilliant, blue and beautiful. Good grief, he was gorgeous. So gorgeous and all she could think about was how great he'd felt up close and every cell suddenly yearned for the impact.

Her own eyes widened as she read his deepening

expression—was there actually a touch of chagrin there? Why?

'Thanks.' It was a whisper. It wasn't what she'd meant to say at all.

HIS CAR SAT low to the ground, gleaming black and ultra expensive. The little badge on the bonnet told her that with its yellow background and rearing black horse. He unlocked it, opened the door. She started as the door and seemingly half the roof swung up into the air.

She sent a sarcastic look in his direction. 'That's ridiculous.'

'No, Bella, that's ridiculous,' he said, pointing back to her Bambini.

She bent low and managed to slide in without popping right out of her top. The interior was polished and smooth and impeccably tidy and also surprisingly spartan. She tried to convince herself the seat wasn't that much more comfortable than the one in her own old banger. But it was—sleek and moulding to her body.

Owen took the driver's seat, started the engine— a low growl. 'He's called Enzo.'

'I'd have thought it would be more plush.'

He shook his head. 'It's the closest thing to a Formula One racing car you can drive on conventional streets.'

'Oh.' Like that was fabulous?

Her feigned lack of interest didn't stop him. 'I like things that go fast.'

She looked at him sharply. He was staring straight ahead, but his grin was sly and it was widening with every second.

Coolly as she could, she gave him her address. The sooner she got home and away from him, the sooner she could forget about it all and get on with her new life.

THE FIRE VEHICLE outside her house should have warned her—nothing ever went smoothly for Bella. There was always some weird catastrophe that occurred—the kind of thing that was so outrageous it would never happen to other normal people. Like being caught in a ripped fairy dress in the supermarket by her only one-night stand—the guy who'd given her the best sexual experience of her life.

'Looks like there might be some kind of trouble.' He stated the obvious calmly as he parked the car.

She stared at the big red appliance with an impending sense of doom intuitively knowing it was something to do with her. She'd have done something stupid. But behind the truck, the house still stood. She released the breath she'd been holding.

'I'm sure whatever's happened isn't that major.'

So he figured it had something to do with her too. She might as well walk around with a neon sign saying 'danger, accident-prone idiot approaching'. But her embarrassment over everything to do with him faded into the background as she got out of the car and focused on whatever had gone wrong now.

As she walked up the path, one seriously bad

smell hit her. The couple from the downstairs flat were standing in the middle of the lawn. A few firemen were standing next to them talking. Silence descended as she approached, but they weren't even trying to hide their grins. It was a moment before she remembered her fairy dress and quickly put her hand to her chest. Wow, what an entrance.

'You left something on the hob.' The head fire guy stepped forward.

She'd what?

'I think you were hard-boiling some eggs.'

Oh, hell—she had been, the rest of the box because they'd been getting dangerously close to their use-by date and she hadn't wanted to waste any. She'd decided to cook them up and have them ready for the next day, and then in the rush to get to the café and pack all her party gear, she'd forgotten all about them.

Isla, her neighbour, piped up, 'They had to break down the door—we didn't have a key.'

The doors to both flats were narrow and side by side. Only now hers was smashed—splinters of wood lay on the ground, and the remainder of the door was half off its hinges.

'I'm so sorry,' she mumbled.

She trudged up the stairs and almost had a heart attack when she saw the damage to the door up there too. The whole thing would have to be replaced as well as the one downstairs. Bye bye bond money. And she'd probably be working extra hours at the café to make up the rest of it.

She stared around at the little room she'd called home for a grand total of two weeks. Her first independent, solely occupied home. There was almost no furniture—a beanbag she liked to curl into and read a book or watch telly. But it had been hers. Now it was tainted by the most horrendous smell imaginable and she couldn't imagine it ever being a welcome sanctuary again. She'd spoilt things—again—with her own stupidity.

'You can't stay here.'

She nearly jumped out of her skin when Owen spoke.

'No.' For one thing the smell was too awful. For another it was no longer secure with both doors broken like that. She wouldn't sleep a wink.

She saw him looking around, figured he must be thinking how austere it was. When his gaze came to rest on her again, concern was evident in his eyes. She didn't much like that look. She wasn't some dippy puppy that needed to be taken care of.

'Can I drop you somewhere else?'

Her heart sank even lower into her shiny slippers. The last thing she wanted to do was call on the family. Having finally broken out she wanted to manage—for more than a month at least. If she phoned them now she'd never get any credibility. The two months' deposit on the flat had taken out her savings, but she didn't care. She'd wanted to be alone, to be independent, and she'd really wanted it to work this time. She could check into a hostel, but she had no money. She had nowhere to go. She'd have to stay here, put a peg on her nose and her ear on the door.

He took a step in her direction. 'I have a spare room at my place.'

She looked at him—this stranger whom she knew so intimately, yet barely knew at all.

'Grab a bag and we'll get out of here. Leave it and come back tomorrow.' He spoke lightly. 'It won't be nearly so bad then.'

She knew it was a good idea but she felt sickened. It was the last straw on a hellish day and her slim control snapped. Anger surged as she stared at him. Irrationally she felt as if he were to blame for everything. 'Is your name really Owen?'

He looked astonished. 'Of course. Why do you ask?'

'I asked at the hotel reception for you.' She was too stewed to care about what that admission might reveal. 'They had no record of any Owen staying there.'

He paused, looked a touch uncomfortable. 'I wasn't staying at the resort.'

She stared at him in disbelief.

'I have a holiday house just down from it.'

A holiday house—in one of the most exclusive stretches of beach on Waiheke Island? Who the hell was he?

He looked away, walked to the window. 'No strings, Bella,' he said carelessly, returning to her present predicament. 'All I'm offering is a place to stay for a couple of days until this mess gets cleaned up.'

Bella pushed the memories out and internally debated. She didn't have much in the way of personal possessions—nothing of any great value anyway. The most important stuff was her kit for the parties and that was in her car. It wouldn't take five minutes to chuck a few things into a bag. And maybe, if she took up his offer, she could keep this latest catastrophe to herself? Her family need never know.

Slowly, she swallowed her remaining smidge of pride. 'Are you sure?'

'Of course.' He shrugged, as if it was nothing. It probably was nothing to him. 'I work all hours. I'll hardly notice you're there.'

She knew she could trust him; he certainly didn't seem as if he was about to pounce. He'd gone running away in the night, hadn't he? Humiliation washed over her again. But she had little choice—her family or him. She picked him—she'd lost all dignity as far as he was concerned already. Maybe she could keep the scrap she had left for her father. 'OK.'

Owen failed to hide his smile, so turned quickly, heading down the stairs to deal with the fire crew. He fixed the bottom door enough to make it look as all right as possible from the outside and gave a half-guilty mutter of thanks for her misfortune. He wasn't afraid to take advantage of this situation—not when she'd so coolly cut him loose that night. Because that flick of desire had blown to full-on inferno again—from a mere five minutes in her company. And now he had the perfect opportunity to have even more of her company—one night, maybe two. Enough to find out what had gone wrong, and then to finish what had started.

Bella stuffed a few clothes into a bag—not many—while dwelling on the glimpse of that wide, wicked, Waiheke smile he'd just flashed. It would only be one night. Two, tops.

Not taking sexy black lingerie. Not taking sexy black lingerie.

Somehow it ended up stuffed at the bottom of the bag.

CHAPTER SIX

THINGS CAME IN threes, right? And Bella had had her three—her dress, the wine and now her flat. Surely nothing else could go wrong with this day?

'Is there anyone you should call?' Owen asked, opening the car door for her.

She shook her head. 'I'll take care of it later.'

'Then let's go.'

She sat back and tried to relax as he turned the car round and headed back towards the centre of town. He slowed as they hit what had once been the industrial district with lots of warehouses for storing the goods that came in on the harbour. Only now most of the warehouses had been converted—restaurants, upmarket shops and residential conversions in the upper storeys. It was the ultimate in inner-city living with theatres around the corner, Te Papa the national museum, the best film house in the country and shops, shops, shops. All less than a five-minute walk away.

He pulled in front of one warehouse. On one side of it was a restaurant, the other a funky design store.

But there was nothing in the ground floor of this one. The windows were darkened. His car window slid down and he reached out to press numbers of the security pad that stood on a stand in front. The wide door opened up and he drove the car in. In the dim light she saw a big empty space—save for a mountain bike and some assorted gym equipment. It immediately reminded her of his muscles. She looked away. There was a lift to the side and a steep flight of stairs heading up in a straight line. He stepped forward, tackling the stairs.

'My apartment is on the top floor.'

Of course it was. On the third level there was another security pad, another pin number. The guy was clearly security conscious. Once inside she blinked—her eyes taking a second to cope with the transition from gloomy stairwell to bright room. It was huge. At first glance all she saw were wooden floors, bricks, steel beams. Half the roof had been ripped off and replaced with skylights—flooding the place in fresh, natural light. There was a huge table in the centre, surrounded by an assortment of chairs, but it was the long workbench that ran the length of one wall that caught her attention.

'Is your computer screen big enough?' She stared in amazement at the display of technology lined up on it. 'Have you got enough of them?'

He grinned. 'Actually most of them are in the office on the second floor.'

'So what, these are just for fun?'

He gave her a whisker of a wink, a faint finger-

print of the humour he'd had that night on Waiheke.
Then it was gone. He walked ahead of her, leading
her to the kitchen area, and she watched awkwardly
as he put items into the fridge and freezer.

'Most of the apartment has yet to be done. After
getting my room and the kitchen done I just ran out
of—'

'Money?' she interpolated hopefully. Surely she
couldn't have been so far wrong about this guy.

'Time,' he corrected, smiling faintly. 'Business
has been busy.' He looked about. 'The basic design
is there but I haven't had the chance to get the last
bits done yet.' He glanced at her. 'I'll show you to
your room.'

It was on the far side of the living area. There
were more rooms heading down the corridor next
to it, but through their open doors she could see that
they were empty. In the room he stopped at, there
was just a bed and a chest of drawers.

'Sorry it's so bare.'

She shook her head. 'I'm used to less.'

'I'll make up the bed.'

'I can do it.' She didn't want him in the room any
more than necessary.

She took a look out the window—it overlooked
the street; she could see all the shoppers. There was
a seriously yummy smell wafting up from the Ma-
laysian restaurant next door. 'You must eat out all
the time.'

He answered from the doorway. 'They do me
take-out packages. But I try to cook a few nights a

week. The downside is the rubbish collection—before six o'clock every morning all the bottles from the night before get tipped into the recycling truck. Makes a hell of a din.'

'I'd have thought you'd be well up by then anyway.' She shot him a look. 'Working.'

That hint of humour resurged, warming her. It was then she fully recognised the danger—she was still hopelessly attracted to him. If he turned on the smile charm again she'd be his in a heartbeat.

She kicked herself. He wasn't offering anything but a room, remember? And she didn't want his sort of gratitude. Tiredness swamped her and the fairy dress slipped lower. She desperately needed a shower. Desperately needed to get dressed in something far more concealing. 'Do you mind if I use the bathroom?'

The amusement in his eyes became unholy. 'Sure. Follow me.'

He led her back into the main space, and across it. Her footsteps slowed as she spied what was through the doorway he was headed to—a very big bed with most definitely masculine-coloured coverings.

'We'll have to share the bathroom—is that OK?'

'Um…sure,' she mumbled. 'That's fine.'

She was in his bedroom. Her skin was prickling with heat.

'The bathroom is one of the things yet to be finished.' He was talking again. 'There's a loo near the kitchen, but the only shower and bath at the moment are the ones in the en suite for the master bedroom.'

The master bedroom—his bedroom—this bedroom. Oh, life couldn't be so cruel.

He was watching her with that wicked twinkle faintly sparking in his eyes. 'It's a really nice shower.'

She was quite sure it would be. She wanted to ask if there was a lock on the door, but thought better of being so rude. She hurriedly looked away from him, only to get an eyeful of his walk-in wardrobe space—and all the suits that were hanging there.

Suits.

Completely thrown, she followed where he'd wandered into the bathroom. It was her turn to stop in the doorway.

He stood in the centre of the room. He turned towards her, his smile satisfied. 'It's something, isn't it?'

She nodded. It was all she could manage.

'When I get the chance I'll get the rest of place up to standard too.'

It was beautiful. A huge wet play area that oozed with refined elegance. All the fittings were obviously expensive. The colourings were muted—dark grey, black with sparse splashes of red. A shower space with ample room for two and the biggest bath she'd ever seen.

She railed against her own appreciation of it. Materialistic was not her—there were other, more important things in life. And yet there was no way she couldn't indulge in such classical luxury. No way she couldn't stop thinking of him in there too.

'Take as long as you want,' he said, passing her

so closely she shivered. 'You'll find everything you need in here.'

She sagged against the door after he closed it behind him. What she wanted and needed had just walked out.

THE KITTEN HEELS of her slippers echoed on the wooden floors as she walked back through to the kitchen. She could smell the most delicious smell. So good it wiped the final traces of the rank burnt-egg odour from her senses.

He was barefoot and looking like that careless, gorgeous hunk of a guy she'd met that wild night. Again she was transported back to the moments when she'd felt the firmness of his denim-wrapped thighs between hers. When he'd pulled her close on the dance floor, even closer in her room... Some-where inside she softened...and immediately she sought to firm up again.

This was the guy who'd been so keen to get away he'd sneaked out in the crazy hours.

This was the guy who wasn't anything like she'd thought, who'd totally misled her—hadn't he?

Now he was standing in his designer kitchen stirring something in a wok with a quick hand. She hovered near the edge of the bench and watched as he added the now diced beef into the mix. Another pot was on the hob and, judging from the steam rising, was on rapid boil.

He glanced up at her. 'You must be hungry.'

Yes, her mouth was definitely watering. And it

wasn't the only part of her growing damper. She shifted further away from him. 'How many?'

'How many what?'

'How many are coming to dinner? You could feed an army with a steak that size.'

'Just me.' He laughed. 'And now you.'

'You really are a tiger,' she murmured, turning to look at the living area again, not really meaning for him to hear. 'So your office is on the level downstairs?' She tried to go for some safe conversation.

'Yeah,' he answered. 'I'm not sure what I want to do with the ground-floor level yet. Not a restaurant, that's for sure. Maybe retail?' He shrugged.

He could afford to leave it untenanted? Inner-city space like this would be worth a fortune. He must be worth a fortune. Her heart sank lower.

How could she have been so wrong? Stupid. Most women would be thrilled to discover someone was actually a kazillionaire. But it just emphasised to Bella her lack of judgment—and the fact she was so out of place here. She'd never be the girl for anyone as successful as this; she was too much of a liability, too much of a joke. Moodily she stared at the dream space again.

But like a bee to honey she was drawn to look back, watching as he poured in an unlabelled jar of the something that smelt heavenly. Intrigued, she couldn't not ask. 'What's that?'

His wicked look was back. 'The restaurant down the road gives it to me on the sly.'

'It smells incredible.'

'And that's nothing on how it tastes.' He nodded to a slimline drawer. 'You'll find cutlery in there. Put some on that tray, will you?'

She was glad for something to do. It meant she had to turn her back on him and not watch the impressive cook on display.

'So how long have you been living in that flat?' he called to her above the sizzling sound of the searing meat.

'Two weeks.'

'Really?' He'd moved so he could see her and she could see the lift of his brows.

'I've only just moved to Wellington.'

'Why the shift?'

'To further my career.' The wedding had been the catalyst. The last push she'd needed to finally get out of there and turn her dreams to reality. Only, already it was falling apart.

'Oh?'

'There are good theatres here. The movie industry is based here.'

'There are good cafés here,' he added, full of irony.

She tossed her head. 'There are.'

'So why now?' He was putting food on plates and she was so hungry she could hardly concentrate on what she was saying.

'It needed to happen.'

'You've got work already?'

She nodded and admitted it. 'I've got a job at one of those good cafés. And I'm going to hit the audition circuit.' She'd already scoped the talent agencies. Knew which ones she was going to target. Hopefully they'd take her on. And then it was a matter of keeping trying and hoping for Lady Luck to smile on her.

He lifted the plates onto the tray. Noodles with wilted spinach and slices of seared beef. Her mouth watered. She hadn't had a meal as good as this in weeks.

'Wine?'

She hadn't noticed the bottle of red standing on the bench.

'Thanks.'

He added the bottle to the tray, glanced at her, all irony again. 'Can you manage the glasses?'

'I think so,' she answered coolly.

She followed him up the stairs she hadn't even noticed earlier. They literally climbed to the roof—to a door that took them right out onto it.

The air outside was warm and not too windy. Most of the roof was bare, but there was a collection of plants in pots lined up close together. As he led her around them she saw they created a hedge. On the sheltered side a small table stood, with a couple of chairs, and a collection of smaller pots holding herbs, a couple holding cherry-tomato bushes. It wasn't a huge garden, but it was well cared for. And the view took in the vibrant part of the city, gave them a soundtrack that was full of life.

He balanced the tray on the edge of the table, unloaded the plates with such ease she knew he'd done it countless times before. Just how many women had dined on his roof? It was, she speculated, the perfect scene for seduction.

Well, not hers. Not again.

But she sat when he gestured and he sat too. He seemed bigger than she recalled. His legs were close under the table and it would be nothing to stretch out and brush hers against his. She felt the flush rise in her cheeks and took a sip of the wine so she could hide behind the glass.

'I've organised for your car to be taken to my local garage. I'll get them to check the tyres too. A couple looked a little bald.'

Bella's nerves jangled. The wine tasted sharper. She swallowed it down hard. She couldn't afford new tyres and the last thing she wanted to be was even more indebted to him. A night in his spare room she could deal with. But nothing more. And fixing up her car was well beyond her at the moment. She didn't want to be dependent on anyone. Certainly didn't want to be beholden to him.

'I'd really prefer that you didn't,' she said with as much dignity as she could muster. 'I can take care of it myself.'

And she would. She was over having people interfering and trying to organise her life for her, as if they all thought she couldn't. As if they thought the decisions she made were ill judged.

He didn't reply immediately—coolly having a sip of his wine and seeming to savour it while studying her expression. 'At least let me arrange to have it brought here. It'll be a sitting duck left in a super-market car park like that.'

She bit the inside of her lip. He was right. It was the ideal target for teenage joyriders—irresistible, in fact. And she loved Bubbles, would hate to see her wrecked, which she would be if any boy racers decided to have a laugh in her. Besides, she suddenly remembered all her party gear was in the back. She certainly couldn't afford to replace all that in a hurry. She knew that once again she couldn't refuse him.

'OK,' she capitulated in a low voice. 'Thanks.'

She sampled some of her dinner. He was right, the sauce was divine—and so was the way he'd cooked the meat in it. But she couldn't enjoy it as much as she ought—the day's events were catching up with her and she realised just what the small fire in her flat had meant. The silence grew and while she knew she should make the attempt she couldn't think what to say. It was like the white elephant in the room—that subject she was determined to avoid. How did people play this sort of thing? How would some sophisticate handle it? How did she pretend bumping into the guy she'd had the hottest sex of her life with was no big deal? But it was a big deal.

Because she wanted it again—badly. Only he'd walked away so quickly, so easily and seemingly without thought to where it had left her.

And now, seeing him in his home environment, she knew he was nothing like the guy she'd pegged him as. He was way out of her league and, judging by the blandly polite way he was dealing with her, he was no longer interested anyway.

He rested his fork on his plate and looked at her. 'So tell me about the wedding.'

She lowered her fork too. So he did remember about that—did he remember he'd offered to be her date too? She shrugged the question off. 'What's to tell?'

OWEN LIFTED HIS fork again and determinedly focused on his food. It was just like that night on Waiheke—one glance and all he wanted to do was take her to bed. For that time in the bar he couldn't have cared less about work and the commitments he knew were burdening him. Not until he'd had her. But then those commitments had pulled. He'd cursed it at the time, mentally swearing as he'd worked through the early hours answering the questions his client had been struggling with.

He'd walked from her. He'd had to work—that was his first priority. It was the one thing he knew he could be relied on to do, and all the while he'd been doing it he'd been thinking of her—of the most spectacular sex of his life. But then, only a few hours later, he'd tried her number, wanting to apologise for letting her down about the wedding and for walking out so fast, but found it rang to someone who'd never heard of her.

Stung, he'd decided it was for the best—a one-off, as most of his encounters were. It was the way he liked it—simple, uncomplicated, with no threat of someone wanting something more from him, emotionally or financially. He'd been appalled to discover years ago that he didn't have the 'more' emotionally to give. When Liz had tried to force a commitment, he'd realised damn quick how much he didn't want the burden of it. He couldn't meet high needs, high maintenance, high anything. He didn't want the responsibility of family and forever and all that. Casual, brief, fun. That was all he offered and all he wanted.

But it still niggled. She'd cut at his pride.

Tony's Lawn Mowing Service. He wouldn't forget that low point in a hurry.

'Was it fun?' He wanted to see if she'd refer to it. Would she even apologise? But instead she was looking at him as if he were the one who had something to be sorry about. Well, he didn't think so.

But he didn't want to challenge her—not yet. He'd bide his time—see if the sizzle was still there for her as it was for him. Because if it was, and he was pretty sure it was, then he wanted to rouse it. He wanted her wanting him again—and not hiding it. That would be the moment to strike. And once he'd heard her reason, had her apology, he'd have her.

He figured it couldn't be as good again—it had been a unique set of circumstances leading to that explosion between them on Waiheke. Sex that good definitely wasn't possible a second time—it would be fun, but it would be finished. Maybe then he'd get some sleep again.

'The wedding was nice.' She spoke in a resigned voice. 'Beautiful food, fabulous setting.'

And a beautiful bridesmaid—he knew that for a fact. 'And the company?'

Her smile was filled with rue. 'Was as expected.'

'You didn't enjoy it.'

She screwed up her face. 'Not parts of it, no. But some things were great.'

'Your family approves of the groom?' He got the impression family approval was something of a major in Bella's life.

'Oh, yes.' The answer came quickly. 'Hamish is a nice guy. He loves Vita. He makes her happy. But that's not why Dad was so happy to have him marry her.'

'No?' He couldn't stop the questions, found he was more and more intrigued as her face grew even more expressive.

She rolled her eyes. 'Money. It all comes down to doing the maths and in the spreadsheet Hamish has it all. He has the right job and went to the right school. Drives the right car, lives in the right suburb. That's the measure. Visible, measurable success.'

Success, huh? He thought of her tiny unfurnished flat, her barely road-safe car, the bad budget wine she'd been about to buy. He felt a twinge of sympathy for her father. 'Maybe he just wants security for her.'

'What sort of security?' she scoffed. 'It wouldn't matter to him if he was a complete jerk, so long as he could check the right boxes he'd be happy.'

He sensed the hurt in her again. Figured he knew

its source. 'Let me guess—you had a boyfriend who didn't measure up.'

'Actually, no. He was exactly what my father wanted.'

A crazy spurt of competition flared through him. 'How so?'

'He had it all.' She ticked off her fingers. 'An accountant. Very successful. Has the car, the apartment. Really good at team sports, the works. The whole family loved him.'

'So what went wrong?'

'He wanted me to wear something more conservative.'

Owen stared at her, only just holding back the burst of laughter. He couldn't imagine Bella allowing that in a million years. Not this woman who was currently wearing some huge flowing blouse and a skirt that was so long it practically dragged on the ground. And he was spending far too long mentally pushing the whole ugly lot off her.

She stared at him, all defiance. 'Nobody tells me what I should or shouldn't wear.'

'That was it?' he asked.

'That was just the start.' She stabbed another bite of meat. 'I'm not interested in someone who wants to change me. Or who wants me to be something I'm not.'

Fair enough point. And he was pleased he'd been right. The guy must have been blind to not see how expression of her individuality was a cornerstone for Bella. 'So what happened to him?'

'He was the best man.'

His mouth dropped. 'At the wedding?'

She nodded. 'He's Hamish's best friend. But it's OK.' She smiled saccharine sweet. 'He's still part of the family. Probably will be part of the family because now he's dating Celia.'

'Cousin Celia?' Owen felt the cold chill ripple through him. Was that why Bella had played so wildly with him? Because she'd wanted to show them all she didn't need them? Just wanted a hot date to throw in their faces? He'd known at the time that that was part of it and he'd enjoyed playing along. But once they'd been behind closed doors there'd been a genuine, raw passion in her—an intensity that he hadn't expected. And he'd found an answering need rising in him. A hunger that had been extreme and that hadn't been fully fed. He'd wanted more and had thought she did too.

Now he knew better. So that wildness had purely been driven by rebound and pride? No wonder she hadn't wanted to know him after and had given him a false number. He'd just been a convenient tool for the evening. His fingers curled tighter round his cutlery. Maybe he wasn't going to bide his time after all. Maybe he would have a go for the way she'd treated him that night—right about now.

But Bella was still talking. 'They're all so pleased, because he is such a great guy,' she continued. 'But of course, they do feel for me. I mean, it must be so hard, seeing him with my cousin like that. After he broke my heart and all. But he just fell in love with Celia, you see. And she really is his perfect match.'

Owen stared at her for a second, not sure if she was being sarcastic or not. Then he caught the glint in her eye. And he started to laugh. Couldn't help it, and the knot of tension loosened again.

Bella smiled too. 'I can see the funny side. I can. But they all think he broke up with me. They just can't believe that I'd have ditched him. It's beyond their comprehension that someone like me would have thrown away a catch like him.'

It soothed him no end to hear she'd been the one to dump the jerk. 'Does what they think really matter so much?'

'Maybe it shouldn't.' She looked at her clear plate. 'But it does.'

'Why?'

'I just want them to respect me.' She pushed back her chair and stood. 'I want them to respect what I do.'

Owen stood, picked up his plate and headed after her. He could see some of the problem. It might be hard, for the conservative type her family seemed to be, to respect someone who wore a Walt Disney dress and drove a car called Bubbles.

He followed her back inside, down the stairs, struggling with the fact his desire for her wasn't abating at all. How was he going to manoeuvre this the way he wanted? Could he really do patience?

'So what was the best bit of the day?' He put his plate on the bench, near where she now stood, filling the sink with hot water and detergent. 'Assuming there was a best bit.'

She turned and smiled then, a brilliant, genuine smile that made him snatch a quick breath.

'Seeing my sister so happy.'

BELLA COULD SEE she'd surprised him. She rinsed the plates and pots and stacked them in the dishwasher. She felt a bit embarrassed about all she'd just unloaded—but once she'd started babbling she couldn't stop and it meant there weren't those heavy silences. The last thing she'd wanted was to sound like some little girl whining about her family not taking her seriously. She was hard to take seriously because she did tend to make stupid mistakes. But that didn't mean that what she did contribute wasn't worthwhile.

She certainly hadn't meant to harp on about Rex. Celia could have him. She honestly didn't want him. He wasn't her type at all. And based on what she could see around she was determined to think Owen wasn't either. People who had this kind of success were conservative, weren't they? They worked hard, played safe, climbed to the top—from the looks of things Owen was definitely at the top. And conservative people just didn't 'get' Bella. No wonder he'd skipped out as soon as he could. No wonder he was Mr Reluctant now. She refused to embarrass him by throwing herself at him. She would be nice, polite, not make a fool of herself—any more than she already had. But she couldn't help appreciating his closeness as he sorted out the dishwasher and switched it on.

'I'm really tired,' she said. 'It's been quite a day.'

'Sure has,' he agreed—those soft, gentle tones again like on the beach as they'd headed to her studio.

Heart thudding, she turned, quickly, awkwardly, to head to her room. But just as she was about to leave it hit her how kind he'd been. He hadn't lectured her about her many mishaps of the day, hadn't teased her mercilessly as her family and friends would have. He'd just accepted it. Dealt with it. Helped her.

And she really appreciated it.

She turned back, still feeling completely awkward. 'Owen, thank you,' she began formally.

He walked up to her then and, now she'd looked up at him, he captured her gaze with his—with the vivid intensity of it. He put a finger on her lips and she was held fast.

'Leave it. It's not a problem.'

Like a statue she stood, mesmerised once more, filled with the memory of how well they'd fitted together. How wonderful his body had felt. How much she'd like to feel it again.

His focus dropped, flickered over her face and then lower. His finger followed, leaving her mouth to touch the hollow just below her collarbone, brushing back her blouse to reveal the skin. 'Is this new?'

What? Oh, the unicorn, the fake tattoo she always

wore for parties. She put one on all the kids too. It was part of the fairy ritual.

'It's temporary,' she whispered. She didn't know why she was whispering, it was just that her voice wouldn't go any louder as his thumb smoothly stroked the small spot.

And at her words a touch of seriousness dulled the gleam in his eyes. A half-smile curved one side of his mouth, but it wasn't one of tease or wicked intent. He stepped back. 'Sleep well.'

Disappointment wafted through her. So he wasn't interested. It had been a night of craziness for him and not one he wanted to repeat. For now she was back in his life but only, like her tattoo, temporary.

What had happened today might not be a problem for him. But it was for her.

CHAPTER SEVEN

OWEN SAT BACK in his chair, letting the debate wash over him as two of his young design team warred over the best way to progress a new program they were working on. They had a meeting with the client in just an hour's time and they had to decide before then. He watched disinterestedly as they both tried to secure his vote with impassioned speeches aimed in his direction. He wasn't really listening.

He hadn't seen Bella leave this morning. Figured she must be on an early shift at the café she was working at. The fairy dress that had haunted him all night was slung over one of the chairs so he knew she hadn't skipped out on him already. Although he suspected she wanted to. He studied the fabric, saw her in it in his mind's eye. The outfit was demure, no parents would object, and yet she looked so damn sexy, so edible. Like a silver-wrapped bon bon—one that he wanted to unpeel and devour in one big bite. No wonder she was asked if she did adult parties. He'd been awake all hours, still seeing her in it—and the curve of her breast almost not in it.

She had this whole slightly incompetent thing going—she had a car that looked as if it had a bad case of multicoloured measles and tyres so bald you could practically see your reflection in them. As for the hard-boiled eggs… He could still feel the mortification that had emanated from her in great waves. It hadn't been hard not to laugh. Unlike her neighbours and the firefighters, he'd seen under the blushes to the hurt beneath, and the fear. The clarity of it all surprised him. He wasn't usually one to tune into the deep feelings of others, but with her it had been so acute he'd almost felt it himself. And crazily he didn't want her to feel alone. He didn't want her to be alone. Alarming, when being alone was the one thing he liked best.

But she'd been faced with a situation where she'd been feeling desperate—desperate enough to come home with him, because he knew she hadn't wanted to. And that, despite those occasional signs pointing the other way, made him keep the brakes on.

She hadn't wanted to see him again—had deliberately given him the wrong number—and then had been forced to accept his assistance. Assistance he'd been careful to offer casually—knowing instinctively that if he'd come on strong she'd refuse and he hadn't wanted that. Because he was certain there was still a strong attraction there—she might not like it, but the chemical reaction between them was undeniable.

Now, somehow, he was going to find out why she didn't like it, and then he was going to get rid of it.

It slowly dawned on him that the room had descended into silence. They were all looking his way. And then he saw that the attention of his team wasn't on him or the lack of conversation. They were all fixated on a spot over his shoulder.

He heard slightly laboured breathing and turned to look behind him. And he was glad he was sitting down. Because the zip on his trousers was instantly pulled really tight. If he were to stand it would be obvious to all the world what this woman did to him. As it was he might have given it away with his mouth hanging open for the last— How long was it already?

She was standing only a few paces into the room, the door to her bedroom open behind her. She was wearing an old, thin, white tee shirt. It was oversized, the sleeves coming to her elbows, the hem only just covering the tops of her thighs. Good thing it reached even that far because that, it seemed, was it. Her only other adornment was a thin white cord coming from each ear, in her hand the tiny MP3 player. Even from this distance, in the silence of his colleagues, he could hear the faint strains of the music playing in her ears.

He clawed back the ability to move and glanced at the table, catching the surreptitious smiles between his workers and saw Billy openly staring at her. He couldn't blame him. He swung his face back towards her himself, unable to look away for long.

Her mouth had opened. She might have apologised but it wasn't audible. He saw her take in another deep shuddering breath. And then she turned, and walked back into the bedroom. As she'd moved her breasts had moved too, making it more than clear that there was no bra on under there.

'Excuse me.' Her voice was louder that time, her profile fiery as she darted back into the bedroom.

Owen stared after her. She had surprisingly long legs for someone who really wasn't that tall. He remembered them around his waist and wanted to wrap them there again—preferably now.

Instead he turned his head back to his team.

'One sec, guys,' he managed to mutter. He swivelled his chair right around before standing so his back was to them as he rose. Gritting his teeth and praying for self-control, he headed after her.

She was across the other side of the room, but turned back to the door as he entered. He glanced about for a moment to buy some more control time before looking at her again. The glance took in her rumpled bed. It didn't help his focus.

'I'm so sorry,' she mumbled, cheeks still stop-sign red. 'I was listening to my music and didn't hear you all out there.'

'I should have warned you, but I thought you'd gone. We have meetings up here every so often.'

All he wanted to do was slide his fingers under the hem of that ratty old shirt and find out for sure if her bottom truly was as bare as her legs were. Looking down, he could see the outline of her nipples. Her glorious, soft warm breasts that he longed to cup in his hands and kiss as he had that magical night on Waiheke.

He was twisting up inside with the effort of trying to control his want, knowing he had to get back to that meeting when all he wanted was to back her up against the bed and take her. The way he was feeling right now it wouldn't take long. Just a few minutes. Fast and furious.

But he knew it wouldn't be enough. He needed longer with her—he needed a whole night.

'I'll be on my way in a moment.' She was still mumbling.

He looked into her face then and the hunger in it jolted him. She was staring—as if she hadn't seen him before, her silvery blue eyes wide. He wondered if she knew how transparent they were. The desire shone in them, the dazed surprise as she looked him over. But at the back of them he could also see hesitation. And that was the bit he didn't understand. What had happened that night? And how could he right it? Nothing could happen until he did. He wanted her as willing and as wild as she'd been at the beginning.

So with sheer force of will he turned away, and, acting as normally as he could, went back to his incredibly boring meeting.

When she emerged from the bedroom the next time she was clothed in the black trousers and shirt he figured was her work attire. He rose and walked her to the door, shielding her from the overly curious stares of his colleagues. He bet they'd be curious. They'd never seen a woman here before. He was glad she'd emerged from one of the spare rooms. He knew he had a reputation for short term, and that was a reputation and a reality that he wanted to keep. It was a good way of keeping gold-diggers at bay. But he wasn't glad about the way Billy was still eyeing her up.

'Are you going to the café?' Of course she was, but he wanted to have some sort of conversation with her, wanted to hold her there for just a fraction longer.

She nodded, still not looking at him, clearly eager to escape.

'But you haven't had breakfast.'

'I'll have something at work.'

She'd slipped out the door before he could think of anything else stupid to say.

He usually worked most of the day up in his apartment, liking the light and the space to think freely— away from the phones and noise of his employees. But today, after the meeting, he stayed down on the second floor with them. Keeping away from the sight of that damn dress and the scent of her.

He was going to have to win her over again. How? Make her laugh? Do something nice for her? He had the suspicion he needed to be careful about that— she'd got huffy over his offer to take care of her car. So what, then?

Annoyed with himself for spending so long thinking about her, he forced himself to work longer and harder. And when that failed he went out and got physical.

BELLA HAD HAD a long day. She was well used to working in a café but was more tired than usual from standing and smiling for so many hours. She'd spent the whole time seeing Owen looking the ultimate stud in that suit. Devastating, distracting, delicious— and totally beyond her reach.

Now she was sitting at his big table, desperately trying to sew the sleeve back onto the offending fairy dress. She'd had a call from one of the parents who'd been at yesterday's party. She had a four-year-old niece who was having a party this weekend and would she be able to attend? Of course she would. She needed the money too badly to say no. She needed to get out of Owen's apartment before she threw herself at him desperate-wench style.

Sighing, she tried to thread the needle again. She was having more luck with her party entertaining than she was with her serious acting. She'd phoned up one of the theatres and had felt totally psyched out when the artistic director started asking about what training she'd had and so on. She'd stumbled, like the amateur she was. He'd said they had nothing now but to keep an eye out in the paper for the next auditions call. She didn't know what else she'd expected, but it was disheartening all the same.

Then Owen got home. She stared as he gave her a brief grin and headed to the kitchen. He'd been to the gym or for a run or something because he was in shorts and a light tee and trainers and there was bare brown skin on show. He was filmed in sweat and breathing hard. She was fascinated. Her own pulse skipped faster, forcing her to take in air quicker too.

He reached into the fridge and pulled out a bottle of water. Seeing him swigging deeply like that, Bella totally lost her stitch. She struggled once more to rethread the needle.

He wandered closer, staring just as hard back at her with an expression she couldn't define. The thread slipped again.

'Repairs not going so well?'

Major understatement. She'd scrubbed so hard at the hem to get the wine stains out and had only partially succeeded. She was gutted because it was a one-in-a-million dress and if she didn't get it sorted she wouldn't be able to work. She couldn't afford a new one and she couldn't afford to get this one fixed. She was going to have to do it herself. She squared her shoulders. Determined to do it, refusing to send an SOS to her father, refusing to give up.

'Let me have a go.' He went back to the kitchen, washed his hands, dried them and then reached for the fabric.

Stunned, she handed it over. 'You really were some sort of Boy Scout?'

He glanced at her then, his eyes full of awareness, and she kicked herself for bringing the memory of that night out into the open. She flushed.

He looked back to the needle, lips twitching. 'Actually, no, but I figure I can't do as bad a job as you are.'

'Thanks very much.'

He sat in the chair next to hers. Suddenly antsy, she moved and took a quick walk around the room before returning to stand over him. He'd been out running for over an hour. She could see the '68' minutes frozen on his stopwatch where he'd recorded his time. Yet his breathing was now normal. Fit guy. But then she knew that already. She could feel the heat from him and all it did was make her uncomfortably hot and her breath came shorter and faster still—as if she were the one out marathon training.

He didn't look too competent with the needle, though.

'Damn.'

Sure enough he'd pricked his finger.

She felt mightily glad to see he was a little useless at something.

He looked up at her, his eyes suddenly all puppy-dog apologetic. 'Sorry,' he said. 'Tell you what, I'll get my dry-cleaner to take it—they do mending as well.'

'No.' She shook her head.

'Bella, I have to. I've smeared blood on it now. I owe you.'

She looked at the dress; sure enough, there was a big spot right on the cute capped sleeve.

'Oh.' Her heart lurched.

'It's the least I can do.' He really did look sorry. 'I'm sure they'll be able to fix it.'

She hadn't got the wine stains out. She'd have no luck getting the blood mark either. Damn it, he'd put her in the position of having to accept his help again. 'OK.'

He slung the dress back over the chair. 'They'll have it back in twenty-four hours.'

Just as he turned away she caught sight of his wicked grin and the suspicion that he'd done it deliberately flew at her. She opened her mouth to protest, but the words died on her tongue as she thought about it. She loved that dress. She needed that dress. She could pay him back after the party, couldn't she? She really had no option.

'I'm starving.' He stretched. 'Let's do pizza.'

Take-out pizza she could handle. It was cheap; it was yummy. Her sense of independence surged. Hell, she could even buy it.

'Just give me a couple of minutes to shower and change,' he called as he headed to his room.

She was opening all the kitchen cupboards and drawers when he got back.

'Looking for something?'

'Phonebook,' she muttered.

He stared at her quizzically for a moment. 'Ever heard of the Internet? Anyway, we're not ordering in, we're going out.'

'We are?' Nonplussed, she stared at him. Since when? But he was halfway to the door already.

She called after him as he sped down the stairs. 'Going out where?'

He grinned up at her as she descended the last few hundred steps. 'My favourite.'

It was a colourful Italian restaurant about five doors down from his warehouse. Not quite the cheap and cheerful she'd imagined. More refined than relaxed, but they didn't seem to mind his casual jeans and shirt and her charity shop special skirt.

Bella had kittens as she read the menu—and saw the prices.

Owen seemed to read her mind. 'My treat. A further apology.'

That was the point where she finally baulked. 'No.' She was not going to have him call all the shots like this, and certainly not have him pay for everything. It made the situation sticky.

'Pardon?' He looked at her. The air almost crackled.

'No, thank you,' she enunciated clearly. 'You've already done far too much for me, Owen.'

He'd frozen. Clearly he didn't hear the word no very often. She was going to have to remedy that. 'You don't have any brothers or sisters, do you?' she asked.

'No,' he said, surprised. 'How did you figure that?'

'You're too used to getting your own way.'

He stared at her; she met the scrutiny with a determined lift to her chin. 'You think?' He suddenly stood. 'Let's get out of here, then. We'll do your precious takeaway.'

'I'm paying.' Assertiveness plus, that was the way.

'Fine.' His lips were twitching again.

The rooftop was as warm and seductive as the night before and Bella soon realised she would have been far safer in the overpriced restaurant. Desperately she went for small talk—anything to distract her from how hot he looked, how hot she felt. And to stop her from making a fool of herself. 'Where are your parents?'

'Mum's in Auckland, Dad's in Australia.'

So they'd split up. Somehow it didn't surprise her. 'Were you very old when they busted up?'

He looked cynically amused, as if he knew how she was analysing him. 'I was nineteen.'

'Really?'

Owen smiled at her surprise. 'Twenty-three years of marriage gone. Just like that.'

'Did one of them have an affair?'

'No,' he answered. Not to his knowledge. But that was the point, wasn't it? He hadn't known about any of it. He'd been so obtuse. Maybe it would have been easier if one of them had. 'They just grew apart.'

She was frowning. 'So what, they just woke up one day and decided to call it quits?'

That was how it had seemed to him at first. A bolt from the blue. Utterly unexpected, unforeseen. But if he'd had an ounce of awareness, he would have known. It still pained him that two of the most important people in his life had been slowly imploding and he hadn't even noticed. He'd been too preoccupied with himself and his work and all his great plans.

'They were unhappy for a long time. I never knew. I was too busy with school and sport and socialising to notice. But they agreed to stick together until I was through school and then separate. In those teen years it seemed every other mate's parents were busting up. I thought mine were the shining example of

success. Turns out they just wanted to protect me—
stop me going off the rails like so many of those
mates then did.'

He didn't want to know that level of ignorance
again. Part of him was angry with them for not being
honest with him sooner, part of him respected them
for the way they'd loved him. More of him was angry
with himself for being so blind. And he couldn't be
sure that he wouldn't be that blind again, so he wasn't
up for that kind of risk.

She'd stopped eating her pizza and was staring at
him with such expressive eyes, it jabbed him inside
to look into them. He stared at the box between them
instead and kept on talking to cover it.

'I think they got bored with each other. They had
different interests. The only thing holding them together was me.' Together forever just wasn't a reality—not for anyone. If his parents couldn't make it,
no one could. He cleared his throat. 'It wasn't acri-
monious or anything. Don't think it left me scarred
or anything. We can all get together and do dinner.
They were both totally supportive when I decided
to quit university to concentrate on developing my
company.'

NOT SCARRED? BELLA doubted that. This was the man
who swore never to marry. Who said it wasn't worth
the paper it was written on. While many men could
claim commitment-phobia, his seemed more vehe-
ment than most. If that wasn't scarred she didn't
know what was. But maybe there was more to it. Her

newly assertive, independent persona took a bite of pizza and went for it.

'And so you've just been working on your company ever since? No serious girlfriend?'

'What is this?' Irritation flashed. 'The Spanish Inquisition?'

So there was someone. 'Just answer.' She pointed her pizza at him. 'Has there really been no one serious in your life?'

'All right.' He took a huge bite of pizza and answered out the side of his mouth. 'I had a girlfriend. A long time ago.' Then he shut his lips and chomped hard.

'What happened?'

He shrugged, eventually swallowed. 'Nothing much.'

'Did you live together?' Why did she need all the details? She couldn't help but want all the details.

'For a while.'

The niggle of jealousy was bigger than she expected. 'What happened?'

'She met someone else. They're married now. Has a kid—two maybe.'

She stared at him, shocked. 'She left you?'

He looked levelly at her. 'I'm not a good companion, Bella.'

'What makes you say that?' Good grief, the guy was gorgeous.

'When I'm working on a project, that's my world, that's all there is. For those weeks, months, whatever, other things pass me by.'

She frowned. 'Are you working on something now?'

'Yes.'

Yet it seemed to her that nothing much passed him by. 'You don't think you're being a little hard on yourself?'

'I didn't notice my folks falling apart. I didn't notice her falling apart.' His face hardened. 'I'm selfish, Bella, remember?'

She stared, her mental picture elsewhere, thinking. From what she'd seen of him, it didn't quite ring true—yes, he did what he wanted, but he did what others wanted too. But he'd totally closed over now, moodily staring at the half-eaten pizza.

She wanted to lighten the mood. 'So what, you just lock yourself away and do geeky boy hacker things?'

His blue eyes met hers and sparked again. 'I have programmers who build the software, Bella. Then I use the programs to do the work that needs doing.'

'I'm surprised you need the programmers, Owen,' she teased, pleased to have his humour back. 'Why don't you get all your precious computers to do it all for you?'

He chuckled. 'There's one thing that computers can't do. Something that I can do really, really well.'

'What's that?'

'Imagine,' he answered softly. 'I have a really, really good imagination, Bella.'

She stared at him, reading everything she wanted to read in his expression—heat. She was a dreamer—

her father had told her off for it. That she wouldn't get anywhere sitting in a daydream all day...

'Someone has to dream it up.'

Someone like him. He was so enticing. Did he know what she was imagining right now? She suspected he might because that look in his eye was back.

Confusion made her run for deflection. 'I could never sit at a computer all day.'

'I could never stand on my feet slaving after people all day in a ton of noise.'

'I like the noise of the café. I like watching the customers as they sit and people-watch. I like the face-to-face contact.'

'I like face to face.'

'Really?' She didn't quite believe him. She had the feeling he holed himself away in that big apartment and thought up things her brain wasn't even capable of comprehending. And then he sold them. She'd been wrong—he was more entrepreneur than anything.

His grin turned wicked. 'And body to body.' He leaned closer, his voice lower, his eyes more intense. 'Skin to skin.'

OWEN GRINNED AS he saw the change in her eyes again. The sparkle went sultry. When he stepped close to her, when he spoke low to her, she coloured, flustered. But he wanted her more than flustered, he wanted her hot—and wild. And now he saw the way to that was so much simpler than he'd thought. All he had to do was get close to her. And she wanted to know about him? He'd tell her about him.

'A couple of years ago I sold the business to a conglomerate for many millions of dollars.' He was upfront, knowing money wasn't something that rang her bell. She seemed to take a strange joy in being broke; it was almost as if she deliberately mucked up—as if it was some sort of 'screw you' signal to her dad.

'So what did you do with all your millions?' she asked, her tone utterly astringent.

There, see? He'd known it would go down like the proverbial lead balloon. 'What do you think I did with it?'

'Bought yourself a Ferrari,' she snapped, 'and a few other boy toys. A plush pad in the centre of the city. An easy, playboy lifestyle.' Her eyes were like poisoned arrows pointing straight at him.

He batted them away. 'Yes to the Ferrari—it was my one big indulgence. But not so many other toys. As you've already seen the plush pad in the city isn't so plush—half of it still has to be plushed up.'

He paused, took in her focused attention. Good, it was time his little fairy saw things the way they actually were.

'I put half into a charitable trust and built a think tank with the other. The people you saw in that meeting yesterday have some of the brightest and best minds you'll find anywhere. Total computer geeks.' He winked at her. 'I get them together and they work through problems, building new programs.'

'That you can sell and make lots of money with.'

'That's right. We take the money, give half away and get on with the next idea. I like ideas, Bella. I like to think them up and get them working and then I like to move on to the next big one.'

'You don't want to see them all the way through?'

He frowned. 'I don't like to get bored.' He didn't like to be complacent. He didn't like to be around long enough to 'miss' anything. It was better for him to keep his mind moving. 'As for the easy, playboy lifestyle—sure, occasionally. But for the most part I work very long, very hard.'

'Why? When you're wealthy enough to retire tomorrow?'

'Because I like it.' Because he couldn't not. Because he needed something to occupy his mind and his time. Because he was driven. Because he couldn't face the void inside him that he knew couldn't be filled. Because he was missing something that everyone else had—the compassion, the consideration, the plain awareness and empathy towards others. His relationship with Liz had made him feel claustrophobic. The family she'd threatened him with had proved to him he wasn't built for it and he had bitterly resented her for trying to force him into it. He would not allow that pressure to be put on him again. But he'd have a woman the way he wanted—he'd have Bella the way he wanted.

'For all that success—' he underlined the word, knowing the concept annoyed her '—I'm still the guy who made you laugh that night.' He tossed the pizza crust into the box and stood. 'I'm still the guy who made your legs so weak you couldn't stand.' He took a step back, determined to walk away now. He spoke softer. 'I'm still the guy who made you alternately sigh then scream with pleasure.' He paused. He'd leave her knowing exactly what his intentions were—plain and simple. He spoke softer still. 'And I'm the guy who's going to do it all again.'

CHAPTER EIGHT

BELLA STAYED IN her room until well after nine the next morning, sure that by then Owen would be downstairs overseeing his group of geeks, coming up with some program to bring about world peace or something. Last night had been the most frustrating night of her life—even more frustrating than after he'd left her bed on Waiheke, and she hadn't thought anything could top that.

After his outrageous comments, he'd gone. With a smile that had promised everything and threatened nothing he'd walked downstairs—presumably to his room. The door had been closed when she'd summoned the courage to leave the roof. What had she been supposed to do—follow him?

She'd badly, badly wanted to. But she didn't, of course, because her legs had lost all strength again—just with his words.

Now, as she moved quietly across the warehouse, she saw his bedroom door was closed. She knocked gently, just to be certain. When there was no reply she opened it and walked on in. Halfway to the bathroom door on the other side she realised that the big lump of bedding on the edge of his bed was moving; it actually had a lump in it—him. He sat up—all brown chest on white sheets, hair sticking up in all directions and wide sleepy grin. 'Good morning.'

She froze, halfway across the floor. 'I thought you'd be at work already.'

'No.' He yawned. 'I didn't get much sleep last night.'

She felt the colour flood into her face.

'I had a call from New York that went on for a while.'

Her colour continued to heighten. She started to back out of the room. At least she was wearing trackies now under the tee shirt. After the embarrassment of yesterday she wasn't running the risk of encountering all those people when she was half starkers again.

'No, don't worry,' he said, swinging his legs out of the bed and reaching for a shirt on the floor. 'Use the bathroom. I'm going for a run.'

She stopped in the doorway. He'd stood up from the bed. Naked except for the shirt he was holding to his lower belly. He was magnificent. Rippling muscles and indents and abs you wouldn't see anywhere other than the Olympic arena. He yawned again, stretched his free arm, showing his body off to complete perfection.

He was doing it deliberately. He had to be. She

swallowed—once. Took a breath. Blinked. Swallowed again. Still couldn't seem to move her legs.

'Bella?'

She turned and walked then, straight back to her bedroom. Where she threw herself down and buried her burning face in the cool of the sheets.

Damn it, Owen. If you're going to do it, do it.

HALF AN HOUR later she figured he'd gone and be out for another hour at least. So she headed to the kitchen—she needed a long, very cold drink. As she downed the icy water she heard the door slam.

She turned, and there he was wearing loose shorts and a light tee. He was puffing, sweating a little. He stalked towards her. Straight towards her and he didn't seem to be stopping.

'You're back already,' she blurted.

'Yeah,' he muttered. To her acute disappointment he veered off course, halting and reaching into the fridge. 'It was short but intense.'

She held onto her glass, leaned back against the sink and stared.

'I ran up and down the stairs for twenty minutes.'

She quickly lowered her glass to the bench. He stood facing her, strong and fit, and she was breathing harder than he. It was early morning, broad daylight, she was stone-cold sober, and she wanted him more than she'd ever wanted anything.

He leaned back, resting on the bench opposite her. 'What are you thinking?'

'N-nothing.'

There was a silence where he looked at her with such amused disbelief and she wanted to squirm away from the knowledge in his eyes.

'Come here.'

She hesitated.

'Here.'

She walked, one whole step, aiming for nonchalant, before stopping, stupidly wishing she weren't still wearing her loose, ugly trackies and old tee shirt.

'Come right here.'

'What?' she asked as she moved fractionally closer, her mind tickled with an alternative meaning to his words, and a delicious mix of anticipation and alarm rose when he straightened. She took another tiny step.

'Why don't you do the "nothing" you've been thinking about for the last five minutes?' He smiled then, took a step to meet her when she stopped short. 'Or is it longer that you've been thinking about "nothing"?'

Her mouth opened but nothing came out.

His gaze dropped to it; she could almost feel him roving over the curves and contours of her lips. She desperately wanted him to. His eyes flicked, coming back to snare hers. There was that warmth in them, the glow was back—the light that had seduced her so completely on Waiheke. And she couldn't walk away from it.

She knew he was waiting. But she was frozen.

And then it seemed that words might not be necessary.

His breathing was more rapid now too—faster than when he'd first got back from his run. And the glow in his gaze had become a burn that was steadily gaining in intensity.

A shrill, tuneless series of beeps shattered the silence.

He didn't step away. 'Someone's trying to call you.'

She shook her head, unable to tear her gaze from his. 'It's just my phone telling me it's almost out of battery.'

'Recharge it.'

'I can't,' she confessed. 'I left the power cord at my flat.'

A smile stole into his eyes. The phone whistled the ugly tune again.

He reached forward, slipping his hand into her pocket and pulling out the phone. She thought, hoped, he was going to throw it away. But then he looked away from her, flipped it open and stared at it. Frowned. Pushed a couple of buttons.

'What's wrong? Is it not working?'

His head jerked in negation. 'I have a cord that should work with this,' he muttered, but his mind had clearly moved to something else. Suddenly she wanted her phone back. She reached, but he held it up high, still pressing buttons.

'What are you looking for?' she asked.

'Tony's Lawn Mowing Service.'

'What?'

'That was the number you gave me.' He gave her a hard look. 'That was why I couldn't get through to you. The phone number you gave me was completely wrong.'

Oh. Hell. 'Was it?' Her voice sounded weak, even to her.

He shot an even harder look. 'Accidentally on purpose.'

Her face fired up. The tension between them burst through her defences. 'You were in such a hurry to leave. I didn't want to be sitting around half hoping for you to call. Better to knock it out there and then.'

He moved, tossing the phone to the side, taking the last step forward so he was smack in front of her, blocking her exit. 'Only half hoping?' His smile teased but his eyes were laser sharp.

Her blush deepened and inside she wanted to beat her head against a wall—so he had tried. Now she felt more defensive than ever. 'Well, you didn't bother to give me your number,' she said miserably. 'Or even tell the truth about where you were staying.'

'That was irrelevant. At the time I was focused on making sure I could contact you. I knew there was no point giving you my number. You never would have called me. Would you?'

Her blush deepened. No. She never would. She'd been too mortified at the way he'd slunk off into the night. 'You just up and left me.' Even she heard it—how much her words betrayed her.

His smile twitched. 'I can see I have some work to do.'

'What sort of work?'

'Convincing you how much I want you. How much I wanted to stay that night.'

'If you'd wanted to stay, you could have.' A little petulant, still unforgiving.

He shook his head. 'Responsibilities, Bella. People were relying on me.'

'Priorities. Choices.' She'd been relying on him. Unfair of her perhaps, but she'd fallen—just like that. And she'd wanted him by her side. She'd enjoyed having him as a buffer between her and her family. But even more, she'd just wanted him at her side again—inside.

'I had every intention of calling you. I tried to call you.' He paused. 'You were the one who made the choice to stop that from happening.'

Humiliation at her exposure rose. Yes, she'd deliberately sabotaged any chance he might make contact because she'd been so sure he wouldn't and she didn't want to keep on hoping for ever that he would. Because she would have hoped—hoped and hoped and gone on hoping for evermore. And at the same time she'd been so sure he wouldn't. She didn't want to be that much of a loser any more.

His fingers were gentle but quite firm on her jaw as he turned her face back to him. He spoke very clearly. 'What you have yet to learn, Bella, is that I let very little stand in the way of what I want.'

'And what do you want?'

'You.'

She was melting inside, every bone liquefying.

'And the thing is…' he inched closer '…I get the distinct impression that you want me too.'

She was about to puddle at his feet. 'Owen—'

'Now why don't you do what you've been thinking about? Because that's exactly what I'm going to do.'

Her breathing skittered as he stepped closer again.

'I'm going to touch you and kiss you and feel you and watch you.'

She'd forgotten to blink and her eyes felt huge and dry.

'I want to watch you, Bella.' He was so close now. If she moved less than a millimetre, she'd be touching him.

'Do you know how expressive you are? How wide your eyes go when you want something? How pink your cheeks and your lips go?' His voice dropped as he whispered in her ear. 'How wet you get?'

She sucked in a breath. Shaken and very, very stirred. Did he know how wet she was now?

'Do it, Bella,' he urged in that low, sexy whisper. 'Do it.'

Her hand lifted and she spoke without thinking. A whisper, softer than his. 'Take your shirt off.'

For a moment their eyes met and she trembled at the flare of passion in the blue of his.

His hands moved to his top and with a fast movement he whipped it off, tossing it in a direction similar to her phone. He glanced down. The sweat had tracked down, slightly matting the fine layer of hair.

'I should shower.' The first hint of self-consciousness she'd ever seen in him.

'Not yet.' She placed the hand she'd raised on his chest, spreading her fingers on the heat, liking the dampness. She leant forward, licking the hollow at the base of his throat, tasting the salt. She liked him like this—raw, his body already primed for action. The run had just been the warm-up.

His breath hissed out.

Glancing down, she saw just how much he did want this—how much he wanted her. She looked back up and saw he'd seen her checking him out, and his smile had gone sinful.

His hands slipped down, pushing the old tracksuit pants from her waist and down. She kicked them off as he unclasped her bra, then he pulled each strap down her arms so it fell from her. Underneath the tee shirt her breasts were now free.

'Tell me, the other day when you barged in on my meeting wearing this gorgeous old tee shirt, were you wearing panties beneath it?'

Bella hesitated. A smile slowly curving her mouth. 'What do you think?'

His smile grew too. 'I'm thinking no.'

'I think you might be right.'

'We'd better get them off, then.'

He dropped to his haunches, slipped his fingers to her hips and found the elastic of her undies. He tugged and she wiggled—just a fraction—so they slid down. As she stepped out of them she stepped closer to him. He stayed down, looking back up at her.

'Perfect.'

His fingers moved slowly over her thighs, his broad palms warm and smooth as they stroked.

He stood. 'I've been dreaming of you in this shirt ever since ten twenty-five yesterday morning.' Then he kissed her—his mouth moving over hers, his tongue invading with hungry surges, until she was breathless and giddy and he groaned.

'I am having that shower,' he said, taking her hand and leading her to his bedroom. 'Stay there, I'll be two minutes.' He kissed her again. 'Make that one.'

But now that Bella had taken the step, she wasn't letting him get away. She followed him into the bathroom, laughing as he grabbed the shower gel. Sobering as she watched him lather it in his hands, slap it onto his body, and seeing again how truly magnificent he was.

'Bella, if you keep looking at me like that I—'

'I haven't showered either.' She cut him off. Tee shirt and all, she followed him into the steam.

The water ran over her, making the cotton of the tee shirt thick and heavy. It clung to her. He cupped her breast through the sodden fabric, thumb stroking the taut nipple. She rubbed the soapy bubbles over his skin, starting with his shoulders, his chest and then lower.

'Bella…' There was definite warning in his tone. And then he growled, yanked her into his arms and kissed her hard, his hands keeping her close.

The elation ran through her as she tasted his desire, thrilled with the knowledge that it matched her own.

He kissed her until her knees went weak and standing was becoming a major issue. She clung to his shoulders, not wanting to break the bliss of the kiss.

Slowly he peeled the wet tee shirt up and off her body. It landed on the bathroom floor with a loud smack. He flipped the lever and shut off the water. The sudden silence was broken by the occasional drip. But the steam kept rising.

He took a step towards her, and with an impish smile, she took a step back. His eyes lit up so she took another, and another, and then with a giggle she turned and ran, exhilarated as she sensed his speed behind her. It was only a second or two and he'd caught her, dragging them both the last half-metre to the bed, and there they tumbled and rolled.

He rose above her, on all fours, trapping her between his legs, her hands in his. For a moment they paused, both enthralled and excited by the chase—and her surrender.

She deliberately relaxed, parted her legs, and sent him the invitation. He didn't need it. He was already taking—mastering her body by using the magic of his. His hands caressed, his lips kissed and his eyes promised. And within moments she was arching, her hips up high, the tension ready to burst. He kissed her again, so intimately, his mouth fastening onto her clitoris while his fingers played deep within.

Her hands clenched in the thickness of his hair as, oh, so quickly she was there, on the brink and over, her body shaking, twisting beneath his.

'Again,' he demanded, slipping up her body fast, his hand still between her legs. 'Again.' He kissed her hard while his fingers were unrelenting. Slipping and sliding and teasing as he kissed her she felt the sensation inside bridge. His tongue thrust into her mouth and she shook with the need to have that other part of him deep inside her, plunging hard and fast— stirring her to an even greater ecstasy.

She broke free of his kiss as the breath expelled harshly from her lungs and her hips bucked. 'Yes!' she cried, incredulous as one orgasm moved into another, longer, more intense one. And he watched, a fiendishly satisfied grin lighting him as she shuddered beneath him.

And then, instead of that weightless, warm, replete feeling that usually came after ecstasy, she was filled with a ravenous void, the need for completion. It was an overpowering hunger. An intense ache that angered her and drove her to take in a way she'd never done before.

She spoke to him. Short, harsh words while her

hands reached out, greedily touching him, and then her mouth too. And the look of smug arrogance and amusement left his features. Concentration took over, and suddenly he was as exposed as she, his hunger revealed as her words stripped him of his control.

She watched as his breathing became laboured, revelled in his haste to sheath himself with the condom. He swore when it took too long. Swore louder when she took over and teased it down on him cruelly slow, all the while whispering in a way that was clearly driving him to distraction, pausing now and then to press passionate, open kisses across his chest. Her hands worked over his body, pulling him to her. She wriggled beneath him, rocking against him, rotating, telling him not just with her words but with her body how hot she was for him. How badly she wanted him and was wanting him more with every passing moment.

'Now, now, now!' she cried, desperate for the fullness that only he could give. And with a raw growl he responded, thrusting deep.

'Har— Oh, yes! Like that. Like that.' She didn't need to say it. He was already doing it exactly how she wanted. Hard and fast, surging into her, and she worked to meet him, stroke for stroke, her fingers curling into his strong hips.

She was transported into a magical realm where her wickedest, wildest fantasy became raw reality and much, much better—and she told him. What he was doing to her, how he was doing it so incredibly and how much more she wanted.

Until the words would no longer come because her mind could no longer think and it was squeals and sighs and moans that escaped—she couldn't control anything any more. Her hunger, her desire, her response to the pleasure his body brought her. The tension mounted—nothing before had ever been so extreme as this. Until it snapped and spasms ravaged through her, the sensations heightened by his fierce growl and the power he plunged into her.

HE ROLLED TO the side, pulling her over so her head rested on his rapidly rising chest. He chuckled then. A warm, contented sound. 'I have never been so turned on in all my life as when you were beneath me begging like that.'

Embarrassment curled into her. She'd behaved like some sex-starved animal. She'd used words she never thought, let alone voiced. Bella instantly felt the need to retain even some sense of the upper hand. 'I wasn't begging.'

'No?'

'I was ordering,' she declared. 'Demanding, in fact.'

He yanked gently on her hair, tipping her face up so she could see his smile.

'Do it any time. I don't mind.' It was a light, teasing smile. 'I didn't think sex could get better than that night on Waiheke. Now I know different. That was fantastic.' He kissed her then. A slow, sweet kiss. One kiss turned into another. When his hand brushed between her thighs, she flinched.

He broke the kiss immediately, a concerned look in his eyes. 'You OK?'

'Just a bit sensitive.' She flushed. So much pleasure had brought her body to the point of pain.

He kissed her again. Gentle, relaxing kisses that soothed the intense over-sensitivity in her body—changing it to warm softness.

'We'll go slow this time.'

Bella had the feeling it was too late to be going slow at anything.

CHAPTER NINE

'I HAVE TO get to the café.' Bella was on another late shift today. 'Shouldn't you be in a meeting or something?'

'Or something,' Owen muttered drowsily.

Bella moved, trying to slide from the bed, but his big heavy arm tightened, penning her in. 'I have to go,' she protested weakly. 'I can't be late.'

He groaned. But his arm relaxed.

She showered quickly, dressed. He was asleep when she went to leave. She spent a second or two by the bed, simply appreciating his tousled sexiness—even in sleep he was all consuming, all powerful—taking up most of the mattress.

And the flame of delight—of disbelief—glowed brighter in her heart. He'd tried to call her. He still wanted her. Relief, joy, satisfaction—she couldn't wipe the smile from her face. For once it seemed she was going to get something she really wanted. Maybe Lady Luck had finally turned her way.

She was halfway through her shift when she checked her mobile. It had been ominously quiet—

despite Owen recharging it for her. Of course it was quiet—she'd accidentally switched it off. She put it back on and cleared the messages. There were three from her landlord. She listened, wincing at his increasingly irate tones, then drew breath and dialled his number.

Less than three minutes later he was no longer her landlord. Her lease was terminated with immediate effect. He was keeping her deposit as payment for the door and inconvenience. She had the next day to remove the rest of her belongings.

In her break she went to the nearest ATM and got an account balance. She didn't really need to—she already knew the situation was dire. She had to save everything for a couple of weeks to get the bond for a new place. That meant she either had to stay with Owen or hit her family for another loan.

She knew what she wanted to do. But was it wise? Two weeks was a little longer than two days. They hadn't talked about anything remotely heavy like what, if any, future they had. She didn't want to— she already knew. Owen had told her right from the start that he didn't do commitment.

She'd swallow her pride and ask her father. It was inevitable anyway; she was as incompetent as he'd always said. Couldn't even manage a month on her own without stuffing up somehow and needing help.

When she got home later in the evening, Owen was waiting for her, music playing on the seriously fancy stereo, dinner keeping warm in the oven.

'What's up?' he asked the instant he saw her.

Was she that transparent?

'I've been turfed out of the flat. The landlord is keeping my bond. I'm going to—'

'Don't worry about it,' he interrupted carelessly, putting plates on the tray. 'You can stay here, long as you need to.'

Her spirits lifted and sank in the one moment. She hadn't wanted to call on her father, but she didn't particularly want to be in Owen's debt either—no more than she already was. Besides, he didn't do live-in lovers.

'Heaven forbid.'

He turned a startled gaze on her. 'What do you mean "heaven forbid"?'

She grinned, hoping to come across light but inside kind of terrified about his response. 'That's what you said at the bar on Waiheke when I asked if you had a live-in lover.'

He lifted a large iron casserole dish out of the oven, using a couple of tea towels to cover his hands. He carefully placed it on a protective mat on the bench. Only then did he answer—equally light in tone. 'Bella, we were in a bar flirting and being flippant.'

He began ladling the steaming contents of the dish onto their plates. 'I never knew you remembered everything I said so perfectly.'

Everything he'd ever said she'd committed to memory. If only she could learn her lines with the same skill.

'Anyway, you're only staying here till you sort

out a new place of your own, right?' Not as his live-in lover, but a temporary guest. He was making the point subtly, but nonetheless still making it. Fair enough.

'Absolutely,' she agreed. They were just confirming everything—mainly because she felt the need for well-defined boundaries.

'So,' he added, 'we don't need the labels, right? You're a friend staying here.'

'Sleeping with you.' There was that small point.

''Till you've got your new place sorted,' he continued, ignoring her comment, starting to sort eating utensils.

'Is that when we stop sleeping together?' She held her breath.

He stopped fussing in the cutlery drawer and looked at her. 'We stop sleeping together when one or other of us says the word.' He fished out another fork, put it by the plates and caught her eyes with his own once more—not that it was hard; she couldn't seem to stop staring at him. 'And says the word gently, right?'

Right.

He left the tray and put his hands around her waist instead. 'Rules established?' he asked softly.

'I think so.' Better late than never, she figured.

Bed buddies. An indefinite series of one-night stands. Except if she thought about it she'd wonder whether this might be more to her than a one-night stand. She might not be that old or that experienced, but even she could see this could lead to trouble—

for her at any rate. So she vowed to keep that limit
on it—two weeks. She'd have as much of him as she
wanted—and she really wanted—then she'd move
out and end it all. Before her heart as well as her
body got entwined.

EARLY THE NEXT morning she went to the flat and
cleared out the last of her belongings. Gave the whole
place a final clean, but even so the burnt-egg smell
lingered. Back at Owen's warehouse she ran a bath,
sank into it for the best part of an hour and appreciated the beauty of the room. The dark colour scheme
could be austere, but it wasn't. The flashes of red
here and there hinted at a touch of passion—the fire
she knew burned inside him. He was full of vital-
ity, ambition, discipline, drive. The bathroom designer had got a good handle on him. It was very,
very masculine. It screamed bachelor—for life. And
yet, there were twin hand-basins, side-by-side mirrors—one for him and one for the lady currently in
his life, huh? The overnight guest.

All his toiletries were in the drawer beneath the
basin, leaving the bench space clear and uncluttered.
Minimalist. With a spurt of defiance she lined up
her bubble bath, shower gel, shampoo and assorted
moisturisers in pump bottles. So she wasn't his live-
in lover? She was just a friend staying? Fine, but she
was quite determined to make her mark.

HE WAS WORKING at the computer when she got home
from the café late in the evening.

'You'll get square eyes,' she teased.

'You're not even into the Internet?' He spun on the chair to face her. 'What about the social pages?'

'I have no interest in communicating with the people I went to school with when I was five.' Not when they'd all be wealthy lawyers or doctors or married to some famous person, or anything like that, when she was just a waitress.

'But it's a necessity in today's market. You need computer skills to work.'

'I'm not saying I don't have skills. I can point and click as well as anyone, I'm just not interested. Why would I want to stare at a screen all day?'

'What about online shopping?'

'I'd really rather go to the movies.'

'And that's not staring at a screen?' He looked sardonic.

'OK, show me, then,' she challenged. 'One thing that's really interesting.'

He grinned. 'Did you know your sister has put photos of the wedding up on her chat page?'

'No.' Bella froze. 'Has she?'

'There's a really cute one of you with the stripe.'

'No!' she shrieked.

'Yep, up there for anyone and everyone to see.' He spun back to the computer, clicked a few times.

The picture was huge on the big screen. Her skin crawled with embarrassment at the line-up of tall blonde bridesmaids…and her.

'We were supposed to look like daffodils,' she said. 'Only, there's me, the lemon on the end.'

'I'd rather have a lemon any day. So much more flavour.'

She was too aghast at the pictures to feel flattered. 'Anyone can see these? Anyone?'

He nodded. 'I really liked this one myself.'

Another picture flashed up onto the screen. She was in the background, behind Vita and Hamish. He pressed a couple of buttons and zoomed in on her. The wind had blown the fabric tight against her chest and in the cool breeze she had the biggest case of erect nipples ever seen—you could see the outline of everything.

She felt heat rise into her cheeks, then actually felt the hardness in her nipples as he looked away from the screen, back to her, desire in his eyes.

Embarrassed, she let sarcasm mask it. 'You really are into computer porn.'

He laughed. 'Search my hard drive. There's nothing there. But I'll admit to studying this one closely for some time. It was all I had until I found out where you were.'

'Where I was?' She frowned.

'You might not have much of a presence on the web, but your sister certainly does and she gives regular updates on her and her family's activities.'

Bella was appalled. 'She's supposed to be on honeymoon. She's not supposed to be sticking things up on…' She broke off, thinking about what he'd implied. 'You knew I was in Wellington?'

He nodded. 'She mentions in her blog how she missed your family farewell dinner.'

'So you were in the supermarket on purpose?' Oh, my, that was sneaky.

'No,' he laughed. 'That was the Fates being kind.'

'But you knew I'd moved down here.'

He nodded.

'Were you going to keep looking for me?' Her silly heart was skipping like crazy.

'I was thinking about it.' Casually he clicked the picture away.

'Why?'

'Why do you think?' He stood, walked away from the computer and towards her. 'I told you, Bella. I tend to get what I want.'

'But you were so frosty.'

'You'd blown me off, remember? With Tony's Lawn Mowing Service.'

'Only because you blew me off,' she defended, 'and I didn't know it was Tony or anyone.' And without hesitation she went into his arms. 'Do you always know what you want?'

'Generally.' He didn't have to think about the answer long. 'Do you?'

Rarely. She knew what she didn't want, but she didn't necessarily want the opposite of that. And for once, right now, she knew exactly what she wanted.

As his arms tightened she knew what he wanted too.

'I haven't forgiven you for leaving that night,' she confessed.

'I know you haven't.'

'But do you know why?'

'You didn't want to be alone at the wedding.'

'No,' she whispered, able to admit now that that wasn't it at all. 'There were things I had planned for you.'

'Yes,' his matching whisper mocked. 'We still have unfinished business, don't we?' His hands teased. 'Now wouldn't it have been so much easier for me to find you if you had a website? I could have typed in your name and discovered you're a sexy children's party fairy—booked up all your weekends.'

She rolled her eyes. The fairy thing wasn't something she was that proud of. She didn't want all those old school friends knowing that was all her ambition had amounted to.

'I'm going to build you one,' he murmured just before pressing a kiss to her neck.

'Hmm?' Fast losing track of the conversation as his mouth took a path downwards.

'A website. For your party business. It'll take a couple of hours max.'

She stopped tufting his hair with her fingers. 'Owen, you've already done enough for me.'

'Bella, please, let me indulge my geek side.' He chuckled, his breath warming her skin. 'More to the point, let me indulge my trainee's geek side.'

But at that she chilled completely. 'You can't get your employees to build me a website.'

He lifted his head and looked unconcerned. 'Why not?'

'I can't afford to pay you.' She couldn't take more things from him.

He placed his forehead on hers, literally closely watching her. 'It would be a good practice job for the student placement kid. I need something to occupy his time when the team is busy on strategic stuff.'

OWEN REALLY ENJOYED the challenge of getting her to agree to his help. She was always so determined to say no and he liked nothing more than hearing 'yes' from her—although more often than not it was a soft 'OK'. Pricking his finger and staining the fairy dress had been a masterstroke in solving that problem. Building her a website was more of a difficult one. He could see the argument in her eyes. But it was really no biggie and it might be a bit of a confidence boost—make her see herself as the small businesswoman she was. If she took herself seriously, others might too.

'You'd be doing me a favour.' He knew she didn't really believe him. She knew, as well as he, it was a weak argument. But Owen liked to win, it didn't matter how minor the game—and this was minor, wasn't it? Maybe not, because he decided the end justified the means in this case. So he used his best weapon. And as he kissed her the hint of her refusal drowned beneath the rising desire.

The week slipped by. He refused to let her cook—saying he knew what she did to eggs and he wasn't letting her do that kind of damage to anything else. Instead he cooked, enjoying the creativity. He never normally bothered. But night after night he had it ready for when she got home. They ate and then snuggled on the sofa while she gave him a crash course in the great movie classics, starting with Casablanca. He hadn't spent so much time quietly relaxing in ages. And then, through the night, they hardly relaxed at all. Voracious—the more he had, the more he wanted. The passion ran unabated and it only seemed to get better every time.

The question of her staying with him had caused a fleeting awkwardness, but he thought he'd got through it smoothly. This was still a purely temporary situation, right? But he'd suffered a sharp twinge when she'd asked about them stopping sleeping together—he definitely wasn't ready for that yet. A few more days—several more nights. It wasn't done between them.

When he went for his run one morning she went with him—riding his bike. She didn't talk too much. Just a word here and there, and he found it companionable. When he walked into the bathroom after, the scent of her shampoo hung in the steam and disappointment surged when he saw she'd finished already. By the time he got out she was dressed and heading to the door.

'What's the hurry? I thought you were on late shift again.'

'I have an audition.' Her hair hung in a wet rope down her back.

He looked her over. 'You want me to iron that shirt for you?'

'Do you iron, Owen?'

'Not usually.' He ignored her chill. 'I have a service. But I can do it for you if you want.'

Her cool look grew even frostier. 'The only thing I iron is my hair.'

Right, yet she hadn't even bothered with that.

'It wouldn't take a second.' It was a lovely shirt, but the crease down one side didn't exactly give her the professional look.

'I'm running late as it is.'

It was his turn to frown. It was her second audition of the week—and she'd been late to that one too, had said it had gone badly, that she'd fluffed the lines completely.

But she looked so on edge now he stepped aside, letting her go.

Friday night she was on another late shift. Only he didn't feel like staying home and cooking. For once the apartment felt too big, too quiet, too lonely. He raided the fridge, found some not-too-ancient leftovers—enough to satisfy the hunger of his stomach for a while. Then he left—needing to satisfy his other hunger.

She was behind the counter, the one taking the orders, not actually making the coffee. He walked straight up to her, registering with pleasure the surprise in her eyes, the pink in her cheeks, her widening smile. The rush of warmth inside rose so fast it threw him, made him awkward. It wasn't the heat of lust; while that simmered in the background, this was different. This was a buzz, a thrill of delight caused by something else—affection, maybe? Amusement? He couldn't think what else. He took a step back, sat at the long counter facing the window so he wasn't staring straight at her. He pretended to leaf through one of the glossy magazines in the stack, but all the while he was attuned to her sing-song voice as she served the customers.

'Would you like whipped cream with that?' The teasing question had him irresistibly turning to look at her.

She was smiling—it turned sinful as she glanced at him—and everything inside suffered an electrical jolt. She could tempt a hunger striker to a four-course banquet if she asked like that. He'd say yes to her like a shot. His discomfort level increased when he realised it—he already was saying yes to her, all the damn time.

BACK AT OWEN'S house, after her shift, Bella thought how her sense of their boundaries was becoming blurry. One day he was spelling out the terms of their relationship as if it were some business transaction, the next he was incredibly sweet and telling her about his geek-boy attempt to track her down. She couldn't help but wonder if the magnetism between them was made of something stronger than just a few nights of fun.

And he was so good at getting her to agree to everything, she wanted to wrest back some of the power. Wanted to gain that independence she'd been seeking for so long. But more than that, she wanted him to be as sunk in her as she was in him—because she'd fallen for him completely now. He was beautiful, bright and bold and she wanted to keep him.

She didn't have a hope. She wasn't the sort of woman for him—if he ever wanted to commit it would be to someone super successful, beautiful, articulate. Someone who could stand beside him in any situation and do him proud. Someone like Vita. Whereas Bella would be an embarrassment—she'd be the one inadvertently wearing half her dinner on her shirt at a posh restaurant; she'd be the one falling on her face down a flight of stairs at a charity ball. She was always the one making the stupid slip-ups somehow.

But she could be the best sex of his life. She smothered the chuckle at the lack of loftiness in her ambition. Oh, yes, for whatever reason he wanted her body, and maybe, if she could keep him wanting her, she could keep this affair burning for longer. She wanted longer. All she had to do was trap him in some kind of sensual net—where he couldn't say no, where he couldn't get enough.

Now, in his bed, she slowly crawled down his body, towards his legs. The view he'd be getting was one she'd never be brave enough to give anyone else. But with Owen, it was different. He made no secret of how much he liked to look at her. How much just looking at her turned him on. And she wanted to turn him on really, really hard because that was what he did to her. He'd been right the other day—she had been begging—and she was determined to make him suffer to the same degree. To make him want her so much he'd never be the one to utter the words that would end it. He made her feel capable of anything—of making her most secret fantasies a reality.

Dangerous—because right now he was her secret fantasy.

He muttered something unintelligible. His hands came up, moulded round the contours of her bottom, then a finger traversed through her slick heat.

'You want me to stop?' she gasped.

'Oh, no. Please, no.'

She wriggled her hips pointedly and to her mixed relief and regret his hands slipped away. At least now she could try to focus.

'Come on,' he urged. 'You're killing me.'

She nuzzled into him, her hair teasing and twisting round his erection.

'Bella…'

'Roar.'

'Tigress.' His laugh sounded half strangled.

She turned around, so she was facing him as she straddled his legs, bending so her breasts were either side of his penis. 'Watch.'

'Oh, I am.'

She took him into her mouth and twirled her tongue on the tip of him.

His hands were fisted by his sides. Every muscle in his body tensed. 'Bella, stop. Please. I want you. I want all of you.'

'I don't mind…'

He shook his head. 'I want to be inside you.'

She slid the condom down slowly.

'Bella.' His lips barely moved, jaw locked, teeth clenched.

She slid herself down even slower.

His head fell back on the bed and the sound of his groan almost made her come. She bit her lip, the tiny pain keeping her sanity for her, stopping her from falling into an almost unconscious state of bliss. She wanted to remember this look of his forever. She wanted to savour the moment.

Heavy lidded, he looked at her body and then back to her face. She knew that right now he was incapable of speech. She'd never felt more beautiful. More admired. More wanted. And she felt the power surge into her. She moved, slowly, tilting her head so her hair fell, twisting her hips so she rode him, watching him imprisoned by passion beneath her.

But then her attempt to keep in control failed and animal instinct took over. She moved, keeping the feel of him so delicious, and the tension drove her, making her work harder, faster until she suddenly stopped, locked into sensation. He took over, gripping her hips, moving only that little bit more to knock them both over the edge, to those timeless moments of brilliant darkness where muscles jerked and pleasure pulsed through every part of her.

His arms held her close. With supreme effort she lifted her head and looked at him—saw the lazy mix of satisfaction and humour, and madly her desire lurched into life again. She couldn't stop herself seeking his kiss. And with a sinking heart she knew the only person she'd succeeded in trapping was herself.

CHAPTER TEN

THE NEXT DAY Bella left Owen's arms again, using all her will power. 'I have a party on this afternoon. I have to get ready.'

She showered quickly, towel-dried her hair and then slipped into her underwear. She plugged in her hair curler.

'A fairy always needs her wand.' She grinned at Owen, who was still lying in bed but watching through the open doorway. She took a length of her hair and wound it round the rod. A few seconds later she released it and there was a bouncy curl. She did a few more, and then tied long sparkly ribbons into it.

'You really go the whole hog.' He'd rolled to his side, rested his head on his hand and was watching her every move.

She tilted her head, frowning at her reflection. 'I'm in character. I have to look the part, fulfil the fantasy for the child.'

'The perfect party princess.'

'Oh, no,' she corrected. 'I'm not the princess. The

princess is the little girl whose birthday it is. I'm the fairy godmother, there to grant the wishes.'

She started work on her face. 'That's why I'm not in pink—that's their colour. I'm in silver and blue. I have pink wings for the girls, pink wands, tiaras. They get a unicorn tattoo and some glitter gel and then become part of the fairy princess network. I'm just there to help them tap into their imaginations.' She paused. 'Most of them don't even need me really.' Smoothing the glitter down her cheekbone, she paused. 'But there's always one. The shy one, the self-conscious one, the one who feels like she doesn't fit in.'

'So how do you get her to fit in?'

'That's always the challenge.' She smiled. 'Take it easy, gently. It can be hard when, for the others, you need to be effervescent. But I want to try to do it because I just know that inside she really wants to be up there and part of it all.'

'How do you know?'

She turned from the mirror. 'Because that was me,' she said simply. 'I was the self-conscious one.'

His eyes said, Yeah, right. So did his voice. 'I can't believe you were ever self-conscious.'

She smiled in triumph then. 'And that's how I know I'll make it as an actress.' One day. 'I'm good at pretending.'

She turned back to her pots of powder and paint. 'At the end of the day you just want them to have fun.'

'All I ever wanted was the food.' He burrowed back down in the bed.

'Figures.' She concentrated on her eyes, worked in silence for several minutes.

'Do you do boys' parties?' he asked.

At that she slanted him a look, saw the mischief in his face.

He tried to deny it, raising his hands all innocent-like. 'I'm serious. You're missing out on half your market.'

'I do. But admittedly it's more girls' parties than boys'. But there are often boys there—especially the preschooler ones. I have a pirate queen routine that I do for them.'

'You're a pirate?' He was back up on his elbows.

'I make a really good balloon sword.'

'You do?'

She giggled.

'The depth of your talent never ceases to amaze me,' he drawled, then watched her majestic nose wrinkle.

'Yeah right.'

She stood in front of the mirror, clad only in bra and panties, and he was having a hard time concentrating on stringing more than two words together.

'Where is the unicorn going today?'

'Where do you think it should go?' She grinned.

He knew exactly where it should go. On the slope of one of those creamy breasts, where it would peek out from the ruffles of the silver-and-blue dress, drawing the eye to the treasure beneath—not that his eyes needed any more pointers.

She glanced at the clock and gave a little squeal of horror. 'Stop distracting me. Lie there and be quiet. I can't be late.'

He didn't stay lying down but he did stay quiet. He stood, wrapped a towel round his hips to try to be a little decent, and then came right up behind her to watch more closely while she finished her make-up. Silently he studied her as she fixed the tattoo with a damp flannel, as she smoothed glitter gel across her shoulders and chest.

Her eyes met his in the mirror for a moment, then they skittered away, then back once more. He felt his tension—his everything—rising. He needed to know it was the same for her, this crazy, unfettered lust. He drew a breath and blew lightly over her shoulder, down onto the spot below her collarbone where the unicorn tattoo was drying. She shivered. He watched her nipples poke harder against the lace of her bra and he was about to pounce. But speedily she turned, left his space, went into the wardrobe where her dress was hanging. All too soon it was on and zipped and she was walking away.

'Right.' Her voice was high-pitched. 'See you later, then.'

He said nothing, just walked beside her all the way to the door, barely curbing his frustration.

As she reached to open it he reached for her—slid his hand round the nape of her neck, fingers wide so they caught in the curls of her hair. He pulled her to him for a hard, brief, melting kiss that didn't relieve him one iota.

'Later.' He basically growled.

He prowled around the apartment like a caged animal. Wished like hell he'd had her before she went to the damn party. But she'd been insistent on getting there on time. Now, three hours later, he was at bursting point. He'd never known a passion as intense as this. Never known a woman who could take up so much of his brain space either. He thought of her all the damn time. Thought up things he could do for her. Crazy stuff, silly stuff, irresistible stuff. He didn't much like it. Wanted to burn it out—blow it out with one big, hard puff.

Finally he heard the slam of the door downstairs. He went to the top of the stairs and waited. She was trotting up them, the silver fairy dress floating up towards him. His body tightened harder with her every step closer. He was filled with the urge to reach out and grab, to hold onto her in complete caveman style. He wanted to possess. He wanted to brand.

She got to the top and raised her brows as she saw him standing there. He watched the smokiness enter her eyes as she got his unspoken message. He watched as her breathing didn't ease at all—accelerated, in fact.

He took her arm and pulled her inside. The door shut behind them but he hardly heard it because by then he'd got his mouth on hers and he was asking for everything. She opened for him immediately and the rush of need overwhelmed him. He had to have her right now; he couldn't reclaim anything until he did.

He got them as far as the big table, pushed her against it, kissing her deeply while yanking up her dress. He pulled her panties out of the way while with his other hand he undid his jeans.

Her hands were in his hair and she leaned back, kissing him, taking him with her. He broke the seal of their lips briefly, to breathe and to thrust and then he was there and she was wet and hot and moving beneath him, full of life and heat and making him so welcome with a sigh and a murmur of delight. And then there was nothing because he kissed her again—hard and long and fierce while he possessed her with his body, pressing her against the hard wood. Trapping her, claiming her as the passion he had for her trapped and claimed him. He wanted to fight it, but pushed harder against her, into her. Harder and harder until suddenly there was everything bursting through him—colour and light and heat and the taste of her pleasure.

And then there was nothing.

He lifted his head, looked down at her and felt the tinge of embarrassment and guilt as he saw her bruised lips and the dazed look in her eyes. He'd just taken her rough and ready on his table, she still had her dress on, they were still joined and already he was tightening with anticipation about their next encounter.

He still wanted her. How he wanted her. He couldn't get enough.

Irritation, self-disgust, flared. Just sex. That was all this could be.

But just now had been more intense than anything. And here he was doing things, wanting things, thinking things…and it was madness because he knew, ultimately, he couldn't see this through. He didn't want complicated. He didn't want to be committed.

Her gaze ducked from his. She pushed gently at his shoulders. He left the warm embrace and instantly felt cold.

'The party was good, thanks.' She'd pulled up her knickers and was walking to the kitchen.

He grunted then, unable to stop the spurt of laughter bubbling through his annoyance.

'I think I've got another booking.'

He leaned on the table and tried to get his breath back, watching her as she moved around, completely at home in his kitchen. He needed to back out of this, but instead he walked over to her, ran a gentle hand down her arm. Quelled the urge to pull her back into his embrace. 'Are you OK?' he asked. Self-conscious wasn't really him. But it was flushing through, heating his cheeks now.

She looked surprised.

'I'm sorry, that was a little—'

'Barbarian?' she suggested.

He smiled again, still a little uncertain.

She put her glass down and a naughty twinkle lit her face. 'You can ravish me any time, Owen, you know that.'

He did know it. She welcomed him any time, every time. That didn't mean he should take advantage of her. Not any more. Guilt ripped through him. It trebled when he saw the tinge of vulnerability suddenly shadow her eyes. He'd got himself into a mess.

This was why he didn't do live-in anything. This was why he was better off alone. He just didn't have it in him to be the kind of guy a woman like Bella needed—any woman needed. He couldn't promise that he'd be there through thick and thin, or that he'd even see the thin patches. He sure as hell hadn't with his parents.

He didn't want to become bored and careless, as he had with Liz. He didn't want to wake one day and see the lust in Bella's eyes had been replaced with disappointment and bitterness. And he definitely didn't want to be there to see her turn from his arms to someone else's.

His whole body clenched. It was time to push away. It was way beyond time, because it'd hurt—until now he hadn't realised it would. But better now than further along when it would only hurt more.

Then he thought of something else. Something so painful it twisted inside, becoming bitter anger. 'Bella, I didn't use anything just then. I didn't have a condom on.'

He'd just lost it. Seen her. Kissed her. Taken her as fast as possible. And now—what if? He could hardly bear to look at her. He already knew he'd make a lousy father.

Bella carefully kept her weight back against the

bench; her legs still weren't working properly and at the expression in his eyes they were going even weaker. But it wasn't from lust. It was from fear. Because it was fear she could read in his eyes. Fear and regret.

'I know.' She'd had the thought in her head for a split second, but it had gone as she'd been swept away in the chaos and bliss of the moment.

'You didn't stop me.' His eyes had narrowed.

'You didn't stop yourself,' she reminded him. She'd wanted it as much as he had—and he had wanted it. She'd never seen that expression on his face before—that naked need. The desire that he could scarcely seem to control. It had turned her on—for a moment she'd felt nothing but power and then she too had been totally lost. But he still wasn't willing to recognise the strength of it. Right now he looked as if he wanted to run.

'Is there a chance you might…' He didn't even seem able to say it.

'Have a baby?' She wanted to use the b-word. Not just say pregnant. She wanted to see how he'd react to the mental image of a tiny little life—real. A child that shared their blood, that breathed because of them.

The loss of colour in his cheeks was almost imperceptible, but she was watching closely.

His 'Yeah' was drawn out and low.

'There's a chance.' It was a slim chance, very slim as her period was due in only a day or two. But she wasn't ready to let him off the hook just yet. She was hurt from that look, the dread and fear in it. And she wanted to know what it was he was going to say.

He exhaled. 'Whatever happens, you know I'll support you.' His gaze slid from hers. 'Whatever you decide.'

Whatever she decided? So it would be her choice and hers alone. He wanted no part in anything that might be? She squeezed her fingers hard on the bench behind her. Still said nothing, but only because her heart was ripping.

'Whatever you want to do,' he was mumbling now. 'I don't…'

What, he didn't—mind? Care?

She'd known, hadn't she? He'd told her that very first night. And, no matter what she fantasised, the reality was exactly as he'd told it. She'd been warned.

But she hadn't paid attention—had just had the bit between her teeth and gone along for the ride. And the consequences were going to be more serious than she'd ever thought possible.

She'd never had her heart broken before.

So much for independence. She'd gone and got herself totally dependent on someone who could never offer her anything like all that she wanted. She wished he'd go away and she could lick her wounds in private. Regroup. Gather up her shredded pride. But at that her pride came racing back, fully armed.

She crossed the room, picked up the little bag she'd dropped by the door and thanked the heavens that the family today had paid her in cash. She opened the envelope and flung the dollar notes down on the bench next to Owen.

'What's that for?' He looked at it, distaste all over his face.

'That's the money for rent, for the four new tyres that Bubbles has—don't think I haven't noticed them—for the petrol, for the groceries, for all the dinners, the wine, for the website and for the hotel bill in Waiheke.' She stopped for breath. It wasn't nearly enough to cover all that, but it sure felt good to say it.

'I don't want it,' he said flatly.

'I won't have you paying for things for me.' She tossed her head. 'It makes me feel like a who—'

'Don't you dare!' he shouted then, his step closer shutting her up. Anger flushed his cheeks and flashed in his eyes. 'I have never paid for sex, Bella, and I don't intend to start now.'

'Really?' she said scornfully, sounding a whole lot braver than she felt. 'But isn't that what's happening here?'

'You know damn well it isn't.' He spoke through his teeth. 'It's just money. It's meaningless.'

Like the sex? Not to her, it wasn't.

He seemed to read her face and growled. 'Why are you so damn keen to label everything?'

'Why are you so keen to deny everything?' The attraction between them wasn't anything ordinary— surely he could sense that?

'This is just sex, Bella.' His words came like the

cracks of a whip. 'I like it. You like it. That's all there is to it.'

Bella blinked. Bit the inside of her cheek as she absorbed the shock of what he'd said and the depth of his scowl. Humiliation started to seep into her very core.

'Why did you pay for that night in the hotel?' She winced. Did he hear that slight cry in her voice?

'I don't know,' he answered irritably, stepping away. 'It was just a spur-of-the-moment thing. I knew you were tight for money. I just wanted to help you out.'

'Well, I don't want your help.' She spoke quickly, marched to the bedroom, unzipping her dress and walking right out of it, leaving it on the floor. She'd never be able to wear it again without thinking of this moment—the time when he'd taken her so passionately and then turned on her.

'Don't you?' He was right behind her. 'Well, you're certainly not helping yourself.'

'What does that mean?' Furious with the way she felt tears close by, she picked a skirt and pulled on the nearest top she could find.

'You won't let me help you. You won't let anyone help you.'

'That's right, Owen. I won't.' She grabbed a flannel and scrubbed her face hard, blocking the sight and sound of him with water from the tap, stopping any stupid tears from even starting.

When her face was bare and reddened, but masked once more, she turned and headed for the door.

'Where are you going?'

'I have an audition.'

'Now?'

She sent him a glare while slipping into her sandals. 'Yes, now.'

'And you're going like that?'

'Yes.' She walked.

He swore. 'You deliberately sabotage yourself.'

After a minuscule pause she kept walking.

'You do,' he said, seemingly just getting into the swing of getting at her. 'You spend over an hour getting ready for one of your parties and less than five minutes getting ready for an audition that could change your life. It's like you don't really want it.'

She whirled to face him. 'Of course I want it.'

'No, you don't! You're never late to work at the café and yet you're late almost every time to a casting call. Tell me,' he said snidely. 'What do you believe in, Bella? Fairies?' He bent to pick up her dress from the floor, his acidity eating an even bigger hole in her heart. 'Do you really think you've got some fairy godmother who's going to make it all happen for you?'

'Of course not.' She turned back and started walking to the door again.

'Then what do you believe in?'

She said nothing, kept walking. It didn't seem like the moment to mention luck.

'Why don't you try believing in yourself?' he called after her. 'If you don't believe in your abilities, why should anyone else?'

She couldn't not face that. He was in the middle of the room, shaking his head at her. 'Instead you blame anything you can. Your family isn't supportive, you haven't had formal acting training, you haven't had that "lucky" break. But it's not about luck, it's about making the decision to do it and then persevering, putting in that hard work.'

Her anger rose another notch. 'I work damn hard.'

'I know, but not at—'

'But nothing,' she snapped. 'You don't know the first thing about acting, about going to casting call after casting call. It's not about learning the lines and spouting them automaton fashion. There is luck involved. Who's your competition? What look are they after? You have to be in the right place at the right time with the right product. I haven't yet.'

'Then you keep going,' he lectured, her dress hanging from his hands. 'You research. You find out what they want and you give it to them as professionally as you can. You believe and work and eventually it'll happen.'

'You make it all sound so easy,' she said bitterly. 'Like it's some computer program.'

'I know it's not easy. But you have to believe in yourself. You have to have the passion for it.'

'I do have the passion!' She was yelling now. 'God, Owen, what do you want?'

'This isn't about what I want!' he yelled back. 'This is about you and you're not the person you can be yet. You're floating along the edges too scared to dive right in. I don't think you even know what it is you do want. It's much easier to skate along and blame it all on everyone or anything else.'

'Well, what about you?' The viciousness of his attack forced her into fight mode. Red-hot anger ran through her veins, releasing the words from her. 'You're not exactly living life to the full either, are you, Mr Workaholic? And as for this Mr Don't-Get-Near-Me-Because-I'm-Selfish routine... What sort of a rubbish excuse is that, Owen? You're not selfish. Doling out money proves you're not selfish,' she shouted, losing her grip entirely. 'What you are is scared!'

His face whitened, his jaw locked, but she hardly noticed. She was on way too much of a roll now.

'You say you don't want labels, but you're the one trying to squeeze us into the smallest compartment possible. Sex is all it is, huh? Well, how convenient for you. You can just keep your distance and don't have to invest anything remotely risky like emotion or take responsibility. What is it you're afraid of, Owen?' Scathing, she flung him the answer. 'Failing at something for once in your life? Hell, I fail at things all the time, but at least I have the guts to get back up and give it another go.'

She spat her fury and hurt. 'So don't you dare lecture me about hovering on life's edges. You're the one not facing up to what's really going on here. You're the coward!'

Breathless, she stopped, realising what she'd said and all she'd revealed—the degree to which she was involved, how much she wanted more, how she wanted him to accept that there was more…but, oh, my Lord, maybe there really wasn't anything more in this for him? Of course there wasn't—she wasn't anything like the kind of woman he'd really want. She turned, more desperate to get out of there than ever before.

'Who's the coward now?' he roared after her. 'Who's the one throwing the accusations and then walking out without giving me a chance to respond?'

She whirled back, bleeding inside. 'Well, what's the point in my staying just to hear you deny everything and say nothing?' Bitterly, she glared at him.

His hands were fisted in her dress, rumpling it so bad it would have to go back to the dry-cleaners again. His face was still pale and a picture of savage tension. He met her glare with one of his own—just as bitter, just as furious. But his jaw was clamped and as she stared she could see his muscles flex down tighter.

He had no answer to that and she didn't want to hear it anyway. She stalked out of the apartment and slammed the door as hard as she could. It was all so easy for him. He was nothing but killer instinct. Nothing but what he wanted now, now, now. All 'I want that, I'm going to do that…' and off he went and had and did with no regard to consequences. It would serve him right to suffer the consequences for once. Because she was. She couldn't compartmentalise this the way he wanted to—this thing was all too big, for her anyway.

She fumed all the way to the audition and barely

noticed the competition. She was too busy stewing over the argument. Too busy trying to stay mad and not recognise the extent of the break in her heart.

They had to call her name twice.

CHAPTER ELEVEN

BELLA SPENT THAT night alone in the spare room, most of it awake, plotting her way out of there. She was mortified at what Owen had said and what she'd said—and spent hours deciding on the truth of it all. This was just sex for him, and his efforts to help her out—the dress, the website, the way he cooked her dinner—was simply him. He'd stop and help an old lady cross the street—that didn't mean he was on his way to falling in love with her.

She was such a fool. And that was the point, wasn't it? She was such a klutz he couldn't help himself trying to help her. Because that was the kind of guy he was. And now she'd humiliated herself completely by insisting that there was more to it. Of course he hadn't been able to reply—he hadn't wanted to hurt her, and he'd already spelt it out as plainly as he could: sex, that was all there was to it.

'How'd it go?'

Damn. She'd hoped he'd have gone downstairs to work already this morning. Instead he was sitting at the table. She felt her cheeks warm at the sight of it. Truthfully, she'd forgotten about the audition the minute she'd walked out of it. Somehow the lines had come to her. She must have come across like an automaton. Ah, well, chalk another one up to experience.

'Don't ask.'

He looked moody. 'I'm sorry I was so grumpy.'

'I'm sorry I was so ungrateful.' She inched closer. 'I really appreciate everything you've done for me, Owen.' Oh, God, this was awkward.

'It's nothing.' He shook his head. 'No trouble.'

That was right—not for him. 'Please let me pay back what I owe you.'

His expression tightened more. 'It's just money, Bella. It doesn't matter.'

'It matters to me.' She hated being in his debt like this. Hated that all she had to offer in return was her heart, and he'd never want that.

'OK.' He paused, stared hard at the table. 'But only if you stay. I'd like you to stay.' He paused. 'Just until you get yourself sorted.'

There it was, the caveat. She'd been right—he couldn't hold back the offer of assistance, but nor could he offer anything else. Now she felt too awkward to say yes, too awkward to say no.

'OK.' Her reply came out on a heavy sigh. She couldn't see that getting herself sorted was going to happen any time soon, but she'd be out of here regardless. She took a deep breath and tackled the most awkward bit of all. 'I'll tell you as soon as I know.' A few days to be certain, then she'd leave. She refused to think about what would happen if she was pregnant—that was altogether too scary.

He looked back at her, looking as sombre as she'd sounded. She knew he knew what she was referring to. And she knew how badly he didn't want it.

THE NEXT TWO days dragged for Owen. He'd wanted to back off, but only seemed to be digging himself in deeper. He kept reliving that argument. She'd touched a nerve and he'd flared up at her, but he hadn't said anything that wasn't true—had he? He couldn't help the sickening feeling that he'd thrown something precious away before he'd even realised he had it.

Worse, he had the feeling she'd been the one hitting truth on the head at the end there. He couldn't face it—couldn't face her, until he knew whether she was pregnant or not. He couldn't think until he knew. It was like waiting for a jury to return its verdict—were they going to get a life sentence? Either way there'd be guilt and bitterness. And it was worse than Liz—this time he was to blame. It hadn't been Bella's fault at all. The sooner it was all over, the better.

And yet he missed her. How he missed her. He practically had to lock himself into his bedroom to stop from going into hers. His arms ached with emptiness. Sleep was utterly elusive—and so was she. She worked long hours at the café and hid in her room the rest of the time. He spent more time in the offices downstairs to give them both some space.

But truly finding space was impossible while she

was staying with him. And he wasn't ready to ask her to leave yet. He still wanted her with a passion that was tearing him up inside and, more than that, he wanted to make things right. He decided a trip away was the answer. Just a couple of days. Regain perspective and work out what the hell he was going to do if she was pregnant.

She hadn't mentioned it again. Whereas by now Liz had chosen names and been practically putting the baby on the list for the most exclusive schools. Bella was making no demands—making a point of it, in fact. She'd backed right off and had shut down her expressive face. He hated that too—he wished he knew what she was thinking and wanted to know if she was OK.

OWEN HAD WITHDRAWN from her. He was working later, not coming into the café any more. Bella munched on her small bowl of muesli and watched him pack his laptop into his case.

'How long are you gone for?'

'I'm not sure yet. Couple of days maybe, I don't know.'

She nodded.

'You've got the security code?'

She nodded again. She'd take the opportunity to find herself a new flat. She could move into a flat-share with some students. There'd be plenty of cheap ones out in the suburbs. That was her plan. This was the end of the end. She knew it. He knew it.

He glanced into the contents of her bowl and his

cheeky smile appeared. She hadn't seen it for a while and it made her heart ache.

'You're supposed to eat that stuff in the morning, you know.'

She managed a wry grin back. 'Better late than never.'

Both their grins faded.

OWEN LISTENED TO the flight announcements, took another sip of his coffee, gripped his bag that little bit tighter. He should have checked in by now. If he didn't check in within the next minute or so he'd miss his flight. He looked into his cup—he still had half of it to go. It would be a shame to throw away good airport coffee.

Bella hadn't said anything. She'd known he was running away—he could see the reflection of his eyes in hers and knew she saw the truth of it there. But still she was making no demands.

And wasn't that what he thought he always wanted? No demands? For fear he wouldn't be able to meet them? Because he wasn't willing to provide the emotional support someone else needed? Damn it, Bella didn't seem to want any kind of support. And suddenly it was all he wanted to do. He wanted to know if she was OK, if she was scared or secretly excited or desperately unhappy. He wanted to help her deal with however she was feeling. And he wanted her to help him too.

His heart jerked. Maybe she didn't demand because she simply didn't care. He knew that for a lie.

He saw it in her eyes. Every time she'd taken him into her she'd been loving him. Just sex? What a joke.

This time, he couldn't walk away. This time, he didn't want to.

The taxi seemed to take for ever. Driving alongside the water, the lights reflected on it. The aeroplanes looked as if they were going to end up in the sea if they didn't slam the brakes on damn fast. Was that him? Headed for a drowning if he didn't skid to a halt soon?

The apartment was in darkness and for an awful moment he thought she'd gone. Then he saw the large lump on the floor. He flicked on the lights. She was huddled in her beanbag. He took in her pale face, her eyes large and bruised and startled.

'I'm sorry, I didn't mean to scare you.' He put his bag on the table.

She blinked, clearly gathering her wits. 'What happened?'

'Last-minute change of plan.' He paused, inventing a non-excuse. 'I managed to get out of it.'

'Oh.'

He could see her biting back other questions and felt bad because of it. He wanted to answer her, wanted to communicate—a little at least.

He stripped off his jacket, wondering why the hell he was so buttoned up in a suit. It had all been for the show of it. He went to the bench in search of wine.

'I'm not pregnant.' Her voice was low, matter-of-fact. It took a few moments to register what she'd actually told him.

Not pregnant. No baby.

He was glad he was against the bench because he needed its strength for a second. He'd never expected to feel it as a blow. Never expected to feel disappointment. Only now was he seeing it in his mind, her body rounded with a baby, and then holding a child, his child. The ache that opened up in him was terrifying.

'When did you find out?' He managed to sound almost normal as he poured a large glass of red.

'Just tonight.'

He nodded, took a big sip. 'You're feeling OK?'

'Oh, sure. Fine.' She mirrored his nod.

He searched her pale features again and knew she was faking it. She looked miserable. He saw the half-eaten cake of chocolate beside her. For a mad moment he wanted to sweep her into his arms and tell her not to be sad, that they'd make babies together any time she wanted to. She just had to say the word.

But he didn't. He took a breath, another sip of wine and a long minute to regain sanity. He still felt lousy. Why—when this was what he wanted, right? No encumbrances.

'Want to watch a movie?' He walked over to her, touched her shoulder gently. Instantly felt a bit better. 'You can choose.'

'I already have.'

Then he noticed the blinking of the screen—black and white. Casablanca. Again.

'Need anything else—ice cream? Wine?'

'Yes, please.'

WHAT SHE REALLY wanted was a hug. What she really wanted was to know his reaction. At least he wasn't doing back-flips and saying, 'Thank God, what a relief.' She didn't know if she could handle that. Because even though she'd been fighting for independence for so long, the thought of a baby had intrigued her—because it would be his. She'd even lain awake and wondered whether their child would have his brilliant blue eyes or her pale ones. But he wasn't giving anything away.

She decided to find out. She took the wine he offered, and was surprised to see her hand wasn't shaking. 'With your attitude to marriage there's no need to ask. I know you're relieved.'

'I...'

'It's OK, Owen. You don't have to hide it.'

He looked away from her, as if what she'd said had hurt. 'I haven't got what they need.' His voice was low. 'Children deserve more than an emotionally absent father.'

She frowned. Emotionally absent? Owen wasn't absent—he was more real, more vital than anyone she'd ever met. She could see the trouble inside him on his face—something was stirring in him and she didn't think it was altogether because of her. But what? And she remembered what he'd said—what his ex had said—that he was selfish. Why had the woman thought that? What had happened? When it was obvious he was generous, not just financially but in more ways than he'd admit. Suddenly Bella wanted him to see that.

'Who waters your garden, Owen?'

He frowned.

'Your plants upstairs,' she explained.

'What's that got to do with anything?'

'Everything.' She smiled. 'That's noticing, that's remembering, that's caring.' She paused. 'That's all that children need.'

He was shaking his head. 'No,' he said. 'They also need to be wanted.'

Her suspicions solidified as she heard his desolate hollowness. And even though the thought of the answer terrified her, she couldn't stop from asking the question. 'Have you been through this before, Owen?'

OWEN OWED HER honesty. Then she'd see the person he really was, and this whole ending thing wouldn't be nearly so bad—she'd be out of his place in no time. Because no woman would understand the way he'd reacted—especially not one who liked kids so much she actually worked with them. It would be over, and he could move on. 'You know I had that girlfriend, right?'

'The one who said you were selfish.'

'Right.' He grinned without mirth. 'Around the time I was selling the company she told me she was pregnant.'

Bella nodded.

He looked away from her, not coping with the hint of sympathy he saw in her eyes. 'I wasn't remotely keen. I felt nothing. I felt worse than nothing.' He took a breath and said it. 'I didn't want it. How terrible is that? Not to want your own flesh and blood?' He'd felt trapped. He still felt guilty about that.

'She was dreaming up names and was all excited and hanging out for a ring and I didn't want to know a thing about it.' He'd withdrawn and gone remote on her rather than admitting how he felt. Certainly hadn't dropped down on one knee instantly as she'd seemed to expect he would. 'It was a crazy time. I was working all hours negotiating this deal…' That was no excuse; he should have been just a little more interested. But the fact was he'd been wanting out of the relationship for a while already. He just hadn't got round to breaking off with her—too busy to be bothered. And he was still too busy to be able to think it through properly—he'd just avoided the issue for a while. Tried to pretend it wasn't real, tried to swallow the guilt that came with that.

'What happened?'

'She was mistaken. There was no baby.' She'd been late, that was all. When she'd told him, with red-rimmed eyes and a catch in her throat, he'd been so relieved and he hadn't been able to hide it from her. That was when she'd lost it—screamed at him about how selfish he was, how unsupportive, that his heart only beat for his business. And she'd been right. He hadn't wanted her or the baby or any of it. It had got really ugly then, and in the course of the argument Liz had slipped up.

It wasn't that she'd been late at all. She'd made it up—there had never been the possibility of a pregnancy. She'd tried to manipulate him—cornering him just as he was about to come into vast wealth. And she'd done it in such a low fashion—because even though he'd known it probably wouldn't work, his integrity would have insisted that he try. He'd have married her and she knew it. It was just that he hadn't come to the party soon enough for her to get away with it. Whether she'd wanted him or the money he didn't know—he suspected the latter.

He'd been viciously angry then and vowed never to be put in the same position again. No woman would wield that threat over him. He didn't want it—marriage, babies—not ever.

'She met someone else not long after.' He dragged out a cynical smile, feeling sorry for the poor bastard she'd netted. 'She married him, has a kid or two. She's happy.' She'd got what she'd wanted.

And he was happy too, right? Happy with his choices and with his freedom to focus on his work and on fun.

The silence was long. Bella was looking at him, expression clouded. He felt bad—the bitterness that Liz had left him with wasn't for her. This hadn't been her fault—it had been his irresponsibility. He'd broken his own rules, he hadn't played safe—and he should have stopped fooling with her a week ago.

'I'm sorry, Bella.' He met her gaze squarely. 'I should never have put you in danger.' He didn't want to treat her badly, and he probably would have.

'I put myself there too, remember?' She looked away, stood. 'I think I'll go to bed. I'm a bit tired.'

He stood too. 'You OK? Comfortable? Need a painkiller or anything?'

She shook her head, a sad smile twisting her lips. He knew what she was wondering—if he felt the same about this baby-that-wasn't, if he had the same antipathy towards the idea. But he couldn't answer her, couldn't bear to think on it because it was hurting him more than he'd ever thought it could. And what hurt more was the realisation that she'd been right. He was a coward.

He watched her go. For the first time feeling as if he'd missed out on everything.

IT HAD STARTED out as the party from hell. The house had been tiny. The wind had meant there was no way they could be outside. The stereo system had failed. And there had been the most hideous boyfriend of one of the mothers who'd hit on Bella before she'd even got all the way up the path.

She'd worked hard to turn it around for the poor kid. Wished the audience of adults would just go away so she could have some fairy fun with the wee ones. In the end it had been good old-fashioned bubbles that had saved it—as she'd made big ones they'd spotted the rainbows in them. And then she'd read them the tale of the unicorn and the temporary tattoos had come out and the face paints and the magic of make-believe.

Bella parked Bubbles in the garage and braced herself. The week had gone quickly and she still hadn't moved out. Still hadn't the strength to leave the man she ached to love.

Now, with the payment from this party, she had no more excuses. She could give him at least some of the money she owed and get out. She'd phone her father for the rest to start afresh. It was best, because now she'd thought about it, she knew she wanted the whole marriage and kids bit. She couldn't live with less. So she needed to get away and over him.

He wasn't waiting to pounce on her the minute she walked back in. Instead he lifted his head from the paper he was reading in his big chair, took one look and frowned at her.

'Didn't it go so good?'

She sighed. 'It was OK. But the house was tiny—and I mean tiny. And they'd invited twelve kids and all their parents were there.'

It made her skin itchy just thinking about it—all that close contact with complete strangers. The kids were OK. It was the adults who grossed her out. And she simply couldn't perform to her best in an environment like that.

He shoved his paper to the floor and stood. 'Actually I've been thinking about you and your parties.' He paused, then words seemed to tumble from him. 'Why don't you use some of the space downstairs? You could do it up and get all the kids to come here. It would save you from lecherous uncles.'

Bella stared at him. 'You're kidding, right?' He'd never want that—would he?

'No. It might as well be used for something. It'll

get other prospective tenants off my back and it'll only be used part of the time. During the week when my guys are in upstairs it'll be quiet.'

'Isn't it a waste of your resource?'

'It's mine to waste.' He shrugged. 'And it'll only be part of it. Still room for a restaurant if I ever want one.'

Oh, my, she thought as he winked. That sparkle was back and his expression was lighter and Bella felt herself falling once more, mesmerised by his vibrancy.

'I'd have to decorate it,' she said, half dazed. 'I don't have the money.'

'I'll loan you. Start-up costs. You can pay me back once you're up and running. You'll make it back in no time.'

She shook her head, stopped thinking completely. This was crazy.

'Bella.' He stepped near her. 'This is what you're good at. This is what you love. Every time you do a party you come home with bookings for at least one or two more. You're a wonderful entertainer. This is what you're meant to do.'

The idea was so tempting. Her own party space. She'd never even thought of it before. And she'd have such fun designing the venue... Unstoppable ideas swirled through her head.

He was grinning at her, as if he knew.

She inhaled deeply, shook her head. 'Owen, I can't.'

'Why not?'

Because things were complicated between them. She didn't want this to be his latest idea that he'd set up and then skip on to the next. They weren't together any more—were they? She really needed to get over him and on with her life. 'I need to get out and find a new flat. I can't stay here for ever.'

There was another non-committal shrug. 'Maybe, but there's plenty of time for that. Why not focus on building a business first? You could do the food too, couldn't you?'

Of course she could—standing on her head. More ideas teased her—of menus and fun things and dreams and fantasies.

'Tell you what.' He kept talking. 'Why don't you just take a segment downstairs and paint it? See what you think. It might not be right as there isn't an outdoor area. It might not work out at all.'

But it would work out. No outdoors didn't matter, not if she created a grotto indoors. And she knew she could do that. And if they built a pirate ship the kids could climb up it and hunt for treasure and…and…

She looked at him. He was acting so casually about this. And yet, in his own way, he was pushing it. Batting away her arguments with a shrug and his usual 'of course you can' attitude. What was his real agenda? Was there anything more to this than a simple offer of help?

Her mind—and heart—leapt to the most blissful conclusion. Was this his way of keeping her in his life? On the terms that he could handle?

Probably not, she scoffed at herself. This was just

his latest obsession. And once it was set up he'd be onto something else. She was looking everywhere for anything. But the little bubble of hope wouldn't be popped. She'd keep on hoping, keep on dreaming. Maybe, just maybe, he'd wake up to the fact that there was more between them than either of them could have imagined. Or was it just her imagination going overtime again?

'Come on, let's go look at it now.' He took her arm, half dragging her down the stairs. The space was huge.

'We could partition it off.' He stood, arms stretched out marking imaginary walls.

'I'd have to get consents.' Her trailing footsteps echoed. 'There'd be building work to be done. I'd have to buy so much stuff.'

'Yeah, but wouldn't it be great?' His eyes were shining so damn attractively. No wonder he was successful—he could make anyone believe in anything. Passionate, enthusiastic, energetic.

'Look—' he dragged her over to one corner '—you could have a little shop next door here selling things—like the fairy dresses and the tattoos and glittery stuff. And you could paint a mural—throw in a few tigers.'

She was amazed. 'You've really thought about this.'

'Sure.'

She could have different themed parties—art, beading, pirates, jungles, teddy bears' picnics—the list was endless. His enthusiasm infected her—bubbling through her veins.

'Owen.' She was shaking her head, but she couldn't stop the smile.

He smiled back at her. And then he stepped closer, his hands on her arms. She only needed to take a step forward to touch him—and she wanted to touch him so much.

'Think about it,' he said softly.

She was. She read the offer deep within him. On a plate he was handing her everything she could ever want—anything material. But what she really wanted wasn't a tangible thing. And he didn't think he had it to give. But he did—and so badly she wanted him to give it to her. She was a fool, such a fool, but his blue eyes shone even more brilliantly and she couldn't ever say no—not when he looked at her like that.

He whispered again. 'I'm going to kiss you, Bella. So if you don't want me to, you better speak up now.'

Pure, deep, hopeless longing overcame her, rendering her silent, waiting and so willing for whatever he wanted.

But it wasn't the fiercely passionate kiss she expected. It was soft and sweet and so gentle. He stepped closer, his hands lifting to frame her face—so tender. She felt her eyes prickle. She closed them quickly and the bliss simply increased. It rushed from both her toes and the tip of her head—meeting in the middle of her, expanding, taking over the beating of her heart.

Suddenly, somehow, they were on the floor and

he'd rolled, pulling her on top, protecting her from the cold, dusty concrete.

'This is bad,' she breathed. 'This is where the kids will be playing.'

'No kids here now. Only a couple of adults. Consenting.'

'Oh, yes.'

CHAPTER TWELVE

BELLA WAS DUSTING the shelves at the café the next morning, mentally choosing paint colours, when she heard the beep of her mobile. She pulled it from her pocket. Didn't recognise the number. She didn't recognise the voice either—fortunately the woman said she was calling from Take One Agency....

Oh, God. The audition. Just over a week ago and frankly she'd forgotten it. It had been the day she'd had that massive argument with Owen.

'I'm pleased to be able to offer you the part of...'

Bella tuned out—entering shock. She was being offered a part on a national touring show.

'Rehearsals start in Christchurch next week...'

She'd be paid. A full-time job as an actress—in a musical theatre production. Excitement flooded through her. She couldn't believe it. Couldn't wait to get home and tell Owen.

Owen.

She pulled up short. Owen—who was probably designing her a pirate ship this very minute. Owen—who was probably the reason why she'd got the job in the first place. Owen—who had made her so mad she'd gone into that audition all guns blazing and uncaring of the consequences. Owen—who had never made fun of her parties, but who made everything matter.

She had to leave him. Leave the business—while it was still a seed, just a fragment of a dream. For one wild moment she wanted to turn down the part. Pretend it hadn't happened. But as she listened to the woman warble on about the details she knew she couldn't. This was it, her shot at the big time. Do well in this and she could springboard to other, bigger, better shows.

Sydney, London, New York… Her imagination ballooned.

But there was Owen. And she wanted Owen. And she'd thought if she had a little more time, she might show Owen how much he had to offer—and not just in the money sense. But it probably was for the best, because that was the fantasy, wasn't it? Her winning him. She'd soon know anyway. She'd tell him about the part, see how he reacted. Then she'd know for sure if this was still just sex or something else entirely. She spent the afternoon totally excited, totally nervous, totally torn.

She raced home, but he wasn't there and she paced round the big space. Not sure how to tell him. How to act. But when he finally appeared the thrill, the disbelief, the pride all bubbled out of her.

'I got the part, I got the part!' She ran to him, her smile and arms wide.

He caught her, sweeping them both into the embrace, lifting and spinning her, grinning hugely.

'What part?' he asked when her toes touched the floor again.

'On the show.'

'What show?' He laughed.

'It's not the lead or anything,' she clarified. 'But it is a minor character. Well, quite a major minor character actually. And I do understudy the lead, which means in some matinees I'll be the lead.'

He was still laughing. 'This is fantastic. Which theatre? When?'

Her smile suddenly felt a little stiff. 'It's a travelling show.'

'Travelling?' His hands loosened.

She took her full weight, brushed a stray bit of hair back behind her ear and blurted it all. 'Rehearsals are in Christchurch. The show starts there and then tours. If the New Zealand tour is successful, then it'll go to Australia.'

'Wow.' He was still grinning as he stepped away. 'Wow.'

He went straight to the fridge and pulled out a bottle. 'This calls for a celebration, right?'

The cork fired right across the room, bubbles frothed. She watched as he poured, staring at the label. Good grief, she'd only ever seen that sort of champagne in the pages of posh magazines.

'Yeah,' she said slowly. Had he known a celebration was in order?

He handed her a glass. 'When do you go?'

'Later this week.'

'How long do you rehearse for?'

'Almost six weeks, I think. Then the tour starts. I don't know how long that'll be ultimately.'

He was all questions; she had no time to think of anything but the answers. It was a good twenty minutes before they quietened.

'You did it,' he said softly, smiling.

'I did.' She still couldn't believe it—any of it. Especially that she'd be leaving, right when things were getting interesting. She finally broached the subject. 'I'm really sorry about not using the space downstairs.'

'Oh. Don't worry about it. It was just an idea. I have lots of them.' He grinned.

Her heart ached. He really didn't mind.

'You'll have to phone and tell your family.'

She paused. 'Not yet.' She'd see how it went first—make sure it was a complete success that she could be proud of. And she was still nervous about contacting Vita. Her sister was too good at prying and she'd want to do a post-mortem over what had happened on Waiheke.

'This is great,' he said. 'This is really good.'

She supposed it was. An easy, clean finish for him. She'd been the one building dream castles. Seeing them shatter, hurt.

OWEN COULD SEE the shadows entering her eyes and steeled himself not to give in. His heart was breaking—just as he'd found he had one. But he could not do it. He could see the question in her face and he refused to answer it. He was not going to give her the out. He was not going to hold onto her only to have her resent him for it in—what?—six months or a year's time. He was not going to ruin it for her.

She had to go. And she had to go utterly free of him. So he talked it up, went on about how exciting it was, how wonderful. She was finally going to realise her dreams. And not once did he mention how it was tearing him apart inside. Not once did he mention how much he wanted her to stay—to choose him. He gave her no choice. Because he knew that right now, inside, she cared for him. But she deserved to have her chance. For a moment there he'd thought they could have it all, but fate had decided it for both of them. The champagne tasted bitter. He'd put it in the fridge to celebrate something else entirely. He'd been going to cast off the coward label and embrace the risk—of emotion and responsibility—just as she'd challenged. Only now he was forced into a far more brave action—letting her go. The irony of it all really sucked.

BELLA DIDN'T TAKE time off work. Nor did Owen. In some ways it was a relief. She worked the last two days at the café totally on auto. They had pizza one night, Thai the next. Before she knew it, it was the last night. She was flying. He'd insisted. Reckoned he'd got a cheap deal on the Internet. She'd let him. It beat the ferry and bus option. She was always sick on the ferry.

They'd talked and teased and joked their way through sex. And it had always been wonderful and fun. But this was no joke. She was making love to him for the last time and then she was leaving.

There was nothing she could say. There was no way of changing it—there was no time.

And so for the first time she caressed him in complete silence. Kissing and kissing and kissing so there was no chance to voice the secrets lodged in her heart. That she'd fallen in love with him. Wanted to be with him. Wanted to stay.

As he moved down her body she couldn't stop thinking. Couldn't quite give herself over to the lust. Couldn't enjoy it the way she really wanted to. He couldn't and wouldn't give her what she wanted. And what she wanted was taking her away. Acting was what she wanted most, right?

This was their last time—she had to make the most of it. But all she could think was that it was the last time. And that was ruining everything. She wanted to stop. She didn't want there to be a last time.

He must have known because he stopped nuzzling her breasts. Instead he lifted his head and looked in her eyes, framed her face with his hands—so gently. And then he kissed her. He kissed and kissed until she could no longer think. Until there was no room in her head for doubt or pain. Only touch.

And then, when her mind was gone and she was all sensation, he stroked the rest of her, leaning close so he could follow the path of his fingers with his eyes. He stroked and kissed and gently blew on her hot skin. Moving with such powerful gentleness it was almost her undoing. But he too was silent.

She closed her eyes against the message she so badly wanted to read in his and just let him play with her until the need for the ultimate satisfaction grew too strong for both of them.

When he entered her this time she held her breath, tightening around him, closing him into her embrace with her arms and legs and everything. In her head words had returned and she was chanting: not going to let you go, not going to let you go.

But she was the one going. And she didn't know if she really had the strength to follow through on it.

But later, as she dressed, alone in his bedroom, she knew she had to leave. It was to protect herself. She owed herself the chance of meeting her dreams. And she couldn't stay with a man who didn't want long term—not when she did. Marriage and babies were on her wish-list and she couldn't change that— just as she couldn't change him.

She tried to make the goodbye as quick as she could. It didn't dim the pain at all. She wouldn't look him in the face—couldn't. He wanted to take her to the airport, was insistent. It tore her up inside as he objected.

Finally she looked at him, unable to hide the ache. 'Please, Owen. Let me do this myself.'

He stopped then, a shadow passing over his face. 'You don't have to do everything yourself, Bella. It's

OK to have help from people when you need it. Remember that, won't you?'

Yes, it was OK, but not all the time. And she had to do this alone; it was the only way she could.

The taxi was there in minutes and she turned to him feeling as if she had sawdust in her eyes and sandpaper in her throat. He lifted her bag into the boot.

'I'll call you,' he said.

'Actually—' she cleared her throat '—I'd rather you didn't.'

He stared at her.

She didn't want to be half hoping—wholly hoping—for the next however many months or years it was going to take to get over him. She needed it to end now. It was the perfect opportunity. Clean, final. Just how he'd like it. She didn't want him to pretend to offer anything else.

'You don't want me to contact you at all?'

She forced her head to move, slowly, side to side.

He stared at her for a long moment, ignoring the driver waiting patiently in the car.

'OK,' he said quietly. 'If that's what you want.'

She nodded then and looked down, not wanting to misread anything more in his face. Wanting to kill all her hope now. She didn't trust her voice at all.

There was a moment of silence. She knew she should move—the driver was waiting, the meter was ticking already. But all that moved were her lashes as she lifted her eyes, unable to resist one last long look at him. His eyes were still a brilliant blue, but charged with a variety of emotions—confusion? Regret?

She couldn't take any more and turned, got the door open. But as she did his hand was on her upper arm and it wasn't gentle as he grasped and swung her back to face him. The door slammed shut again, she had only a fraction of a second to see the blue ablaze and then he was so close and she shut her eyes. The kiss wasn't gentle either. It was hard and demanding and hurt.

But, as always, she softened for him, opened for him, couldn't say no to him. He could have her and take from her as much as he wanted. And then he softened too, his tongue caressing where moments before his mouth had pressed so fiercely, his fingers lightened on her arm and his lips soothed.

And at last she had the strength—she knew not from where—to twist away from him. He couldn't have everything from her when he wouldn't offer the same. It wasn't fair.

She turned, blindly groping for the door handle again, wrenching it open and scrambling into the seat.

'Drive.' It was sort of a bark but it ended as a broken sob. 'Please just drive.'

CHAPTER THIRTEEN

OWEN THREW HIMSELF into work. He worked and worked and worked. And every minute of the day he thought about Bella. Missed her. Wondered what the hell she was doing—where she was, who she was with, whether she was happy, whether she was missing him. And then he worked some more.

He hadn't thought he had it in him to be so aware of another person. To be driven to meet their needs—to put someone before himself. He'd been so ignorant of his parents' situation, so wrapped up in himself and his ideals and ideas. Only now he saw how they and Liz had tainted his view of marriage and children.

He hadn't been in love with Liz. He'd never been in love with anyone until now. So of course back then he hadn't been ready for a child. The baby-that-wasn't hadn't ever seemed real to him, it had simply been the symbol of a burden he hadn't wanted then and thought he'd never want.

Now he knew that if Bella's child had been real

he would have loved it—because now he knew what it was to love and how uncontrollable love could be.

When Liz had turned on him and told him how lonely he'd end up, he hadn't believed her. He'd never felt lonely. Too busy with his work. Too busy out partying when the need for physical company bit. He'd thought he had it all sussed.

Until now. Now he felt as lonely as it was possible to feel. And it hurt so badly he didn't know if he'd ever recover—he could only try to get used to it somehow.

He supposed it served him right. That the woman he'd found he was able to love wasn't one who needed it. The timing was all wrong. Her career was just starting. She was finally getting to where she'd wanted to be for so long. And he refused to ruin it for her. He didn't want her to resent him.

It was so ironic that when he finally found someone he wanted to care about, to love and cherish, help and protect, she was someone who was determined not to need those things. Bella didn't want help; she didn't want his money. She wanted independence. She'd said it, at the end there, that she needed to do this by herself. She was looking for respect. Trying to fight her family for it, fight him, every step of the way. But couldn't she see there was a balance? He couldn't stand back and watch her futile efforts when there were ways in which he could help. Maybe the way it had ended was all for the best.

Like hell it was.

As the days progressed, so his anger rose. Screw

this true hero thing. It was a con. There was no happiness in nobility—not this sort. He should never have let her go, at least, not without him. She'd tipped his world upside down and then walked out, leaving him in a hell of a mess. Damn it, his wanting to help her wasn't because he thought she was incapable; it was about him simply wanting to support her. No one was truly independent—not even him.

And there he'd been worried he'd get bored with one person for life. He laughed, a bitter, self-mocking laugh. What an arrogant jerk. No one could ever be bored around Bella.

She was full of life—a little kooky perhaps, most definitely a touch accident-prone. But she was also true and sweet and generous and funny. He wanted the warmth she had to offer. And he didn't want to ever give it up.

He couldn't stop the emotion from flowering in him. She was his own magic fairy—she'd brought back his humanity, his humility, his hope. And he wanted to keep her by his side for ever. He chuckled. So he was still selfish. He was about to make his most selfish move ever.

THE REHEARSAL WEEKS flew by. Bella had never worked so hard in all her life. They rehearsed all day and halfway through the evening. After that she collapsed into her little single bed in the tiny overcrowded flat that she was sharing with three other cast members and tried to sleep. Tried not to feel cold and lonely. But it was only when she closed her eyes tight and imagined herself in his big warm bed that she managed to drift off to sleep. In that blissful moment just on waking she'd still think she was there with him, but then she'd open her eyes and remember.

The work was full on but fun. She was glad she'd done all those years of dancing as a kid. Costumes were made, the set was designed, affairs were begun, gossip was spread. It was the mad, bad, bitchy world of musical theatre. She kept her distance from the worst of it. She learnt her part, understudied the other and developed an unhealthy obsession with the Internet. There was a lot on him—had she known she'd have looked sooner. But there was his website and a ton of articles about the savvy young entrepreneur. One of them had an accompanying picture of him in jeans and tee, totally looking like the relaxed guy she'd met that first night.

She couldn't indulge in her usual fix of chocolate, ice cream and red wine without thinking of him, couldn't eat her muesli at odd times of the day, couldn't even have a coffee. Everywhere she turned, everything she did, she thought of him. But worst of all were the nights. When in her lonely, little bed she lay restless, remembering every moment, every move, every touch, every tease.

She worked harder, longer, not wanting her silly heart to ruin this time for her.

There was nothing, no contact from him, just as she'd requested. And she forced that stupid, still sparking hope inside to shrink—day by day.

Opening night was upon her before she knew it. Nerves threatened to swamp her. But as she put on her make-up the security guy came and delivered the most beautiful bunch of flowers to her. There was no note other than her name. No hint of who they might have come from. The speed of her pulse quadrupled. Were they from him? She got through the show on a buzz of adrenalin and bubbling hope. Was he out there—in the audience?

Afterwards she joined in the laughter and excitement of the others, then scurried back to her dressing room, changing into her opening-night party outfit. There was a knock at the door. Heart thundering, she opened it.

'Dad! Vita!' Her jaw dropped. 'It's you.'

'We wouldn't miss it for the world.' Vita threw her arms around her.

'I didn't think you even knew.' Bella emerged from the hug and looked from her father to her sister.

'Well, we wouldn't have if it was down to you.' Vita gave her a sharp look.

She hadn't thought they'd be that interested. Not that she was about to admit that to them.

'Did you get the flowers?' her father asked almost shyly.

'They were from you?' she asked in the wobbliest voice ever.

Her father nodded. 'Vita chose them.'

Her sister smiled at her.

Bella smiled back. She shouldn't feel disappointed. It was wonderful of them to have sent them.

It was even more wonderful that they'd been here for her. But she'd wanted to believe they'd been from Owen. Crushed, she forced out a smile. Her best acting job of the night was required after the performance.

'We're coming again when you get to Auckland,' her father said unexpectedly.

Vita nodded enthusiastically. 'To a matinee when you're playing the lead. All the brothers are coming too. We've booked out a whole block of seats.'

Bella failed on the smile front then, bent her head to hide the sudden tears that were stinging her eyes. She blinked a few times. 'How did you know about that?'

'Someone sent us the details.' Her father spoke.

'Oh?'

'Owen sent an email to the whole family,' Vita said.

'What?' But there was no time for a repeat— now that her father had started talking, it seemed he couldn't stop.

'You were great up there, honey. I was so proud.' He beamed. 'Your mother would have loved it.'

She couldn't hide the tears then, and her father awkwardly put his arm around her, offering her a comfort she hadn't had in years.

VITA AND BELLA sat while their dad went up to the counter to get drinks at the after show party.

'You know, I've always been a bit jealous of you.' Vita smiled. 'Now I'm a lot.'

Nonplussed, Bella just stared at her for a moment. 'You want to be onstage?'

Vita laughed. 'No!' She shook her head. 'All that make-up would play havoc with my skin,' she joked. 'No, it was because you always seemed so confident. You didn't give a damn about what the rest of us were doing, or what Dad thought you should do. You just knew what you wanted and went for it. You've got such determination.'

'You've got to be kidding me.' Bella nearly choked. 'It's not like that at all.'

'But you've always known what you wanted,' Vita said. 'I've never known. I only did commerce because it was what everyone else had done and they seemed to do OK.'

Yes, but the fantasy of what Bella had wanted and the reality weren't panning out to be quite the same thing. 'Is it OK?' she asked her sister.

'Yeah, but I'm not exactly passionate about it.' Vita winked. 'Spreadsheets and tax returns aren't exactly something you live for.' She laughed. 'Whereas you have a job you love. I'm envious of that. But—' she leant forward '—I've got a secret. I'm quitting accountancy and I'm opening my own café.'

'You're what?' Bella was astounded. 'Vita, do you know how hard it is to work in a café?'

'Sure.'

'What does Hamish say?'

Vita's eyes glowed. 'He's really supportive. It's because of him that I'm finally going to do it. I'm doing a catering course and then I'm opening up.

He's keeping an eye out for a good location now. He's such a great guy, Bella.'

'I know.' Bella nodded. 'Wow. That's really cool. Good for you.'

'I'd never have had the guts if I didn't have you as an example, though.'

Bella nearly laughed. If only her sister knew. It had only been because of Owen that she'd got the part. He'd made her so mad. Worst of all he'd been right. But she couldn't think of him any more. 'Thanks so much for coming to the show. And for bringing Dad. I really appreciate it.'

'It was Owen who organised it. What's happening with him anyway?'

'Oh, nothing,' Bella answered shortly, really not wanting to dwell on him. 'We're just friends.'

Vita giggled. 'As if. The two of you the night before my wedding? My God, you had the place steaming up so bad there was practically water running down the walls.'

Bella felt her cheeks blaze.

'He's very good-looking,' Vita said. 'And very successful.'

'What do you know about him?' She couldn't stop her curiosity.

'Bella—' Vita shook her head '—if you were remotely clued in to the real world like the rest of us you'd know too. He made squillions when he sold his web stuff to that multimedia conglomerate.' She looked sly. 'How did the two of you meet anyway?'

Bella shook her head. She sure didn't want to go

there. 'It was nothing. It's over. This was just him being nice.'

'I don't think a guy like Owen would be organising your family for you if it was over—he wouldn't want us getting the wrong idea.'

'I haven't spoken to him in weeks. Trust me, it's over.' This last gesture was just the way he worked, charming to the end, still helping her out. Only now she was trying even harder to forget the heat in that final kiss, trying to stop wondering what might have happened if she hadn't got the part, if she hadn't left town.

Thankfully her father was heading to the table carrying a tray laden with glasses and nibbles. Talk returned to the show and the tour.

SHE GOT TO the theatre early as usual the next day.

'This parcel arrived for you last night too—sorry I didn't get it to you sooner.' The security guy at the theatre door collared her as she made her way in.

'Oh, that's fine,' she answered, heart hammering as she recognised the handwriting on the packet, trying not to snatch the thing out of his hands. She hurried to her dressing room, ripped the end of the bag and tipped the contents out.

A soft toy tiger bounced onto the table. She picked up the plush creature. There was a small card on a ribbon around his neck. She read it. 'Break a leg.'

She didn't need her leg breaking as well, thanks very much. She already had a broken heart. That was more than enough. She tipped the bag upside down and shook it again. Nothing else. No other message. It wasn't even signed. There was no return address on the back.

Bastard. She tossed the tiger across the room. She'd asked him not to contact her, all the while been hoping he would and now he had and with what—a damn toy? For the child he thought she was? She'd wanted more—she'd wanted so much more. This almost felt worse than nothing.

Almost. She frowned at the tiger. Why had she thought that he'd taken her seriously? But for about five minutes there he'd really seemed to want to believe in her and her party business. Hell, he'd even offered to help her paint a jungle mural on his warehouse wall, for heaven's sake.

So what did he mean by this? She was too scared to try to figure it out and too stupid not to start hoping some more.

The tiger seemed to be looking at her reproachfully. She rolled her eyes. It was a toy, for goodness' sake. Inanimate. Stuffed. The reproachful look deepened.

'Oh, all right, then.' She stomped over to it. 'Stop making me feel so guilty.' She picked him up, fingers automatically smoothing his fur. 'Don't think you're sleeping in my bed, though.'

The nights started to blur together. After the excitement of the opening, the thrill of the first reviews, they settled into the performances, tried not to get stale. And the reality of her new life hit her.

She was lonely. The show lasted nearly two hours.

The applause lasted maybe ten minutes at the most. There was no real contact or interaction with the audience. The cast and crew were fabulous, fun. They were a kind of family. But she couldn't quite get into it. Why was it that things were never quite how you imagined they would be?

Early in the mornings that followed, she snuggled deeper into her bed, hugged Tiger that little bit closer, and dreamed.

CHAPTER FOURTEEN

IT WAS THE matinee performance and Bella was taking the lead for the first time. She swallowed her nerves, but found they got stuck in her throat. So she stood in the wings and remembered the fierce look on Owen's face when he'd told her she had to believe in herself.

Believe. Believe. Believe.

As the opening music started she closed her eyes, whispered it to herself one more time and then stepped onto the stage. Looking on it afterwards, the whole thing was a blur. But backstage everyone was effusive in their congratulations and support. Even the director was pleased and told her that if she kept up like that she'd be getting bigger parts very soon. Bittersweet success flavoured her mood as she tripped down the corridor to the dressing rooms.

She stopped. Owen was leaning against the wall outside her door.

She stared. Looked him up and down and up and down and again. Put a hand out to balance herself against the wall because her legs had gone lifeless.

At her dumbfounded appraisal his grin was boyish. 'My mother taught me to dress for the theatre.'

'Even the eleven a.m. matinee show with all the audience aged either under ten or over sixty?'

'It's still the theatre,' he said smoothly.

She took a step closer. The tuxedo was devastating. The jacket fitting so well across his broad shoulders and tapering into his lean hips it just had to have been tailor-made.

Finally her heart started beating again—loud, painful thumping. 'What are you doing here?' She couldn't believe it.

'You were great.' He'd lost the grin and was now serious and not quite meeting her eyes.

'What are you doing here?' She strained to focus. She had to know.

'You really were amazing on that stage.'

He spoke so softly, she almost wondered if he was talking to her or just himself.

'Are you listening to me?' What the hell was going on?

'You have a real gift.'

She couldn't handle any more of this madness.

'I'm getting changed.' She stalked straight past him, into the dressing room, and shut the door. She whipped off her costume, climbed into her usual skirt and top, and wiped off as much of the make-up as she could in thirty seconds. Then she stared at her reflection in the mirror. Had she just imagined that encounter? Was she finally going nuts?

Taking a deep, supposedly stabilising breath, she

opened the door. He was leaning against the jamb right in front of her. The tux was no less magnificent. Her brain went fuzzy.

He straightened. 'Can we go somewhere to talk?'

She searched his features, wanting him to meet her gaze. 'Why are you here?'

He looked at her then, blue eyes blazing. 'Why do you think?'

She expelled a sharp breath as everything inside quivered. She fought the sensation, tensing up—that look wasn't enough. She wanted to hear it. Wanted to know—because what he was here for might not be enough for her. Anger and uncertainty and fear ripped through the delight in seeing him. 'Are you ready to define us yet, Owen? Or are we still not applying labels?'

He glanced away, down the corridor, and she realised he too was tense all over. 'Just give me a minute, Bella.'

'You're kidding,' she snapped. 'How much time do you need?'

'Listen to you.' His sharp smile flashed. 'You really have got your act together.'

'Don't you patronise me.' Frustration trammelled through her. She was ready to slam the door again—in his face.

But in a swift movement he put his hands on her hips and jerked her out of the doorway towards him. 'Never.'

One arm snaked hard around her waist, pulling her home, while his other hand lifted, holding her head up to his as his mouth descended. Her body thudded into his as their lips connected and just like that her fight against him was gone, overtaken completely by desire and ultimately by love.

She was holding her head up all by herself and his hands were all over her, pressing, pulling her closer to his heat and strength. And still it wasn't close enough. Shaking, she threaded her fingers through his hair, holding him, clutching at him, reaching up on tiptoe as her mouth clung to his—giving, seeking, taking, wanting more and more. Pure energy, electricity, sent sparks through her where they touched. She moaned into his mouth, feeling his response—harder, fiercer, deeper. The madness was back and she wanted it to last for ever.

He was the one who eased them out of it. His large hands taking her wrists, lowering them as he slowly lifted his head. For a second she strained up to follow. And then she heard it—the cacophony, the riot. She glanced to the side.

Oh, God, the entire cast and crew were in the corridor, watching them, catcalling and wolf-whistling and cheering.

She turned back and tried to tug free from his grip. She knew her cheeks were scarlet.

'I did ask you to give me a minute.' He grinned at her, but his hands were still tight, keeping her close. 'To get us some privacy. But now I'm not letting go.'

'My flat,' she muttered. 'It's only a few minutes away.'

He guided her out of the theatre, holding her

hand firmly. Still flushed, she could hardly summon a smile for her colleagues as they called goodbye, wished her well and made the odd laughingly crude comment.

'And there was me thinking you liked an audience,' Owen said dryly as they got outside. He opened the door to the waiting taxi. She didn't question, just got in and gave the driver the address. Owen slid in the back seat beside her, reclaimed her hand and passed the time chatting to the taxi driver about the rugby.

But he said nothing as, trembling, she unlocked the door and led the way in. And when she turned in the tiny room and saw him behind her, looking at her with those brilliant eyes, the loneliness and heartache that she'd tried so hard to bury resurfaced in a crashing wave, crushing her. She couldn't believe that he was here. And what if he still couldn't give her everything she wanted? She couldn't settle for less, but she had no choice. She was so bound to him, had such need for him, it terrified her. She blinked as her eyes stung, but still the world went blurry.

'Ah, Bella.' Husky, he reached for her, took her into his arms, wrapping them around her—strong and secure. 'I'm sorry.'

She burrowed her face into his broad chest, gripped his lapels, a bundle of tension and fearful need.

But he said nothing more. For long moments he just cradled her gently, stroking his hand down her rigid back in a long, slow rhythm, until at last she felt her warmth returning, and could relax into him. His arms tightened.

And then she was the one who spoke. 'Vita and my dad came to the show.'

'I know.'

'Opening night.'

'I know.'

'They're coming again, when I'm the lead in Auckland.'

'I know.'

More tears leaked from her eyes. It had all been him. 'It means a lot to me.'

'I know.'

She took in a deep breath, shuddered with it. 'Thank you.' It was muffled, into his shoulder.

His fingers slid up, into her hair. His mouth moved on the top of her head. 'They loved it. They love you.'

'I know.'

'He just wants you to be happy.'

'Yeah.'

'He thought that what made them happy would be the same thing to make you happy. But you're different, Bella. You're you. And you had to work it out for yourself.'

She nodded. 'But what I thought would make me happy hasn't.'

He lifted her chin, frowning at her tear-stained face. 'You're not happy?'

She shook her head. 'Owen, I'm such a mess.' Another tear spilt. 'I thought I wanted all this, but I don't.'

He looked deep into her eyes. 'What do you want?'

You. She was sure he could read her answer. But she refused to say it; it sounded so pathetic. And he wasn't all she wanted. She still wanted everything. 'I'm not going to do the Australian leg of the tour. I'll do New Zealand, but that's it. It's not what I want to do.'

His frown returned, bigger than before. 'But, Bella—'

'I miss the kids,' she interrupted, wanting to explain before she lost the nerve. 'I miss the direct contact. It's make-up on, bright lights, but I can hardly see the audience. It's a big theatre but it seems lonely. They applaud, they leave. By the time I'm scrubbed and changed, there's no one there. There's no interaction.' She lifted her chin, determined to take pride in her decision. 'I know being a children's entertainer isn't exactly the most highly rated job there is, but I'm good with them. I enjoy it. I'm going to go ahead and find my own venue and set up a business like you suggested. It was a good idea.'

He smiled then, a warm, encouraging smile. 'Bella, that's wonderful.'

Pleasure washed through her as she heard and saw his support. He believed in her and how she loved him for it and suddenly nothing else mattered. She'd take whatever he had, for however long, it would be enough—because she loved him.

'Don't look at me like that,' he suddenly begged.

'I'm not kissing you again until I've said what I have to say.'

She leaned that little closer into him and he groaned.

'I'm coming on tour with you.' He blurted the words out.

'What?' She jerked upright again.

'I'm coming with you. Sorry if that's not what you want, but that's what's happening.' He spoke even faster. 'I'm not spending another night apart from you.' He bent his head. 'Ever.'

She gasped at the rush of exhilaration. This kiss was even hungrier and more desperate than the one at the theatre. They clung, fierce, fevered. But again slowly, reluctantly, he drew back. He gripped her hands, stopping their frantic exploration, making her listen.

'I can work with my laptop and mobile. I'll have to fly to meetings every now and then, but I'll be back for the night. Every night.'

She couldn't stop the smile spreading as the glow inside grew stronger, becoming a solid flame of joy. 'OK.'

'And another thing,' he continued after another crazy kiss, his hands failing to stop their own exploration this time, 'the next family wedding you're going to is your own.'

'I thought you didn't believe in marriage.' She gaped. 'That it wasn't worth the paper it was written on.'

'You remember every stupid thing I've ever said, don't you?' he asked ruefully.

'Some of it wasn't so stupid.' He'd changed her life, made her see everything so much clearer. And now her whole body seemed to be singing.

'I want to marry you,' he said softly. 'I'll never want anyone but you. But I need you to tell me if you're not happy and I've not noticed.'

'You'll notice,' she assured him. 'You notice more about me than I do myself.'

'But if I'm buried in work…' He stopped, then almost whispered, 'I don't want to fail you.'

'You won't.' She raised her hand to his cheek, gently smiling. 'And if you do, I can always send you an email.'

'You'd do that?' He chuckled. 'For me?'

'I'd do anything for you,' she quietly admitted, knowing he already knew that.

His arms tightened. 'I never thought I could love anyone the way I love you.' At last she saw the vulnerability in his eyes as he wholly opened up. 'I want to be everything for you.'

'You already are.'

He shook his head. 'I want to do everything with you. I want to give you everything.' He drew in a shaky breath. 'I want you to have our children, Bella. I want your children.'

At that she closed her burning eyes tight, pressed them hard against his jacket again. 'Me too,' she said, and then drew a deep breath. 'But maybe not for a while? I want to make the business work first.'

And she wanted to have some time just with him, to broaden their foundations before they had their family.

'OK. You just say the word. When you're ready, I'll be ready.'

He was going to be there for her, for everything.

She reached up, pulled him down for her kiss and walked backwards, leading him to her tiny bedroom. He glanced around and she melted at the mix of relief and desire in his face. Her legs stumbled and he scooped her up.

'Do me a favour.' He lifted his mouth from hers for a moment.

'Anything.' She pulled it back to her.

'When we get home, can you put on that bridesmaid's dress?'

She paused then. 'It's hideous.'

He shook his head. 'It's beautiful.'

She undid his tie. 'Your eyesight is dodgy from all that staring at screens.'

'You have no idea the number of fantasies I've had involving that dress. All these long, lonely nights where I've had nothing but those pictures.' He stole another quick kiss. 'You have no idea how much I regret missing that wedding. I totally fell for you the minute I saw you in that bar—it was like nothing else. I should have held onto you then and there. Never let you go.'

She melted more. 'It happened right. You were right. I needed to stand up and try. To discover what it was I wanted.'

'And so did I.' He turned and leaned back, landing them both on her bed. But he didn't kiss her; instead he reached behind him, sliding his hand under the sheet and pulling out...Tiger.

Owen's whole expression softened, the lights in his eyes warming, mouth twitching. 'So you got him.'

She nodded. 'He usually comes to the theatre with me but the others were joking about him and I was worried he'd go wandering.'

'Well, sorry, tiger, there's no room in here any more.' He bent his arm back, about to throw him.

'Don't you dare!' Bella scolded, taking the toy from him. 'He's been a good friend to me these past few days.'

'Have you been cuddling him?'

'Maybe.' She tried to play it cool.

He grinned and took the toy from her. 'What a good little tiger, keeping her arms occupied and scaring off any interlopers.'

'As if I'd do that.'

'It wasn't you I was worried about,' he teased. 'It was all these showbiz boys and crew and groupies. They'll all be panting after you.'

'Half of them are gay.'

'And half of them aren't. I wanted tiger here to be the only thing in your arms. And you did a good job, didn't you, boy? Well, I'm back now and you can go sleep somewhere else.'

He stood up and put the tiger on an armchair, facing away from the bed, slung her cardigan over him.

'Happy now?' His eyes were twinkling.

'No,' she answered—all tragedy—but she couldn't hide the happiness any more. It burst out of her. 'Not until you're back here.'

He vaulted onto the bed, kissed her and their passion, too long denied, erupted. As he rose, his strong body braced over hers, she spread her fingers wide across his chest and marvelled. She simply couldn't believe she was going to have it all.

'How did I get so lucky?'

'It isn't luck, Bella,' he muttered as he pushed home. 'It's what you deserve.' He drew closer still. 'You deserve everything.'

She arched, reaching to meet him, wanting to give him as much as he was giving her, so that together they would have it all. And, as his murmurs of love melded to her moans, and the feeling of bliss between their bodies grew, she knew.

She'd succeeded.

* * * * *

THE MORNING AFTER
THE WEDDING BEFORE

Anne Oliver

To Sue.
You're loyal, generous, compassionate and caring, touching people's lives in the best way, and a true friend on life's amazing and unpredictable journey Thank you for always being there! Anne

CHAPTER ONE

EMMA BYRNE REFUSED to give in to the nerves zapping beneath her ribcage like hysterical wasps. She was a sophisticated city girl, she wasn't afraid of walking into a third-rate strip club. Alone.

But she paused on the footpath in King's Cross, Sydney's famous nightclub district, and racked her brain for an alternative solution as she eyed the bruiser of a bouncer propped against the tacky-looking entrance.

Six p.m. on a balmy autumn Monday evening and the Pink Mango was already open for business. Sleazy business. She gulped down the insane urge to laugh—she'd been naïve enough to think the Pink Mango was an all-night deli.

But she'd promised her sister she'd deliver the best man's suit to Jake Carmody, and she would. She could.

Pushing the big sunglasses she'd found in her glove box farther up her nose, she slung her handbag and the plastic suit bag over one stiff shoulder and marched inside. The sound system's get-your-gear-off bump and grind pounded through hidden speakers. The place smelled like beer and cheap cologne and smut. Her nostrils flared in distaste as she drew in a reluctant breath.

Her steps faltered as a zillion eyes seemed to look her way. *You're imagining it,* she told herself. *Who'd give you a second glance in a dive like this?* Especially given her knee-length buttoned-up red trench coat, knee-high boots and leather gloves, all of which she'd left on the back seat of her car since last winter. Which, when she thought about it, could very well be the reason she was garnering more than a few stares...

Better safe than sorry. Thank heavens for untidy cars and a convenient parking spot.

Ignoring the curious eyes, she turned her attention to the décor instead. The interior was even tackier than the outside. Cheap lolly pink and gold and black. The chairs and couches were covered in a dirty-looking fuchsia animal print. A revolving disco ball spewed gaudy colours over the circulating topless waitresses with smiles as fake as their boobs.

At least they *had* boobs.

Most of the early-evening punters were lounging around a raised oval stage leering over their drinks at a lone female dancer wearing nothing but a fuzzy gold string and making love to a brass pole. A hooded cobra was tattooed on one firm butt cheek.

Far out. Despite herself, Emma couldn't seem to tear her fascinated gaze away. *What men like...*

She'd never have that voluptuousness, nor the chutz-pah to carry it off.

Maybe that was the reason Wayne had called it quits.

Shaking off the self-doubt, she blew out a deep, slow breath and turned away from the entertainment. Just what she *didn't* need right now. A reminder of her physical inadequacies.

I don't care if you and Ryan are getting married next weekend, little sister, you owe me big-time for doing this.

'I've got an appointment to get my nails done,' Stella had told her with more than a touch of pre-wedding desperation in her voice. 'Ryan's in Melbourne for a conference till tomorrow and you don't have anything special on tonight, do you?'

Stella knew Emma had no social life whatsoever since the break-up with Wayne. Of course she'd be free. Wouldn't have mattered if she wasn't. As the maid of honour, how could she refuse the bride's request? But a strip joint had *not* been part of the deal.

A man in an open shirt with a thick gold chain over an obscene mat of greying chest hair watched her from behind a desk nearby. His flat, penetrating gaze—as if he was imagining her naked and finding her not up to par—made her stomach heave. A bead of sweat trickled down her back—it was stifling inside this coat.

But he seemed to be the obvious person to speak to, so she moved quickly. She straightened her spine and forced herself to look him in the eyes. Not easy when those eyes were staring at her chest.

But before she got a word out he twirled one fat finger and said, 'If you've come about the job, take off that coat and show us what you've got.'

The hairs on the back of her neck prickled and, appalled, she tightened her belt. 'I *beg* your pardon? I'm n—'

'You won't need a costume here, darlin',' he drawled, eyeing the garment bag over her shoulder. 'We're one down tonight so you can start on the tables. Cherry'll show you. Oi, Cherry!' His smoke-scratched voice blasted through the thick air.

Emma cringed as people looked their way, glad of her dark glasses. She summoned her frostiest tone. 'I'm here to speak to Jake Carmody.'

He shook his head. 'Won't make a scrap of difference, y'know. Seen plenty just like you pass through the door hiding behind a disguise, expecting to make a quick buck on the side.'

'*Excuse me?* Just tell me where I can find Mr Carmody so I can finish my business with him and be *out of here*.'

Those pale flat eyes checked her out some more as a woman approached toting a tray of drinks. She was wearing eighties gold hot pants and a transparent black blouse. Beneath her make-up Emma saw that she looked drawn and tired and felt a stirring of sympathy. She knew all about working jobs out of sheer necessity, and was grateful she'd never been quite so desperate.

'Lady here wants to see the boss. Know where he is?'

The boss? 'There must be some mistake…' Emma trailed off. His PA had told her she'd find him at this address, but…he was the *boss* of this dive?

The woman called Cherry gave a weary half shrug. 'In the office, last I saw.'

He jerked a thumb at a narrow staircase on the far side of the room. 'Up the stairs, first door on the right.'

'Thank you.' Lips pressed together, and aware of a few gazes following her, she made her way through the club, keeping as far away from the action as possible.

The *boss?*

Despite the heat, she shivered inside her coat. His lifestyle was none of her business, but she'd never in a million years have expected the guy she remembered to be involved in a lower-than-low strip joint. He already had a career, didn't he? A degree in business law, for goodness' sake. *Please don't let him have chucked in years of study and a respectable livelihood for this…*

Sleaze Central's business obviously paid better. Money over morals.

She knew Jake from high school. He was one of Ryan's mates, and the two guys had often turned up at home to catch up with her more sociable sister and listen to music. Emma had been either working one of her after-school jobs or experimenting with her soap-making, but there'd been a few times when Stella had persuaded her to chill out with them.

Jake the Rake, Emma had privately thought him. A chick magnet. Totally cool, ever so slightly dangerous, and way too experienced for a girl like her. Maybe that was why she'd always tried to avoid him whenever possible.

Hadn't stopped her from being a little in love with him, though. She shook it away. Obviously her young eyes had been clouded by naïveté and love was definitely not in her life plan. Not ever again.

She heard him before she reached the door. That familiar deep, somewhat lazy voice that seemed to roll over the senses like thick caramel sauce. She *was* well and truly over her youthful crush on him, wasn't she? He was on the phone, and as she paused to listen his tone changed from laid-back to harassed.

The door was open a crack and she knocked. She heard a clatter as he slammed the phone down, a short, succinct rude word and then an impatient, 'Come in.'

He didn't look up straight away, which gave her a moment to slide her sunglasses on top of her head and look him over.

Sitting at a shabby desk littered with papers, he was writing something, head bent over a file. He wore a sky-blue shirt, open at the neck, sleeves rolled up over sinewy bronzed forearms. Unlike the rest of this dive, his clothing was top of the line. Her gaze lifted to his face and her heart pattered that tiny bit faster. God's gift with a sinner's lips…

An unnerving little shiver ran through her and she jerked her eyes higher. His rich, dark hair was sticking up in short tufts here and there, as if he'd been ploughing his hands through it. Her fingers itched to smooth it down—

Good grief, she was lusting after a man who owned a seedy striptease venue—a man who not only used women but exploited them. Wanting to touch him made her as low as him and as bad as those pervs downstairs. But, despite her best efforts to ignore them, little quivers continued to reverberate up and down the length of her spine.

'Hello, Jake.' She impressed herself with her aloof greeting and only wished she felt as cool.

He glanced up. His frown was replaced by stunned surprise. As if he'd been caught in a shop window with his made-to-measure pants down. She blinked the disconcerting image away.

'Emma.' Putting his pen down slowly, he closed the file he'd been working on, took his sweet time to stand—all six-foot-plus of gorgeous male—and said, 'Long time no see.'

'Yes,' she agreed, ignoring the tantalising glimpse of masculine hair visible at the neck of his shirt, the way his broad shoulders shifted against the fabric. 'Well…we've all got busy lives.'

'Yeah, it's all go these days isn't it? Unlike high school.' He came round to the side of the desk with a smile that was like a lingering caress and did amazing tingly things to her body.

She took a step back. She needed to get out. Fast.

'I can see you're busy,' she hurried on, keeping her gaze focused on his black coffee eyes. 'I j—'

'Are you here for a job?'

What? She felt her jaw drop, and for a moment she simply stared while her brain played catch-up and heat crawled up her neck. The sod. The dirty rotten *sod.* 'I phoned your office—your *other* office—and your PA told me you were here.'

Her lip curled on the last word and she tossed the garment bag onto the desk, sending papers flying every which way. 'Your suit for the wedding. If it needs altering the tailor says he needs at least three days' notice, which is why I'm dropping it off tonight. Ryan's interstate, and Stella had an appointment, so I—'

'Emma. I was joking.'

Oh. She glimpsed the twinkle in his eye and took another step back. Twinkles were dangerous. And why wouldn't he joke? Because no way did she measure up to those voluptuous creatures downstairs. 'I don't have time to joke today. Or anything else. So… um…you've got the suit. I'll be off, then.'

He watched her a moment longer, as if saying *What's your hurry?* Beneath the harsh single fluorescent light she saw the bruised smudges and feathery lines of stress around his eyes, as if he hadn't slept in weeks.

Well, good, she thought. He deserved to be stressed for making her feel like an inadequate fool. As if her self-esteem wasn't suffering enough after Wayne ending their relationship, and in this place…

'So, it's *Gone with the Wind* for us two, eh? Hope I can do Rhett Butler justice.' He glanced at the bag, then aimed that sexy grin at her. 'And you're to be my Scarlett for the day.'

She stiffened at the darkly delicious—no, *bad* thought. But her blood pulsed a bit more heavily through her body. 'I'm not your anyone. Why they had to choose a famous couples-themed wedding's beyond me.'

He shrugged. 'They wanted something sparkling and original and wildly romantic—and why not? Might as well have some fun on the big day. Everything's downhill from there.' His long, sensuous fingers curled around the edge of the desk and he aimed that killer smile again. 'Thanks for dropping it off. Can I get you a drink before you leave?'

Good heavens. 'No. Thank you.'

CROSSING HIS ARMS, Jake leaned a hip against the desk, inhaling the fresh, unfamiliar fragrance that had swirled in with her. She was an energising sight for tired eyes. What he could see of her.

Tall and slim as a blue-eyed poppy. Even angry she looked amazing, with that ice-cold sapphire gaze and that way she had of pouting her lips. All glossy and plump and…

He fought a sudden mad impulse to walk over and taste them. Probably shouldn't have made that wisecrack about a job here. But he'd not been able to resist getting a rise out of her. On the few occasions she'd been persuaded to join them she'd always been so damn serious. Obviously that hadn't changed.

The muffled thump from downstairs vibrated through the floor. He rasped his hands over his stubbled jaw. 'If I'd known you were coming I'd've arranged for you to drop the suit at my office. My *other* office.'

She drilled him some more with that icy stare. And he felt oddly bruised, as if she'd punched him in the gut with her…gloved hand.

'I have to go,' she said stiffly.

He pushed off the desk. 'I'll walk you down.'

'No. I'd really rather you didn't.'

The tone. He knew well enough not to mess with it and crossed his arms. 'Okay. Thanks again for dropping the suit by. Appreciate it.'

'Glad to hear that, because it's a one-off.'

'I'll see you tomorrow night at the wedding dinner.'

'Seven-thirty.' She hitched her bag higher. 'Don't be late.'

'Emma…' She glanced back and he thought once again of poppies. About lying in a field of them on a summer's day. With Emma. 'It's good to see you again.'

She didn't reply, but she did hesitate, staring at him with those fabulous eyes and allowing him to indulge in the cheerful poppy fantasy a few seconds longer. And he could have sworn he felt a… *zap.* Then she nodded once and her head snapped back to the doorway.

He watched her leave, admiring the way she moved, all straight and sexy and *classy*. He wondered for a moment why he'd never pursued anything with her back in the day. He'd seen her look his way more than once when she'd thought he wasn't watching.

His lingering smile dropped away. He knew why. Emma Byrne didn't know the meaning of fun, and she certainly didn't know how to chill out. She wore *serious* the way other women wore designer jeans.

Jake, on the other hand, didn't do serious. He didn't do commitment. He enjoyed women—on his terms. Women who knew the score. And when it was over it was over, no misunderstandings. No looking back. But, *hoo-yeah*… He couldn't deny this lovely, more mature, more womanly Emma turned him on. Big time.

The door closed and he listened to her footsteps fade, stretching his arms over his head, imagining her walking downstairs. In that neck-to-ankle armour—which only added to the sexual intrigue. Did she even realise that? He should have escorted her down, he thought again. But the lady, and everything about her body language, had said a very definite no.

Shaking off the lusty thoughts, he rolled down his shirtsleeves. Damn Earl, the SOB who'd fathered him, for dying and leaving him this mess to sort out. No one knew of Jake's connection to this club, with the exception of Ry and his parents and more recently his PA.

And now Emma Byrne.

'Hell.' He checked the time, then shoved his phone

in his pocket. He didn't have time for that particular complication right now—he had an important business meeting to attend. Grabbing his jacket from the back of his chair, he headed downstairs.

CHAPTER TWO

AND SHE'D TOLD him not to turn up late.

'She'd better have a good excuse,' Jake muttered the following evening as he swung a left in his BMW and headed for Sydney's seaside suburb of Coogee Beach, where Emma lived with her mother and Stella. As Ryan's best man he'd had no choice but to elect himself to conduct the search party.

Or maybe she'd decided she didn't want to run into Jake Carmody again so soon.

She'd always been big on responsibility, he recalled, and tonight was her sister's night, so he figured she wouldn't opt out without a valid reason. But she hadn't answered her mobile and concern gnawed at his impatience. He tapped the steering wheel while he waited at a red light. A trio of teenagers skimpily dressed for a night on the town crossed in front of him, their feminine voices shrill and excited.

Maybe Emma wasn't the same girl these days. Maybe she had decided to swap those self-imposed obligations for some fun at last. After all, apart from those few minutes yesterday, when neither of them had actually been themselves, how long had it been since he'd seen her?

His gut tensed an instant at the memory. He knew exactly when he'd last seen her. Seven months ago at Stella and Ryan's engagement party. He knew exactly what she'd been wearing too—a long, slinky strapless thing the colour of moon-drenched sea at midnight.

Or some such garment. He forced his hands to loosen on the wheel. Unclenched his jaw. So what if he'd noticed every detail, down to the last shimmering toenail? A guy could look.

He'd arrived in time to see her leave hand in hand with some muscled blond surfie type. Wayne something or other, Stella had told him. Apparently Emma and Wayne were a hot item.

Maybe Surfer Boy was the reason she'd lost track of time…

Frowning at the thought, he pulled into the Byrnes' driveway overlooking the darkening ocean. The gates were open and he came to a stop beside an old red hatchback parked at the top of a flight of stone steps.

Perched halfway down the sloping family property was the old music studio, where he remembered spending afternoons in the latter days of high school. Early-evening shadows shrouded the brick walls but muted amber light shone through the window. Emma lived there now, he'd been informed, and she was obviously still at home. In the absence of any other car on the grounds, it seemed she was also alone.

Swinging his car door open, he pulled out his phone. 'Ry? Looks like she hasn't even left yet.' He strode to the steps, flicking impatient fingers against his thigh. 'We'll be there soon.'

Pocketing the phone, he continued down the stairs. If *he* could make it on time to this wedding dinner after the hellish day he'd had, trying to stay on top of two businesses, so could Emma. She was the bridesmaid, after all.

Some sort of relaxation music drifted from the window, accompanying the muted *shoosh-boom* of the breakers on the beach. He slowed his steps, breathing in the calming fragrant salt air and honeysuckle, and ordered himself to simmer down.

THE PEAL OF the door chime accompanied by a sharp rapping on her front door jerked Emma from her work. She refocused, feeling as if she was coming out of a deep-sleep cave. She checked her watch. Blinked. *Oh, no.* She'd assured Stella she'd be right along when the family had left nearly half an hour ago.

Which officially made her the World's Worst Bridesmaid.

She stretched muscles cramped from being in one position too long and assured herself her lapse *wasn't* because her subconscious mind was telling her she didn't want to see Jake. She would *not* let him and that crazy moment yesterday when their eyes had met and the whole world seemed to fade into nothing affect her life. In any way.

Rap, rap, rap.

'Okay, okay,' she murmured. She slipped the order of tiny stacked soap flowers she'd been wrapping back into its container and called, 'Coming!'

Running her hands down the sides of her over-sized lab coat, she hurried to the door, swung it open. 'I…'

The man's super-sized silhouette filled the door-way, blocking what was left of the twilight and ob-scuring his features, but she knew instantly who he was by the way her heart bounded up into her throat.

'Jake.' She felt breathless, as if she'd just scaled the Harbour Bridge. Ridiculous. Scowling, she flicked on the foyer light. She tried not to admire the view, she really did, but her eyes ate up his dark good-looks like a woman too long on a blond boy diet.

Tonight he wore tailored dark trousers and a choc-olate-coloured shirt open at the neck. Hair the col-our of aged whisky lifted ever so slightly in the salty breeze.

'So here you are.' His tone was brusque, those black-coffee eyes focused sharply on hers.

'Yes, here I am,' she said, trying to ignore the hot flush seeing him had brought on and reminding her-self where she'd seen him last. The flashback to the strip club made her feel like a gauche schoolgirl and it should not. But she was the one at fault tonight— and the reason he was standing in her doorway.

She gave him a careless smile, determined not to let yesterday spoil this evening. For Stella's sake.

'And running late,' she rushed on. 'I assume that's why you're here?' *Why else?*

One eyebrow rose and she knew he wasn't impressed. 'You had some people concerned.' He said it as if he didn't count himself amongst those people—where had yesterday's twinkle gone?—while he stepped inside and scanned the dining room table covered in the hand-made goat's milk soaps she'd been working on.

'You weren't answering your phone.' His gaze swung back to hers again. 'Not handy when people are trying to contact you.'

Her smile dropped to her feet. Was that *censure* in his voice? 'This from the guy who was too busy at his *other business* to answer his own mobile yesterday?' she shot back. 'You do realise I had to pry the info as to your whereabouts from your PA?'

He nodded, his eyes not flinching from hers. 'So she told me. I apologise for the inconvenience, and for any embarrassment I caused you.'

Emma drew in a deep breath. 'Okay.' She forced her mature self to put yesterday's incident to the back of her mind for now. 'As for me, I have no legitimate excuse for forgetting the time, so it's my turn to apologise that you had to be the one to come and get me.' She tried a smile.

He nodded, his dark eyes warmed, and his whole demeanour mellowed like a languid Sunday afternoon. 'Apology accepted.' He leaned down and brushed her cheek with firm lips, and she caught a whiff of subtle yet sexy aftershave before he straightened up again.

Whoa. Yesterday's tingle was back with a vengeance, running through her entire system at double the voltage. 'So…um…I'll just go…' Feeling off-centre, she backed away, ostensibly towards the tiny area sectioned off by a curtain which she used as a bedroom, but he didn't take the hint and leave. 'Look, you go on ahead. I'll be ready in a jiff and it's only a ten-minute drive to the restaurant.'

He shrugged, stuck his hands in his trouser pockets. 'I'm here now.'

Slipping off her flats, she glanced about for her heels. But her eyes seemed drawn to him as if they were on strings. He dressed like a million bucks these days. Still, those threadbare jeans he'd worn way back when had fuelled more teenage fantasies than she cared to remember. She watched him wander towards her table of supplies. With his hands in his pockets, drawing his trousers tight across that firm, cute butt…

No. Sleazy club-owner. Dragging her eyes away, she scoured the floor for her shoes. 'There's really no need to wait…'

'I'm waiting. End of story.' She heard the crinkle of cellophane as he examined her orders. 'Your hobby's still making you some pocket money, then?'

Irritation stiffened her shoulders. She glared at him. 'It's *not* just a hobby, and it's never been about the money.' *Unlike others who shall remain Nameless.* Exhaling sharply through her nose, she swiped up a black stiletto and slipped it on. 'I have to wonder why it is that helping people with skin allergies seems to you to be a waste of time.'

'I never sa—'

'Why don't you go while I…?' *Calm down.* 'Find my other shoe.'

'So uptight.' He tsked. 'You really need to get out more, Em. Always was too much work and not enough play with you.' He scooped her shoe from beneath a chair and tossed it to her. 'Maybe the wedding'll help things along.'

She caught it one-handed, dropped it in front of her with a clatter and stepped into it, then bent to do up the straps. She'd had it with people telling her how to live her life. Get out more? She let out a huff. She had familial obligations. Had she told him what she thought of the way he was living *his* life nowadays? No.

She finished fastening her shoes and straightened, pushed at the hair that had fallen over her eyes. Forget his uninformed opinion. Forget him, period. She had her *un*fabulous job at the insurance call centre— but it paid the bills—and she had just finished her Diploma in Natural Health. And if she chose to fill her leisure hours working on ways to help people use natural products rather than the dangerous chemicals contained in other products these days, it was nobody's business but hers.

'So how's…what was her name…? Sherry?' she asked with enough sweetness to decay several teeth as she slipped open the top button of her lab coat. 'Will she be missing you this evening?'

His brows rose. 'Who?'

'The one...' *draped all over you* '...at Stella's engagement party. Stella mentioned her name,' she hurried on, in case he thought she'd actually asked. Which she had. But he didn't need to know that.

'Ah...You mean Brandy.'

She shrugged. 'Brandy. Sherry. She looked like more of a *Candy* to me.' With her suck-my-face-off lips and over-generous cleavage. And everything else Emma was lacking. 'You didn't say hello and introduce us. Was that because she was one of your *exotic dancers?*'

'You and your date left as we arrived. Was that just a curious coincidence?'

Jake watched her cheeks flush guiltily and felt an instant stab of arousal. Hell. He kept his expression neutral, but something was happening here. And the hot little fantasy he'd had last night about what she'd been wearing beneath that red coat yesterday wasn't helping.

And now she was undoing the second button of that lab coat, revealing a pair of sexy collarbones and putting inappropriate ideas into his head.

He ground his teeth together as images of black lace and feminine flesh flashed through his mind. 'Are you going to get ready or what?' The demand came out lower and rougher than he'd have liked. Then he held his breath as she shrugged out of the coat, tossed it over the couch.

'I'm ready already.' She flashed him a cool look. 'I use the coat to protect my clothes when I'm working.'

His gaze snagged on her outfit—a short black dress shot through with bronze, hugging her slender curves to perfection. He swallowed. The legs. How come he'd never noticed how long her legs were? How toned and tanned? He did *not* imagine how they'd feel locked around his waist.

Cool it. He deliberately relaxed tense muscles. He'd wait outside, get some air.

But before he could move she picked up an embroidered purse from the couch and walked to the front door. 'Shall we go?'

He walked ahead, opened the door. 'We'll take my car.'

'I'm taking my own car, thanks.' She locked the door behind them, then headed towards the hatchback, her heels tapping a fast rhythm on the concrete.

He pressed his remote and the locks clicked open. 'Hard to get a parking space anywhere this time of night,' he advised. 'And we—make that *you*—are running late already. Stella and Ryan are waiting.'

Swinging her door open, she glanced back at him. 'Better get a move on, then.'

He started to go after her, then changed his mind. She was in a dangerous mood, and he was just riled enough to take her on. And it might end… He didn't want to think about how it might end. Because he had a feeling that anything with Emma would need to be very slow and very, *very* thorough. If you could find your way through those thorns, that was. 'I'll see you there.'

She clicked her seat belt on, turned the ignition and revved the engine. 'Ten minutes.'

EMMA'S STOMACH JITTERED. Her pulse raced. Trouble. She'd seen more than enough of it in Jake's hot brown eyes. As if she was performing some sort of striptease. She'd not given it a thought when she'd peeled off her lab coat. But he had. *Sheesh*. She scoffed to herself. As if he'd give her less than average body a second look when he was surrounded by all those Brandies and Candies and brazen beauties at the Pink Mango.

Flicking a glance at her rearview mirror she caught the glare of his headlights. She deliberately slowed her speed, hoping he'd overtake, but he seemed content—or irritated enough—to cruise along behind her. She could feel his eyes boring into the back of her head.

She let out a shaky sigh and drew a deep, slow breath to steady herself. Easier to blame him than to admit to that old attraction—because no way was Jake the Rake the kind of man she wanted to get involved with on an intimate level.

She accelerated recklessly through a yellow light, Jake hot on her heels. She wasn't herself tonight. Wrong. She hadn't been herself since she'd come face to face with Jake in his dingy office yesterday.

Even as a teenager he'd always made her feel…

different. Self-conscious. Tingly. Uncomfortably aware of her feminine bits.

Her fingers clenched tighter on the steering wheel. She needed to get herself under control. She didn't figure in his life at all, nor he in hers. And tonight wasn't about her or him or even *them*; it was about Stella and Ryan.

She tensed as the well-lit upscale restaurant came into view, and glanced in the mirror again just in time to see Jake's car glide into a parking space she'd been too distracted to notice right outside the restaurant.

Oh, for heaven's sake, this was ridiculous. The restaurant was on a corner and she stopped at a red light, tapping impatient fingers on the dashboard. Seriously, if it wasn't Stella's night she'd turn around and go home, pull the covers over her head and not surface till Christmas—

The thump on the car's roof nearly had her foot slipping off the brake as Jake climbed in beside her. 'Don't you know better than to leave your passenger door unlocked when you're driving alone at night?'

She hated his smug look and lazy tone and looked away quickly. 'Don't you know better than to scare a person half to death when they're behind the wheel?'

'Light's green.'

She clenched her teeth, pretending that she hadn't noticed his woodsy aftershave wafting towards her, and crossed the intersection. 'What are you doing here? There's no sense in both of us being late.' She saw a car pulling out ahead, remembered at the last second to check her rear vision and slammed on the brakes.

'We'll walk in together, *Scarlett*.'

'Don't remind me,' she muttered. She slid the car into the parking spot, yanked the key from the ignition, jumped out and locked her door before he'd even undone his seat belt.

Jake took his time getting out, watching her walk around the car's bonnet to the footpath. Not looking at him. No trace of the blue-eyed poppy tonight, he thought, locking his own door. She was as prickly as a blackberry bush.

The pedestrian light turned green. She left the kerb and he fell into step beside her. 'If we're going to pull this wedding business off, we need to be seen to be getting along.'

She jerked to a stop outside the restaurant. 'Fine.'

Catching her by her slender shoulders, he turned her to face him, noticed her stiffen at the skin-on-skin contact. 'We'll need to have a conversation about that at some point.'

'There's nothing to talk about.'

Light from the window spilled over her face. Wide eyes stared up at him, violet in the yellow glow. He slid his hands down her bare arms, felt her shiver beneath his palms and raised a brow. 'Nothing?'

'Nothing.' She rubbed her palms together, her gaze flicking away. 'It's chilly. I should've brought a jacket. I left it on the bed…'

No, he thought, she'd been distracted. Grinning, he let her go. 'Lighten up, Em, and give yourself permission to enjoy an evening out for once.'

CHAPTER THREE

WITH A LIGHT hand at her back, Jake ushered Emma into the upstairs restaurant. Exotic Eastern tapestries lined the burgundy walls. On the far side, through double glass doors was a narrow balcony crowded with palms. Dreamy Eastern music played softly in the background. The tempting aromas of Indian cuisine greeted them as they made their way towards the round family table already covered in a variety of spicy smelling dishes.

'Apologies, everyone.' Jake nodded to the happy couple. 'Glad to see you've already started.'

Emma murmured her own apologies to Stella while Ryan spooned rice into two empty bowls and passed them across the table. 'We wondered whether you two had decided to play hooky.'

'We thought about it—didn't we, Em?' Jake grinned, enjoying her appalled expression, then turned to Ryan's father.

Gil Clifton, a stocky man with wiry red hair and always a genuine smile, rose and shook hands. 'Good to see you again, Jake.'

'And you. We must get around to that tennis match.'

'Any time. Just give us a call and drop by.'

'I'll do that.'

Gil's smile faded. 'I was sorry to hear about your father. If there's anything I can do…'

The mention of the old man left nothing but a bitter taste in Jake's mouth and an emptiness in his soul that he'd come to terms with years ago. As far as he was concerned Gil and Julie Clifton were the only adult support he'd ever needed. 'Got it covered, thanks, Gil.'

He kissed Julie's cheek. 'How's the mother of the groom holding up?'

'Getting excited. And, to echo Gil's words, if you want to drop by and chat…you're always welcome.'

If Jake was ever to be lost for words now was that time. Ryan's family were the only people who knew about his dysfunctional childhood, and now the whole table knew about Earl. He forced a smile. 'Thanks.'

Emma watched Julie give Jake's arm a sympathetic squeeze. It occurred to her how little she really knew of his background beyond the fact he was Ryan's mate.

'So how's business?' Gil asked as Jake moved to the two empty chairs.

'Busy as usual. Evening, Bernice.'

'Jake.' Emma's mother acknowledged him coolly, then turned the same stony gaze on Emma. 'Thank you for collecting my unpunctual daughter.'

Emma reminded herself she was Teflon coated where her mother's barbs were concerned. The others resumed their conversations while she took the empty seat that Jake pulled out beside her mother and whispered, 'Sorry, Mum.'

'Have to admire our Emma's work ethic, though,' Jake remarked as he sat down beside her. 'It's not easy juggling two jobs.'

'Two jobs?' Bernice bit off the words. 'When one's a waste of time, I—'

'Mum.' Emma counted to ten while she reached for her table napkin and smoothed it over her lap. 'How are you enjoying the food?'

Bernice stabbed at a cherry tomato on her plate. 'You need two *proper* jobs to be able to afford a dress like that.'

Jake smiled at Bernice on Emma's other side. 'And it's worth every cent. She looks sensational, don't you think? Wine, Em?'

'No, thank you. Driving.' She acknowledged Jake's support with a quick nod and reached for the glass of water in front of her. She took several swallows to compose herself before she said, 'I bought it at Second Hand Rose, Mum. That little recycle boutique on the esplanade.'

When her mother didn't reply, Emma turned to Jake. 'I didn't know about your father,' she murmured as other conversation flowed around the table. 'I'm sorry.'

He didn't look at her. 'Don't be.' He tossed back his drink, set his glass on the table with a firm *thunk* and turned his attention to something Ryan was saying on his other side.

Ouch. Emma reached for the nearest dish, a mixed vegetable curry, and ladled some onto her plate. He didn't want to talk about his father—fine. But there was a mountain of pain and anger there, and... She paused, spoon in mid-air. *And what, Emma?*

He clearly wasn't going to talk about it. He didn't *want* to talk about it—not with her at any rate—and she had no business pursuing it. It wasn't as if they were close or anything.

A moment later Jake turned to her again. 'I was abrupt. I shouldn't have been.'

An apology. Of sorts. 'It must be a tough time, no matter how you and he...' The right words eluded her so she reached for the nearest platter instead. 'Samosa?'

'Thanks.' He took one, put it on the side of his plate. 'I've been thinking about you, Emma.' He leaned ever so slightly her way, with a hint of seduction in the return of that suave tone.

She could feel the heat bleed into her cheeks. 'I don't—'

'Have you considered selling your supplies over the internet?' He broke off a piece of naan bread. 'Could be a profitable business for you. You never know—you might be able to give up your day job eventually.'

'I don't want to give up my day job.' *I'm not a risk-taker. Mum depends on me financially. I can't afford to fail.*

'I could help you with your business plan,' he continued, as if she'd never spoken. He lowered that sexy voice. 'You only have to ask.'

His silky words wrapped around her like a gloved hand and an exquisite shiver scuttled down her spine. She could imagine asking him…lots of things. She wondered if his sudden interest and diversionary tactics had anything to do with taking the focus off his own family problems. 'I don't have time to waste on the computer, and I told you already it's not about the money.' *Business plan? What business plan?*

'Lacking computer confidence isn't something to be embarrassed about.'

'I'm n—' With a roll of her eyes she decided her protest was wasted—men like Jake were always right—and topped up her curry with a broccoli floret. 'I'm flat out supplying the local stores. I don't need to be online.'

'It would make it easier. And if your products are so popular why wouldn't you want to see where they take you?'

She would—oh, she *so* would. Her little cottage business was her passion, but technology was so not her; she wouldn't know where to start with a website, and her meagre income—which went straight into the household budget—didn't allow her to gamble on such a luxury. 'As I said, there's no time.'

'Maybe you need to change your priorities. Or maybe you're afraid to take that chance?' He eyed her astutely as he broke off more bread. 'The offer's always open if you change your mind.'

Was she so easy to read? An hour or so with Jake and he saw it already. Her fear of failure. Of taking that step into the unknown. He was the last person she'd be going to for help; she felt vulnerable enough around him as it was. 'Thank you, I'll keep it in mind.'

Over the next hour the meal was punctuated with great food, toasts to the bride and groom, speeches and recollections of fond memories.

Jake watched on, feeling oddly detached from the whole family and the getting-married scenario. What motivated sane, rational people to chain themselves to another human being for the term of their natural lives? In the end someone always ended up abandoning the other, along with any kids unlucky enough to be caught up in it.

Then Emma excused herself to go to the ladies' room and Julie claimed Bernice's attention with wedding talk. He breathed a sigh of relief that for now he wasn't included in the conversation.

A moment later he saw Emma on her way back and watched, admiring her svelte figure and the way her hips undulated as she walked. Nice. Last night's fantasy flashed back and a punch of lust ricocheted through his body. She'd been fire and ice yesterday at the club, and he couldn't help wondering how it might translate to the bedroom.

He saw her come to an abrupt halt as a newly arrived couple cut across her path. His eyes narrowed. Wasn't that…? Yep. Wayne whoever-he-was. Jake watched on with interest as Wayne's dinner partner hugged his arm a moment then walked to the ladies', leaving Emma and Surfer Boy facing each other.

More like facing off, Jake thought, studying their body language. Even from a distance he could see that Emma's eyes had widened, that her face had gone pale and that Surfer Boy was trying to talk himself out of a sticky situation fast. Emma spoke through tight lips and shook her head. Then, turning abruptly, she headed straight for the balcony.

Uh-oh, he thought, *trouble in paradise?*

EMMA'S WHOLE BODY burned with embarrassment as she hurried for the nearest sanctuary. She pushed blindly through the glass doors and took in a deep gulp of the cooler air.

He'd had the nerve to introduce the girl. *His fiancée.* Rani—a dusky beauty, heavy on the gold jewellery—had flashed a brand-new sparkle on the third finger of her left hand and said they'd been seeing each other for *over a year.*

While Emma and Wayne had been seeing each other. *Sleeping* with each other.

The bastard.

He'd broken it off with Emma only a month ago. Said it wasn't working for him. No mention then of a fiancée. Obviously this Rani girl had what it took to keep a man interested.

The worst part was that Emma had let her guard down with him. She'd done what she'd sworn she'd never do—she'd fallen for him big time.

Shielded by palm fronds, she leaned over the railing and stared at the traffic below. But she wasn't seeing it—she was too busy trying to patch up the barely healed scars and a bunch of black emotions, like her own stupid gullibility. She'd been used. Deceived. Lied to—

'Emma.'

She jumped at the sound of Jake's voice behind her. Embarrassment fired up again. He must have seen the exchange. No point pretending it hadn't happened. 'Hi.' She ran a palm frond through her stiff fingers. 'I was just talking to an ex.'

'A recent ex, by the look of things.' Warm hands cupped her shoulders and turned her towards him. He lifted her chin with a finger, and his eyes told her he knew a lot more than she wanted him to. 'Should I be sorry?'

She shook her head. 'I'm not very good company right now.' Shrugging off the intimacy of his touch, she looked down at the street again, at the neon signs that lit the restaurants and cafés.

'You didn't answer the question, Em,' he said softly. 'But, if you ask me, I'd say he's not worth being sorry over.'

'Damn right, he's not. That was his *fiancée*. According to her, they've been together over a year.'

'Hmm. I see.'

'Unfortunately for me, I didn't.' She stared at the street. 'We were both busy with work and after-hours commitments, but we always spent Friday nights together.' Frowning, she murmured, 'I wonder how he explained that to her?'

'Friday nights?' There was a beat of silence, then he asked, 'You had, like, a regular slot for him, then?'

She watched a couple strolling arm in arm below them and felt an acute pang of loss. 'We had an understanding.'

'He *understood* that you scheduled him into your working life like some sort of beauty session?'

Her skin prickled. Wayne had actually been the one doing the *scheduling,* and Emma had been so head over heels, so desperate to be with him, she'd gone along with whatever he'd asked. 'He had a busy schedule too.' Obviously. 'But Friday night was ours. And he was cheating all along.'

Why the hell was she telling Jake this? Of all people. She turned to him, dragged up a half-smile from somewhere. 'I'm fine. I was over it weeks ago.'

'That's the way.' He smiled, all easy sympathy, and gave her hand a quick pat. 'The trick is not to take these things too seriously.'

These things? Being in love was just one of *these things?* 'And you'd be the expert at that particular trick, wouldn't you?' She and Wayne had had an understanding. He'd betrayed her and *that was serious*.

To her surprise, he spoke sharply. 'Contrary to what you may think, I don't cheat.'

'Because you're not with a woman long enough.' As if *she* would know his modus operandi these days…she wasn't exactly a social butterfly. She looked up and met Jake's eyes—dark, intense, like Turkish coffee. 'Sorry.' She shrugged. 'It's just that you're here, you're male, and right now I want to punch something. Or someone.' Her gaze flicked down to the street. 'Nothing personal.'

He shoved his hands in his pockets. 'Emma, yesterday—'

'You live your way, I live mine.' She waved him off. 'We're not teenagers any more.'

But was she living her life her way? she wondered as she paced past the balcony's foliage and back. Or was she living for other people?

After her father had died, leaving them virtually penniless, Emma had spent years working menial jobs after school so that they wouldn't have to sell her maternal grandmother's home, and then had supported herself through her studies. Her mother had been diagnosed with clinical depression soon after their father's death, and Stella had taken on the role of main carer, but Emma had been the one with the ultimate financial responsibility.

She didn't mind giving up her time or her money, but her mother was recovered now and Emma's sacrifices went unacknowledged and unappreciated.

And now she'd discovered the man she'd loved had been cheating on her for God knew how long, and in Jake's opinion it was because she was so focused on her work.

But Jake knew nothing about it, and she intended for it to stay that way. It did *not* excuse Wayne. Even the fact that the girl was more exotic than she was, more voluptuous…more everything…was no excuse. She was tempted to run downstairs and tell him what she thought of him, let Rani in on his dirty little secret—except she never wanted to see him again and she'd only make herself look like a fool.

'If nothing else, I expect honesty in a relationship.'

'You call a regular Friday night bonk a *relationship?*' he said.

She met his stare with a defiant stare of her own. 'It suited us.'

'It suited *you.*'

She bit her lip to stop unwanted words from spilling out. 'I thought what we had was what he wanted too.'

'Yeah, I'm sure it was.'

His dry comment riled her further. She rubbed the chill from her arms while inside her the anger and hurt and humiliation burned bright and strong. Better him thinking she was an idiot than knowing the embarrassing truth—that she was a naïve, gullible idiot.

'Sometimes I get so damn tired of doing what everyone else wants. What other people expect…' She trailed off when she saw Wayne and Rani outside an Italian restaurant on the street below. While his *fiancée* studied the menu in the window he glanced up and met Emma's eyes.

Renewed outrage surged through the other emotions in a dark wave. She refused to step back, refused to be the one to break eye contact. How dared he? Their weekly love-in had been a lie. They'd been seeing each other for months and the whole time he'd been deceiving her.

Making a fool of her.

In an uncharacteristic move, she made a rude hand gesture…and it felt good. Especially when Wayne looked away first. She spun away towards Jake, finding an oddly reassuring comfort in his presence. 'And sometimes I just want to live my own life and to hell with everything and everyone.'

'So start now, Em,' he said, his voice gentle yet firm. 'Change your life. Do what you want for a change.'

She stared into those dark eyes holding hers. What *did* she want?

All she saw was Jake.

Every rational thought flew away. Every drop of sense drained out of her as she stepped nearer to him, her eyes only leaving his to drift to his mouth.

What I want…

Before she could warn herself that this was a Really Bad Idea, she launched forward, cupped his jaw between her hands and plastered her lips to his.

Her heart gave a single hard jolt, and a little voice whispered, *This is what I've been waiting for.* The sizzle zapped all the way to her toes and back again before frustration and fury liquefied into heat and hunger. She flung herself into the moment, indulging her senses. The warmth of his mouth against hers was a counterfoil for his cool, refreshing scent—like moss on a pristine forest floor.

Caught off guard, Jake rocked back on his heels before steadying himself, and her, his hands finding purchase on the smooth slope of her hips as he kissed her back.

Emma. Her taste—new and unforgettably sweet. The fragrance of soap and shampoo and woman all wrapped up in the texture of skin-warmed silk beneath his fingers.

She was a rising tornado of emotion and needs, and it whipped around the edges of his own darker desires. The word *complication* lurked somewhere at the back of his mind. He shrugged it away and instead, sliding his palms around to her back, hauled her closer and settled in to savour more of the exquisite sensations battering him.

'Ohh…' The sound was exhaled on a strangled gasp as firm hands pushed at his chest. She jerked out of his hold, eyes wide. 'I didn't… That was…'

'Nice,' he finished for her. His hormone-ravished body protested the gross understatement even as he knew she was just using him to get back at the drivelling idiot probably still watching the performance from the other side of the street.

As quickly as it had blown in the whirlwind subsided leaving only a tantalising whisper as she stared up at him, rolled her lips between her teeth and said, 'I don't know why I…did that.'

'You were upset. I was here.' Enjoying the way her eyes reflected her conflict, he couldn't help but grin. 'Have to tell you it wins hands down over the punch you threatened to dole out earlier.'

'I…need to see if Mum's ready to go home.'

'Emma.' He lifted a hand, dropped it when she

edged farther away. 'Don't beat yourself up. It was just a kiss. And I'm sure Wayne got the message.'

She flinched as if he'd hit her. '*He* wasn't the… He wasn't look— I was… Oh, forget it.'

And in the light filtering through from the restaurant he glimpsed twin spots of colour flag her cheeks before she whirled around and made a dash to the door.

Shoving his hands into his pockets, he leaned a hip against the railing while he waited for his body's horny reaction to subside. *You kiss me like that, honey, I ain't gonna forget.*

It was too bad she'd come to her senses so quickly. He didn't mind being used when it came in the form of a beautiful woman in distress—particularly when the woman had seemed oblivious that she *had,* in fact, used him. He looked down at the street. No sign of the scumbag.

He could still smell Emma; the fresh, untainted fragrance lingered in the air, on his clothes. The flavour of that one luscious kiss still danced on his tastebuds. The surprise of it—of *her*—like the first green sprout emerging from the carnage of a bushfire, still vibrated along his bones. She'd reacted without thinking for a hot and heavy moment there, and he'd enjoyed every second.

So had she.

And he wasn't going to let her forget either. Her weekly love-in arrangement proved she did casual. And she expected honesty from her lover. They had something in common on both counts.

He watched her walk towards a group who were preparing to leave and smiled to himself. The upcoming wedding weekend was looking better and better.

EMMA GULPED IN a calming breath, drew herself tall, and walked unsteadily towards her table, trying not to remember she'd just kissed Jake Carmody senseless. Correction: *she* was the one who was senseless. The dinner left-overs had been cleared away. Only a rumpled and food stained red tablecloth remained. And a few curious faces were aimed her way.

'Emma…' Stella trailed off, her gaze sliding over Emma's shoulder.

The back of Emma's neck warmed. Her cheeks scorched. 'Um…sorry.' Was it possible to speak more than one word at a time? She waved a hand in front of her face. 'Needed some air.'

'We were starting to wonder whether you two had slipped away without—'

'Jake and I were just catching up.' She collected her purse. 'Mum, are you ready to leave? I've got some work to do before I go to bed.' She didn't wait for an answer, moving around the table saying her goodnights.

'Can I get a lift with you?' Stella reached for her own bag. 'Ryan's taking his parents home, and I want a couple of early nights this week.'

'Sure.' Emma steered clear of Jake, muttering a quick goodnight without looking at him, and from a safe distance on the other side of the table, then headed for the stairs.

'You okay, Em?' Stella asked beside her as they drove home. 'You're awfully quiet.'

'Wayne came into the restaurant while we were there,' she said, her voice tightening. 'With his fiancée.'

'Oh. Oh, Em. I'm sorry. You guys split up— what?—only a month ago?'

'What did you expect?' her mother piped up from the back seat. 'If you mixed with the right people like your sister, instead of hiding away in that studio night after night, y—'

'I'm not hiding.' Emma sighed inwardly. Stella had nursed their mother, then fallen in love with a wealthy man; in Bernice Byrne's eyes her younger daughter could do no wrong. 'I enjoy what I do, Mum.'

'Like you enjoyed cleaning other people's toilets and stocking supermarket shelves after school too, I remember. Just another excuse not to meet people.'

Emma pressed her lips together to stop the angry words from rushing out. *Yeah, Mum? Where would we be if I hadn't? In a rented bedsit on the wrong side of town. Not in Gran's home, that's for sure.*

'Mum, that's not fair.' Stella spoke sharply.

'It's not, Stella. But then, life's not always fair— right, Mum?' Emma glanced at her mother in the rearview mirror. 'And sometimes it makes us hurt and lash out and say things we shouldn't. So I forgive you. You're not sorry about Wayne, Stella, and neither am I. And I don't want to talk about it. *Him.*'

'No, you'd rather kiss that good-for-nothing Jake Carmody behind the palms like some floozie,' her mother muttered.

Emma jolted, her whole body burning with the memory. And her mother, of all people, had obviously seen the entire catastrophe. Something close to rebellion simmered inside her and made her say, 'Jake's hardly a good-for-nothing, Mum—he has a well-established practice in business law.' She couldn't help feeling a sense of indignation on his behalf.

The strip club aside, she knew enough about Jake to know he'd worked hard all those years ago, taking jobs where he could get them to pay his way through uni.

Whereas Ryan came from old money. He'd graduated in the sciences and held a PhD in Microbiology—all expenses paid by Daddy. Then he'd volunteered his skills in Africa for a couple of years before hooking up again with Stella.

From the corner of her eye she saw Stella shift in her seat and turn to look at her. Suddenly uncomfortable, Emma lifted a shoulder. 'What?'

'Jake *kissed* you?' she said slowly. 'Like a proper kiss?'

'Not exactly.' Emma couldn't resist a quick glance at her mum in the mirror again. 'Mum got it right. It was more like…I kissed him.' As she relived that moment something like exhilaration shot through her bloodstream. 'What about it?'

'Ooh, that's so…hmm… You and Jake?'

Emma heard the smile in her sister's voice, could almost hear her mind ticking over.

'Wouldn't it be cool if—?'

'*Not* me and Jake. You know him. Every red-blooded female in Sydney knows him. Didn't mean anything.'

'But—'

'No buts.'

'Okay. *But*… The wedding will give you two time to catch up. You liked him well enough when we were younger, I remember.'

'Yeah—in a galaxy far, far away.'

'Not that far, Em. He lives in Bondi now. Only an hour's stroll along the coast…if you feel inclined.'

'I don't. I won't.'

But she couldn't blot him from her mind when she crawled into bed that night. She *had* been looking forward to seeing Jake again, even if it was only to assure herself she was well and truly over him.

But she didn't want to catch up with a seedy strip club owner who used women for his own purposes—both for his personal satisfaction and his burgeoning bank account.

But, oh, that moment of insanity…his lips on hers, his hands tugging her against the heat of his hard, muscled body…

And it *was* insanity. She stared up at the music room's low stained ceiling and tried not to hear the thick elevated thud of her heartbeat in her ears. She could have kept it simple. A friendly few days in the company of a good-looking guy. But she'd kissed him like one of his Brandies or Candies…and she'd changed everything.

CHAPTER FOUR

STIFLING A YAWN, Emma glanced at her watch and wondered if Stella's hen's party would ever end. Twelve-thirty. The male stripper had done his thing and left to raucous feminine laughter and a wildly improper proposition or two over half an hour ago. The girls were now sitting around Emma's table drinking what remained of a bottle of vodka.

Emma had sat on one glass of wine the entire evening. She needed a clear head. She still had half a dozen orders to fill when the others left.

Emma glanced at the bleary-eyed girls in various stages of intoxication as Joni poured the remains of the vodka into her glass and laid the bottle on its side on the table. 'Don't any of you girls have to work in the morning?' she asked.

'It's Friday tomorrow,' Joni said, spinning the bottle lazily between two fingers. 'Nothing gets done on a Friday anyway.'

'Well, I don't want to be a party pooper but I've got work to finish tonight.'

Karina pointed at her. 'You need to get a life,

Emma Dilemma.' She downed her drink, slapped her glass on the table and slurred, 'Seriously. Your hormones must be shrivelling up with neglect. When was the last time you got laid?'

'Kar, give it a rest.' Stella shot Emma a concerned look. 'She broke up with her boyfriend a few weeks ago.'

Karina squinted at Emma through glazed green eyes. 'You had a *boyfriend?*'

Emma could see it in Karina's eyes—*How did you find the time?*—and her whole body tightened. 'He wasn't a boyfriend as such…' She picked up her glass, touched the rim against her lips. 'He was convenient. More like a bed buddy.' Even if Wayne *had* seen their relationship that way, in Emma's book bed buddies didn't cheat. When the gaggle of giggles subsided she angled her glass in Karina's direction. 'You'd be familiar with the concept of bed buddies.'

'Totally.' Karina grinned. 'Way to go, Em,' she enthused, then raised a hand. 'Okay, enough of the true confessions. We're hungry, aren't we, girls? And since you're the only sober one here, Emma Dilemma, how about being a good little bridesmaid and fetching us a burger from that shop down the road?'

'And fries,' Joni added, stuffing another chocolate in her mouth.

'I'll go to the drive-through. It's closer.'

Karina shook her head. 'Nuh-uh. We want real hamburgers with proper meat—not that cardboard stuff.'

'Yeah,' Joni agreed. 'With lashings of bacon.'

Stella leaned to the side and massaged Emma's neck a moment. 'Come on, Em. I *looove* you, sis,' she cajoled in a boozy voice, then pulled her purse from her bag. 'My treat.'

Emma pushed up. Anything for peace. 'Okay. Providing you take your orders and eat them somewhere else. I've got to work.'

'You're a good sport, Em.' Karina stood, slung an arm around Emma's neck. She patted Emma's backside, then grinned hugely. 'Off you go, now.'

'TOLD YOU THEY'D still be awake,' Ryan said as the limo pulled into the Byrnes' driveway.

They'd dropped off the rest of the guys from the bucks' night, but Ry had got it into his head to kiss Stella goodnight before going home, and Jake—well, he was along for the ride. It was his responsibility to ensure nothing happened to Ryan before the big day. It had nothing to do with Emma living here too.

'Not sure they'll appreciate us gatecrashing their evening.' With a few beers under his belt, Jake stretched his long legs out in front of him. He'd assured Stella he'd look out for Ryan, and he'd done a pretty good job. He glanced at the slightly worse-for-wear groom-to-be. Mostly. Then he looked down to the well-lit studio. 'What do you suppose the girls get up to on a hens' night?'

'We're about to find out.' Ryan was already fumbling with the door.

'Steady, mate. I promised Stella I'd get you home in one piece.'

'Whoa…' Ryan murmured as the limo's lights swept an arc across the driveway, whitewashing the unexpected view of a female figure half-in, half-out of a car. 'Nice arse.'

Jake blinked at the flash of leggings-clad backside poking out of the open door, then took his time to admire the slender thighs and shapely calves rising from a pair of silver stilettos. A spark of interest danced along his veins. 'Careful,' he murmured with a grin. 'You're practically a married man.'

'Doesn't mean I'm dead.'

But Jake's attention had focused on what looked like a neon sticker in the shape of a hand on the girl's backside. 'What *is* that?' He squinted. The words *Pat Me* glittered in gold. 'Don't mind if I do,' he murmured, still grinning. His grin faded. 'Isn't that Emma's car?'

'Reckon you're right.' Both men looked at each other. '*Emma?*'

They turned back to see her unfurling from the car's depths. Dropping a loose soda can into the carton on her hip, she righted herself only to freeze in the headlights like a stunned, lanky-legged gazelle.

Incredulous, Jake felt his whole body tense as he took in the view. *Hot.* Over the leggings she wore a slinky white sleeveless top with a scooped neckline, blanched in the glare and highlighting enough curves to start her own Grand Prix.

'Eyes off, buddy.' He cleared his suddenly dry throat. 'She's about to become your sister-in-law.'

But Jake wasn't honour-bound by any such restriction. Eyes still feasting on the mouthwatering sight, he unfolded himself and climbed out, leaning an elbow on the open door. Cool air hit him. He could smell burgers.

'Emma. Wow.'

He gave himself a mental kick up the backside. *Well said.* Spoken like a freaking teenager. Where the hell were his sophisticated, urbane conversational skills? But his brain didn't seem to be functioning because all his blood had drained below his belt.

She seemed to come out of her daze, eyes widening as they met his. 'You're not supposed to be here,' she said, tight-lipped, as she turned and headed for the door at a rate of knots.

'Careful…' he called. Too late—he was already moving forward as he saw her stiletto bend and her ankle crumple. He heard her swear before she landed on that watch-worthy rear end in front of him, the carton she'd been carrying landing beside her.

Ryan rescued the carton with a muffled, 'I'll get Stella,' and made his escape as Jake squatted beside her. 'Emma?' He reached for her elbows. 'Are you okay?'

Emma groaned, but not nearly as much from the pain shooting up her calf as from her spectacular fall from grace in front of *this* man. She felt Jake's hands on her, his warm breath washing over her face, and closed her eyes. 'Just let me die now.'

She heard that rich caramel chuckle of his. He had both her shoes off before she could stop him. Gentle fingers probed her ankle, and a voice laced with calm concern and a hint of amusement said, 'So this is what you girls get up to on hen nights. Ry and I were wondering.'

She started to shuffle away from him but felt her leggings snag on the rough cement. She heard a strange sound, like Velcro parting, and stopped abruptly. 'I'm okay,' she said, gritting her teeth. Or she would be if she didn't die of embarrassment first. 'Now go away.'

He moved around behind her, slid his hands beneath her arms and hauled her upright so that his body was in intimate contact with her back. His big, hot *masculine* body. Her practically naked back. And nothing but thin torn jersey between her bare bottom and his…pelvis. Liquid heat spurted into her cheeks, along her limbs and everywhere their bodies touched.

'I told you I'm fine.' She tried to shrug away from the intimate contact but he didn't budge.

'Test your weight on it,' he ordered.

Her ankle tweaked when she set it on the ground but she stifled a wince and said, 'See? Fine.'

'Yeah, I can see.'

Ryan and the girls spilled out of the studio just as Jake swept her up into his arms. In an automatic reaction she clutched at his shoulders, and for an instant of lunacy she wallowed in the strength and heat surrounding her.

Being held against Jake's chest and carried inside was like being lifted into the clouds. She gazed up at his square shadow-stubbled chin. And just above that were…those lips.

Instant tension gripped her insides and refused to let go. Had she so quickly forgotten she'd kissed those lips? And *how?* That she'd flung herself at this man in an instant of heightened emotion was going to have to live with the reminder for the rest of her life? Or until after the wedding at least.

'It's going to be okay, Stella, don't worry,' she told her sister as Jake set her on the saggy old couch. Right now she was more concerned with that ripping sound she'd heard. 'Pass me that sarong on the armchair, will you?'

'Are you chilled?' Stella said, her voice anxious. 'Do you want a blanket or something?'

'No—and stop hovering.'

Stella pulled the sarong off the chair. 'I'm not hovering.'

'Are too.' She grabbed the proffered garment. 'Thank you.'

'Um… Before I go, I should tell you that Karina…um…' She exchanged a look with Jake, who shook his head.

Emma darted a glance between the two of them. 'What?'

Stella let out a strangled sound behind her hand. 'Never mind.'

Squatting in front of Emma, Jake prodded her ankle and began issuing orders. 'Get rid of the girls, Stella. And then you might like to kiss your fiancé goodnight and send him on his way.'

Hearing their cue to leave in that no-nonsense masculine tone, the girls scuttled out with muffled giggles.

Panic rose up Emma's throat. 'No, stay, Stell. Let Jake go.' She glared at him, winding the sarong about her torso as high as possible under her arms. 'I bet he has a million things to do.'

He met Emma's eyes full-on for a few seconds, then studied her foot again. 'Some ice would be good here, Stella, before you go.'

Seconds later Stella produced a pack of frozen peas from Emma's fridge, handed it to Jake. 'I feel responsible...'

'Don't,' Emma said, tight-lipped. 'If these guys hadn't turned up everything would've been all right.'

'So this guy'll take care of it.' Easing the improvised cold pack around Emma's ankle, Jake waved her sister off. 'You have guests to see off and a fiancé to farewell. You've called the girls a taxi, right?'

Stella nodded.

'Okay, go to bed.'

'If you're sure...' Stella's eyes flicked between the two of them.

Emma couldn't decide whether there was a glint of something playful in her sister's baby blue eyes, but her voice was concerned enough when she said, 'Phone up to the house if you need anything, Em.'

Then she disappeared outside with the rest of the gang, leaving Emma alone with Jake. The voices faded and the bustling atmosphere disappeared, leaving a tension-fraught anticipation in the gaping stillness. So still that Emma could hear the nearby surf pounding the beach. The sound of her heart beating at a million miles an hour. Jake had to be able to hear it as well. Fantastic. She groaned inwardly.

'But you have to go too,' she told him. 'The limo…'

'I can call him back. He's booked and paid for till 3:00 a.m.' His voice lowered a notch. 'Unless you want me to stay longer?'

His head was bent over her foot so she couldn't see his eyes. Just the top of his glossy dark head and those impressive shoulders making the fabric of his sexy black shirt strain at the seams. Before she could tell him no, not on his life, he straightened.

'It doesn't seem to be swollen. You sure that's the only casualty?'

'Yes.' In his line of work he might see more than his fair quota of bare backsides, but he wasn't going to see hers. She squeezed her still smarting butt and trembling thighs tighter together. 'I can take care of myself.'

'It's not your cute *derrière* I'm interested in right now, Emma,' he said, and she wondered if she'd voiced her thoughts. *And what did he mean 'right now?'*

Her cheeks flamed and she pushed the frozen pack of peas away. 'I can walk.' Holding the edges of the sarong together, she rose, ignoring the glint of pain in her ankle, and took three tentative steps. 'See? Now I want to go to bed. I appreciate your concern, but I'd like it if you'd leave.'

He ignored her. 'You should rest it. You need to be fit for Saturday.' He picked her up again and moved swiftly across the room and past the privacy curtain. He set her on her bed, laid the peas against her ankle again, then placed his hands on either side of her lower legs. Looked into her eyes. 'And, remember, as best man I've got the first dance with you.'

He'd come to her rescue and allowed her to keep her dignity. And now he sounded so genuinely caring that a wry half-smile tugged at her mouth.

'With you to remind me I'm not likely to forget.' She had to admit it felt good to be pampered for once in her life, to have someone care enough to look out for her and not even remotely laugh at her embarrassment. She relaxed a little. 'Thank you. I feel like a kid again. All I need is the warm milk and honey.'

'Warm milk and honey?'

'Mum's panacea for everything. Rather, it used to be.' *Twenty years ago.*

Jake knew Emma had always been a keep-to-yourself kind of girl, whereas outgoing, fun-loving Stella had made friends easily. He knew, too, how Emma had changed when her father had died.

Leaning in, he watched her gorgeous eyes widen, smelled her soft feminine scent. 'No milk and honey, but this—' he touched his lips chastely to her forehead '—might help.'

He heard the barely-there hitch in her breath and drew back. His gaze dropped to her mouth and lingered. Unglossed but luscious. So tempting to lean down and… He felt his blood pressure spike. His good deed damn well wasn't helping *him*.

Don't. Her lips moved but no sound came out.

'Why not?' he murmured. 'You kissed me the other night and I can't return the favour?'

'That was…different.' Her voice was breathless and he got the impression she'd have pressed her rigid spine through the wall if she could.

'Yeah,' he said, recalling the firestorm which had engulfed them both for one unguarded moment. 'It was.'

'It was impulsive and selfish and I used you.'

Straightening up, he looked at her eyes, almost violet in the dim light from the single naked globe above the bed. 'I didn't mind. And, if we're being honest here, you didn't mind either.' He saw colour bleed into her cheeks and patted her leg. 'Take it from me, Surfer Boy wasn't right for you.'

'And you'd know that how…?' She stared at him out of soulful eyes. 'I sure as heck don't know Jake Carmody. You work in the sex industry.' Her voice rose with disapproval. 'You *own* that…that place. So you… It follows naturally that you're not ashamed to use and exploit women—often women with no other choices—to make money. And it's just *wrong,*' she went on. 'Does—?'

'I didn't buy the strip club. I inherited the place when Earl died.'

She frowned. 'Earl? Who's Earl?'

'My father.'

'Oh…' A slow exhalation of breath accompanied

the word. She curled her fingers beneath her chin. 'So…your dad owned it.'

'Not "dad". That word implies some sort of familial bond and there wasn't any.' He refused to allow regret to intrude on his life. He didn't need family. He didn't need anyone. 'And before you say I should shut it down and walk away and there'd be one less sleazy club in King's Cross I have the staff to consider. I've found a potential buyer but we're negotiating; I want to ensure a fair deal for everyone.'

'Oh. Yes. Of course. I…' She trailed off, and maybe her eyes softened, but he couldn't be sure because for once in his life he wasn't really seeing the woman in front of him.

He scratched the niggling sensation at the back of his neck that he'd learned long ago to recognise as insecurity. He hadn't felt it in years. He made his own rules, controlled his circumstances, his life. Himself. Always.

Not this time.

He clenched his jaw against the feeling that the rules had suddenly changed and his life was veering off course. And he might have left then but for Emma's soft voice.

'Your mother…is she…?'

'She lives in South America. She doesn't keep in touch.' After nearly two decades, her abandonment still had the power to slice at his heart. He'd always made a point of not getting personally involved in other people's lives because it would involve opening up his own.

'Do you have any siblings to help? Extended family?'

'No.'

'That must be tough for you, handling everything on your own.'

He shrugged dismissively. 'I'm a tough guy.' It was baggage he'd left behind years ago and he wasn't going there. Not for anyone.

She nodded slowly and smoothed the sarong over her legs. 'Look, I'm sorry if I sounded over the top, it's just that I have very firm thoughts about men who use women for their own purposes.'

He knew she was thinking of Surfer Boy. 'Acknowledged and understood.'

'Still, I am sorry about your dad…I can see it hurt you. If you wa—'

'Okay. Let's leave it at that.'

'So…um… How did it go with the guys' night?' She didn't seem in such a hurry to kick him out now, and he didn't know whether that was a good thing or not.

'Ry may need me to remind him tomorrow that he had a good time.'

'Did it include a visit to King's Cross by any chance?'

'Every bucks' night worth its mettle has to include a stop somewhere in King's Cross.' Unfortunately. He must be the only straight guy in Sydney who didn't find striptease a turn-on.

'Well, we girls enjoyed our own private stripper right here.' With a theatrical flick of her hair she drew her knees up to her chest, tucking the edges of the sarong beneath her feet.

'And how did that go?'

'Man, he was *hot.*' The instant the words were out her hands rushed to her cheeks. 'I've never seen a guy strip…well, not that way.' She sucked in her lips. Her cheeks were pink beneath her hands.

'Am I detecting a double standard here?' He couldn't resist teasing her. 'Okay for the girls to look but not the guys?'

'Oops!' Her pearl-tipped nails moved to her lips. 'Can I say I didn't look?'

'Afraid not.' He leaned closer. 'I have to tell you, you looked hot too, last night, in that sexy little number.'

Her smile, when it appeared, was a delight to behold. 'It *was* fun dressing up and feeling attractive for a change.'

'You should try it more often.'

'Try what?' Her smile disappeared. Her hands fell away from her face. A shadow flickered in her eyes—a blue moon sinking into an inky sea—as she crossed her arms and hugged her shoulders. 'Looking attractive? Gee, thanks heaps.'

'Fun, Emma. Just try having some fun.' He was barely aware that his hands had somehow moved towards her thighs, so close he could feel the heat from her body, and barely caught himself in time.

He jerked back and away. Pushed to his feet. If he stayed he was just un-sober enough to show her something about having fun…and he didn't want to think about the consequences if he did.

Not tonight.

'Since you don't seem to need me for anything, I'm going to see if I can catch up with Ry after all. I haven't heard the limo leave yet.' He didn't know what demon prompted him to add, 'The night's still young. Might as well enjoy my evening off…'

He winked—he *never* winked—leaving Emma staring wide-eyed at him as he lifted a hand, then turned and walked away. ''Night.'

He let himself out and headed towards the limo at the top of the drive. He needed the brisk evening air to cool his groin. So much for keeping his past where it belonged. He'd moved on, made something of himself. Until Earl had died and all the old bad had rushed back.

He didn't need Emma messing with his head, trying to make everything all right. Maybe he should just keep things as they were. Acquaintances. Casual friends.

He came to an abrupt halt. Except…now he'd tasted her on his lips, enjoyed the slippery slide of her lithe womanly body against his. Seen and felt her respond as a woman did to a man she fancied…

Friends, *hell*. It was too late for that.

CHAPTER FIVE

'DID YOU EVER see such a view?' Emma leaned over
the balcony outside the room she was sharing with
Stella for the night. 'You sure know how to pick
a wedding venue. It's like some god has spread a
knobbly green carpet over the Grand Canyon, then
sprayed it with a fine indigo mist.'

'It helps that one of Ryan's uncles owns the place,'
her sister said cheerily behind her.

Nestled on the edge of the escarpment at Echo
Point, in the famous Blue Mountains west of Sydney,
the exclusive boutique hotel was pure luxury. The
majestic view of Jamieson Valley stretched out below
them, equally breathtaking. As evening approached,
soft golden light coloured the sky. Inky pools were
swallowing up the valley floor, and the sun's last rays
hammered the streaks of exposed rock with vermil-
ion, carving deep purple shadows between.

Stella joined Emma at the balcony's wooden rail.
'The guys won't be seeing anything like this where
they are.'

'No,' Emma murmured, drawing her tracksuit jacket closer as the air chilled. The guys and Ryan's parents were spending the night at a cosy little bed and breakfast in Katoomba, a two-minute drive away. 'But I'm sure they'll find something to entertain them.' Her tone was more caustic than she'd intended.

She was still brooding over the way Jake had swaggered out of the studio last night. She couldn't stop wondering what he'd got up to afterwards. Her fingers tightened on the cool wood. He'd *winked* at her. She knew exactly what he'd got up to.

And why on earth was she tying herself up in knots over it? It was precisely the kind of behaviour that reminded her that he had been, and obviously still was, a chick magnet. And why he was such a knee-buckling, sigh-worthy *experienced* kisser…

'So, Stella.' Forcing him from her thoughts, she linked arms with her sister and guided her back to the little glass table. 'Ryan can't wait for tomorrow. He's going to make a wonderful husband, and you're going to have lots of babies and live happily ever after, the way you always dreamed.'

She picked up their Cosmopolitan cocktails and offered a toast. 'To your last night as a single woman.'

As she sipped, Emma's gaze drifted inside, through the floor-to ceiling glass doors, to the two four-poster double beds with their embroidered snowy white covers and mountains of soft lace pillows.

Ryan's parents had footed the bill for the entire wedding and the wedding party's accommodation here tomorrow night. Ryan was their only child, and for them this extravagance was a drop in the ocean.

'You're marrying money, Stell. We might have been rich too if Dad hadn't made those bad investments just before he died.'

Stella nodded. 'Yeah, Mum never got over losing her inheritance that way.'

'She never got over *Dad.*' Even now their mother was in her own beautifully appointed room down the hall, alone. 'She let him destroy her,' Emma went on. 'Even beyond the grave she's still letting him colour her life grey.'

Emma reminded herself that she wanted no part of that pain. Wayne had temporarily clouded her vision with his good looks and smooth-talking charm, but now she saw everything through the crystal-clear lens of experience. No man would ever have that power over her again.

Stella set her glass down and touched Emma's hand. 'You've kept us together all these years with a roof over our heads and I want to thank you—'

'It was my responsibility as the elder sister to keep us safely off the streets.' She shook her head. 'You looked out for Mum—I had it easy compared to you. But I wanted a career too. All you ever wanted was to find the right man and get married.'

'Yeah.' Stella sighed. Then she smiled, her face aglow with a bride's radiance. 'But now I'm marrying Ryan I'll be in a position to help out. I've already decided—'

'Stella—'

'He and I have discussed it.'

'For Mum, then. Not for me.'

Stella met her eyes. 'You don't want to give away a bit of that independence and find someone to love and share your life with some day?'

'Love? No.' Because Stella's question had unsettled her, she cupped her suddenly cold hands beneath her armpits. 'I prefer lust. Less complicated.'

'You're hurting after what happened with Wayne,' her sister said gently, 'and that's okay because—'

'I told you last night. It was lust, not love.'

'Bed buddies?' Stella murmured, then shook her head. 'I don't believe you for one minute, Em. And I don't care what you say. You *do* want love somewhere down the track when you're over the love rat. I remember when we were kids and used to talk about the men we were going to marry. Your man had to own a house by the sea, he had to love animals, 'cos Mum refused to let us have pets and he had to own a cupcake shop.'

Emma smiled at her childish fantasies. 'What about your ivory castle?'

'We're staying in one in France.' Stella hugged her drink close to her chest. 'Not ivory, but a real medieval castle with its own resident ghost.'

Emma heard the signal for an incoming text and dug her phone out of her pocket to read the screen.

'*How's the view where U R? J*'

She frowned as a butterfly did a single loop in her stomach. She texted back: '*Glorious.*'

Setting the phone on the table, she reached for her drink and considered switching the thing off. She needed a clear head for tomorrow, and interacting with Jake beforehand—in any way, shape or form—wouldn't do her any favours.

A moment later another text appeared. '*Did U bring work?*'

She sipped her drink and looked at her phone a moment before answering: '*Yes.*'

Seemed he wasn't put off by her one-word texts, because the next one appeared a moment later.

'*Not allowed. This weekend is about having fun.*'

Fun and Jake…? A shiver tingled down her spine. He was a man who definitely knew how to have fun. She texted back: '*Is she a blonde?*'

'*I have a certain brunette in mind. Meet me downstairs 4 a drink.*'

The shiver spread to her limbs. '*Spending evening with sister. Remember her? 2moro's bride.*' She switched her phone off, shoved it back in her pocket.

'Who are you texting?'

'Jake.' She threw Stella an accusatory glance.

'Anything wrong?'

'He asked me to meet him for a drink.' She felt Stella's gaze and looked away, out over the darkening valley and the gold-rimmed purple clouds in the distance.

'Something you're not telling me, here?' Stella asked behind her.

'No.' She had the niggling feeling she was being set up by her sister.

'Jake likes women, but he's a good guy. Nothing like the love rat. He's not into commitment right now and, as you've clearly pointed out, neither are you… so are you going?'

'Of course not.' She turned around and met her sister's scrutiny full-on. Stella had a half-smile on her lips, as if she didn't quite believe her. Emma glared back. 'This is our last night together—you and me.' And she wanted to place some orders and research some alternative suppliers on her laptop at some stage.

'Well, I'm going to have a long soak in that to-die-for spa tub.' Stella rose, collected their glasses and walked towards the door. 'I won't miss you for an hour or so if you want to change your mind.'

'Nope.' Emma followed her in. 'I've got my music to keep me company.' So much for placing orders. Right now she couldn't remember a single item she needed, and music seemed a more soothing option.

The hotel's phone rang as Emma closed the balcony's glass doors and Stella stretched out on her bed to pick up. 'This is the bride's room,' she announced, with a bounce in her voice. 'You're speaking to the bride, who's just about to enjoy her own candlelit spa bath.' She grinned over at Emma, then rolled onto her back, listening to whoever was on the other end of the phone. 'Uh-huh. In the lobby. Ten minutes. Okay.'

Emma's pulse blipped. She sat on her own bed and unravelled her earphones. 'No.'

'But it's Ryan.' She hugged the phone to her chest. 'The guys had Chinese take-out and he has a fortune cookie for me—isn't that sweet of him?'

'It's not sweet, Stell, it's subterfuge.' Emma lay back and closed her eyes. 'Jake put him up to this, and I'll bet you your fortune cookie that it's Jake, not Ryan, down there.'

'Please, Em. You have to go to make sure. I can't see him now before the ceremony. It's bad luck.'

'And Ryan would *know* that.'

'*Pleeease?*'

'Fine,' she huffed, and sat up, clipping her iPod to her jacket.

'She said fine,' Stella told her caller, and hung up then grinned. 'Thanks, bridesmaid.'

Emma grabbed an elastic band from the nightstand and dragged her hair back into a tight ponytail. 'Only for you, and only because it's your wedding day tomorrow. Then I'm going for a run.'

'Take your time,' she heard Stella call as Emma let herself out of the room and headed for the stairs.

JAKE DISCONNECTED WITH a satisfied grin. 'You don't need me for a while, do you, Ry? She said yes.'

Ryan was stretched out on the couch, checking out their honeymoon destination on his tablet PC but he glanced up as Jake pulled on a clean T-shirt. 'You're a sneaky devil.'

'Make that *smart* and sneaky.' He stuffed his wallet in his jeans. 'And your fiancée's as much to blame as me.'

'Then she's a sneaky devil too.' He tapped the screen. 'I don't know why I'm marrying her.'

Jake grinned and waggled his brows. 'Having second thoughts? It's not too late to back out, you know.'

'Ah, but the reception's paid for. Why waste good grog?'

'There's that.' His humour fading, Jake sat down on the end of the couch and studied his best mate. 'Seriously, Ry. Why the big commitment?'

Ry looked up, and Jake saw the furrows of concentration in his mate's brow smooth out and the corners of his mouth tip up. 'When you meet the woman you want to spend the rest of your life with you'll know why.'

'But *married?*' Jake mentally shuddered at the word. 'Why would you want to spend your life with one woman? Man wasn't meant to be monogamous.'

'Says who?'

'I read it in an article. Somewhere. A reputed scientific journal, if I remember right.'

'Okay, well, *this* man's monogamous.' Ry resumed tapping his screen.

'Maybe *now,*' Jake said. 'I remember when you and those twins—'

'Past history. I was at uni and Stell and I weren't seeing each other then.'

'But how do you *know* she's the one?'

Ry's finger paused. 'When I saw my children in her eyes I knew.'

Jake stared at the guy he'd thought he knew. 'Crikey, mate—break out the violins.'

Ry squinted at something on the screen, slid a finger over its surface. 'Just because you're not into the matrimonial thing doesn't mean others aren't.'

'Fair dinkum—*your children in her eyes?*'

Ry looked up, a lopsided grin on his face. 'Yeah. We want kids. A whole bunch of 'em.' His expression sobered. 'I guess the bottom line is I love Stella. For better or worse. I don't want to imagine my life without her.'

Jake didn't want to imagine a life without women either. But *one* woman for ever? Absolutely for worse. But a curious sensation gripped his chest, as if somehow Ryan had betrayed their friendship and left him standing on the outside looking in.

'So, are you going to tell me why you're playing sneaky devil?' Ry asked, his eyes focused on the screen once more.

Jake rose to hunt up the keycard for the room. 'Because the girl needs a kick up that seriously sexy backside—'

'Which I didn't notice, remember?'

'Yeah, I remember.' Something that might feel like possessiveness—if he were the type—clawed at the back of his neck. He didn't care for the sensation and rubbed it away, swiping the keycard from the bottom of his bed. 'She needs to come out of that shell she's been living in for the past however many years. There's more to life than work.'

Ry looked up, expression thoughtful. 'And you're going to be the one to show her? Careful. That's Emma you're talking about—she's not just any woman. And she's my future sister-in-law.'

'I'm aware of that,' he muttered, fighting the scowl that came from out of nowhere to lurk just beneath the surface of his skin. He planted a grin on his face and grabbed his jacket. 'Trust me.'

The moment the door shut behind him his smile dropped away, his own words echoing in his ears. Problem was, could he trust *himself?* But from the moment Emma Byrne had walked into the club in that sexy red coat, those blue eyes smoking and sparking with every challenge known to man, he'd not been able to think past getting her naked. He'd never intended acting on it—he liked his women without prickles, after all—but then there'd been that kiss at the restaurant… Sparks that hot demanded at least some sort of exploration.

He decided to walk the short distance to sample autumn's crisp mountain air. Cold. Bracing. Invigorating. Mind-numbing. Just what he needed. His breath puffed in front of him as he strode along Katoomba Street towards the girls' hotel.

After tomorrow it would never be the same between him and Ry again. He passed a warmly lit café, packed with Friday-evening diners, and hunched deeper into the warmth of his jacket. It reminded him that back in that room with Ry he'd felt…shut out. As if Ry was about to join a club Jake wasn't eligible for. Would never be eligible for.

Clenching his teeth against the chill, he crunched through a pile of autumn leaves, sending them scattering and twirling along the pavement in noisy abandon. He didn't want to join the matrimonial club.

Shut out.

His mother had shut him out of her life too. 'You look just like your father,' she'd accused her five-year-old son.

Jake was reminded of that every time he looked in a mirror. She'd left her cheating husband and young look-alike child for a new life and a new marriage. Rejected him—her own flesh and blood.

And, yeah, he might be his father's spitting image—but had he inherited Earl's genes? He'd learned a lot about women in his formative years. After all, how many kids got to grow up in the back room of a strip club? With the smell of cheap perfume and sex in their cramped living arrangements. Falling asleep to carnal sounds through his tiny bedroom's paper-thin walls.

As a teenager blocking out those same sounds while trying to finish homework, because he'd known that to escape the place, to take control of his life and become a better man than his father, he needed to study.

Jake knew how to have a good time. A good time involved no strings, no stress. No emotion. Was he like his father in more ways than looks? He clenched his jaw as he turned a corner and the hotel came into view. *Shoot me now.*

He picked up his pace. Earl had used women, whereas Jake respected his partners. The women he associated with were professional career types more often than not—unlike Earl's. They were confident, intelligent and attractive, and they understood where he was coming from. He made it clear up front that he wasn't into any long-term commitment deals and they didn't expect more than he wanted to give.

It was honest, at least.

EMMA WAS BRACED to see Jake, not Ryan, waiting in the lobby. So she took the three flights of stairs rather than the elevator. Deliberately slowly. Admiring the delicate crystal lighting along the hallway, the local landscape paintings on the walls as she reached the top of the ground floor. The thick black carpet emblazoned with the hotel's gold crest.

But seeing Jake standing at the base of the sweeping staircase as she descended, one bronzed hand on the newel post, dark hair gleaming beneath the magnificent black chandelier, with his jacket slung over his shoulder like some sort of designer-jeans-clad Rhett Butler…

Her hand was gliding along the silky wooden banister or her legs might have given out. She might even have sighed like Scarlett; she couldn't be sure. She was too busy shoring up her defences against those dark eyes and the heart-winning smile. Because she knew in that instant that this man could be the one with the power to undo her.

Slowing halfway down, she leaned a hip against the staircase, sucked in a badly needed breath. *Stay cool,* she told herself. *Cool and aloof and annoyed.* He thought he'd tricked her into coming but she knew better. Didn't she? She frowned to herself. She was here, after all.

Because Stella had asked her.

Right. Straightening, she resumed her descent, concentrating on not tripping over her feet, her eyes drawn to him no matter how hard she tried to look away. That sinner's smile and those darker-than-sin eyes…

'Are you feeling all right?' he asked when she reached the bottom step.

She looked at him warily. 'Why wouldn't I?'

'You looked as if you were swaying there for a second or two. I thought you were going to swoon, and then I'd have been forced to play the hero again.'

'I did not sway. Or swoon. And you are *not* my hero. I'm guessing there are no fortune cookies either.'

He grinned. 'You're guessing wrong.' He took her elbow, led her across the glittering marbled foyer.

At intervals floor-to-ceiling glass columns illuminated from within threw up a clear white light. He stopped by a little coffee table with two cosy leather armchairs. 'Sit.'

She did, gratefully, sinking into the soft black leather.

He pulled two scraps of paper from his jeans pocket, checked them both, then placed one on her lap.

'This isn't a fortune cookie.'

'I have to admit Ry and I ate them. But we saved you girls the messages.'

She unrolled the little square. '"A caress is better than a career".' Where the heck had he found *that* little gem? 'Says who? *And* it would depend on who's doing the caressing.'

But her traitorous thoughts could imagine Jake's warm, wicked hands wandering over her bare skin… Lost in the fantasy for a pulse-pounding moment, she stared unseeingly at the paper in front of her. *For heaven's sake.*

She forced her head up, regarded him with serene indifference. 'This isn't from a fortune cookie. You made these yourselves.'

He spread his hands on his thighs, all innocence. 'Why would I do that?'

'To get me downstairs, perhaps?'

His smile came out like sunshine on a cold day. 'You have to admit it's inventive.'

'Deceptive, more like.'

'Hey, Ry has to take some of the credit.'

She felt the smile twitch at the corner of her mouth. 'What does Stella's say?'

'"Two souls, one heart". Appropriately romantic, Ry thought.'

And Cool Hand Jake didn't, obviously. 'She'll probably sleep with it under her pillow tonight.' Desperate to distance herself from his enticing woodsy scent and the thought of those coolly efficient hands on her heated body, she pulled her earphones out of her tracksuit pocket. 'Okay, now that's out of the way I'm off for a run.'

'Not so fast.' He reached over, circling her forearm in a loose grip. 'You're going to say you've got soap orders to type up or some such rubbish when you get back. Right?'

Right. If she could only remember what... The heat of his hand seemed to be blocking her ability to process simple thought. 'I—'

'To avoid me.'

She swallowed down a gasp. He was flying too close to the truth, and it threw her for a loop. 'Why would you matter th—?'

'You know it. I know it.' Cutting her off, he leaned forward, his hold tightening a fraction, his eyes boring into hers. 'Admit it.'

'Why?' Little spots of heat were breaking out all over her body.

'I matter to you.' He smiled—grinned, actually—

teeth gleaming white in the light. 'How much do I matter, Emma?'

She pushed a hand over the crown of her head, her mind a jumble. 'Stop it. You're confusing me. This is the last evening I'll see my sister before she gets married. I...I'm going to spend the evening with her—a maid of honour thing.'

'Of course. And you can. In a little while.' His thumb abraded the inside of her wrist, sending tiny tingles scuttling up her arm. 'She won't mind,' he continued in that same liquid caramel tone. 'In fact I'm betting she's enjoying her soak in the spa right now.'

'It *was* you on the phone.'

'Guilty.' He grinned again, totally unrepentant. As if he pulled that kind of stunt all the time to bend women to his will. 'She's confiscated your laptop, by the way.'

'*What?*'

'Your sister agrees with me that you need time out from work.'

She gaped at him, incredulous. 'You two discussed my *needs?*' The image popped into her mind before she could call it back, along with the overly explicit, overly stressed word, and the whole calamity hung thick in the air like a sultry evening.

His eyes turned a warmer shade of dark. 'Not all of them. But we'll get to that. Stella wants you to enjoy her wedding, not be distracted by orders and schedules. She's concerned about you. And frankly—'

'What do you mean, "we'll get to that"? Get to what?' Her voice rose on a crescendo. A couple of heads turned their way.

'This isn't the place,' he murmured, his voice all the quieter for her raised one.

Changing his grip, he pulled her up before she could mutter any sound of protest. He was so close she could feel the heat emanating from his body, could smell expensive leather jacket and freshly showered male skin.

'The place?' she echoed. 'Place for what?'

He entwined his fingers with hers. 'Why don't we take a walk and find out?'

CHAPTER SIX

EMMA BLINKED UP at him through her eyelashes. It took her a scattered moment to realise she was still holding her earphones in her free hand and that her other hand was captured by the biggest, warmest hand it had ever come into contact with. She told herself she didn't want to be holding his hand...but who was she kidding but herself?

'*Run,*' she managed, pulling out of his grasp. 'I was going for a *run.*' And if she was sensible she'd keep running all the way back to Sydney.

'I'll join you.'

She glanced at his leather jacket and casual shoes, deliberately bypassing the interesting bits in between. 'You're hardly dressed for it.'

'I'll try to keep up.' *His* gaze cruised down her body like a slow boat on a meandering river, all the way to her well-worn sneakers. 'What about your ankle?'

'It's fine.' He'd be offering to carry her next, so she conceded defeat. 'Okay, we'll walk.' Stuffing her earphones back in her pocket, she accompanied him outside and onto the street.

The air had a cold bite and an invigorating eucalypt scent that called to her senses, and she breathed deep.

'I saw a little café on the way here,' he suggested.

'I didn't come to the mountains to be shut in a stuffy café with a bunch of city slickers up for the weekend.'

'Of which we're two,' he pointed out.

'I want to see the Three Sisters by night and sample some mountain air. Come on, it's a ten-minute walk to Echo Point.'

He took her hand again. 'What are we waiting for?'

They followed the hotel wall that enclosed the beautiful garden where tomorrow's ceremony would take place until it gave way to bushland fenced off from the road. Beyond, the ground fell away more than two hundred metres to the valley floor. Neither talked, but a feeling of camaraderie settled between them. Both were absorbed in the mutual appreciation of their surroundings.

The minute the famous Three Sisters rock formation came into view Emma came to an awed stop. 'Wow.' She hung back from the main vantage point where a few tourists were milling about, unwilling to share the moment with strangers.

Floodlit, the Sisters gleamed a rich gold against the black velvet backdrop, surrounding trees catching the light and providing a lacy emerald frame. The never-ending sky blazed with stars.

She sighed, drinking in the sight. 'Aren't you glad we didn't go for coffee?'

'That first glimpse always packs a punch, that's for sure.'

His voice rumbled through her body and she realised he'd let go of her hand while she'd been taking in the view and was now standing behind her, his chin on top of her head.

'Did you know the Aboriginal Dreaming story tells us there were three brothers who fell in love with three sisters from another tribe and were forbidden to marry?' She hugged her elbows, and it seemed natural to lean back into Jake's warmth.

In response, a pair of rock-solid arms slid around to the front of her waist. 'Go on. I'm sure there's more.'

'A battle ensued, and when the men tried to capture them, a tribal elder turned the maidens into stone to protect them.'

'And right there,' he drawled lazily, 'you're viewing a lesson to be heeded about the dangers of love and marriage.'

She turned within the circle of his arms. 'The sad thing is the sisters had no say in any of it.'

'But you do,' he murmured against her brow. And bent his head.

Warm breath caressed her skin and her heart began to pound in earnest. He was going to kiss her… And she wasn't in a fit state to be running anywhere.

Her legs trembled and her mind turned to mush as anticipation spun through her and she looked up. His face was so close she could feel the warmth of his skin, could see its evening shadow of stubble. He had the longest, darkest eyelashes she'd ever seen on a man. And his eyes…had she ever seen such eyes? As bottomless as the yawning chasm they'd come to view.

Then a half-moon slid from behind a cloud, bathing his perfect features in silver, as if the gods had hammered him so.

'You can tell me no.' He loosened his hold around her waist slightly. 'Right here in front of the Sisters you can exercise your free will as a modern woman. Push me away if you want. Or you can accept what we've been tiptoeing around for the past few days and kiss me.'

'Tiptoeing?' she whispered. 'I haven't—'

'And it's time it stopped.'

'Kiss you…?' Her words floated into the air on a little white puff as she looked up into his eyes. Dark and deep and direct. Had he mentioned free will? Her will had suddenly gone AWOL; she'd felt it drift out of her and hang somewhere over Jamieson Valley with the evening mist.

His gaze dropped to her mouth. Strong fingers curled around her biceps. 'And this time I'm warning you I'm not letting you go until I'm good and ready.'

The way he said it, all male attitude and arrogance, sent a shiver of excitement along her nerve-endings. Emma heard a whisper of sound issue from her throat an instant before his lips touched hers.

Then she was lost. In his taste: rich and velvety, like the world's finest chocolate. His cool mossy scent mingled with leather. The warmth of his body as he shifted her against him for a closer fit.

She should have stopped it right there, told him no—he'd given her the option. But her response was torn from her like autumn's last leaf in a storm-ravaged forest. Irrational. Irresistible. Irrevocable.

Voices ebbed and flowed in the distance but she barely heard them above the pounding of her pulse, her murmur of approval as she melted against him like butter on a barbecue grill. Her arms slid around his waist to burrow under his jacket, where he was warm and solid through the T-shirt's soft jersey.

Jake felt her resistance soften, her luscious lips grow pliant as she opened for him, giving him full access, and he plunged right in. Dark, decadent delight. Moans and murmurs. Her tongue tangled with his, velvet on satin, and her taste was as sweet as spun sugar.

Dragging her against him, he moved closer, his fingertips tracking down her spine, over the flare of her backside, where he pressed her closer so he could feel her heat.

So she could feel his rapidly growing erection butting against her.

He felt the change instantly—subtle, but sure. A tensing of muscles. A change in her stance. She didn't move away and her lips were still locked with his, but…

Breaking the kiss with a good deal of reluctance, he leaned back to look at her. They were the same age—both twenty-seven—but she looked impossibly young with her hair scraped back from her face, her eyes huge dark pools in the moonlight, her mouth plundered.

He stroked a finger over the groove that had formed between her brows. 'You're thinking too hard.'

'One of us should.' She didn't look away. Nor did the frown smooth out.

'Okay. Talk to me.'

She took a step back. 'This…thing between us is getting way too complicated.'

'Seems pretty straightforward to me. So I'm proposing a deal,' he went on before she could argue, resting his hands on her shoulders. 'This weekend neither of us talks about work.' He touched his forehead to hers. 'We don't *think* about work. We're both between partners, so we'll enjoy the wedding and each other's company…and whatever happens *happens*. No complications. One weekend, Emma.'

'One weekend.' She leaned away, her eyes clouded with conflicting emotions. 'And then what?'

'Put next week out of your mind, it's too far away.'

Come Monday they'd go their separate ways. Back to real life and working ridiculous hours. Emma and the Blue Mountains would be nothing but a warm and pretty memory.

'Think about this instead,' he said, sliding his hands down her upper arms. 'Neither of us wants to be tied down, and we both work our backsides off. We deserve some playtime.'

'Playtime?' She stared up at him, her eyes the colour of the mist-swirled mountains behind her. 'No deal. Not with you.'

'Why not? Afraid you might enjoy yourself?'

She rolled her lips together, as if to stop whatever she'd been about to say, then said, 'I just don't want to play with you, that's all.' She turned and began walking back the way they'd come.

'Liar.' Grabbing her arm, he walked around her, blocking her path until they stood face to face. 'Tell me you didn't enjoy that kiss just now.'

She studied him a moment. 'I didn't enjoy that kiss just now.'

He laughed. 'You started it. That night at the restaurant. You blew me away with your enthusiasm and got me seriously thinking about you. And me. I haven't stopped thinking about you and me—together—since.'

'I told you, that kiss was an overreaction to a particular circumstance,' she said primly. 'And what are we—kids? *"You started it",'* she muttered with a roll of her eyes, but he thought he saw a hint of humour there too.

She looked so delightful he couldn't resist—he planted a firm smacking kiss on those pouted lips then grinned. 'I'd better get you back. Stella'll be starting to think I've kidnapped you.'

Grabbing her hand, he tugged her alongside him along the path towards the hotel. The weekend had barely begun, plenty of time to convince her to change her mind.

'So. Seen any good movies lately?'

She kept up a brisk pace beside him. 'No.'

'Me neither. Stella mentioned you swim every morning, come rain or shine. Is that true?'

'Yes.'

'So…if I were to change my early-morning jog—'

'One weekend.' She jerked to a sudden halt and looked up at him. 'And whatever happens happens?'

A strand of hair had come loose and blew across her eyes. He smoothed it back, tucked it behind her ear. 'We'll take things as they come. It'll be good, I promise.'

Oh, yes, she knew. Emma stared into those beguiling eyes. 'I bet you say that to all the girls.' She couldn't believe she was having this conversation with Jake Carmody.

She resumed walking, hoping she was headed in the right direction. Everything seemed surreal. The moonlight distorting their combined shadows on the path in front of them. The sharp eucalpyt fragrance of the bushland. The way her body was responding to his proximity even now.

His seductive charm really knew no bounds. No wonder women swooned and fell at his feet. She firmed her jaw. Not *this* woman. Still, she didn't have to swoon, exactly…

He was suggesting what amounted to nothing

more than a weekend of sex and sin. Heat shimmied down her spine. A weekend on Pleasure Island. She had no doubt Jake could deliver, and couldn't deny the idea called to her on more than one level. But was she game enough? Why not? It wasn't a lifetime commitment, for heaven's sake.

Since her father's death eleven years ago she'd worked her butt off to make things better for them all. Jake had made it clear to her that it was past time she took something for herself. One weekend to be free and irresponsible. And this weekend, with Stella leaving home and the love rat a disappearing blot on her horizon, was it perhaps a good time to start?

They reached the hotel and she hesitated on the shallow steps out front. Her cheeks felt hot and super sensitive, as if a feather might flay away the skin.

She turned to say goodnight and met his gaze. The heat from that kiss still shimmered in his eyes, and it took all her will-power to keep from flinging herself at him and kissing him again.

Deliberately she stepped back, aware she hadn't given him an answer and just as aware they both already knew what her answer would be. She turned towards the building.

A liveried porter swept the wide glass door open with a welcoming smile and warm air swirled out. 'Good evening, madam.'

'Good evening.' She smiled back, wondering if her cheeks and lips were as pink and chapped as they felt. From the safety of distance, she turned to Jake once more. ''Till tomorrow, then.'

'Get a good night's sleep.'

His smile was pure sin. *You'll need it*—no mistaking that message in those hot dark eyes, and her heart turned a high somersault. It continued its gymnastics all the way up the three flights of stairs.

Stella was bundled in a fluffy white hotel robe on the couch, watching a TV cook-off, when she entered.

'Traitor.' But there was no sting in the word as Emma pulled out the fortune cookie note and dropped it on Stella's lap. 'For you.' Because her legs were still wobbly, she flopped down on the couch beside her.

'"Two hearts, one soul." Ooh, I've gone all gooey inside.' Smiling broadly, Stella tucked her legs up beneath her. 'What does yours say?'

She shook her head, that overly warm sensation prickling her skin. 'Never mind.'

Stella stuck out her hand, palm up. 'Come on—give.'

'Oh, for heaven's sake.' Emma dug into her pocket again, then glued her attention to the TV screen, but she wasn't seeing it. 'It's not romantic, like yours. And that's okay because I'm not a romantic like you.' She pressed a fist to her lips to stem the flow.

'"A caress is better than a career". Of course it's romantic, silly. It's telling you to take time out and enjoy… To…*Em*.'

'Where's my computer, by the way? Jake said… never mind.' Emma could feel Stella's gaze on her and jerked herself off the couch without waiting for an answer. 'I'm going to take a bath.'

'Oh. My. Lord.'

'What?' She was in the process of ripping off her tracksuit jacket but stopped at her sister's tone. 'What's wrong?'

Stella was staring at her. And pointing. 'What have you done with my sister?'

'What are you talking about?' She shrugged her shoulders. Ran a hand around her neck. 'What's he done?'

'Ha!' Stella jabbed her finger in the air again. 'I should be asking what *Jake's* done with my sister.'

'No. It's nothing. Don't you say one word to Jake or I'll—'

'*Not* nothing.' Stella craned forward, studying Emma as if she was counting her eyelashes. 'My big sister with fresh whisker burn around her mouth. And stars in her eyes. She's never had stars in her eyes. *Never.*'

'Don't be ridiculous.' Panicked, Emma swiped at her mouth, then sucked in her lips and backed away. Tugged her T-shirt over her head and threw it on her bed. 'Do you know how cold it is outside? The air… A hot bath…'

'Emma Dilemma.' Stella grinned. 'You've just had it on with best man Jake.'

'*No.* It's such a cliché to get it on with the best man. I kissed him, that's all. No. He kissed me. We kissed each other. He started it. No biggie, okay?'

Stella shook her head. 'My sister never gets flustered when she talks about a guy. *Never.*'

Emma fumbled through her suitcase. 'He's not a guy, he's Jake. And I'm not flustered. It's nothing.'

'It's something.'

She yanked her pyjamas from her overnighter and blew out a breath then turned to Stella who was watching her with her chin on the back of the sofa. 'Okay, it's something. But it's just a weekend something. Or not. I haven't decided yet.'

Stella smiled. 'You know you'll have this room all to yourself tomorrow night…?'

'Not another word.' Emma flung up a hand. 'You breathe so much as a syllable of this conversation to Jake or anyone else and I'll sabotage your wedding night.'

And, swiping up her cosmetics bag, she fled to the bathroom.

CHAPTER SEVEN

THE WEDDING DAY dawned bright and clear. And cold. Clad in her complimentary terrycloth robe, Emma took her early-morning coffee onto the balcony to admire the cotton balls of cloud that hid the valley floor. From her vantage point she could see the garden below, where even now staff were setting out chairs, toting flower arrangements, twining white ribbon and fairy lights through the trees.

A few moments later Stella stumbled out, hair wild, eyes sparkling. 'Good morning.' She leaned a shoulder against Emma's. 'It's just perfect. Isn't it perfect? Not a cloud in the sky. By afternoon it'll be warm and still sunny. Hopefully… Can you believe I'm getting married in a few hours' time?'

Emma dropped a kiss on her sister's cheek on her way back inside. 'And there's a lot to get through before that happens.' She checked her watch. 'Breakfast is due up in ten minutes. The hairdresser will be here in half an hour.'

WITH LESS THAN an hour to go, the bride's dressing room on the first floor was pandemonium. Underwear, costumes, flowers. A blur of fragrance and colour. Sunshine streamed through the window. Champagne and orange juice in tall flutes sat untouched on a sideboard, along with a plate of finger food.

Stella was with Beth, the wedding planner, and her two assistants—one aiming a video camera and catching the memories. The excitement, the laughter, the nerves.

In one of the full-length mirrors Emma caught a glimpse of her reflection in a strapless bustier. Crimson, with black ribbon laces at the front, it looked like something Scarlett O'Hara would have approved of. She yanked the ribbon tight between her breasts and tied it in a double knot, staring closer.

Wow. She actually had breasts today. Enhanced by the bustier's support, they spilled over the top like something out of a men's magazine. The garment pulled in her waist and flared over her hips, leaving a strip of bare belly and the tiny triangle of matching panties tantalisingly visible. A pair of sheer black stockings came to mid thigh, held up by long black suspenders.

For an instant she almost saw Jake's reflection standing behind her, his eyes smouldering as he leaned over her to dip a finger between—

The tap on her shoulder had her spinning in a panicked one-eighty. 'What?' Her breath whooshed out and her heart skipped a beat. 'Stella. Sorry. I was—'

'A million miles away.'

Not as far as that. 'I'm here. Right here.' She gave

a bright smile, then forgot about her erotic meanderings as she gazed at the bride. 'Oh, my! Gorgeous.'

Stella's figure-hugging floor-length Guinevere gown was bottle-green crushed velvet. A dull gold panel insert in the bodice gleamed with tiny emerald beads, replicated on the wide belt cinching in her waist. Full-length sleeves flared wide at the wrist and fell in long soft folds. Her coronet of fresh freesias, tiny roses and featherlike greenery complemented her rich auburn hair.

'You look stunning, Stell. Radiant and stunning. I can't wait to see Lancelot's face when he gets a load of you.'

'Neither can I.' She looked down at Emma, waved a hand. 'Um…are you planning on wearing something over that? I'm sure the guys won't mind, but this is my day and I know it's selfish but I want all the attention.'

'Getting there…' With the help of Annie, one of the assistants, Emma stepped into a voluminous skirt and shimmied into the bodice. 'I told you, Stella. You should have been Scarlett, not me.'

'And I told you already, Scarlett's the brunette. She's playful and coquettish and I really, really wanted you to be that woman today. Whereas Guinevere was pale and intense and totally and unconditionally in love with Lancelot.'

'Well, you'll have that attention,' Emma said, admiring her sister. 'Ryan, not to mention the rest of the male population, won't be able to take his eyes off you.'

Annie slipped buttons into the tiny loops at the back of Emma's dress, then handed her black lace gloves and a parasol.

'Don't forget the bridal bouquet.' Emma passed Stella a simple posy of flowers to match those in her hair. She paused with her sister at the top of the wide sweeping staircase. 'We're a clash of eras, aren't we?'

'We are. But it's going to be fun. For both of us.' Stella squeezed Emma's hand. 'Thank you for helping to make it a perfect day.'

'It's not over, it's just beginning.'

The harp's crystal clear rendition of 'Greensleeves' floated on the air as they arrived at the garden's designated bride spot. At a signal from Beth, the music segued beautifully into Bach's 'Jesu, Joy of Man's Desiring.'

'You're up,' Beth murmured to Emma. 'And don't forget to *smile*.'

She'd taken but a few steps along the petal-strewn manicured lawn when she saw Jake and Ryan up ahead. She forgot about smiling. The garden might look like a fairytale. The costumed guests might look magnificent or they might be naked for all Emma knew, because her peripheral vision had disappeared.

Rhett Butler had never looked so devastating. Black suit, dove-grey waistcoat and dark mottled cravat beneath a snowy starched shirt. His eyes met hers and he smiled. A slow, sexy, come-away-with-me smile.

'*Hi,*' he mouthed.

'*Hi,*' she mouthed back, and, *Oh, help*. Her knees

went weak but she seemed to be moving forward. What was wrong with her? No man had ever captivated her this way.

Deliberately freeing her gaze, she aimed her smile at Ryan instead, looking regal in a black tunic and cowled top over silver-grey leggings and black knee-high boots. The Clifton family crest was emblazoned on his tunic—she could make out a lion and a medieval helmet in the black-and-gold embroidery.

Not that he was looking at her; his eyes were for his bride, a few steps behind. As they should be. Emma wondered for a quickened heartbeat how it would feel to have someone look at her that way, with shiny unconditional love. She rejected the thought even as it formed and concentrated on keeping her smile in place, her steps smooth and measured.

Jake's eyes feasted on Emma. The deep colour complemented her lightly tanned complexion. A wide-brimmed hat shaded her face, and he couldn't quite read her eyes, so he contented himself with admiring the seductive cleavage and the way the crimson fabric hugged every delectable curve as she moved closer.

His fingers flexed in anticipation of becoming more intimately acquainted with those curves. How long would it take him to get her out of that dress? To lay her down on the grass right here in the sunshine and plunge into her while the birds sang and the cool wind blew up from the valley....

Then she moved out of his line of sight to take her place beside the bride. Probably just as well, because any longer and it might become obvious to all where his thoughts were.

He turned his attention to Ry and Stella, and watched the couple blindly promise to handcuff themselves to each other till death did them part. A life sentence, no parole. His collar itched on Ry's behalf, and he shifted his shoulders against the tight sensation inside his shirt.

They looked happy enough. But it never lasted. There were exceptions, of course. Ry's parents—Henry VIII with a fake red beard and Anne Boleyn—were holding hands, eyes moist.

He glanced at the girls' mother in her white Grecian goddess robe, looking, as always, eternally constipated. Her marriage disaster had turned her into a bitter and twisted woman. Nevertheless, she was still beautiful. He imagined Emma would look as beautiful in thirty years' time.

But he didn't want to contemplate Emma's lovely face marred with that same perpetually pinched expression, those sparkling sapphire eyes clouded with sadness.

Who in their right mind would take the marriage risk? Only those temporarily blinded by that eternal mystery they called love. Not him, thank God.

Formal photographs followed in the gardens, then on to the decking overlooking the mountains as the sun lowered, turning the sky golden and the valley purple.

Emma couldn't fault Jake's behaviour. He was the perfect gentleman. The perfect Rhett. He only touched her when the photographer required him to do so. During the five-course meal he was seated next to Ryan at the top table, so conversation between them was limited, but there was a heated glance or two when the bridal couple's heads didn't block the view.

After the speeches guests chatted over music provided by a three-piece orchestra as the desserts began coming out of the kitchen. Anne Boleyn, aka the mother of the groom, made her way to the top table.

'Beautiful ceremony, my darlings. It must be your turn next, Emma.'

'Oh, I don't think so.' Emma smiled back, then lifted her champagne glass and swallowed more than she should considering her duties. 'It's not for me.'

'Ah, you just have to find the right man.'

Smile still in place, Emma set her empty glass on the table with a thunk. 'And isn't that the killer?'

'And Jake?' Ryan's mother smiled in his direction. 'When's some clever woman going to snap you up and make an honest man out of you?'

'Alas for me, fair lady.' He put his hand on his heart. 'You're already taken.'

Laughter from the bridal couple. 'You never know, Em,' Stella murmured into her ear as her new mother-in-law walked back to her chair. 'He could be closer than you think.'

'What I'm thinking is it's about time you two cut that white skyscraper.'

The guests applauded as Stella and Ryan laughed into each other's eyes and fed each other cake. Weddings, Emma thought. They always whipped up those romantic, dreamy, nostalgic emotions. It was hard not to be caught up in the euphoria.

She deliberately veered from those too-pretty thoughts and watched Karina knock back one glass of champagne after another. Emma pursed her lips, remembering the *Pat Me* sticker she'd discovered stuck to her backside after the hens' night. She narrowed her gaze as Karina plastered herself all over one of Ryan's cousins up against a wall. Weddings also came with too much booze and indiscriminate physical contact.

But when Ryan and Stella took to the floor for the bridal waltz to the seductive beat of 'Dance Me to the End of Love', she knew her own moment of up close was imminent and her legs started to tremble.

Jake rose and held out his hand, his eyes as beguiling as the song. 'I think it's our turn.' Emma caught the undertone in his voice and her whole body thrummed with its underlying message that went way beyond the dance floor and upstairs to that big soft bed.

When he grasped her fingers to lead her into the dance space there was something…different about the contact. And in the centre of the room, when he slid his hand to her back, firm and warm and possessive, she felt as if the floor tilted beneath her feet.

They'd never danced together, and his proximity released a stream of endorphins, stimulating her senses. The throb of the music echoed through her body. His cool green aftershave filled her nostrils.

The sensuous brush of his thighs against hers beneath the heavy swish of her full skirt had her breath catching in her throat.

'Sorry,' she muttered, missing a step and trying to create some space between them—she needed it to breathe, and to say, 'I'm not a very good dancer.'

'Lucky for you I am.'

She flicked him a look. 'Lucky for you I'm feeling congenial enough to let you get away with that.'

Was there *anything* in the seductive sciences he wasn't accomplished at? She sincerely doubted it as his palm rubbed a lazy circle over her back, creating a deliciously warm friction and at the same time drawing her closer and causing her to misstep—again.

'Is it the dance, or is something else distracting you, Em?'

How typically arrogant male. But she smiled into his laughing eyes. 'Do men always have sex on their minds?'

His answering grin was unrepentant. 'Pretty much.' He dipped close and lowered his voice. 'It's on your mind too.'

She dragged in a breath that smelled of fine fresh cotton and hot man and tried not to notice. 'I'm finding it hard to concentrate on the steps, that's all.'

As Ryan swept his bride past them Emma saw Stella's eyes twinkling at her and looked away quickly. Apart from the bride and groom and Ryan's parents they were the only couple on the floor. 'People are watching us.'

'And why wouldn't they? You look amazing.' The hand holding hers tightened, and his thumb whisked over hers as he leaned in so that his cheek touched her hair. So that his chest shifted against her breasts. 'You feel amazing,' he murmured into her ear. 'Forget the audience. Listen to the music.'

Forget the music. Listen to the Voice. Her head drifted towards his shoulder, the better to hear it. When other couples joined them on the dance floor he swept her towards the window with its panoramic views. Not that she was interested in any view right now except the one in front of her.

He crooned the song's lyrics about wanting to see her beauty when everyone had gone close against her ear. She nearly melted on the spot. 'You think I've changed my mind?'

'Honey, I don't even need to ask.' His hand tightened around hers and then she realised that couples were swirling around them and they were standing still. And close. That the fingers of her free hand had somehow ended up clinging to the back of his neck. That the song had changed to something more upbeat.

How long had they been standing there? How long had she been showing him exactly how she felt? That those options she'd thought she had were down to one? Somehow she managed to yank herself into the present and remember her bridesmaid duties.

She let her hand slide down the smooth fabric of his jacket, slipped the other one from his grasp. 'I need to go.'

'Are you sure?' He lifted the heavy mass of hair from her shoulder with the back of his fingers and stroked the side of her neck, then linked his arms loosely around her waist, trapping her against him. 'Because I'm kind of enjoying where we are right now.'

She felt a series of little taps track up her spine.

'How many buttons would you say this dress has?' He slipped the top one from its tiny loop. Then another.

Her breath caught and her blood fizzed through her veins like hot champagne. 'What do you think you're doing?'

He swirled a finger beneath the fabric. 'Your skin feels like warm satin. How many buttons?' he asked again.

'Twenty two.'

He muttered a soft short word under his breath.

'Is that a problem?'

His eyes burned into hers. 'I've never encountered a problem with female clothing I couldn't solve one way or another.' And with a slow sexy grin he released her. 'Okay, you're free. For now.'

For now? But she couldn't deny the thrill of knowing he wanted her. That he was already figuring a way to get her out of her dress. That the women casting admiring glances his way were not even on his radar tonight—Emma Byrne was.

His proprietorial hand at her back manoeuvred her through the dancers as she made her way towards the bridal table. A middle aged Fred and Wilma Flintstone twirled by, a gay couple dressed as King Arthur and Merlin, a Beauty and a Beast.

'Who's the Roman warrior chatting up Bernice?'

Emma followed Jake's gaze to a nearby table and snorted a half laugh. 'He won't get far with Mum.' But to her surprise her mother smiled at something the middle-aged guy said. Then laughed. 'Amazing.' Emma smiled too. 'Maybe I should invite him around some time as a distraction when I'm fed up with her.'

'Hang on—that's Ryan's Uncle Stan from Melbourne. Divorced last year and looking good. Go, Stan.'

Emma took that moment to break away. 'I have something I need to take care of.'

Leaving the sounds of laughter and music behind, she made her way to the honeymoon suite in another wing of the hotel with a basket of rose petals. A glance at her watch told her she had half an hour before the happy couple were due to leave the party and celebrate the end of their special day.

More than enough time to catch her breath and take a moment. Letting herself in with the keycard she'd been given at Reception, Emma flicked on the light. A soft glow filled the room, glinting on the massive brass bed and lending a rich luxury to the sumptuous gold and burgundy furnishings. She leaned a shoulder against the door, drawing in air. She really needed to increase her daily workout.

Rubbish. Emma knew her lack of fitness wasn't the reason her lungs felt as if they'd shrunk two sizes.

She could try telling herself her underwear was laced too tightly. The ballroom had been badly ventilated. She'd had too much of the fizzy stuff.

But there was only one reason, and thank God he was downstairs—

'Need a hand?'

That familiar seductive drawl coated the back of her neck like hot honey, causing her to jolt and drop her little basket. She drew in a ragged breath. His question, which wasn't a question at all, could only mean one thing, and it wasn't an offer to help sprinkle her rose petals over the quilt.

'Jake…' The word turned into a moan as a warm mouth bit lightly into the sensitive spot where shoulder met neck. She simply didn't have the strength or the will to pull away. 'What are you doing here?'

He soothed the tender spot with his tongue and her toes curled up. 'What do you think I'm doing here?' In one fluid move he spun her around. The door swung shut behind them and he rolled her against the wall, his hands hard and hot and heavy on her shoulders.

He didn't give her time to answer or to think. One instant she was staring into a pair of heavy-lidded dark eyes, the next her mouth was being plundered by the wickedest pair of lips this side of the Yellow Brick Road.

He lifted his mouth a fraction and his breath whispered against her lips. 'Is that clear enough?'

Perfectly. And just clear enough to have her remember where they were and what she'd come here to do. 'Are you out of your mind?' She pushed at his chest. Uselessly. 'Housekeeping could show up here any minute.'

'Then we've got a minute.' He grinned, dark eyes glinting. 'Better make the most of it.'

Excitement whipped through her as his hands rushed down, his thumbs whisking over taut nipples, the heat of his palms searing her skin through the satin as he moulded them around her waist and over her belly with murmurs of appreciation.

There was nothing of the suave, sophisticated gentleman from this afternoon except perhaps the scent of his aftershave. This man was the wickedly handsome rogue bent on seduction that she'd always known him to be. Nothing for her to do but to look into those eyes and oh-so-willingly acquiesce.

He gathered handfuls of her voluminous skirt in his fists at either side of her, creating a cool draught around her knees as he ruched the fabric higher. 'Do you want to tell me to stop?' he murmured, leaning down to sip at her collarbone.

Only to stop wasting time. A moan escaped as the tips of his fingers grazed the tops of her stockings, then came into smooth contact with naked flesh. He slid one sensuous finger beneath a suspender and up, to track along the edge of her panties.

He grinned again as he tossed her skirt up over her breasts. 'How many layers have you got on under here?'

'I don't remember...' Moisture pooled between

her legs, dampening her silk knickers, and she didn't know how much longer she could remain upright.

He watched her eyes while his finger cruised closer, curling inward, between her thighs, along the lacy edge of her knickers, almost but never quite touching where she wanted him to touch her most. And the spark she saw in his gaze ignited a burn that wasn't about to be extinguished any time soon.

'Jake… Housekeeping—'

'Tell me what you like. What you want.'

The husky demand turned her mind to mush, and she arched wantonly against his hand. Forget Housekeeping. 'Anything. Everything.' Clutching her skirt, she let her spinning head fall back against the door. 'And quickly.'

He stepped between her legs, the sides of his shoes pushing her feet wider. One sharp tug. Two. The sound of fabric ripping. And she felt her knickers being whisked away from her body by impatient hands.

She trembled. She sighed. She hissed out a breath between her teeth. 'Hurry.'

'No.' His thumb found her throbbing centre. 'A job worth doing…'

'Ah, *yesss*…' A slow, sensuous glide over her swollen flesh—one touch—and the burn became a raging inferno. *So* worth doing…

How could one finger cause such utter devastation? Her eyes slid closed. Golden orbs pulsed across her vision. She felt as if she was standing on the rim of a volcano, yet she was the one about to erupt.

He touched her a second time, and she flew over the edge and into the hot and airless vortex, her inner muscles clamping around him.

She flattened her palms against the wall for balance, her breathing fast and harsh. She felt him step away on a draught of air, and opened her eyes in time to see him grin with promises yet to be fulfilled as he slipped out through the door.

CHAPTER EIGHT

OH...MY. GOD. EMMA sucked in a much needed calming breath. If she'd had the luxury of time she'd have slid down the wall and possibly passed out for the rest of the night.

He'd touched her twice. *Twice.* That was all it had taken to bring her to the most intense orgasm of her life. And then he'd nicked off like some pirate in the night, stealing her breath and her composure and leaving her with the possibility of facing Housekeeping alone.

Out. She realised she was still clutching her skirt up to her chest and pushed it down quickly, her cheeks flaming, at the same time thanking her lucky stars that no one had turned up yet.

A hank of hair fell over one side of her face. She pushed it behind her ear. Panicked all over again, she scanned the floor for her knickers. No sign of them. Picking up her forgotten basket, she stumbled to the bed and dumped the petals in the centre, arranging them in a hasty circle. She placed the two heart-shaped soaps she'd made with Ryan's and Stella's names in gold leaf in the centre, then made her way quickly downstairs, where the couple were preparing to farewell the guests.

She didn't see Jake amongst the crowd until he appeared in the doorway ten minutes later. Their gazes clashed hotly across the room. He was the only one who knew she was naked beneath her gown and her cheeks flamed anew. She prayed he'd stay away from her for the next little while, because they both had their respective duties before the social part of the evening was over.

Neatly sidestepping as Stella threw her bouquet in Emma's direction—she wasn't falling for that old trick—she saw Jake follow the bridal couple out.

She moved among the guests, catching up with friends and relatives. She was on tenterhooks, expecting Jake to tap her on the shoulder at any moment, and she didn't know how she was going to hide the guilty pleasure from her expression.

The band was still playing and guests lingered, enjoying the music. Some danced; others gravitated towards the bar next to the lobby. A while later, when Jake still hadn't shown his face, the glow cooled, to be replaced by an anxious fluttering in the pit of her stomach. Was he coming back? Was he expecting *her* to look for *him* after his impromptu seduction?

She didn't know what game they were playing—had no idea of the rules. *Damn him.* Collecting her hat and parasol from behind the concierge's desk, she made her way towards the bar.

JAKE WAVED RY and Stella off and headed straight for
Reception. Business taken care of there, he stopped
to collect a couple of sightseeing brochures on his
way to the lobby bar.

He found a comfortable armchair in the corner,
from where he could see the ballroom, and signalled
the waiter. He knew Emma was still in there. He'd
give her some space but if she didn't materialise in
ten minutes he was damn well going in there and
hauling her out.

Folding the brochures, he slid them into his jacket
pocket. His fingers collided with silk. Emma's panties. He remembered her surprise, the passion in those
deep blue eyes, when he'd stripped them off. The way
her lips had parted on a moan of pleasure when he'd
first touched that intimate flesh.

His body tightened all over again. The next time
Emma writhed and moaned against him… He smiled
to himself in anticipation. He had definite plans for
the way their evening was going to go.

Han Solo and Princess Leia exited, with a lone
cowboy in tow. No sign of Emma. He exhaled sharply
through his nostrils and rechecked his watch. Was
she saying a personal goodnight to everyone in the
bloody ballroom?

His order arrived with a paper napkin and a bowl
of peanuts. He set the unopened bottle of champagne
and two glasses on the floor beside his chair and
reached for his beer.

'Good evening, Rhett.'

Jake took a second or two to catch on that the

sultry come-hither voice was directed at him. He glanced up to see a well-endowed woman in her mid-thirties or thereabouts, in an embroidered medieval get-up, holding a cocktail glass brimming with blue liquid and a cherry on a stick.

He lifted his glass and drained half of it down then set it back on the table. 'Hi.'

She took his half-smile as an invitation and spread herself out on the chair opposite him, placing her glass up close to his. She lifted the little stick to her mouth.

'So.' He kept his eyes off the cleavage obviously on offer and leaned back, crossed his legs. 'Who are you tonight?'

Slipping the cherry between her glossed lips, she tossed her mane of auburn hair over her shoulder and aimed a killer smile at him. 'The Lady of Shalott.'

He took his time to say, 'No Mr Shalott?'

She giggled. The sound grated the way feet scrabbling down a rubbled cliff face to certain death grated. Clearly she thought he was interested in her as the night's entertainment. And at some other time he might have been interested. Or not.

'There *was* no Mr Shalott. It's a poem,' she informed him, in case he didn't know.

'Yes, Tennyson. Tragic circumstances. The girl loved Lancelot but he really wasn't that into her, was he?'

She leaned forward on the edge of her chair. 'But he didn't *know* her. If he'd taken the time, things might've turned out different.'

'But not necessarily for the better. Lancelot had his eye on someone else. The lady would've been disappointed.' A thought occurred to him and he tried to recall if he knew her. 'You and Ry weren't…?' He jiggled a hand in front of them.

She grinned. 'No. I had no idea the groom was going to be Lancelot. I'm Ryan's cousin. Kylie. From Adelaide.'

'Ah…yes. Cousin Kylie from Adelaide.'

He'd heard about Wily Kylie—two husbands down, on the prowl for her third. He suddenly needed a drink, and lifted his beer.

Following suit, Kylie raised her glass and tapped it to his. Her eyes drifted to his mouth. 'To a good night.'

Not if I hang around here it won't be. Like an addict, he suddenly craved the woman he'd partnered all day, not this silicone bimbo looking for rich husband number three. *Emma.* A woman with a real body and a smile that could quite possibly melt his heart if he wasn't careful.

'And a good night to you too.' He drained the glass and set it down on the napkin, then picked up his bottle and glasses, rose and executed a bow. 'Welcome to Sydney, Lady Kylie, enjoy your stay.'

He didn't wait for a reply, simply turned on his heel and headed towards the ballroom to find Emma.

EMMA'S HANDS SHOOK so much she could barely swipe the keycard through its slot. On the third try she managed to let herself in and lean back against the door. She felt physically ill—as if the five-tiered wedding cake had lodged in her stomach.

One hand clenched on her parasol, she rubbed her free hand over her heart and up her throat. Jake hadn't come near her since their upstairs 'encounter'. For want of a better word. Never mind that she'd stupidly tried to avoid him; that was totally beside the point.

Flinging her hat into the air, she watched it sail across the room. She'd been hanging around in the ballroom, expecting him to come and find her. But he hadn't. When it came to guys like him she really was *so* naïve.

Then *she'd* found *him*. In the lobby bar…with a woman who *looked* like a woman, not some underdeveloped teenager.

The soft knock at the door behind her had her whirling around. Heart pounding in her throat, she yanked the door open.

Jake leaned on the doorjamb, his jacket slung over one shoulder, shirtsleeves rolled back. His hair was a little mussed, his cravat was gone, and the top button of his shirt was undone, leaving his throat tantalisingly exposed. He dangled a bottle of champagne and two glasses in his free hand.

His eyes met hers. They burned with such hot, unsatisfied hunger her throat closed over and she couldn't raise so much as a whisper. All she could think was he'd come for her. *Her*.

He lifted the bottle. 'You going to let me in? Or do you want the entire floor to know the best man's planning a hot night with the bridesmaid?' He grinned as he slid sideways and passed her, brushing his liquor-tinged lips over hers on his way. 'I hope you hadn't planned on starting without me.'

She took a moment to catch his meaning, then a wild fire swept up her neck and into her cheeks. All she managed was a gurgling sound at the back of her throat.

She closed the door and leaned back against it, heart pounding as she watched him toss his jacket over the couch, watched the way his muscles bunched beneath his shirt. His hair held the gleam of burnished gold threads amongst the brown.

He glanced back at her as he walked to a little round table topped with a crystal vase of fresh blooms. 'You weren't running out on me, were you?'

'You…you were otherwise occupied.' She found her voice.

He frowned. 'I was *waiting* for you.'

'I didn't know.' The door felt hard, the row of buttons digging into her spine.

He set the bottle and glasses down, brows raised, eyes dark as midnight. 'You *didn't know?* Jeez, woman.'

'I thought maybe you'd…' *found someone more desirable, more attractive* '…changed your mind.'

'What? This weekend's about you and me, remember?'

Her chin lifted. 'I never agreed.' Exactly.

'You…' He shook his head, eyes changing, finally

comprehending. 'Come on, Emma, do you really think I'd go for that type downstairs?'

'I...hoped not.' She swallowed, relief softening her limbs, and allowed herself a smile. 'Because then I'd have to hit you with my parasol.'

He grinned back at her, eyes wicked. 'Maybe I'll let you. Later.'

'Um...' Was she really up for an experienced man like Jake?

He popped the cork off the champagne bottle. 'Tonight's been a foregone conclusion all along, and we both know it.'

Yes. And for this moment, for what was left of the weekend, or for however long this spark burned, she knew without a doubt she wanted to make love with Jake more than her next breath.

He set the bottle down. 'Come here and kiss me.'

She needed no second bidding. Crossing the few steps between them, she flattened herself against his chest, her arms circling his neck, fingers diving into his hair as she fused her mouth to his.

Heat met heat. Not sweet and tender—not even close. Not with Jake. Nor did she want it so. This melding of selves and mashing of lips was a dark, dangerous mix of pent-up passion and long-held desires. Exactly what she wanted.

Hard hands dragged her closer, then zigged down her spine to press her bottom against him so that she could feel the steel ridge of his erection. Persuasive pressure. Promised delights.

He lifted his lips to murmur, 'Emma, Emma, you've been driving me crazy all evening. All week.'

His admission thrilled her to her toes. 'Same goes…' Dazed and dizzy, she arched her hips against his hardness and clung to him, welcoming the scrape of evening beard as he worked his lips and teeth up her throat, down the side of her neck, over her décolletage.

Impatient hands skimmed over her breasts, kneading and squeezing, deft fingers finding her aching nipples through the satin and rolling them into hardened peaks.

The delicate fragrance of the valley's sweet-scented wattle and eucalypt from the arrangement on the table mingled with the hot scent of aroused man as he laved the swell of her breasts above the neckline of her dress, then bent his head lower to nip and suck at her nipples through the fabric.

He made a sound of frustration, lifted his head and leaned back slightly to look at her. Light from the chandelier wall bracket glinted in his eyes, but the heat, the purpose she saw there, burned with its own fire.

'How many buttons did you say?'

Oh. 'Buttons…' She raised her arms to help but he didn't give her time. In a frenzy of movement, he fisted his hands in the fabric at her shoulders and yanked. She felt the satin give way down her back as buttons popped and pinged. 'Uh…'

'I know a dressmaker…'

Of course he did.

Dropping to his knees, he pushed the ruined garment and accompanying petticoats to her feet. She stepped out of the mound of puddled satin, kicked it away, leaving her wearing nothing but her laced bustier and stockings.

'You're gorgeous,' he murmured, voice husky. A corner of his mouth kicked up in a wry smile. 'And armour-plated yet again.'

Goosebumps of heat followed his gaze as it swept up her corset-trapped body to meet her eyes. 'Not quite. You do have my panties…don't you?' she finished on a slightly panicked note.

'They're mine now.' He looked down at the feminine secrets exposed below the suspenders, then back, his eyes burning. 'I want to see all of you.'

He knelt in front of her, took off her shoes then unhitched her stockings, warm hands gliding them down her legs, breath hot on her naked skin. She lifted each foot so he could slide them off and toss them away.

Hands shaking, she started to fumble for the laces. Her breasts weren't… 'I'm not—'

Laying a finger on her lips, he shook his head.

Taking her hands in his, he spread them wide so that their bodies bumped in all the right places, then, fingers entwined, brought them in close and began to waltz. Tiny steps, his thighs pressing against hers. He swayed her towards the massive four-poster bed. She could almost hear the dusky beat of Stella's chosen song that they'd danced to earlier.

She felt the corner of the bed against her thighs

as he backed her up against the bedpost. Watching her, he turned her hands palm up, kissed the inside of each wrist, where her pulse beat a rock concert's applause, then curled each finger around the smooth wooden bedpost above her head.

'And don't let go,' he ordered, squeezing them for good measure, fingers trailing down her raised arms, leaving little shivers sparkling in their wake.

The erotic pose triggered within her an avalanche of wild needs and urgent demands. Her breasts thrust upwards, straining at the bustier's confines, nipples tight to the point of pain and on fire for his touch.

'Jake…' She sighed. Wanting it all. Wanting it now.

His eyes swept over her and his smooth seduction vanished in the blink of an eye.

His fingers scrambled for the laces. When she loosened her hold on the post in a frantic effort to hasten the process he grabbed her wrists, pinning her in place, a firestorm in his dark gaze. '*Stay.*'

A thrill spiralled through her body, clenching low in her belly as he renewed his task. His hands weren't steady, she noticed, and his breathing was ragged. He swore, then a hand dived into his trouser pocket and reappeared with a miniature Swiss Army knife. A handful of condoms spilled onto the floor.

She glanced down at them, then met his eyes. 'Boy Scout?'

'Just prepared,' he muttered thickly.

His eyes darkened. She knew his intent, and her pulse kicked into a wild erratic rhythm. No trace of the suave urban sophisticate—just prime, primitive male. She loved that he'd lost control with *her*—plain and ordinary Emma Byrne.

He flicked the tiny blade open and nicked the first ribbon. The second. Her breath sucked in. So did her stomach. His knuckles grazed a nipple as he worked his way down. The erotic response echoed in her womb, drawing it tight at the same time softening and moistening the internal muscles, slackening her inner thighs.

'Jake…'

Snick, snick, snick. 'I'll buy you another one.'

'Doesn't…matter…it's…only ribbon.'

The undergarment fell apart and slid to the floor and her breasts spilled free. And suddenly it didn't matter that she didn't have the breasts she'd like to have, because he was looking at them with awe and appreciation.

'Gorgeous,' he whispered. 'Absolutely perfect.'

Dropping the knife, he filled his hands with her, thumbs whisking over the tight buds, rolling and pinching them between his fingers until she thought she'd pass out with the pleasure. Wayne had never, *never* worshipped her body the way Jake was doing.

She writhed against the post, tilting her hips and arching her back. Closer…she had to get closer… She needed more. Him inside her. *Now.*

A groan rumbled up his throat and she heard the sharp rasp of his zipper. Without taking his eyes off hers, he somehow produced a condom that hadn't fallen from his pocket and ripped the foil packet open with his teeth.

Her breath stalled in her throat as he quickly sheathed himself. 'Hurry.' Anticipation and that aching, devastating need had reached flashpoint.

Hard wide palms clamped onto her hips, a sensuous vice, holding her in place. With unerring precision he plunged deep and hard and true. A torpedo finding its target. Invading her, stretching her, filling her.

Where he belonged.

Somewhere in a dark corner of her pleasure-fogged mind she fought that concept even as she embraced it. Then all thought melted into oblivion as she gave herself wholly over to layer after layer of sensation.

His hard thighs abraded hers through the rough weave of his trousers while he hammered into her. The sound of his laboured breaths, shockingly harsh in the room's stillness, and her own rapid sighs of response.

The golden light pulsing behind her eyes as she felt her climax building, building... Her legs threatening to give way, she clung tighter to the satin-smooth pole behind her, then Jake's hands were covering hers, holding her upright. From heads to toes their bodies collided, naked skin to fully clothed.

She was slick, hot and unbearably erotic, and Jake couldn't remember the last time he'd been so turned on. She bucked against him, all wild, wanton woman, meeting his thrusts with an eagerness and energy that rivalled his own.

He hadn't expected Emma to be so utterly responsive, and the pleasure of it, of *her,* slapped through him, sharp and viciously arousing. Clenching her hands between his own he drove into her, the urge to plunder and possess riding roughshod over anything sane and rational.

He'd not known it could be like this. That need for a woman—for one woman—could be so desperate, so powerful, so consuming. Some kind of madness had seized him.

She came in a rush, all but sobbing his name, her internal muscles clamping around him, silky walls of heat that triggered his own climax.

Their joined hands slid down the sweat-slicked post and he released her, and they flopped onto the bottom of the bed together in a tangle of sated limbs, their ragged breaths filling the air.

'Come here,' he murmured when he felt able enough to move again, shifting up the bed and dragging her with him. He hauled her on top and she lay spread-eagled over his body like one of those ragdoll cats. Against his thundering heart, he felt hers pounding in unison.

'Do you realise this is the first time we've actually been horizontal together?' she said drowsily.

'Mmm,' he answered, almost as lazily. Her body fitted seamlessly against his, curves to angles, womanly soft where he was hard, as if she'd been made exclusively for him. She made him feel like the king of the universe. Already he was becoming aroused again, his body stirring as she arched a bare foot over his calf.

'Hey, you gonna get naked with me or what?' Her voice was slurred with fatigue.

He tilted her face so he could look at her, skin peach-perfect and sheened with a translucent film of moisture, eyes still glazed with residual passion.

Emma.

An unfamiliar feeling stole through him. One he wasn't sure how to deal with. He eased her off to one side. Her hair was in disarray; he smoothed it away from her face and kissed her damp brow. 'Give me a minute.'

In the bathroom he dealt with the condom, then splashed cold water on his face. He'd just had wild sex with Emma. *Emma.* Looking away from the frown he glimpsed in his reflection, he swiped a towel and dried his face.

When he came back she'd burrowed beneath the quilt and was fast asleep, dead centre in the middle of the bed, one arm flung across a pillow, long dark lashes resting on cheeks the colour of dawn.

She looked tiny, all alone in that master bed. As if the snowy mountain of quilt might swallow her up.

Vulnerable.

That odd feeling intensified. He watched the slow rise and fall of the quilt as she breathed. He'd not anticipated this...this surge of emotion. What had he done?

He should go back to his own room, he thought,

even as he stripped off his shirt, tossed it over the chair. Collect a few essentials. She might need some space. Hell, *he* needed some space.

But he toed his shoes off, shoved down his trousers and jocks and stepped out of them. Retrieved the condoms from the floor, dropped them on the nightstand, then slipped into bed beside her.

She snuggled against him with a sleep murmur. Her warmth seeped into his bones, her exotic fragrance…fresh and floral and exclusively hers, surrounded him. He'd never forget that exotic fragrance. And when this attraction had run its course…

He closed his eyes.

Tomorrow. He'd think about that tomorrow.

CHAPTER NINE

THE SOUND OF a man's steady breathing woke Emma. A hard-muscled, hairy thigh was draped over one leg, its weight effectively pinning the lower half of her body in place. A warm hand curved around her left breast.

Jake.

Her heart leapt and her body burned as images of last night with the man of her dreams flooded back. She knew it was morning because a dull apricot light shimmered behind her eyelids, but she didn't open her eyes. She lay still, not wanting him to wake yet, because she wanted to replay every glorious, mind-blowing minute. Her skin felt as if it had been rubbed all over with a stiff towel.

He'd made love to her again while the soft darkness cocooned them in its blanket of intimacy. Horizontally this time. And slowly, skilfully. Sinfully. The way only a man with Jake's experience could.

And again and again. Always different, always amazing.

Her eyes blinked open and she turned her head

on the pillow to study him. As innocent as a baby but she knew better. Those perfectly sculpted lips, so relaxed in sleep, could wreak absolute havoc. Everywhere. A quicksilver shiver ran through her.

His hair was sticking up and it was an odd feeling knowing she'd had something to do with it. She smiled to herself. She itched to run her fingers through its silky softness again. Couldn't wait to feel the weight of his body on hers, to feel him come inside her again. Now. Tonight. Next week.

But reality intruded like a thief, stealing away the lovely feeling and her smile faded. This weekend was all he'd offered. All they'd agreed on. Just for fun.

And that was all she wanted too, right?

So make the most of it, she told herself, determined to ignore the feeling tugging at her and pleading for more. *Live in the moment.* They still had a late checkout and the rest of the day to spend together however they chose. A lot of fun could be packed into those few hours.

Easing her leg from beneath his, she slid a hand down between smooth sheets and hard-muscled belly... She found him semi-erect and wrapped her fingers around him. His eyes snapped open and that innocence disappeared in an instant, replaced with hot, not-quite-sleepy desire as he hardened beneath her palm.

'Good morning,' she murmured, and slid her hand down his satin-steel length and up again. 'Sorry to wake you... Actually, I'm not sorry.' She squeezed gently. 'I've got big plans for the day.'

He stuck one hand behind his head and watched her. A smile teased the corners of his mouth. 'Have you, now?'

'Mmm.' Positioning her top half over his chest, she rubbed against him once, twice, enjoying the rasp of masculine hair against her nipples, before reaching down to cup the heavy masculinity between his thighs. *Very big plans.* Resting her chin on his breastbone, she looked into his eyes. 'What about you? Any ideas?'

'I'm up for anything.' His smile was wicked and wide awake, like the rest of him.

She pushed the quilt down and took her time to admire the magnificent view of tanned skin over hard-packed muscle…and the proud, arrogant jut of his masculinity. 'I noticed.' Before he could flip her on her back and have her at his mercy again, she took charge and straddled him, reaching for a condom. 'Let's start the day on a high.'

A short while later, snuggled against him, she stretched lazily. Sunday mornings didn't get any better than this.

'Speaking of high,' Jake said, running his fingertips up and down her arm. 'What else are you up for today, Emma?'

A sneaky premonition snaked down her spine. 'Depends.'

'I'm thinking there's a playground of world-famous tourist attractions within walking distance that we should make the most of.'

She knew, and her stomach was already doing

somersaults. Did she want to be suspended two hundred and seventy metres above the forest floor on a wire cable? Or be slung down the side of a cliff on the steepest funicular railway in the world?

Her whole body recoiled. She wasn't a fan of heights and she didn't care who knew it. 'Or we could explore the local galleries, or take a drive to Leura and have lunch in one of the cafés before we head home,' she suggested hopefully.

He grinned and shook his head. 'Come on, Em, where's your sense of adventure?'

'I lost it somewhere. Really,' she insisted, when his grin remained. If anything it broadened. 'I think maybe I used it all up in this room,' she finished. She stared at him, her whole body blushing at everything they'd gotten up to last night. Suddenly feeling way too naked, she sat up, pulling the sheet over her breasts. 'Is this...*us*...weird?'

His grin faded, and for a long moment he didn't answer while they watched each other. In the stretched silence she heard a service trolley lumber past the room, the clatter of dishes. Had she ever seen his eyes so dark? Something behind that gaze had her heart stumbling around inside her chest... It was supposed to be just physical. *A weekend on Pleasure Island, remember?*

'You're thinking too hard again.' Jake reached out, smoothed her hair behind her ear. 'I rebooked my room. I want another night with you. What do you say?'

Yes, please?

One more night. Her pulse was on a fast track up the side of that mountain. Free and irresponsible was calling her, and she wasn't ready to go back to her boring job and busy *unsociable* life just yet.

'It'll mean a very early start tomorrow if we're going to make it to the city in time.'

'I've decided to take tomorrow off. You?'

'Monday's busy. I've got—'

'Stay with me. Call in sick.'

'I can't just take a day off.'

His brows rose. 'Why the hell not? Your sister just got married. Your boss'll understand.' His voice turned low and smooth and seductive. 'If you want, I can convince him you need the day to recover.'

She frowned. How she chose to use her recreational time was one thing, her job was quite another. An income was a necessity. A one-night stand, even a two-night stand, was a luxury.

And didn't every woman deserve a little luxury now and again?

Still... 'I haven't interfered in your working life, Jake. Please respect mine. And, just so you know, my boss is a woman, and it happens she's a real soft touch when it comes to love and romance.' She leant over and soothed his lips with hers. 'I'll organise it myself.' And deal with the repercussions later.

'Good decision.' She felt his fingers on the back of her head, holding her still while he turned her smooch into a meltingly irresistible kiss.

'Are *you?*' he murmured against her lips a moment later.

'Am I what?'

'A soft touch when it comes to love and romance. You feel soft enough…' He drifted a finger over her cheek, a bare shoulder.

She drew back, shrugged off the words and the associated emotions she didn't want or need. Jake and love and romance were mutually exclusive. In that they were equally matched. But she couldn't quite look him in the eye, and drew circles on the crisp pillow-case with a fingertip. 'I don't want the complication of either in my life.'

'You're a career girl.'

'At least you can count on your career.' Unlike counting on a man.

'Okay, career girl. We'll both play hooky tomorrow and then take a leisurely drive back to town.' He sat up, swung his legs over the side of the bed and reached for his trousers on the floor. 'I need to go back to my room, take a shower and change. Meet me downstairs for breakfast in half an hour and we'll discuss our plans.'

'Okay.' She watched him pull last night's clothes over his magnificent taut backside. The way the muscles in his shoulders bunched as he shrugged into his shirt. Biting back a sigh, she rose and picked up the terrycloth robe she'd worn the night before, which still lay on a nearby chair. She tied the sash and followed him to the door.

'See you in a little while,' he said, bending to kiss

her before opening the door. Then Emma saw his shoulders tense as he came to an abrupt halt.

'Jake.'

She heard her mother's chipped ice voice and Emma's skin flushed to the roots of her tousled bedroom hair. Shrinking into her robe, she hugged the lapels up to her chin with both hands.

'Good morning, Bernice.' Jake's back was towards Emma, and if he was surprised or embarrassed his voice gave no sign. 'Em's about to take a shower,' she heard him say as he sauntered out, his jacket and waistcoat slung over a shoulder. 'You just caught her in time.'

Emma sucked in a fortifying breath. 'Mum.' She moved forward and pulled the door wider while she imagined slamming it shut. 'Jake was…just leaving.' Obviously. And he seemed to have taken her thought-processing skills with him.

Her mother stalked in, missing none of last night's carnage strewn across the floor. 'I came to tell you I'm driving back with Ryan's Uncle Stan.'

Was that a flicker of *excitement* in her mother's eyes? But when Emma blinked it had vanished. 'That's…great, Mum…' She trailed off. What to say?

'I wanted to make sure you'd arranged a lift, but I assume now that you're driving back with Jake.'

Emma heard the underlying criticism loud and clear. 'Thanks, but actually I'm staying on another night.' Defiance streamed through her veins. 'Make that *we're* staying another night.'

Her mother had been staring at the rumpled bed but she swung to face her. 'What about work tomorrow morning?'

'I'm taking the day off.'

'Have you no sense of responsibility, girl? And with a man like Jake.' She exhaled her disapproval audibly through pinched nostrils.

'I never take time off. As for Jake, I like him, Mum. And so does Stella.' She hugged her arms to ward off the chill in her mother's eyes. 'He's an interesting, honest, hard-working man. I make my own decisions about the men I choose to see. And my own mistakes.'

'So you already think he's a mistake, then?'

Maybe it *was* a mistake, but she'd never know if she didn't take the risk. Jake had liberated something inside her last night and she wanted explore it, even if it was only for what was left of the weekend. 'I want a chance to find out.'

'Very well, then,' her mother replied, tight-lipped. The stony expression remained as she moved to the door. 'I'll see you at home.'

'Right. Drive safely.' Emma maintained an outward calm until the door closed with chilling formality, then swung around to lean back against it and slap her palms on the smooth wood. And a big goodbye to allowing her mother to put a blot on the morning.

It was only a little risk, she told herself, gathering her discarded garments and all the loose buttons she could locate. She tossed them into her suitcase, took out her casual clothes. A relaxing day playing tourist in the Blue Mountains was just what she needed.

And tonight… Her newly energised body tightened at the thought. It was going to be fun. Just fun.

CHAPTER TEN

AFTER WAVING THE newly married couple off on their honeymoon, Jake convinced Emma to walk to Echo Point again later that morning. The air was cold but the sun was out for now, turning the Three Sisters a stark orange against the blue-tinged foliage. A bank of clouds was building; it would rain before nightfall.

'So Stan's driving your mum home,' Jake said as they gazed over the valley. Bernice finding him in Emma's room had been an unexpected and awkward moment. 'Did she give you a hard time?' Neither of them had spoken of the episode over breakfast, but it needed to be said.

'No more than usual.' Emma spoke casually, but he saw her posture dip as she leaned on the railing as if it might prop her up. 'I hope Stan can put her in a better mood.'

'If anyone can cheer Bernice up, Stan's your man.'

Hanging on to the rail with both hands, she leaned back at a crazy angle and looked at the sky. 'You know what? I don't want to think about her *or* work today.'

'Good girl.' He covered her hands with his. 'To-day's for us.'

'Sounds perfect.' Turning to him, she tipped her face up to his, last night's sparkle still dancing in her eyes. She wore a faded tracksuit, scuffed sneakers and her hair was tied back into a loose coil which hung between her shoulderblades. Without make-up, her face glowed with good health except for some luscious-looking peach-coloured lipgloss.

She looked…radiant. Last night's gymnastics had done her a world of good. 'Let's go.' Keeping her hand clasped firmly in his, he headed towards a walking trail which pointed to Katoomba Falls.

Seeing the spectacular World Heritage sights with Emma, he discovered their mutual enjoyment of exploring nature on foot. She shared his interest in the environment and the native flora and fauna they came across. Ancient ferns, rainbow lorikeets. They even glimpsed an echidna fossicking in the bushland nearby.

He persuaded her to cross the valley on the Sky-way with the promise of lunch at the revolving restaurant at the other end. She buried her face against his chest as they swung out into space so high that the shadow of their cabin was the size of a newborn's thumbnail on the Jurassic forest below.

Jake couldn't remember a day he'd enjoyed more in a long time. Simple things like sharing a can of soda while they sat on a rock with the breeze at their backs and listened to the crystal sounds of the nearby Katoomba waterfall.

He was as interested in Emma's mind and her opinions as he was in her body. Connecting with her, seeing that rare smile and finding out what they had in common, was as much a part of the day as the hot, lingering looks they exchanged, knowing the evening ahead promised to be as special as the last.

By mid-afternoon it was becoming increasingly difficult to keep his hands off her, so they cut the sightseeing short and made a fast trip back to the hotel and his suite.

Later, surrounded by white candles in the gleaming black spa of the stunning black bathroom, with its wide uninterrupted view, they sipped bubbly and watched the constantly changing panorama. A curtain of rain filled the valley floor, a blur of dull gold with the setting sun behind as the shower moved through in brilliant contrast to the encroaching stormy black sky.

But the best view was right in front of him.

Emma's hair was catching the sun's last feeble rays, and the soft glow of candlelight shone on her cheeks as daylight faded.

She was facing him across a mountain of bubbles, and in those sapphire eyes, with their stars and luminosity, he could see a load had been lifted. She'd let herself go for once in her life and had a good time.

How long would it take for the pressures of real life to tarnish that glow and eclipse the sparkle? After tomorrow's short return journey to the urban rat race it was back to business for them both.

Which made it all the more important not to waste a single second of what was left of tonight.

He took her glass, set both flutes on the side of the spa, then slid forward, knees bent, so that his legs came around hers and her belly came into contact with his. Put his hands on her shoulders so he could look right into those eyes. 'You're a pleasure to be with, Emma Byrne.'

Emma stared into his warm brown eyes. She was going to pay for that pleasure sooner or later. This weekend had been one amazing adventure after another, one she'd remember for ever.

'Hey, that's supposed to make you smile, not frown.'

'I'm not fr—'

'You are. You get that little line between your eyebrows…' He smoothed it away with a fingertip. 'Okay, I've got something guaranteed to make you smile.' His deep voice rumbled between them and he pressed closer, his burgeoning hardness hot and impatient against her belly.

'Mmm…'

'See? Smiling already.' He nipped his way up the side of her neck to the sensitive spot beneath her ear. 'How am I doing?' Tugged her earlobe between his lips, making her tingle.

'Pretty well.' His hands were a slippery delight on her shoulders.

'Only pretty well?'

She closed her eyes the better to savour it. Him. 'You can do better.'

A slow hand cruised down to her left breast to toy with her nipple. 'How about this?' He moved his mouth over hers and murmured, 'Is this good?'

'Mmm. Good.' *Very good.* She sighed and her lips opened under his probing tongue. It wasn't only his fabulously sexy body and his skill as a lover, it was their easy rapport, their shared interests.

Or was it something deeper?

Before she could ponder or react to that significant and scary thought he surged forward, his hands on either side of her face, his dark eyes holding hers. Slowly, slowly, he pushed that glorious hardness inside her. Slow and slippery and…oh, he was persuasive. Addictive.

'Tell me it's the best you ever had,' he demanded against her lips, withdrawing inch by excruciatingly exquisite inch, leaving her breathless and arching her hips in anticipation.

'Ha!' she managed. 'Isn't that what you guys all want to know?'

'Tell me you want more.' He leaned back just enough for her to see the wicked glint in his eyes and withdrew.

'Yes,' she moaned. 'More.' And moaned again as he pushed inside her, faster now, on a wild ride to paradise.

'Come with me.' His words sounded harsh and ragged against her ear as he came deep inside her.

'Coming,' she gasped as she rode over the edge of the velvet chasm with him.

JAKE HAD CHOSEN the room for its awesome view and the gas fire. The flames that licked over attractive smooth river stones provided warmth and intimacy. They sat in matching hotel robes on the rug in the flickering glow and shared the cold lobster and mango salad Room Service had delivered earlier.

He watched Emma slip a slice of mango between her lips. Tousled damp hair framed her face. Her eyes reflected the fire's orange glow, turning them violet and mysterious.

He wanted to know more of her secrets. More about the product line she'd developed and why she was so passionate about it that she'd spend so much of her free time immersed in it and yet not pursue its potential further.

Was it a front to hide behind? Was she lonely or a natural loner? Was she a risk-taker or not?

She was different to the women he usually got involved with. *So* different from the synthetic types to be found in King's Cross. Emma was sparkly and refreshing, a glint of dew on spring grass on a sunny morning. Her body was slender, firm, natural. Curves in all the right places and they were all real.

'Taste.' She swirled a sliver of lobster into the buttery sauce and held it to his lips. 'It's divine.'

He opened his mouth and let her feed him. Chewed a moment, savouring the flavour, the slight pressure of her finger against his lips.

The room's muted glow cast intimate shadows. 'Nothing beats romance, huh?'

She wiped her fingers on her napkin, her movements a little jerky. Her eyes were still on his but rather than the dreamy violet from moments ago they were quicksilver-black. 'I don't do romance.'

The flat comment surprised him. 'No?' He waved an all-encompassing hand around the room—the flickering firelight on the walls, its warmth against his skin. 'What do you call this? The candlelit spa we just enjoyed?'

'Ambience.'

'So define romance.'

'Hearts and flowers and pretty words.' Silver sliced through her gaze, a knife's glint against ebony. 'I don't need them and I don't want them.'

'Why not?' He saw the pain in her eyes before she looked away. 'Surfer Boy wasn't the romantic type?'

She shrugged. 'That's just it. He was. Something special every Friday night and a dozen red roses every Wednesday, with a pretty note to say he was thinking of me...'

Her story didn't make sense to Jake. 'You weren't being totally honest with me about him the night of the dinner, were you?'

'Just because I don't want rom—'

'It's in your eyes. That's why you're not looking at me.'

'I'm...' Her shoulders drooped. 'Okay. I didn't slot him into my schedule. He slotted me into his. And I let him. Because, you see, I was stupidly in love with him.'

Jake reached out, trailed a finger down her cheek.

'He's even more of an idiot than I thought,' he murmured.

She shook her head. 'Romance is a lie to cover a lie.'

'It doesn't have to be, Emma.'

'No romance, okay? No lies.'

'Okay…' He pressed her down and rolled her onto her back on the rug, unknotting her belt and spreading her robe wide. 'Does that mean I can't tell you you're the sexiest woman I've ever made love to by firelight?'

She reached for his robe, pushing it away, fingers stretching and flexing over his shoulders, her eyes duelling with his, a smile on her lips and that little dimple in her cheek winking as he lowered himself on top of her. 'I'm okay with that.'

THEY HAD A late checkout on Monday morning so they spent it in bed and then enjoyed a quick lunch in a charming little rustic café before returning to Sydney. Emma had phoned in sick to work—something she'd never done before.

On the trip back she was almost tempted to open her laptop which Jake had returned to her, and catch up on the orders she'd neglected. But she knew she'd not be able to concentrate. Her mind was chock-full of distracting thoughts. So she watched the scenery flash by, and with it the slow return from fairytales and magical rides—of any kind—to civilisation and real life.

Real life. Depressing thought. Closing her eyes,

she feigned sleep as they reached outer suburbia and let her mind drift back over the past two days.

She heard Jake speak on his mobile with his PA about some problem with a client that couldn't wait, enjoying the deep, authoritative timbre in his voice, remembering how it sounded when he came deep inside her.

Emma's phone signalled an incoming text. She considered ignoring it, but her responsible self wouldn't allow her to. She opened it and stared at the message. 'I don't believe it,' she murmured.

Jake glanced her way. 'Something wrong?'

'Mum's gone to Melbourne. With Stan.'

'Good for her.' Jake's voice was laced with a smile.

Emma texted back a reply before slipping her phone back into her bag. 'She's never done anything so impulsive in her life.'

'Then it's time she did.' With his eyes on the road, Jake put a hand on her thigh. 'Stan's a good guy. She'll be fine.'

'Of course she will.' She hoped. Because she wasn't looking forward to the fall-out if things went wrong.

'Your mum's a hard woman, Em,' he said, moments later. 'I know she was ill for a long time...'

'Clinical depression.' Emma hugged her arms, remembering the stress she and Stella had endured as a result. 'She's recovered now, but the after-effects linger on.' *And on.*

'Your dad's death caused it?'

She shook her head. 'She was depressed long before that. Dad didn't love her and there were other women.'

'Why didn't she just kick him out or walk away?'

'Because he had absolute control of her money. Remember, her generation isn't ours. And maybe she *wanted* to play the martyr.' The angst spilled out and it felt good. Really good. As if she was sweeping it out of her life. 'Just before Dad died he invested what was left of her inheritance and lost the lot.'

She heard Jake exhale loudly. 'That's tough, Emma. That's why you were always working?'

'I couldn't let the house be sold. It would've finished Mum off. Stella, being the nurturing soul she is, took on the role of carer.'

'So, forgive me if this offends you, why the hell does Bernice treat you the way she does? And why do you let her?'

A question Emma had asked herself often enough. 'Mum never appreciated the financial side of what I was doing—she just didn't see it. And Stella's been there for her in a more physical and emotional way.'

'So you erected a barrier to protect yourself from the rejection.'

'I guess I did. She doesn't get to me any more.'

He glanced at her. 'I disagree, Emma. It's still there.'

She shrugged—maybe he was right—and watched the glimpses of the ocean through the windscreen as they neared Coogee. 'She allowed my father to ruin her life. It spilled over to her daughters.'

And it reminded Emma why she wouldn't allow herself to think of what she and Jake had as anything more than a sexy encounter. She'd enjoyed it for what it was. But never again would she rely on anyone for her own happiness.

It felt odd, pulling up in her driveway in the middle of a work-day afternoon. She felt as if she'd lived a lifetime since she'd been home.

Jake switched off the engine, and the sudden silence in the car's confines seemed to shout. She busied herself searching her bag for her keys then realised she was already holding them.

She felt his gaze as he said, 'I guess you'll want to jump straight on your laptop and check out those orders that have piled up in your absence.'

His tone suggested that even if *she* wasn't down from the clouds and quite ready to settle to work just yet he was. He was probably used to switching from pleasure to business without a blink.

She fought down an absurd disappointment and turned with a smile fixed on her face. 'It doesn't go away, does it? Even when we do.'

He smiled back. 'Okay, then.' He pushed open the door and walked around to the boot to take out her belongings.

She took a careful, calming breath before climbing out and following him to the front door. She unlocked it and he ushered her past him and inside.

'Where do you want your gear?' he said behind her.

'Here's fine.' She gestured beside her and turned

to him, suddenly feeling like a stranger in her own surroundings. Everything felt different and she didn't know what to say. How ridiculous. She was experiencing morning-after awkwardness *now?*

He set the suitcase down and placed the garment bag on top, then straightened.

'Thanks.'

'No worries.'

She didn't know what to do with her hands and clasped them in front of her. How did you say goodbye to a man you'd just spent the past couple of nights having the best sex of your life with?

You said it casually, as if it happens all the time. 'Thanks for a great weekend.'

'My pleasure.' A flicker of heat darkened his gaze. *Mine too.*

'I'll let you get to it, then.'

No *We'll have to do it again sometime.* 'Yes. Better get started. So…I'll see you…around.' God, did she sound needy? Clingy? Desperate?

He nodded, those dark eyes fixed on hers but giving nothing away. 'I'll give you a call some time.'

'Right.' Tomorrow? Next week? Next year?

He bent to kiss her. Just a brief brush of those expert lips over hers. Then he must have changed his mind because his arms slid around her waist and pulled her close. Her mouth opened beneath his and she let him in, tasting him as his tongue slid over hers. Her heart thudded against her chest and she clung to his shirt a moment before he lifted his head.

His eyes had changed, she noticed, like hot treacle. But she instinctively knew he wasn't going to act on it, so stepped back first. *At least maintain a little dignity.* 'Bye, then.'

'Catch you later.'

As he turned to leave his mobile buzzed and he yanked it out of his jacket pocket. 'Carmody.' He paused on Emma's doorstep, not looking at her while he listened to the caller. He didn't look back, walking into the sunshine, his attention already focused elsewhere.

Emma closed the door and listened to the purr of his car's engine as he drove off. She rubbed a hand over the familiar ache in her chest. It couldn't be love. Not again. She wouldn't let it be.

CHAPTER ELEVEN

EMMA FOUND IT tough going over the next couple of days at work—unable to concentrate, thinking of Jake, remembering their time together, wishing she could see him again even if it was just to remind herself that he was a one-weekend wonder. But she didn't hear from him.

Get over it. They'd had a fling. One wild, sexy weekend of pleasure. He'd never promised more. He'd been totally upfront with her. At least he'd been honest, and after Wayne that counted for a lot.

She felt different, though. Being with Jake had given her a new-found confidence in herself. As a woman, as a lover, as a person. She wanted to take on the world. She wanted to get serious about her business.

She wanted to see him so she could tell him that.

Meanwhile she filled her orders and surfed the internet for new soap-making recipes and considered how she might extend her client base.

On Thursday evening, humming along with her favourite jazz CD, she collected the ingredients together for honey soap. She melted glycerin bars and honey, poured it into a shallow pan, then melted the goat's milk, adding it to the mix. She'd just set it aside to cool when she heard the doorbell chime and went to answer it.

Jake.

He was leaning on her doorframe, reminding her of the last time she'd seen him standing there, and her heart tripped and she was breathless all over again. A burst of happiness sang through her veins as she met his warm brown eyes. Tonight he wore a luxurious-looking cream jumper over black trousers.

Her smile was spontaneous. 'Hi.'

'I was on my way out and passing this way…' The timbre of his deep, familiar voice turned her insides as hot and syrupy as the mix on her kitchen bench. 'Have I caught you at a bad time?'

'No…no.' She forced the surprise and excitement from her voice. *Act natural. He's on his way out, after all.* 'Come on in. I'm just finishing some soaps.' She turned, casting a deliberately casual glance over her shoulder as she moved to the kitchen. 'What brings you by?' When he didn't answer, she stopped at the kitchen table and turned. He almost crashed into her.

'You,' he said, his eyes melting into hers.

The heat from his body seemed to shimmer right through her. He smelled of warm wool and apple and cinnamon pie.

'More specifically, your soaps.' He rubbed his knuckles together audibly. 'It's my PA's birthday next week. I'd like to buy some for her.'

'Uh-huh. Well…' She swished her own hands down her coat. Her palms were sweating. 'I've got some pretty flower-shaped ones with a "Happy Birthday" imprint somewhere. I'll—'

'No birthday imprint.' He caught her arm as she started to move away.

'Oh. Okay…' She blinked once.

'She doesn't want anyone to know.' He lifted a shoulder. 'She's shy about birthdays.' Jake lowered his voice, curling his fingers around the lab coat's thick fabric. He felt Emma's gentle warmth beneath, the smooth muscle over bone against his palm, before letting his arm drop to his side. 'I thought I'd take some extras into the office at the same time. Let some of the staff try them out.'

'Really?' Surprise and humour glinted in her eyes and her lips curved and he knew she was wise to his game.

'Really.' He smiled back. 'What can you recommend?'

She moved to the plastic containers stacked along the wall. 'They're all made with goat's milk for sensitive skin, but I have a range of fragrances. How about amber, which has a sweet woody note suitable for both sexes? Or vanilla? Or, for something extra special…' She pulled out a container, carried it to the table. 'I've got some gorgeous little cupcake shapes in different fragrances—vanilla, blueberry, cinnamon, coconut. They're my favourite stock and very popular. I can pack them in a little basket for you if you want.'

He grinned. 'Do you wash with them or eat them?'

She opened the box, closed her eyes briefly and inhaled the fragrance, her ecstatic expression reminding him of when she'd come apart in his arms. She lifted out a pretty pink sample that matched the colour in her cheeks. 'I love cupcakes to death, but I wouldn't recommend eating these.'

Amazing, this transformation from the solemn girl who'd greeted him at her door only last week. The obvious joy she got from her creative work. The sparkle it put in her eyes and the glow it brought to her cheeks. And she was right; this was no mere hobby. Little wonder she'd been insulted he'd called it such. She had something unique here, a marketable product.

He leaned a hip against the table. 'Have you given any more thought to expanding this business online? Because I see a different woman standing here tonight. One who might be willing to take that chance now.'

'Maybe I *am* a different woman.' He noticed her eyes had turned a darker hue as she looked at him. 'You've had something to do with that. And I *am* thinking about it.' She picked up a green cake, held it to his nose. 'What do you smell?'

'Fresh mown grass?'

'It gives a bathroom a pleasant scent.' She set it down. 'So many fragrances. I love them all.'

'Which one do you use?' He leaned in to catch more of that scent he'd missed over the past few days, heard her tiny intake of breath.

'Tahitian Fantasy.' Her breath hitched again. 'Why are you really here, Jake?'

Her husky voice vibrated against his lips as he set them on her smooth neck. 'Nothing like a little Tahitian Fantasy. Because I wanted to see you again. Are you okay with that?' His hands drifted to her waist, lips tracing a line over the fragrant flesh beneath her ear.

'Ah…yes…'

'Good, because I can't seem to stay away.' He nipped at her earlobe. 'What's in it?'

'The tiare flower. Tahitian gardenia.' She arched her neck. 'It has healing properties.'

'I've got this itch…'

'Where?' she murmured.

'Everywhere,' he murmured back, moving nearer, pressing open-mouthed kisses up her neck, over her jaw. 'I itch every damn where.'

'That sounds serious.' She stepped back to see his eyes, her own dancing as she slid his sleeve up to his elbow, fingers lightly massaging his forearm. 'Do you exfoliate?'

He had to lean forward so he could drop a lingering kiss on her lips. 'Only when I'm with you.'

Her blue eyes twinkled up at him. 'Ha-ha.' She picked up a dark-coloured soap that looked like congealed breakfast cereal. 'Honey and oatmeal,' she said, and gave his chest a light prod with one finger. 'Sit down…if you've got a moment?'

'For you, yes.' He yanked out a chair and watched her fill a shallow bowl with warm water.

The last time he'd been in her place she'd been uptight and defensive and prickly. Tonight she was the relaxed woman he'd enjoyed the weekend with.

Was it only four nights ago? It felt like four weeks. He'd spent those nights in a kind of limbo, caught between wanting to call and ask if he could come over and reminding himself they'd agreed on a weekend and the weekend was finished.

Had she spent the last few nights thinking of how good they'd been together? In bed and out of it? She was fresh, honest and fun to be with. He regretted putting a time limit on their affair.

'It's almost as good as sex.' Her words had him sitting up straighter as she carried the bowl to the table, set it in front of him along with a handtowel.

'What is?'

'Push up your sleeves and put your hands in the bowl.' She moistened the soap in the water and worked it between her palms till it glistened, then slid it over and around his hand in a slow, slippery massage. 'Good?'

He watched, fascinated, her small fingers with their short neat nails gliding over his, between his. He looked up, met her eyes. 'Very good. Exceptionally good. But... Do I need to work on my bedroom technique?'

The twinkle in her eyes sharpened. Her lips stretched into a full-on smile. 'Okay, that was my selling point before the weekend. Damn—now I'll have to think of something else.'

'We could always test the theory again, just to be sure…'

'There's nothing wrong with your technique, Jake.' She twined her fingers against his. Silky heat on silky heat.

'Nor yours.' He reciprocated, pressing his thumb into her palm and drawing lazy circles, watching her cheeks pinken, her eyes turn to liquid pools of blue desire.

His own vision was growing hazy as they continued to watch each other while they made out with their joined hands. 'Do you give all your clients the personal treatment?'

She leaned in so that her lips were a whisper away from his. 'Only the ones who knock on my door.'

'I've been thinking,' he murmured back, 'there's no reason why we can't continue seeing each other, is there?'

Her whole body stilled. 'What are you saying?'

He soothed his lips over hers just once. 'I like being with you. Don't look too far ahead. Let's just enjoy the ride. What do you say?'

'Uh-huh…'

He lifted her damp fingers to his mouth, kissed them and released her. 'In the meantime, I've got an appointment in King's Cross. If tonight goes as planned, tomorrow the Pink Mango could be looking at a new owner.'

She continued to stare at him, unblinking, gaze unfocused. 'Uh-huh.'

But she didn't seem to hear him. 'Don't congratulate me yet,' he said anyway. He wiped his hands on her little towel, then pushed up. 'Talk to you tomorrow evening.'

'Uh-huh.'

He folded the towel, set it on the table. 'I'll let myself out.'

He smiled to himself when he heard her call, 'Yes!' as clear as crystal as he walked to the door.

FOR EMMA, THE following work day dragged. Unlike what was happening with Jake, which seemed to be taking off at warp speed. She couldn't focus on anything except their unexpected sexy interlude last night.

He liked being with her. He wanted to be with her some more. It brought a smile to her lips every time she remembered. So often that her co-workers cast more than a few Emma-had-got-lucky glances her way over the course of the day.

She left the call centre five minutes before closing time; something she'd never done before. She tapped along with the beat of the latest pop song on the radio as she drove home, looking forward to Jake's call.

It was nearly six o'clock when he rang. Emma picked the phone up on its first ring.

'It's done,' he said without preamble. 'The Pink Mango's history.'

She almost heard the drum-roll of satisfaction in his voice and smiled. 'Hooray for you.'

'Can you clear your evening schedule and come out to celebrate with me?'

Her smile broadened. 'Consider it cleared.'

'I'll pick you up in thirty minutes?'

'*Thirty* minutes?'

'You'll look gorgeous whatever you're wearing,' he said, obviously familiar with the female ritual, 'and I've got somewhere casual in mind.'

Thirty-five minutes later, after three changes of clothes, she'd decided on her best jeans and an ivory jumper with a bright turquoise-and-orange scarf when he arrived.

Seeing him was like cresting the top of a roller-coaster wave, all excitement and anticipation. He wore black jeans and a black T-shirt beneath an often washed black, white and navy flannel shirt, open down the front. Definitely casual.

'Hi.' She sounded as breathless as she felt.

'Hi.' With one arm still propped against the door-frame he tugged on her scarf, pulled her towards him and kissed her.

He tasted *sooo* good, and she felt herself rushing down the other side of that slippery breaker. Then he straightened, and with a wickedly hot twinkle in his eyes, said, 'If we don't get moving we might never get there.'

'Wait up. You forgot something last night.' She picked up a little cellophane-wrapped basket from the shelf by the door and held it out with a grin. 'Tell your PA happy birthday from me.'

He nodded, eyes twinkling. 'How much do I owe you?'

'Nothing. Free sample.'

'Are you sure?'

'Positive. Promotion's good for business.'

'Okay, but don't forget to write it off as an expense.'

Moments later they were cruising along a well-lit Bondi street bustling with Friday-night shoppers. But Jake bypassed the usual restaurants and turned into a suburban street.

She looked out at the luxury homes, roofs glinting in the streetlights. 'Where are we going?'

He pulled up in front of a buttercream wall. Beyond, Emma could see an expansive red-tiled roof. 'Welcome to Jake's Place. Home of great food and magnificent views.' He pressed a remote and the gates swung open revealing a large two-storey house.

'Wow.' She took in the view as the car came to a stop under an open carport. A long curve of beach, dark now but for a couple of lights blinking near the horizon. 'It's magnificent, Jake. You've achieved so much in such a short time.' The location alone had to be worth a fortune.

He swiped the keys from the ignition, his gaze on the black waves laced with a fine line of white in the distance. 'The bank still has a share, but we're getting there.'

Reaching across the console between them, he cupped the back of her neck with one hand, unclipped her seat belt with the other, his gaze hot with smouldering promise. And before she could blink he meshed his lips with hers.

He'd had no intention of jumping her until he'd

fed her, but when Jake looked into those sapphire eyes which had kept him from the precious little sleep he'd managed over the past few nights, every thought flew out of his mind bar one. Having Emma.

'Have you missed me?' he murmured against her lips. When had he ever asked that question? he wondered vaguely, and was stupidly happy when he felt her lips curve against his mouth.

'Yes.' She sucked in a breath.

His impatient fingers found the hem of her jumper and rushed beneath to feel the firm, warm flesh of her torso, the ridges along her ribcage, and higher to the curve under her breasts. Her nipples tightened as he swirled his fingers over the crests. Beneath his hands he felt the same urgency that whipped through his own body as she strained against his palm.

'Emma…' The breathless sound registered somewhere as his own voice. 'Missed you too.' Flicking the clasp, he loosened her bra, shoved it up and out of the way so he could feast on the sweet taste of an engorged nipple. He slid his palm between her thighs, cupped her hard through the hot denim, felt her shudder and arch in response, heard her muffled sigh as she forked her fingers through his hair and pulled it tight against his scalp.

He heard a rushing noise in his ears; it might have been the sea, or her ragged breath, or the fizz of his own blood. All he knew was if he didn't get out now he'd have her here, in the car, before sanity could prevail.

Swearing and fumbling with the latch, he pushed

the passenger door open. Somehow they were both out of the car and stumbling together towards the house.

His keys… In the car—somewhere. The hell with them. He had her up against the wall, mouths fused, teeth clashing, his raging erection pressing into the soft give of her belly before either of them knew what had happened.

Did she have any idea how much power she wielded over him? He never lost it like this. Her pupils were dark and dilated when he lifted his head to watch her while he snapped open the top button of her jeans.

She returned the favour, hard little knuckles against his belly as she loosened the stud.

There was a harsh zipping sound as they freed each other. And then he was lifting her against the wall and pushing into her familiar sultry heat, his tongue mimicking the action as it dived inside her mouth to drown in her taste.

Fast, furious, frantic. No time to think. Just blind, burning lust, passion and pleasure. She seemed to struggle for air, and he lifted his lips, as breathless as she, and watched her, head thrown back, neck pale and slender in the cool wash of light angling in from the street.

Then his mouth was there, on that galloping pulse, her smooth fragrant skin. Exquisite taste. Pure sensuality.

But the need she conjured in him as he rode the wave to completion, this desperation, as if she was tearing something from deep within him, was beyond his experience.

Moments later, his body still humming, he lowered her to her feet, rested his brow against hers. 'What is it with you? I can't seem to get enough—'

Protection. He froze. He'd not given it a thought. Not given Emma's welfare or safety a thought. What kind of man did that make him? He lifted her chin with a finger and stared into her eyes. 'We just had unprotected sex, Emma.'

'We didn't use a condom, no.' She didn't look fazed or alarmed. Her eyes were clear and calm, like the sea on a summer day.

'I…if anything happens…'

'It won't. I'm still on the pill.'

He relaxed a little. 'You didn't tell me.'

'You didn't ask.' She lifted a shoulder, then wiggled back into her jeans. 'And I wasn't as sure about you then…'

He caught her drift. 'I'm healthy, Emma.'

If they'd been in full light he'd have sworn her eyes darkened, and she rolled her lips together in that way she had before saying, 'I wanted *you* inside me, not a piece of rubber.'

Her words hit hard, right where his heart suddenly pounded like a hammer on steel. His fingers tightened as he adjusted his own clothing. 'I should've been more careful. I always use condoms.' Just not this time.

'I take care of my own protection,' she said.

Emma didn't want to talk about it. Not another

word. *Oh, no.* Her heart suddenly cramped, twisted as she realised the full import of what she'd just admitted. She'd wanted that closer connection with him. Craved it like an addict. *Dangerous.* Had she made the right decision to continue seeing Jake after all?

She rubbed a hand over her chest. 'It's cold out here,' she said, hugging her arms. 'Can we go inside?'

He mumbled something about keys and walked to the car, fishing around in the luxury interior a moment before coming back, keys in hand. 'Come on— you can take a look around while I cook.'

She used the time alone to refocus her thoughts while she explored Jake's domain. The décor was essentially masculine but comfortable. Lots of glass, dark furniture with splashes of colour—maroon, grey, red. The wood-panelled kitchen was surprisingly clean and tidy, putting hers to shame. But then, he had enough cupboard space and mod cons for the both of them. An office with two computers and three monitors, and a fortune in the latest technology in the living room.

The upstairs bedrooms were mostly empty except for Jake's. A massive king-size bed dominated the room with its tan and navy quilt and minimal furniture. She backed away from the reminder that other women had no doubt enjoyed themselves there and hurried downstairs.

He'd slapped a couple of thick steaks on the grill and was slicing an avocado when she returned to the kitchen, but he waved away her offer of help so she wandered to the living room. Windchimes filled the balcony beyond the floor-to-ceiling windows, the sound tinkling and clacking in the gentle breeze. Solar-powered balls of crackled glass slowly spun multi-coloured lights over the deck.

He appeared moments later with the aromatic steaks, a bowl of healthy-looking salad and a loaf of crusty bread.

They ate while a blues CD poured music out of the speakers with only the solar-powered balls for lighting— 'ambience', he was quick to point out— and washed it down with a nice cabernet sauvignon while they watched a passenger ship track north, myriad tiny lights blazing.

He topped up her glass. 'What's the latest on your mum?'

'She's still in Melbourne. Staying in Stan's house, of all places. *And* she's still deciding when she'll come home.'

'Having a new man in her life's obviously done her good.' He grinned. 'Maybe she'll be a little more mellow on her return.'

'Maybe.' It helped that Jake understood, and Emma was glad she'd opened up on that topic; it felt good to share.

He rose, collected their plates. 'Why don't you go make yourself comfortable on the couch and I'll make coffee? What's your preference?'

'Cappuccino, please. With extra chocolate?'

While he attended to the coffee machine she

walked out onto the deck to feel the salt breeze and hear the sound of the sea. She told herself that she was right where she wanted to be. With a guy whose company she enjoyed. She refused to let herself think beyond the ride he'd promised.

When she walked inside he'd brought the coffee and a bowl of dark chocolates and she snuggled against him on the couch. She listened to his heart beating strong and solid against her ear, the fresh fragrance of sun-dried clothes and his clean scent in her nostrils. He turned on the TV. Some old adventure movie was playing. She tuned out, closed her eyes, and moments later felt herself drifting…

'You're tired,' he murmured. 'Stay the night.'

The spell she was falling under shattered like glass. She kept her eyes closed but her mind was instantly alert. Unlike their fantasy weekend in paradise, this was the real world. And in the real world she was…falling in love with this man.

Even as the words formed in her mind she was shoving them away, squeezing them out of her heart. She refused, *refused* to fall in love again. She'd been there, done that, and had the scars to prove it. Her mother had fallen for a man who'd not loved her and it had brought nothing but pain and misery to herself, her husband and her daughters—even long after he'd died.

'You're thinking too hard again.' He curled a hand around her head and stroked her hair. 'You won't need pyjamas, and I've got a spare toothbrush.'

Oh, yes, she'd bet he did.

'So…spend the night with me?'

She opened her eyes, looked into his and felt her heart tumble further. 'I can't,' she all but whispered.

A puzzled crease formed between his brows. 'I'll drive you back in plenty of time in the morning. I can even wait while you get your swimsuit and drop you off at the beach if you want.'

'We'll see each other, Jake, but I won't be staying nights.'

A beat of silence. 'I'm not Wayne, Emma,' he said quietly.

'I know. I just need my space for a bit. This is all happening too fast.' She couldn't help it. She reached up, touched his clean-shaven jaw. 'Okay?'

'Okay. I won't pressure you. It's too soon. I get that. But if you change your mind…'

She nodded, feeling the strength drain out of her. 'Thanks. But you're right. I'm tired and, if it's okay with you, I'd like to go home now.'

He exhaled a slow, deep breath, then pushed off the couch. 'I'll get my keys.'

WHEN A WOMAN didn't want to spend the night with him, he… He what? Jake frowned at his darkened ceiling later that night. He couldn't remember the last time.

He swung out of bed, dragged on old shorts, T-shirt and sneakers, then headed downstairs and out into the salty night air. The chill spattered his skin with goosebumps as he made his way along a couple of streets to the beach. Black waves surged and thumped on the sand as he jogged off the road and onto the esplanade.

She had good reasons, he reminded himself, and it wasn't personal—the scumbag surfer had done a real number on her.

He'd respect her space, give her time. That fragile heart of hers was still healing, and no way was he going to be responsible for further damage. Meanwhile they could continue to enjoy what they *did* have, keeping it casual.

A car skidded to a stop a short distance away, drawing his attention. The back door swung open, something flopped onto the road and the vehicle sped off. What the…?

Switching direction to the way he'd come, he increased his pace.

The small bundle of dirty fur moved, and two frightened eyes looked up at his. Jake's heart melted. 'Hey, fella. Steady.' He looked the dog over, murmuring soothing noises. No ID. Beneath the matted white fur he was skin and bone, and alive with fleas. Abandoned in the middle of the night. Poor little scrap.

'Come on, Scratch. We'll find you some place safe.' Sliding a finger beneath the grimy collar, he picked the little guy up and set off for home. In a different life he'd have kept him, but he had no choice but to hand him to the nearest animal shelter first thing.

With Scratch contained in the laundry, with a bowl of water, a left-over sausage and an old cushion to sleep on, Jake's thoughts turned to Emma again as he climbed the stairs to snatch a couple of hours of sleep.

She was sexy, had a sense of humour, and was good company in and out of bed. If she wouldn't stay the night he'd accept that. Because she was Emma. She wasn't only a lover, she was a friend. There was something so easy about being with her, and she brought more to his life on so many levels than any woman ever had.

Careful, mate. He was starting to sound like Ry. *Hell.* He flopped backwards onto his bed. That was one very dangerous thought.

CHAPTER TWELVE

THE SEA WAS as calm as glass on Sunday morning, but the air chilled Emma's body as she waded in for her morning workout. The sun had lifted out of the ocean, spreading crimson and gold across the sky.

Sliding beneath the surface, she kept close to the shoreline between the red and yellow safety flags, swimming hard until her limbs warmed and softened. She trod water, watching the sun glimmer on the surface, and waved to a regular fellow swimmer before heading back the other way.

Jake had come by yesterday evening, late and tired. Working his day job and dealing with the sale of the club would take a toll on anyone. She'd made popcorn on one occasion and they'd made love—on every occasion. On the couch. In her tiny shower stall. In her too-small bed. But he hadn't stayed. She'd been unable to sleep for the rest of the night, knowing there was a big warm man in a big warm bed a few kilometres away who'd have been happy to share.

She headed for her towel farther up the beach.

Sunday mornings brought out tourists and locals alike. Walking up the shallow steps towards the lawns bordering the esplanade, she watched a group of families set up for a picnic breakfast.

Only now, with Jake in her life, was she realising how isolated she'd let herself become over the years. She needed to make an effort to go out and socialise more.

She wrung out her hair, tied it into a high ponytail, then changed into her track suit in the change rooms, dumping her swimsuit and towel into her hold-all.

On such a beautiful day she didn't want to go home and deal with business, shut away from people and life. She'd splash out on a take-away hot chocolate on the way home. She might even add a cake to her order and sit at an outdoor table on Coogee Beach Road and people-watch awhile.

A big guy with a black-and-white dog on a leash was approaching when she reached the traffic lights. He waved and she pushed up her sunglasses. Jake? With a dog?

She waved back, and suddenly that sunshine seemed a whole lot warmer. The whole world seemed that much brighter. He was looking at her as if he wanted to eat her while he waited for the lights to change.

He crossed the road and kissed her right there on the footpath. 'Hello, gorgeous girl,' he said when he let her up for air. 'Mmm—salt.'

She licked his familiar taste from her lips. 'I wonder why.' He was a beautiful sight, even in a ratty

T-shirt smudged with what looked suspiciously like doggy paw prints. She bent to pat the gorgeous black-and-white pooch of indeterminate pedigree at his feet. 'I didn't know you had a dog.'

'He's not mine, unfortunately. I walk him for an elderly neighbour who can't get out much these days. Say hello to Seeker.' He patted the dog's head. 'Shake hands, boy.'

At Jake's command, Seeker sat down and lifted a paw, big puppy eyes looking up at her and a doggy smile as wide as the beach. 'Oh, aren't you *gorgeous?*' She squatted down to ruffle his well maintained fur and was rewarded with a sloppy kiss. 'I always, always wanted a dog, but Mum said no.' *And hadn't she decided her perfect man in her perfect world would love animals?*

'I still do, but these days with my lifestyle it wouldn't be fair, so I get my animal fix with Seeker, here. Some people don't deserve pets.' He frowned. 'I had to turn an abandoned dog in to a shelter yesterday.'

'That's so sad—not to mention criminal. If you can't give a pet the time and love it deserves, don't have one. I'm going for hot chocolate. Would you like to join me? We can get take-away and walk if you like.'

His grin was one-hundred-percent contagious. 'I would. I didn't stop for breakfast. Had to give Seeker his doggy bath.'

'You groom him too?'

'It's part of the fun. He's all mine every Sunday morning unless I'm out of town. There's a dog-friendly park a ten-minute walk away. I can let Seeker off the leash. I've got his *B-A-double-L*.'

She laughed. 'He's gorgeous *and* smart.'

Like you, Jake thought, watching her bury her face in fur.

'So how come I've never seen you down here before?' she said, straightening.

'I don't usually come this far. I was on my way to see you, as a matter of fact. Good timing—I was hoping to catch you on your way home from the beach. If not I was going to hunt you down at your place and interrupt you.'

'Oh? Why?'

Because I can't get you out of my mind. I want to be with you all the damn time. 'Can't a guy see his favourite girl?'

She blushed, and her smile was the best thing he'd seen all morning. 'I thought you said you were going in to the club today.'

'I am. Later.' He'd delayed his meeting with the buyer by a couple of hours—something he'd never have done for any other woman. He slung an arm around her shoulders with an unnerving feeling that with Emma he was swimming in uncharted waters. 'But here you are, so let's get that breakfast you promised and take it to the park.'

'*I* promised?' She smiled up at him, the light in her eyes reflecting the sun's sparkle off the sea. 'I never promised breakfast.'

'Okay, you buy the hot chocolate; I'll spring for the rest.'

They took their purchases to the park: two hot chocolates and a couple of cupcakes drizzled with icing. They shared half a soggy bacon and egg burger with wilting lettuce and mayonnaise, and let Seeker snaffle the other half.

After a vigorous game of chase-the-ball, which Emma threw herself into with enthusiasm, Jake suggested they walk back to his place, return Seeker on the way, and he'd drive her home on his way to the club.

They headed towards Bondi. Emma jogged a few steps ahead with Seeker, chasing a white butterfly, her slim figure as watch-worthy as any catwalk model, her ponytail bouncing and swinging in time with her steps.

They'd been lovers just over a week. With a little of the edge gone after those first frenzied encounters he'd expected the attraction to fade somewhat, as it invariably did. It hadn't. They'd had fun this morning. She'd not fussed over her sea-damp hair and lack of make-up like other women he dated would. Her tracksuit was smeared with paw-prints and covered in fur.

He'd never in a million years considered asking a woman to come out and play ball with a dog in a park on a Sunday morning. With Emma it came naturally.

'Hope you weren't worried,' he said when they reached Mrs G's front door.

'Of course not, Jake.' The white-haired lady

turned her smile on Emma. 'And you found your friend.'

'Mrs G, I'd like you to meet Emma. Emma, this is Grace Goodman—everyone calls her Mrs G.'

'Pleased to meet you, Emma. Jake was hoping to run into you.'

Emma smiled up at him, then at Grace. 'Nice to meet you too. We've had a lovely morning.'

'I don't how I'd manage without this young man here,' Mrs G told Emma. 'He's taken good care of both of us since my Bernie died. I broke my hip last year, and I can't get out like I used to.'

'Afraid I can't stay,' he said, with an apology in his grin and handing the leash to Mrs G. 'Got work.'

Grace shook her head. 'You work too hard. You and this lovely girl here should be out enjoying your-selves.'

Emma smiled at him. 'Work comes first.'

He knew Emma understood. She believed it as much as he—something some of his other lovers hadn't. But he was also working on the playtime her life had been lacking. The idea of convincing Emma to let him take the rest of the day off with her was tempting, but he had to meet the new club owner and go over the books.

They farewelled Mrs G, then picked up his car. He dropped Emma home first. But he lingered over a long hot kiss before letting her go. 'See you tonight.'

On Tuesday Emma had a rostered day off—and her first luncheon date with Jake.

Since Jake had clients all morning, she was meeting him at his office. His *real* office, which he shared with two other professionals. In a respectable building in the commercial heart of the city.

She rode the elevator to the fourteenth floor, smoothed the lapel on her black jacket as she stepped into a bright reception area with wide windows and glimpses of the Harbour Bridge between the skyscrapers. A dark-haired woman with exotic eyes that hinted at her Asian heritage greeted her with a professional smile at the desk. So different from the first time she'd met him at his place of work—and in so many ways.

Emma smiled back. 'I'm Emma Byrne and I'm here to see Jake Carmody.'

'Oh. Emma, hello.' Her professional smile widened to friendly interest. 'I'm Jasmine. Jake told me to expect you. He's with someone at the moment. Can I get you a coffee or something while you wait?'

'Thanks, I'm fine.'

'And thank you for sending in the soaps. They're a real hit. I'm making a list of people wanting to buy more.'

'That's very kind of you.'

'Are you sure I can't get you a coffee?'

She shook her head, smiling back. 'I'll just admire the view.'

'It's not nearly as spectacular as where you're going for lunch. I booked the table.' She lowered her voice to a conspiratorial whisper. 'Oh, and I probably wasn't supposed to tell you that.'

Emma had expected to grab something in the little café downstairs, and was pleasantly surprised. 'I didn't hear a thing.'

'Don't plan on getting any work done for the rest of the afternoon. I— Excuse me a moment,' she said when the phone rang. 'Carmody and Associates.'

Ten minutes later Jasmine was still handling what seemed to be a complex call. Emma glanced at her watch and flicked through another magazine. Maybe they should postpone their lunch for another time. He was obviously busy.

Even as she considered it, she heard a door open and Jake's voice in the corridor. '…Any time—and don't worry. It's all going to be fine.'

'Thank you, Jake,' a woman's voice said. 'For everything.' Her voice trembled. 'You've given me a chance to start over and I'll never forget it.'

'Just put it all out of your mind for now, and concentrate on spending some quality time with Kevin while I get things rolling.'

The woman appeared first, in jeans a size too big on her too-thin frame and a faded black top slipping off one shoulder. Her hair was scooped into a knot on top of her head and she carried a thumb-sucking toddler on her hip.

Familiar…Emma racked her brain, trying to place her as Jake followed close behind. He walked the woman to the elevators on the other side of Reception, squeezed the woman's bony shoulders as she entered the lift.

Then Emma remembered where she'd seen her. The waitress from the Pink Mango. Cherry.

Obviously a woman like her couldn't afford to be paying Jake for his professional services, yet he was treating her with the care and respect he'd offer any fee-paying client.

Then he turned and saw her, and his frown cleared and his face lit up. 'Emma. Sorry to keep you waiting. Unexpected delay. Hang on a sec, I have something for you.' He disappeared again into his office.

Jasmine, still on the phone, smiled at Emma and rolled her eyes as she spoke to the caller.

Then Jake returned with a fluffy black-and-white stuffed dog. 'According to the tag, his name's Fergus.'

'Oh…' A warm squishy feeling spread through her body. 'You got me a dog.'

'I hope you like stuffed animals.'

'I did, I do. I guess I never grew up.' She'd mentioned never having pets and he'd bought her the next best thing. 'Thank you.'

He jerked a thumb at the busy Jasmine to indicate they were off, then walked Emma to the elevator. It was crowded with office workers headed out for lunch. He flagged down a cab, then they took a short ride to the Centre Point Tower.

She stared up at the famous landmark, as high as the Eiffel Tower. 'We're going up there?'

'I know you hate heights, but I'm sure you'll enjoy the food,' he said as they shuffled towards one of the elevators that shot sightseers to the observation deck, the Skywalk and other adventures Emma had never felt the urge to discover. 'Don't look till we're there.'

She slipped her hand in his and looked up at him. 'Maybe it's time I did.' Steeling her stomach muscles for the inevitable drop, she let out a nervous laugh. 'I might even surprise myself and enjoy it.'

And she didn't shut her eyes once all the way to the top—which seemed to take for ever. The three-hundred-and-sixty-degree revolving restaurant afforded magnificent views of Botany Bay and as far away as the Blue Mountains. She was so proud of herself she even ventured to the slanted window for a quick dizzying glimpse to the street way below.

Jake's hand on her shoulder and his 'Congratulations' made it even more special. She might never have had the nerve to try if he hadn't been there to encourage her. But her legs were still shaky as she set Fergus on the edge of the table.

Jake ordered white wine and a shared seafood platter for starters. He'd made the right decision about the venue—seeing the almost shy pleasure in Emma's eyes when she'd faced her natural fear was worth it.

'Any other plans for your day off?' he asked, setting the menu aside.

'I have an appointment with a potential client at two-thirty.'

'New client?' He leaned forward, interested. 'That's great, Em. Where?'

'It's a new natural products shop in the mall where I work.'

'So we've plenty of time.' He raised his glass. 'Cheers.'

'Cheers.' She tapped her glass to his.

'Emma, I've been thinking about you getting your products out there. Letting people sample them. Why don't you ask one of the shops you supply if you can set up a display one Saturday morning or during late-night shopping hours? I'll give you a hand. You might sound out this place this afternoon, since they're new, and see if they're interested.'

The seafood platter arrived and she selected a prawn. 'That's an idea.'

'We'll need to set up a website first, in case customers ask, and get some business cards printed so they can contact you.'

'You really think my products are good enough for all that hoopla?'

'*Hoopla?*' Had no one ever encouraged her to aim for the stars? 'Are you kidding? After that sensual demonstration the other night?' He pointed the crab claw he was holding her way. 'You'll never know if you don't give it a go. Honey, have a little faith. In yourself *and* your products.'

'I'm trying to. I *do*,' she corrected, and gave a half-laugh. 'Force of habit. I'm not used to others sharing my enthusiasm, and I'm still getting accustomed to the different mind-set.' Setting her palms on the table, she leaned forward with a grin. 'Of *course* you have confidence in my products; why wouldn't you? They're the best you ever tried, right?'

'Right.' He grinned back. 'We'll make a start to-

night,' he decided. 'I'll come over when you get home
and we'll make plans.'

Emma took another sip of cool fruity wine while
she thought about his ideas. She didn't want to let
him—or herself—down, especially when he was
so busy. Surely she could try it on her own? Even if
she just let him help her with the IT side of things?
'You're very generous with your time, Jake. As if
you haven't got enough to do with your practice and
winding up the club. Are you sure?'

'Of course I'm sure. I want to help you any way
I can.'

'Cherry obviously thinks you're pretty wonderful too.'

He looked slightly stunned. 'You know Cherry?'

'I recognised her from the club. I didn't know
she had a child, though. I guess you don't think of
people in that industry as being mums and having
otherwise ordinary lives. She looked pretty down...'
She waved a hand. 'Sorry, it's none of my business.'

'Cherry and her kid were evicted from their accommodation a couple of weeks ago. She came to
me for help.'

Emma understood that feeling, that desperation,
all too well. She'd had to work after school to help
pay the bills when her mum had been too depressed
to get out of bed for weeks on end. 'That's a horri-
ble, gut-wrenching feeling, and even worse with the
added responsibility of a child. What about women's
shelters?'

'Do you have any idea how many homeless people

there are in Sydney?' His expression changed, and his eyes met hers with an understanding she'd not expected. 'Maybe you do.'

Emma nodded. 'It wasn't that desperate with us, but it so easily could have been. So Cherry came to you?' She remembered the woman's tremulous and relieved voice outside Jake's office. Cherry saw the kind of man Emma saw. An approachable man, an honest man, someone she could trust to help her and her child in a time of desperate need. A man who was generous with his time and expertise. 'It shows how highly she thinks of you.'

But he shook his head as if it was nothing. 'She needed a place for the night, for herself and Kevin. I told her there was a room at the back of the club she could use until we sorted something out. She's staying there for the time being.'

'If anyone can help it'll be Jake Carmody.'

They didn't talk for a moment while they sampled more of the delicious food. 'So…who looks after Kevin when Cherry's working?' Emma asked between mouthfuls.

Jake chose a prawn, peeling it carefully while he answered. 'The girls take shifts. They're a tight bunch. Protective. Mostly they're just people trying to make a living the best and sometimes the only way they know how.'

Emma didn't miss the slightly defensive tone. As if he had a personal interest or understanding. She speared a piece of pickled octopus. 'So what happens next? Obviously that can't work for ever.'

'I've bought a place. It needs some work, but I'm using the sale of the club to finance it. Temporary accommodation for people like Cherry to stay until they get themselves on their feet. I've asked Cherry if she'll run it. It'll get her out of the club scene.'

She took a moment to consider his words before she answered. He seemed so sure—as if he'd thought this through over a long period of time. 'This is very important to you.'

Jake nodded, selecting another crab claw, snapping it open. Damn right it was. It was the only good thing to come out of his inheritance: an ability to make a change for the better. If he only helped one person it would be worth it.

'I've been around that strip club for a big chunk of my life, Emma. Seeing women and their kids come and go. Seeing their lack of power over their own circumstances, the hopelessness in their eyes. Wanting to do something to break the cycle. That's why I went into law. I may not have had the world's best upbringing, but I've turned it around, I think.'

He saw her shift closer, elbows on the white tablecloth, her fresh, clean fragrance wafting towards him. 'I reckon you have,' she said softly. 'You should be careful, Jake, a girl could fall hard for a guy like you.'

His head shot up. Her eyes… Maybe, just *maybe,* there was a hint of those for ever stars in that blue sparkle? He shredded another prawn while his heart tumbled strangely. 'Not a girl like you, Emma. You're too smart.'

The little crease dug between her brows as she popped an olive in her mouth. 'Why not a girl like me?'

Careful. The last thing Emma needed right now was another crack in that heart. 'We're both career types, you and me,' he said, avoiding her gaze. 'Work hard, play hard.'

But were good times all he really had in common with Emma? He'd never discussed the club or his up-bringing or his reasons for his choice of career with anyone. Not even Ryan. Though his mate knew of his father's business they'd never talked about it. Yet he'd talked about it with Emma. But she didn't need to know his whole life history.

Shaking the thoughts away, he lifted his glass, drained his wine, then said, 'Tell me more about this shop you've discovered that's going to help send your new career soaring…'

EMMA DROVE HOME, her mind abuzz. The new shop was happy for her to promote her products with a display—this coming Friday evening, no less, to co-incide with their first week of trading.

Jake was the only one who'd ever shown an inter-est and inspired her to take the plunge. Jake's encour-agement and support had lifted her spirits and caught her enthusiasm. With his help she might just be able to make it work. Correction: she *would* make it work.

With his help so many people were better off, she thought. She thought too, how he'd chosen a career so he could help people like Cherry—the girls and their plights had made a lasting impression on him.

Because he'd grown up around the strip club. For how long? she wondered. Had his mother been a stripper? How long had it been since he'd seen her? She remembered the fleeting expression in his eyes when he'd spoken of her, just once, on the night of the hens' party—at odds with the casual indifference in his voice.

She hadn't let herself become interested in his past because what they had was based around the present. But now she simply couldn't ignore it. His past had shaped him into the man he was. He might be fun-loving, casual and outgoing but there were shadows there too.

She switched direction and headed for his place. There was so much more she wanted to know.

CHAPTER THIRTEEN

EMMA PRESSED THE intercom on the wall outside Jake's home. 'It's me,' she said, when he answered. 'Let me in.'

The gate slid open and by the time she'd reached the door Jake was waiting for her, naked but for a towel low around his hips. 'I thought we arranged to meet at your place, but if you've come to share my shower…' His sexy grin faded when he realised she wasn't smiling back. 'Something wrong? Didn't it work out with the new clients?'

'No, no, nothing like that. It went well, really well, and I'll tell you about it later. But…' She waved a hand. 'Can we talk?'

He gestured her inside. 'Let's go to the living room.'

She followed him, then went to the window and looked out at the sea while she took a calming breath. She didn't know how it was going to go. Whether he'd resent her for what he might see as an intrusion on his privacy. But this was too important to ignore.

'I've been thinking about what you said this afternoon,' she said slowly. 'About Cherry and the place you've bought. How important it is to you.'

'It is, yes. Is that a problem for you?'

'Of course not.' She turned to face him. 'But why buy a place? Why be personally involved? Why not give to a homeless charity instead? *Why* is it so important?'

Jake listened to her rapid-fire questions while he dragged in a slow, slow breath. Having Emma come into his life was one of the most life-changing events he'd ever experienced. To his surprise, he discovered he wanted to answer them, to have her listen and understand. His only concern was if once he started he might not be able to stop.

He crossed the room, gripped her shoulders loosely and steered her towards the couch. 'Sit down.' He sat down beside her, fisted his hands on his thighs. Took another breath. 'I lived there, Emma. The back of that strip club was home sweet home. So I know first-hand what it's like to be powerless.'

'Oh…Jake.' She lifted a hand, thought better of it and drew it back. 'How long?'

He shifted a shoulder, always uncomfortable with sympathy. But that wasn't what she was offering. Just support and a willingness to listen with an open mind. He'd never realised he'd needed it until now.

He gazed through the windows into the deepening twilight. 'I was five when Mum left in the middle of the night. I hadn't started school yet. I had no friends. Can't blame her, Earl cheated on her as regular as clockwork. She worked late-night shifts cleaning offices, so I saw all sorts come and go at our apartment. One night she just didn't come home. It was like losing an arm.' Or a heart.

Emma didn't speak, but he felt her reaching out to him with streamers of warmth that touched the dark, secret places inside him.

'It was lonely and isolating—after all, I could hardly ask schoolmates to come over and play. As I grew up I understood what had happened, and I swore I'd never be like *him*.' His fists tightened against his thighs. 'But the one person I'd counted on, the one person I'd loved and trusted, left me there. She didn't take me with her and it hurt like hell.'

He felt her hands cover his fists and looked into her moisture-sheened eyes.

'Your mum stayed in a loveless marriage, Emma, but she stayed. Even a mum who gives you grief is better than no mum at all—at least yours had some compassion, some sense of loyalty. But then, that's my opinion. We're always going to see it from our own perspective.'

'How do you know she went to South America?' she said softly. 'Did she come back for you?'

'She sent a postcard once, when I was ten. New continent, new husband, new life. Anyway, after she'd left Earl didn't see the point in paying rent on two places and we moved in to the back of the club. At least I had a roof over my head and food in my belly.'

'A child living in the back of a strip club?' Her

eyes changed—ice over fire—and she exhaled sharply. 'The authorities? Didn't they ever catch up with Earl?'

He shrugged, remembering times when he'd been ferried to some stranger's home in the middle of the night. 'Earl was clever. Always one step ahead. It wasn't so bad,' he went on. 'The girls used to make me breakfast sometimes before they went home. They helped me with my homework. Substitute mums of sorts.'

'Your young life must have been very confusing. How did you cope with it all?'

He wrapped a hand around the back of his neck. 'Kept to myself. Studied. Swore one day I'd get out. I was seventeen when I left and found a part-time job and a room to rent.'

'I'll never understand a mother leaving her own flesh and blood.'

He remembered the despair and heartbreak he'd seen too often in his mother's eyes. The guilt that had tormented his youth. The pain of that rejection and abandonment he'd never really got past. 'Because when she looked at me she saw him.'

'Ah…' She shifted closer, the fresh, untainted scent of her skin filling his nostrils. 'But you're *not* him. And she's missed out on knowing someone amazing.' She combed her fingers over the back of his hair. 'You're kind and generous and thoughtful. You're also a man of integrity, and don't let anyone tell you different or make you feel less or they'll have me to deal with.'

A band tightened around his heart. Even knowing his past, she didn't judge. 'Using my inheritance to pay for a safe house is one way of addressing the injustice. My mother didn't benefit, but others will.'

'You're one special guy, you know that?' Her compassionate blue gaze cleared and brightened, and she touched the side of his face with gentle fingers.

He hauled her against him so he could feel her generous warmth against the cold. 'I need that shower.' He needed the water's cleansing spray and her caring hands to rid himself of unwanted memories. Memories that no longer had a place in his life. He closed his eyes. 'You want to wash my back?'

'Does that mean I have to get naked too?'

He drew in a breath and opened his eyes. She was smiling. He touched her hair. 'Unless you want to drive home dripping wet or wearing my bathrobe.'

'Yeah, there's that. Whatever would I do if the car broke down on the way?'

Or you could stay here...

Only he didn't say it. She might be ready to hear it now, but he didn't want rejection of any kind tonight. He undid the top button of her blouse. 'You *want* to get naked too?'

'Try stopping me. You know what?' She pressed her lips to his chest. 'I even have some spare soap left over in my bag from this afternoon's meeting.' She opened her mouth and flicked out her tongue, leaving a damp trail as she worked her way up to his Adam's apple then his chin. 'There's a new fragrance I'm trialling...' She let her hands wander over his hips, drawing tight little circles through the terry towel with her fingers. 'Eygptian nights. Musk and sandalwood.'

'First Tahiti. Now the East. A round-the-world tour, huh?'

She grazed her fingers over his hardening erection. 'More like a journey of discovery,' she whispered, drawing the towel away. 'Just the two of us.' She reached behind her neck, unfastening her zip and sliding it down so that her dress slipped to the floor. Stepped out of her panties and unsnapped her bra, tossed it away. 'One back scrub coming up.'

AT EMMA'S PLACE later that evening, Jake worked with her on a website design for Naturally Emma. They drank instant coffee and ordered business cards and composed her website pages. It helped take their minds off the earlier conversation. There was a new understanding, a comfortable silence between them as they worked.

Emma took shots of her products for Jake to upload to her computer. She was literally bouncing off the walls with enthusiasm. And nerves. 'Where will I put the extra stock?'

'You'll find a place. I have an empty room under the house if you need it.'

'What if this thing explodes? How will I keep up?'

'Now, *that's* the confidence I like to hear.' He smiled at her, the computer screen's glow reflecting the encouragement etched on his expression. 'You'll give up your day job and employ someone to help you.' He stretched his arms over his head, then reached out to take her hand. 'You'll be fine. If you need help I'm here.'

She breathed deep. 'You don't know how much it means to have you in on this with me, if only to get me started.'

As usual, he shrugged off the praise. 'No worries. I'll have the website ready for you to look at tomorrow night.'

When Jake left, she worked on into the wee hours. She made a start on some mini soap samples and selected a collection for display.

The following day Emma took off in her lunch-break to slip further down the mall and make arrangements with the shop, collected her business cards from the printer, then caught up with Jake in the evening and approved the website.

Naturally Emma. She stared at the screen, biting her lips, hardly able to believe it was really happening. The lavender background with elegant flowing script and artistic design. The photos. The little piece about her background and qualifications that she'd composed.

'Only two nights to go,' she said, hugging her arms.

'I'll be here to pick you up,' he said, rising. 'But I need to get going. I've got some of my own work to catch up on.'

'I'm sorry. I've monopolised your time.'

'Not at all. Glad I could help.' He pulled her up for a quick kiss. 'Get some sleep.'

THE MALL WAS bustling with late-night shoppers when Emma and Jake carried her boxes in at five-thirty on Friday evening. Lights gleamed on the shiny store windows, the smell of roasting nuts and popcorn mingled with perfumes and hair treatments. Elevator music tinkled in the background, along with the ever-present underlying tide of urban chatter.

Kelsey, the shop's proprietor, had set up a table for the products just inside the entrance, and was serving a customer as they arrived. She smiled and waved when she saw them.

'I've got a severe case of killer butterflies,' Emma told Jake as she pulled stock from her box and began arranging it on the table. Her hands weren't steady, her pulse was galloping, and she really, really wanted something to moisten her dust-dry throat. 'What if no one stops by?'

'Looking at you, why wouldn't they?'

She glanced at Jake over her box. He was smiling at her, his eyes full of encouragement. He believed in her, she couldn't let him down. She couldn't let herself down. 'I'd rather they look at the products, but thanks.' She swallowed. 'Would you mind getting me a bottle of water? I forgot mine.'

'Sure.' He put down the box he'd been emptying. 'Back in a moment.'

Kelsey, with curly red hair and moss-green eyes behind her rimless glasses, stepped up as Jake walked away. 'Your guy's a superstar.'

Her guy. Emma started to deny it then stopped. Her heart took a flying leap. Yes, she realised. He was. 'None of it would've happened without his support.' She drew out a cellophane-wrapped basket full of soaps and held it out. 'This is for you. You can take them home, give them to friends. Whatever. I hope your new venture's a success.'

'Oh, Emma, thank you. It's beautiful.' Kelsey admired the basket with a smile, turned it in her hands. 'I think we'll both do well. People look for natural products these days. I'll leave it here for now, so customers can see it. Thanks so much. Oh, I've got a customer...'

JAKE SLOWED AS he arrived back, then stopped, watching Emma talk to a couple of elderly ladies. The shop's downlights glinted on her glossy dark hair. She wore the same white top she'd worn for the hens' night, with a slim white knee-length skirt. Tasteful, professional. A chunky gold bracelet jangled on one wrist as she gesticulated.

She'd ditched the nerves, obviously, and was deep in animated conversation, smiling, eyes alive with friendly interest. Calm, in control, and the sexiest girl in the mall. In all of Australia. How different was this Emma from the Emma he'd seen wearing that top only two weeks ago?

He felt a twinge around his heart—he seemed to be getting a lot of those lately—and his fingers tightened on the red foil balloon with its twirling ribbons he'd purchased on impulse after remembering her edict about no flowers.

He shook his head. No matter what she said,

Emma was a woman made for hearts and flowers and pretty words, and he was discovering, to his surprise, that he wanted very badly to give them to her. Because, unlike with his previous lovers, with Emma they would mean something more than traditional and often empty gestures.

He watched her pack soaps into a bag, pass it to one of the women with a smile as they handed over their cash. They continued down the mall. Then a guy in a snazzy business suit stopped at her table.

Jake watched Emma smile some more. Watched her flick back her hair as she talked. Pretty boy leaned closer, head tilted to one side, listening. Nodding. He picked up a soap flower and held it to his nose.

Jake scowled and wasted no time making his way to her table. 'Sorry I took so long, honey.' Slight emphasis on the endearment as he handed her the balloon and her water, then nodded at Mr Businessman. 'How's it going, mate?' He stuck out his hand. 'Jake Carmody. Emma's accountant.'

The man shook his hand. 'Daniel McDougal.'

Beside Jake, Emma made a noise at the back of her throat, setting water and balloon aside. 'Thanks.' Then she darted him a disconcerted glance. 'Jake, Daniel is from Brisbane. He owns a large health food chain and is interested in trialling my products up there.'

'That sounds great.' Jake nodded again. 'I'll let you two get on with it, then.' He dropped a firm hand on Emma's shoulder, let it linger a few seconds longer than necessary. 'If you need me, my phone's on. I'll be back to help you pack up.'

'MY ACCOUNTANT?' EMMA said on the way home.

'Yeah.' Why the hell had he got so proprietorial back there? He didn't *do* proprietorial. He dismissed the unsettling notion from his mind and concentrated on the traffic. 'Because I'm coming over on Monday night to look over your financial records,' he said. If this was going to take off, Emma needed someone she trusted from the get-go to help her manage the financial side.

'Oh. Okay. Thanks.' She bopped her little balloon against his arm. 'And thank you for tonight.'

'Pleasure.'

He glanced her way. She had a dreamy expression on her face. He looked away quickly. *Accountant? Sure.* She knew exactly what had gone through his mind.

ON SATURDAY EMMA caught up with all the things she hadn't been doing, such as grocery shopping, washing and cleaning. In the evening Jake took her to a little out-of-the-way café where the pasta was hot and the jazz was cool.

She was thrilled when Jake asked her to share dog-walking duties the following morning. They took Seeker for his walk before Jake went in to the office to catch up on his own neglected work.

Emma spent the afternoon looking forward to

seeing him again at dinner while she put together a gourmet beef casserole and whipped up a batch of Jake's favourite lemon poppyseed cakes.

But how long would this thing with Jake last? How long before he tired of her? The way her father had tired of her mother and taken a mistress. The way Wayne had tired of her and found Rani. A guy like Jake with good-looks and all the charisma in the world could have any woman he wanted.

He'd never mentioned anything lasting. *Don't look too far ahead,* he'd told her. *Enjoy the ride.*

And it was one amazing ride.

She could handle it if—when—it came time to let go. Whatever happened, she'd be fine. Because he'd changed her, made her a confident woman who could meet life head-on. She loved him. But a wise woman knew if her love wasn't returned there was nowhere for it to go. She hoped she was strong enough now to let him move on. At some point.

She needed to stand on her own two feet with this business. And she could. He'd given her the belief in herself to give it a really good go. After he'd shown her what to do with the accounting side of things she was going to say thank you very much and be her own businesswoman.

WHEN JAKE ARRIVED after work on Monday night, Emma was looking more than a little harassed.

At the front door they spent a moment with their lips locked before she broke away with a sigh. 'This is impossible,' she said, walking to her work spot at the dining room table. She flicked at an untidy pile of papers, sending a couple sailing to the floor. 'I can't do figures. It's a mess.'

'First off—calm down.' He took her hands in his. 'I'm in business law. That makes me a figures guy. Brew us a coffee while I look over your books.'

She stared up at him, eyes panicked. 'Books? I don't have books. I have paper. Piles and piles of paper.'

'Okay. Why don't *I* make us coffee while you gather them together? Then I can take a look. And don't worry. That's what I'm here for.'

'But it's *not* your worry. I have to be able to do it on my own...'

She trailed off, but not before he heard the hiccup in her voice. A sombre mood fell over him, a dark cloud on a still darker night. He squeezed her hands that little bit firmer. 'I'll be available for however long you need my help.'

She looked away at the clutter on the table. 'I'm not a complete moron. I should be able to handle it myself.'

'You're not and you will,' he reassured her. 'I'll sort it, show you how it all works, then you can take over.'

A few hours later he'd organised her paper filing system into some sort of order. He'd set up an accounting program on her laptop and entered her details. All he had left then was to show her how to manage it.

He'd hardly been aware, but at some point she'd finished packing and stacking and made another coffee. He sipped his, found it stone cold. Stretching out the kinks in his spine and neck, he turned to see her zonked out on the couch, fast asleep, a book on the Pitfalls and Perils of Small Business still open on her stomach.

He didn't get nearly enough time to watch her in that state, so he took the opportunity while it presented itself. Turning his chair around, he straddled it, resting his forearms along the back.

Her waterfall of glossy dark hair tumbled over the side of the couch. Her long, dark eyelashes rested on pale cheeks. Her mouth…a thing of beauty, full and plump and turned up ever so slightly at the corners, as if waiting for one chaste kiss to awaken her…

Her eyes would open and that glorious sapphire gaze would fix on his and he'd kiss her again…not so chaste this time…

His lips tingled with sweet promise. His heart beat faster, re-energising his bloodstream, reawakening sluggish muscles. Desire unfurled deep in his belly. Amazing—this feeling, this need for her, never waned. In fact, it was stronger than ever.

But he touched only her silky hair. She needed her sleep. She looked pale, worn out. He should leave, let her rest. They'd catch up tomorrow. But he couldn't leave her to finish the night on that spring-worn couch.

Gathering her in his arms, he carried her to bed,

laid her down, and for his own peace of mind pulled the quilt right up to her chin.

She stirred and looked up at him through sleepy eyes…

And it was as if he saw all the days and nights in a-fantasy-filled future when he'd wake and lose his heart over and over every time he gazed into those captivating blue depths—

When I saw my children in her eyes…

A bowling ball rolled through his chest. His throat tightened as if the air was slowly being squeezed out of him by an iron fist, and for a few crazy seconds he thought he might black out.

But his moment of panic slid away like an outgoing tide over hard-packed sand, replaced by a shiny and unfamiliar warmth which seeped deep into his heart.

Love.

It had to be love. What else could it be? He'd not recognised it before because he'd never experienced it. Never believed in it. Not for him. Love had always been an unknown. His childhood had been one of rejection and indifference. His entire adult existence had revolved around relationships that never lasted. The women in his life had been about fun and good times. He'd never really taken the time to get to know them on a deeper level. Hadn't wanted to. Maybe he'd been afraid to.

But he knew Emma. And she'd opened his eyes and his heart to a different world. A world where life held more meaning than he'd ever imagined.

'Jake…Wha…?' Her drowsy murmur drifted away.

'Sleep, sweetheart,' he murmured against her temple, and she snuggled into her pillow, eyes already closed again.

He woke before dawn, still fully dressed on top of her quilt, his eyes snapping open to the fading sound of a car's tyres screeching in the distance. Emma was spooned against him as warm and soft as a kitten. He shifted carefully off her bed and let himself out into the pearl-grey of early morning.

He hurried to his car. He had plans to make before his working day started.

CHAPTER FOURTEEN

JAKE WAS WEARING a groove in the floorboards in
Emma's studio. He'd left the office at lunchtime,
dropped by Emma's workplace and asked her for
a key so he could work on her computer. She'd told
him she'd be home by six.

It was now twenty minutes past.

The mustard chicken and orzo casserole he'd ordered from his favourite gourmet kitchen was in the
oven. A bottle of her favourite bubbly was chilling
in the fridge, along with a couple of his favourite
gourmet cupcakes.

He'd cleared the work from her table and covered its scarred surface with a cream lace cloth he'd
found in her kitchen drawer, placed on it a bunch of
red poppies he'd bought.

Should he have taken her to some fancy restaurant instead? No. He didn't want a bunch of strangers intruding. He wanted to share the moment with
her. Only her.

A beam of light arced through the window and
the familiar engine's sound had him reaching for gas
lighter and candles.

GRABBING THE PLASTIC carry bag of fried chicken and a bottle of fizzy stuff from the passenger seat, Emma swung her bag over her shoulder and almost danced down the steps. She couldn't wait to tell him her news. She hadn't phoned. She needed to say it in person.

'Honey, I'm home,' she sing-songed as she pushed the door open.

She was met by some herby, aromatic fragrance. On the table, tall red poppies speared out of a jar alongside two squat red candles already lit.

Jake was pouring fine pink champagne into two glasses that were far too elegant to have come from her cupboard. *He* looked too elegant, in slim-fitting black trousers and a snowy-white shirt that looked as if it had just come out of a box.

'Seems you beat me to it.' She set down her own cheap bottle of fizz on the sideboard and admired the candlelight reflecting on crystal and silver. 'This looks wickedly romantic.'

'I thought it was time I took a chance on the romance bit. You don't mind, do you?' Hands occupied with wine and glasses, he grinned and leaned forward so that she could plant an enthusiastic kiss on his lips. He smelled of some exotic new fragrance.

'I don't mind. Taking chances is what it's all about, right?' Overflowing with excitement, she sashayed over to the oven, peeked at the delicious-looking meal inside. 'And I bought take-away. You should've let me know you were planning a seduction.'

'I wanted to surprise you.'

'You did. And I've got—'

'Everything's ready. Sit.'

He didn't appear to hear her. Okay, this wasn't the moment, she decided. He'd obviously gone to a lot of trouble. 'It smells yummy.'

'It tastes even better.' Pulling out her chair, he waited till she was seated, then walked to the oven. He removed the casserole, set it on the table, then sat down opposite her.

'You okay?' She studied him. 'You seem a little...' she circled a finger in the air '...preoccupied.'

His mouth kicked up at one corner as his gaze drifted over the front of her shirt. 'If I am, it's your fault for looking so sexy after a day at work.'

'And don't you know just the right things to say?' While he spooned the meal into shallow bowls, she fingered a poppy. 'I didn't know poppies had blue centres.'

'These do.'

'Made-to-order poppies? Hmm. You *have* put thought into this.'

'They remind me of you in that sexy red coat of yours. Tall, slim. Blue-eyed. Gorgeous.' He raised their glasses, handed her one. 'To happiness.' Did his eyes look different tonight? Deep and dark... Maybe she was imagining it.

Because everything looked different tonight. From the sunset to the sea, even her old studio apartment. Everything *felt* different tonight. Her life was about to change.

'To happiness.' She took a sip, then set her glass down. She was bursting to talk but she squashed it. She didn't want to spoil his evening's plans. She wanted him to see her make time and enjoy the meal he'd obviously taken so much thought with first. The crystal flutes were sparkly new and very expensive. He'd used her best silver cutlery and china and her grandmother's tablecloth.

She spread a matching cloth napkin over her knee. 'Did you cook this yourself?'

'It's from a gourmet shop in Bondi. I shop there so often the owner's thinking of making me a partner.' He passed her a bowl. 'I'd have cooked, but today's been a bit of a rush.'

So while they ate she asked him about his day. One of his colleagues in the office was taking on a high-profile case. He'd almost finished entering her data on the computer.

How was it going with Cherry and Kevin? He'd driven Cherry to the safe house and they'd chosen paint for the walls. Cherry and a couple of the other girls were starting that job next week in their spare time.

When they'd polished off the last cake crumb from their plates and were enjoying their filtered coffee, Jake decided the moment was right now. He took a gulp of coffee to moisten his throat and steady his nerves. His fingers tightened on the little box in his trouser pocket.

'Emma, I—'

'I have some news—'

Both spoke at the same time.

She was clutching her hands together beneath her chin. Her sapphire eyes shone like stars, reflecting the candlelight.

A premonition snaked down Jake's spine and his breath snagged in his chest. Why did he suddenly feel as if the floor was about to give way? He nodded once. 'You first.'

Her shoulders lifted and she leaned forward. Her familiar fragrance curled around his nostrils.

'You talked about taking a chance earlier—on romance. And it's been lovely. Everything. Thank you for making the evening so special.'

He acknowledged that, but didn't speak.

'I've taken a chance too. I've been offered work in Queensland. *Real* work. Work I love, work I've wanted all my life but never had the opportunity to do.'

Jake was having trouble processing the words. *Queensland*. He was grateful he was sitting down because his legs suddenly felt like lead stumps. 'Queensland?'

'I know. Isn't it exciting? I can't believe it.'

Neither could Jake. 'Where? Who? You've made plans?' *Without discussing it with me?*

'You remember Daniel McDougal? From the mall last week? Well, he was so impressed with my products he had them analysed and everything, consulted with his partners, and rang me this afternoon. He wants to invest in my product line *and* take me on as a consultant to liaise with his client base all around the state.'

Daniel McDougal. Mr Pretty Boy. 'But what do you know about him? Aren't you jumping in without the facts? God, Emma, you can't just—'

'Turns out he's Kelsey's cousin. You know—the owner of the shop? I talked to her, and checked him out on the internet to make sure. Danny's a real success story up there.'

So it was *Danny* now? Jake clenched his jaw. 'You don't have to make a decision right away, Emma.' But she didn't seem to be listening.

'He's got stores around Australia. He's booked me an airline ticket for tomorrow morning to meet the staff and look over the factory before I commit to anything. He emailed me the information. I have a copy right here. Since you're the expert, I'd be grateful if you'd check it out?' She reached into her bag, pulled some papers out, set them on the table.

Damn right he'd check it out. He picked them up with a restraint he was far from feeling. 'This isn't something you simply say yes to, Emma.' He flicked through the first couple of pages. 'There are other considerations to take into account.' *Us, for starters.*

'Of course, and I know that. Jake, put those pages down and look at me.'

He did. He'd never seen her so happy. That sparkle in her eyes, excitement glowing in her cheeks.

'We've got something special,' she said. 'But it was only ever temporary, I'm realistic enough to know that. I'm a career girl, you said so yourself.

This chance to do something meaningful with my life is what I've been waiting for. And if it wasn't for you I'd never have had the courage to go for it. I have to try or it'll all have been for nothing. Do you understand?'

His fingers clenched beneath the table. 'Yes.' She was thinking with her head, not her heart—she was doing the right thing. He knew she had to give it a shot. Because if he told her he loved her and asked her to stay and she missed out on her big opportunity he'd never forgive himself. He forced himself to smile. 'I'm proud of you, Emma. You've come so far.'

Her answering smile and the dancing sapphires in her eyes faded a little. 'It's such a big decision, and I have to make it on my own, but… Oh, Jake, I…' She bit down on her lip. 'I…I almost wish I could ask you to make the decision for me. *With* me.'

Damn. Her heart was bleeding into the mix, threatening to sabotage everything. He needed to leave soon, because he didn't trust himself not to try and change her mind—and that would be the worst thing he could ever do for her.

'That's the old Emma talking. Don't listen to her. You know what you want, so go for it.'

A memory of his mother flashed through his mind. She'd left him too. The circumstances were at opposite ends of the spectrum but the hurt was the same. All these years he'd never allowed a woman into his heart, and in a couple of weeks Emma had managed to do what no other woman had.

'Emma. You're a very special woman and I've

enjoyed being with you. But circumstances seem to have made the decision for us. And I want you to go. I want you to have that opportunity to shine because I know you will.'

Rising, he swiped his jacket that hung over a chair, shrugged it on—he'd never felt so cold. He picked up her papers. 'I'll look this over and get back to you.'

'Jake, wait.' She pushed up, eyes wide. 'Why are you leaving so soon? Didn't you have something you wanted to tell me just now? You let me have my say—it's your turn.'

He shook his head. 'I was going to tell you I'm flying out too—tomorrow morning. A client's set up a new business in Melbourne and wants my advice.' He waved a hand over the table. 'The meal was to… sweeten things.' He smiled again but it felt as if his lips had turned to stone. 'Turns out it was a celebration after all. And if I know anything about women, you'll need the rest of the night to sort what you're taking and pack.'

He took her in his arms, kissed her beautiful lips just once. Inhaled the scent of her shampoo, drifted his fingers over her silky cheeks as he stepped back and looked into her eyes one last time.

'Go, Emma, and make me proud.'

CHAPTER FIFTEEN

EMMA YAWNED AS the taxi pulled into her driveway at ten p.m. on Thursday evening. She paid the cabbie, jumped out to key in the gate's security code, then collected her cabin bag from the footpath.

As she rolled it across the pavers she saw her mother exit the back door, the old cardigan she'd wrapped around her shoulders flapping in the breeze as she came to meet her.

Just what she didn't need right now, but Emma pasted on a smile. 'Hi, Mum. You're back.'

'Yesterday. I got your text. How was Brisbane?'

'Warm and sticky.' And lonely.

'Jake dropped by this afternoon to drop this off for you.' She held out a large envelope. 'Said he'd rather leave it with me than in the letterbox.'

'Thanks.' She frowned. 'I thought he was going to Melbourne.' It must have only been an overnight stay. Emma knew she should wait until she was alone, but she needed to see what Jake thought of the offer of employment. She so needed to see his handwriting. Anything. Something of him.

She slid the documents out. A green sticky note was attached to the top page.

Hi Em. Looks OK.
Remember, go with your gut—if you think it's
right, do it. And good luck.
J.

'My offer of employment.'

Emma blinked back tears as she slid the contents back into the envelope. Forty-eight hours ago she'd thought it was worth more than gold. Now she knew it wasn't. A successful career was an empty one if she couldn't share it with the man she loved.

Rubbing the chill air from her arms, she reached for the handle of her case. 'I hope you were pleasant to Jake?'

Her mother pursed her lips, but then seemed to relax a little, and something like a smile twitched at her lips. 'Bit of a charmer, that one. Done all right for himself, hasn't he?'

'Yes. He has.'

'Come inside for a few moments.' She turned and began walking the way she'd come.

The kitchen, when Emma entered, was warm and smelled of fresh-baked cinnamon cake. She hadn't smelled that comfortable homey aroma in this kitchen in years.

Her mother pulled a carton of milk from the

fridge. 'Would you like a hot chocolate? I could do with one myself.'

'Thanks.' Emma sat down at the kitchen table. 'You've been baking.'

'Stan's coming up to Sydney tomorrow.' She put milk in the microwave, then set slices of fresh buttered cake on the table. 'Try this and tell me if I got it right. I tried a new recipe.'

Emma took a slice and broke a piece off, bit into it. 'Mmm—yum.' She dusted off her fingers. 'So how long will Stan be staying?'

'Not sure yet.'

'He's staying here?'

'Yes.' Her mother stirred chocolate powder into the hot milk and poured it into two mugs, then carried them to the table and sat down.

Emma cupped her hands around the mug and blew on the steaming surface. 'This smells good.' Almost as good as the old milk and honey fix. 'So...things are going well for you two?'

'We have a lot in common.'

'That's great, Mum. What are you planning while he's here?'

'We'll take it as it comes. What about you and Jake?'

Emma could feel her mother's eyes on her and stared into her mug. 'He... We...' She swallowed the lump that rose up her throat.

'He was the mistake you thought he might be?'

Still staring at her mug, she said, 'It was one of

those get-it-out-of-your-system things…' Only she hadn't.

'So you're going to Brisbane to work?'

'I thought I was. But I've changed my mind.'

She flashed Emma a look. 'Why?'

'Mum, why did you stay with Dad when you had so many reasons not to?'

'I had two children.'

Emma's jaw tightened. 'And you made us pay for your unhappiness. Every day of our lives.'

She saw her mother flinch, then she put her mug down and folded her arms on the edge of the table. 'Yes. I did. I'm sorry for it. I was wrong.'

Emma studied her, thoughtful. Jake's mother had abandoned her child and he'd suffered the consequences his whole life. Emma's had stayed, even if it would have been better for all if she hadn't. But maybe her mother had been too afraid to leave— afraid of the changes it would bring. The way Emma had been afraid.

Basically her mother had made what she'd thought was the right decision, and it wasn't Emma's place to judge.

'Sorry, I shouldn't have said that,' Emma murmured.

'It needed to be said. I needed to hear it. But a good man, a man who takes the time to look beneath the hard shell and find the woman inside screaming to be let out…' Her mother's voice softened. It was a tone Emma hadn't thought her capable of, and an unexpected smile brightened her whole demeanour. 'Well, he can change your life.'

Emma nodded. 'Yes. He can.' Stan had instigated the change in her mum without Bernice even being aware of it. And wasn't that what Jake had done for Emma?

Friday

'GOOD AFTERNOON, CARMODY and Associates.'

'Hi, Jasmine, it's Emma Byrne.'

'Emma, hi.' There was a smile in Jake's PA's voice that wasn't only professional courtesy. 'What can I do for you?'

Emma's fingers tightened on the phone and she rolled her lips together before saying, 'I was wondering…is Jake there?'

'Yes. He's free at the moment. Do you want me to put you thr—?'

'No.' She swallowed. 'Thanks. I wanted to know… I want…' She sucked in a deep breath. 'Actually, I was hoping you could help me…'

JAKE CHECKED HIS watch, then pressed the intercom. 'Jasmine? Looks like your friend's a no-show. Why don't you give him a call, tell him to reschedule? I'm knocking off early—'

'She'll be here,' she assured him. 'Do me a favour and wait a few more moments.'

Jake was already shutting down his computer with his free hand. Jasmine hadn't mentioned her friend was a woman. The only woman he wanted to see walking through that door was a million miles away.

'I gave her my word you'd see her tonight,' Jasmine continued. 'Hang on…' He heard a muffled sound then, 'I can see her from the window. She's walking into the building now.'

EMMA REFUSED TO let the nerves zapping beneath her ribcage win. She was a woman on a mission and nothing was going to stand in her way. So she wasn't afraid of walking into an office high-rise to face the most important meeting of her life.

Six p.m. on a chilly autumn evening in Sydney's CBD and the business day was over. Workers were trickling out of the building on their way home.

Her work was just beginning. The most important work she'd ever done. The most important work she'd ever do. She'd promised herself she'd talk to Jake Carmody, and she would. She could.

Shrugging her bag higher, she marched inside. A couple of men in snazzy business suits exited the lift. She clutched the miniature hat box at her waist as she passed them. Did they know her life was on a cliff's edge? Could they hear how hard her heart was pounding? She hit the button for the fourteenth floor and watched the numbers light up while her stomach stayed on the ground floor.

The doors slid open smoothly and she stepped out. Jasmine looked up and smiled, collecting her bag from her desk on her way out. 'Go straight in. He's getting a little impatient.'

'Thanks.'

Emma heard him on the phone before she reached the open door. That deep, lazy voice that rolled over her senses like caramel sauce. Only three days, but she'd missed hearing that voice. She loved that voice. She loved the man it belonged to. It was time she took the big, scary leap and let him in on that fact.

She took a fortifying breath, then knocked and entered.

He was sitting behind his desk and looked up sharply, eyes widening when she closed the door behind her.

'Something's come up. I'll speak to you tomorrow,' he said into his mobile without taking his eyes off her. He disconnected and set the phone on the desk. 'Emma.'

'Hello, Jake.'

'I'm expecting a client…' He studied her face. 'I'm guessing it's you.'

'Jasmine told me you'd be here. She asked you to wait, so thank you.'

His eyes raked over her coat and she felt a flush rise up her neck. Heat, desire, longing. Her body reacted to his gaze as if it had been programmed for his exclusive use, and her nipples hardened beneath her finely woven cashmere jumper. She wished she knew what he was thinking, how he felt about her turning up without calling first.

He checked his watch. 'I was about to leave. I need to get home.'

Her heart clenched so tight she wondered that her blood still pumped around her body. Her fingers tightened so hard on the little box she wondered it didn't implode. 'A…date?' She had to force the words out.

He stared at her with those beautiful, dark, unreadable eyes. 'What do you think, Emma?'

'I think…if it was…I'd try to talk you into cancelling because I need to talk to you first.'

'No need—there is no date.' He was turning his mobile over and over in his hands. Watching her. 'How was Brisbane? Is the new job everything you wanted?'

'Yes. And no.' She focused on those eyes. 'It's everything I wanted in a career. Double the income I'm making at the call centre. A spacious office with my name on the door. The chance to build my own business on the side. A chance to travel.' She sucked in her lips. 'But it's not enough.'

'Not enough.' Rising, he came around to her side of the desk, leaned his backside against the edge. 'Why isn't it enough, Em?'

He enjoyed being with her, she knew that. He made love to her as if she were a goddess. He believed in her. But did he love her? How would he respond if she asked him? There were no guarantees in life and love, but wasn't taking that leap of faith what it was all about?

She tightened her fingers on the little box and sucked in a lungful of air. 'It's not enough because I want more. I want it all. What's the point in being successful if you're lonely?' She pushed her gift into his hands. 'I love you, Jake. I need you in my life. No matter what else I do or don't have, I need you.'

He shook his head slightly, as if he couldn't believe what he was hearing, then looked down at the box. Back to her.

'Open it.'

She forgot to breathe as he lifted the lid. He met her eyes. A slow smile curved his lips and her breath whooshed out. He lifted out the cupcake with its red heart piped on top.

'It's not soap. It's chocolate—you can eat this one.'

'I'm not so sure I want to. It's too special.'

She twisted her trembling fingers together in front of her. 'Jake…do you love me back? I really, really need to know if I'm making an idiot of myself here…'

'Emma.' He set the cake and its box beside him on the desk, then covered her hands with his. 'I know that when I'm with you, when I look at you, I have this feeling inside me that makes Everest seem like an ant hill. It makes me want to go out and climb its highest peak with my bare hands. It gives me a reason to get up and watch the sun rise and thank the universe for bringing you into my life. I'd say that's love, wouldn't you?'

'Yes. Because that's how you make me feel too.' She was beyond terrified that she might have let this chance slip through her hands. It gave her strength to continue. 'I came here to say…to ask…Jake, will you marry me?' The last words rushed out on a trembling breath.

His eyes darkened, warmed. And his slow smile was the most wonderful, heartbreakingly beautiful sight she'd ever seen. 'That's going to be one hell of a story to tell our children some day.'

Our children. Her heart blossomed with all the possibilities of a future together opening up inside her. 'So…is that a yes?'

He brushed the back of his hand over her cheek, the side of her neck, leaving a shimmer of heat, the scent of his skin. 'I'm not planning on having our kids out of wedlock, sweetheart.'

He bent his head towards her and she rose on tip-toe, slid her arms around his neck and pressed her lips to his with all the pent-up emotion and love she had inside her. He kissed her back without hesitation, without reservation, dragging her close so that she could feel the fast, hard beat of his heart against hers.

Finally she drew back so she could see him, cupped his treasured face in her hands. 'I was afraid to love you. Afraid of its power. It can lift you up, but it can bury you so deep you can't see a way out. I saw what it did to my mother. I saw how she let it destroy her.

'But when I went to Brisbane I realised I wasn't like her. You showed me that, by pushing me out of my comfort zone and allowing me to see another side of myself. And I want to thank you for the rest of our lives.'

He smiled down at her. 'And I want to let you.' Then his expression sobered. 'I was afraid too, but wouldn't admit it—even to myself. I've never let anyone close. It was easier to play the field and move on. But with you I couldn't seem to let you go. Until you told me about the new job. I wanted you to have that career you worked so hard for. That success. I had to let you go and find it for yourself, even though I knew I loved you.'

'It's not enough. Not without you.' She tugged his hand. 'Can we get out of here?'

'Sure thing.' Tightening their clasped fingers, he headed for the door. 'I've got a surprise for you.'

Jake handed his address and a healthy wad of notes to the parking attendant on their way to pick up Emma's car. 'Find someone to take care of it and there's enough cash for a cab back,' he told him, then, slinging his arm around Emma's shoulders, he hustled her along the street. He wondered that his feet touched the ground. Half an hour ago he'd been at the lowest point in his life and now he was flying.

A short time later he kissed her on the front door step. 'Welcome home. I love you, Emma, and I'm never going to tire of hearing myself say it.'

'I'm never going to tire of h—' A long, low whine interrupted, vibrating through the door, followed by a whimper and a series of sharp barks. '*What* is that?'

He unlocked the door and a flurry of paws and joyous barks greeted them. 'Meet Scratch.'

'You bought a dog? So *that's* why you had to get home.'

'He's the abandoned dog I told you about.'

'And you rescued him.'

'I just couldn't bring myself to leave him at the

shelter, so I picked him up yesterday.' He bent to scratch behind his silky ears. 'I think we rescued each other—didn't we, boy?'

'We were all in need of rescue,' Emma murmured. 'Hey, there, you little cutie, you.'

Jake watched her wasting no time getting acquainted, crouching down so Scratch could sniff her and approve. With a joyous yelp he rolled onto his back, his tongue lolling out, adoration in his eyes.

Jake squatted beside Emma to scratch the dog's tummy. 'So what do you think—you and me and a crazy pooch? You didn't know he was part of the deal—you sure you still want to marry me?'

'Are you kidding? He seals the deal absolutely.'

He looked at Emma, his heart overflowing with that mysterious thing called love. It had eluded him all his life but now… Now he had it all.

A few moments later, with Scratch tucking into his dinner, Jake put the little velvet box into Emma's hands. 'To make it official.'

Her eyes widened. 'What's this? How…?'

'I was going to propose to you the other night. Until you told me your news.'

Realisation dawned in her bright blue eyes. 'So *that's* why you went to so much effort. Oh, Jake. I was so focused on myself I didn't—'

He placed a finger on her lips. 'Just open it.'

'Oh, my…' she breathed. 'It's beautiful.'

Three diamonds on a platinum band winked in the light. 'One for you, one for me, one for the kids we're going to make,' he told her, sliding it onto her finger.

He lifted her off the floor, twirled her around and around until they were both dizzy, then waltzed her to his bedroom the way he'd waltzed her to bed that first time they'd made love.

He tugged on her belt. 'I'll have you know the first time I saw you in that coat I wondered what you were hiding beneath it. Now…take it off and let me see.'

LATER, EMMA CUDDLED against him in his king-size bed. Scratch snored doggy snores in his basket nearby. 'I think I'd like to stay right here for the rest of the weekend.' She stretched, feeling satisfied, in love, and entirely too lazy.

'Sounds like a plan. But I doubt Scratch will agree.'

'Our house by the sea and a dog,' she murmured. 'This really is home. What a wonderful life…'

'And what do you want to do with that life…' he nuzzled the sweet taste of her breast '…besides making love endlessly till dawn?'

'I want to concentrate on Naturally Emma. Danny's still going to market my products in Queensland, and I might go up once a month to see how it's going.'

'Maybe I can accompany you sometimes. As your accountant.'

'Nuh-uh. If you accompany me it'll be as my husband.'

'Even better.' His hand created a warm friction over her belly. 'I'm shifting some of my office work home. When I decided to take on a dog I made the commitment to be home more.'

'We'll neither of us ever get any work done.' She drew a line up his shin with her toes and draped her top half over him like a scarf.

His laugh was more of a choke as his arms went around her to pull her all the way on top. 'Reckon you're right.'

She buried her face in the musky warmth of his neck and breathed in his scent. 'I'm always right. I asked you to marry me, didn't I?'

'So...how does a wedding as soon as Ry and Stella come back from their honeymoon sound?'

She lifted her head so she could look into those warm coffee eyes and see his love for her shining through. 'Perfect.'

* * * * *

Harlequin Presents stories are all about romance and escape—glamorous settings, gorgeous women and the passionate, sinfully tempting men who want them.

From brooding billionaires to untamed sheikhs and forbidden royals, Harlequin Presents offers you the world!

Eight new passionate reads are available every month wherever books and ebooks are sold.

HARLEQUIN
Presents®

Revenge and seduction intertwine…

Harlequin Presents welcomes you to the
world of The Chatsfield:
Synonymous with style, spectacle…and scandal!

Step into the gilded world of The Chatsfield!
Where secrets and scandal lurk behind
every door…

Reserve your room!

SPECIAL EXCERPT FROM

 HARLEQUIN®

Presents

*Harlequin Presents welcomes you to the
world of **The Chatsfield**;
Synonymous with style, spectacle...and scandal!*

*Read on for an extract from Chantelle Shaw's glittering
new edition to this series:* **BILLIONAIRE'S SECRET**

* * *

"NICOLO, WAKE UP."

He groaned again.

Desperate to rouse him, Sophie touched his shoulder. "Nicolo..." She let out a startled cry when he suddenly gripped her wrist and gave a forceful tug. Caught off-balance she fell on top of him.

"What's going on?"

"Nicolo—it's me, Sophie."

"Sophie?" His deep voice was slurred.

"Sophie Ashdown—remember me? You've been dreaming...."

There was silence for a few moments. "I grew out of wet dreams a long time ago," he drawled finally. "This is no dream. You feel very real to me, Sophie."

To Sophie's shock he tightened his hold on her wrist and moved his other hand to the small of her back, pressing her down so that she was acutely conscious of his muscular body beneath her. Only the sheet and her nightdress separated them. Sophie could feel the hard sinews of his thighs. She caught her breath as she felt something else hard jab into her stomach. Nicolo was no longer caught up in a nightmare; he was awake, alert—and aroused.

She hurriedly reminded herself that it was a common phenomenon for males to wake up with an erection, and it did not mean that Nicolo was responding to her in a sexual way. The same could not be said for her body, however.

"For goodness' sake, let me up," she said sharply, frantically trying to ignore the throb of desire that centered between her legs. To Sophie's horror she felt a tingling sensation in her nipples and prayed that Nicolo could not feel their betraying hard points through the sheet.

The pale gleam from the moon highlighted the hard angles of his face and the cynical curve of his mouth. Trapped against him, Sophie breathed in the spicy tang of his aftershave. It was a bold, intensely masculine fragrance that evoked an ache of longing in the pit of her stomach. Nicolo was the sexiest man she had ever met, and she was shocked by her reaction to his potent masculinity. "You were having a nightmare," he insisted. "I was trying to wake you. What other possible reason would I have for coming to your room in the middle of the night?"

* * *

*Step into the gilded world of **The Chatsfield**!*
Where secrets and scandal lurk behind every door…
Reserve your room!
August 2014

HARLEQUIN®

Presents®

Revenge and seduction intertwine…

Don't miss the final book in Susan Stephens's dazzling Skavanga Diamonds series!

Diamond-dynasty heir Tyr Skavanga has returned to the cold north haunted by the terrors of war. But one person has managed to defy his defenses….

The exotically beautiful, innocent Princess Jasmina of Kareshi is strictly off-limits. With their reputations at stake, can they resist the electrifying connection between them?

HIS FORBIDDEN DIAMOND

by

Susan Stephens

**Available August 2014,
wherever books are sold!**

HARLEQUIN®

Presents®

Revenge and seduction intertwine…

Maisey Yates's

stunning contribution to the
Fifth Avenue trilogy in:

AVENGE ME

Austin Treffen never had the means to prove the dark
corruption that his father hides behind money and
power—until he meets Katy Michaels. But beneath
their intense attraction lies a heady mix of guilt, grief
and resentment, the need to protect…and the need
for revenge.

*The first step to revenge in the **Fifth Avenue** trilogy*

Austin has the plan…

June 2014